the Seamstress of Ourfa

Armida Publications is a member of the Independent Publishers Guild (UK),
and a member of the Independent Book Publishers Association (USA)

www.armidabooks.com | Great Literature. One Book At A Time.

Summary:
The Seamstress of Ourfa richly recreates the culture of the Armenian community in Ourfa
at the tail end of the Ottoman Empire. The eponymous seamstress, Khatoun, creates
beautiful dresses that leave her customers' husbands dizzy with desire, while her sister
in law Ferida cooks sumptuous feasts to sustain a growing and lovingly described group
of relatives and the waifs and strays they adopt. The author creates a finely textured
sense of family, only slowly making the reader aware that the date is creeping nearer to
1915 and the genocide of the Armenian people in Turkey. When the horrendous events
of those years start to unfold, the traditions and lives of the Armenian people are
slowly yet inexorably torn apart. *The Seamstress of Ourfa* does not shy away from the
painful realities of those years, but manages to maintain a sense of cultural continuity
into the 1960's, where the author's surviving family reunite in Nicosia, Cyprus.

[1. FICTION / Cultural Heritage. 2. FICTION / Family Saga.
3. FICTION / Literary. 4. FICTION / Women . 5. FICTION / Historical / General.
6. FICTION / Family Life / General. 7. FICTION / Biographical.]

Cover design by: Annie Damianou
anniedmn.com
contact@anniedmn.com

Motifs by: Victoria Harwood Butler-Sloss

First edition: June 2018

ISBN-13 (paperback): 978-9963-255-59-7

the Seamstress of Ourfa

Victoria Harwood Butler-Sloss

ARMIDA

I'm thirty-four and I meet a man with very blue eyes
who looks inside me. He tells me he can see me at
sixteen, at eight, as a child when he makes love to me.
His eyes open and close very slowly next to my face.
Sometimes they half close and look down and they are
grey-green, cool, and then they slide up and pierce me
with open sky. Sometimes he lies close and breathes
into my mouth and the breath is sweet, whatever
we've done. I clutch momentarily at the edges
of this deep drop into his love, then free-fall,
my chest open to the heart,
and drift in on his sweet air.

For William with love.

Ասոււած Յոգիս Լուսաւորէ

Sept 21st 1967- March 13th 2018

Acknowledgments

None of this would be possible if not for my family. Iskender Agha Boghos, Khatoun Khouri, Umme Ferida, Alice Avakian, Haygaz Avakian, Takouhi and Verginia Avakian, John Harwood, Jack Patey, Billy and Ann Patey, Robert Gombie Harwood, Arum and Roibhilin. You continue to give my life stories. Thank you.

Also, John Tracy Clinic where I sat and wrote in between classes; they know how much I love them.

Brenda Richie for employing me and providing a quiet office with a fountain where I finished the first draft in between ordering flowers, checking mail and feeding the baby.

Colin Thubron for telling me to do it.

Marianne Jean Baptiste, Akure Wall, Marilyn Acons and Cynthia Bond for reading early pages and heaping encouragement.

Aminatta Forna for many many things, including the number of times she pushed me, introduced me and shared a glass of wine over gossip.

Elise Dillsworth for totally believing in me and making me laugh through every rejection.

Aline Ohanesian for continual support and for spending that hilarious afternoon with me checking the veracity of expletives in other languages.

Kumru Bilici and Leyla Servet Konuralp for always answering questions so snappily on Facebook.

The Book Club girls for nagging me non-stop to give them a book to read.

Krista Gelev, for research and help with indexes.

Edith Weil, Julian Beeston, Virginia Mileva, Kyla Gelev, JC Barros, Ayala Elnekave and the esteemed Mary Woronov for allowing me to exploit their patience and artistry.

Annie Damianou for the beautiful cover, Kate Ivanova for feeling my pain when I cut two chapters, James Mackay for his eagle eye and Elena Lipsos for her fine-toothed comb. You all helped over the finish line.

And of course, Haris and Katerina at Armida for kittens and tashinopita while editing and the birth of this book. Thank you.

Everything's a story.

Dorak

Tarsus

MEDITERRANEAN SEA

Nicosia

Famagusta

Map detail from:
The Treatment of Armenians in the Ottoman Empire 1915-16
by Viscount Bryce, G.P. Putnam & Sons, 1916.

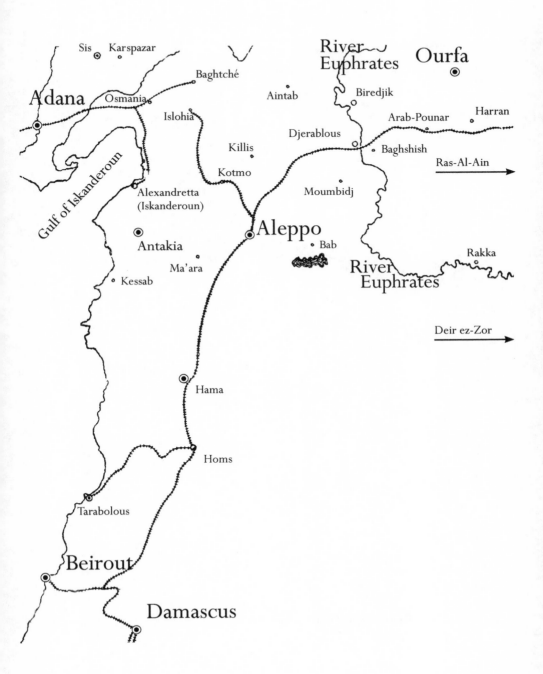

Map of Ourfa, hand drawn by Victoria Harwood Butler-Sloss

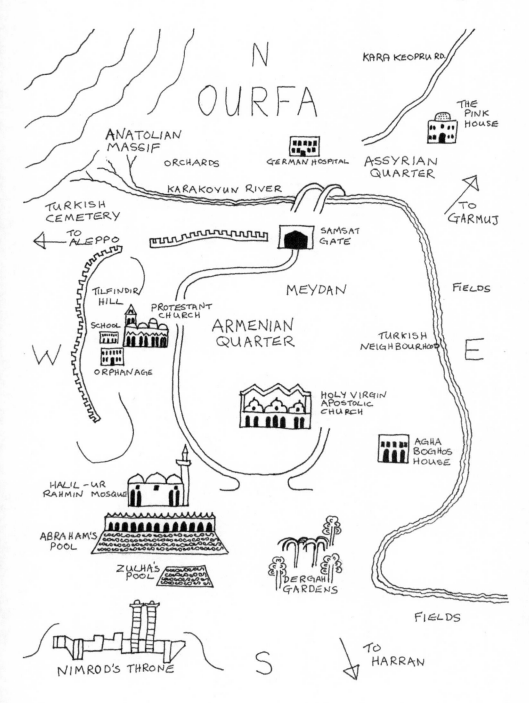

Who I Am

Nicosia, Cyprus, July 1968
Vicky

She's heading towards me at speed, her black plastic slippers slapping the tiled floor as she comes. I think she's an adult but I'm not sure. Her face is wrinkly but she's only a finger taller than I am and I'm seven. She must be Nene Khatoun, my great-grandma who is very, very old. As ancient as the hills, Mummy says, and everyone knows ancient things shrink. Here she comes, making a beeline for my corner. Luckily there are lots of people between us and she can't get round them easily. She has to keep stopping to get her balance. Eyes quick, I search for someone to help me but everyone's busy.

The room is full of people. My family I'm meeting for the first time. They live here in Cyprus and Mum, Rob and I came on an aeroplane across the sea from England to see them. Now we are drowning in them. In the middle of the room is an old man in a dressing gown and a blue crocheted hat and he's crying. He's got Robert stuffed under one arm and Billy under the other.

"Tvins! Tvins!" he's screaming, even though they're not. Robert is my brother and Billy is my cousin even though they do look alike.

Jumping up and down next to the old man is a lady with red hair and a film star dress. She's kissing both boys and messing up Rob's parting and singing a song, *"Achoognered bidi oudem, kitignered bidi oudem."*

I know what she's saying, even though it's Armenian. I understand that much. She wants to eat Robert's eyes and nose! Before I can warn him, before I can move, I am finally attacked. The midget great-granny has me locked in her arms. She smells of mothballs and onions and her lips turn in over her pink gums which hold no teeth. There's a cave in her mouth that wants to suck me in. I don't know if I want to cry, or faint, or have a comforting wee in my pants but as I look into her eyes, only inches above mine, she says my name and the whole world stops.

"Vicky."

She winks at me, undoes the top button of her spotty dress and I climb in, crack open her ribcage and nestle into her heart. In here I feel the safest I have ever felt in my life. It's my blue eiderdown and lentil soup and Fleur in 'The Forsyte Saga' after a hot bath in winter. It's new, like a pomegranate split open, ready to eat. It's the taste of milk and honey. The smell of lily-of-the-valley in our front garden in Bromley, especially after the rain. She is the rain. The rain that runs down the windowpane that I follow with my finger on long car journeys. She is with me now and for always, the angels sing. All ways.

"Always dreaming!" Mummy says, yanking at my arm. I'm in shock — being dragged back to earth so rudely. That's parents for you — they teach you manners and then they don't use them. Mummy wants to introduce me to all the people in the room. I look over at Nene Khatoun and she nods. Suddenly I can hear *her* voice even though it's Mummy's lips that are moving. Nene Khatoun can speak to me without opening her mouth just like they do on the telly, on magic shows. Telepathy, it's called. Or ventrilolilolism, that thing with a creepy doll. I listen to Nene Khatoun's voice inside my head, watching Mummy's Coral Frost lipstick move, *woowah woowah*. Nene Khatoun is telling me important stuff.

"It won't make any sense now but will in the future," she says. "It's about who you are."

I listen hard. I know I may have to depend on these words one day. Mum pushes me in front of the red-haired lady in the lovely dress, wipes my eyebrows and tugs at my hem. The lady has stopped singing that song and is smiling at me. Colgate, three ways clean.

"This is Auntie Verginia, Mummy's sister," Nene Khatoun's voice says. "She'll show you her *dzidzigs* when she gets undressed. Look at them. Her body is not as loud as her laugh."

Auntie Verginia does laugh a lot. She sticks her fist in her mouth and bites it and does a little dance. I wonder what her *dzidzigs* look like under her clothes. She smells like a film star. As soon as I have pecked her on the forehead someone else grabs my face and smooshes it together. I look like my favourite dolly after Robert squashed it with his chair leg.

"This is my little girl, my daughter, Alice. Your Grandmum. Same person, just different names. Listen to her when you can't

hear me. She saw things at your age that a child cannot unsee."
Nene Khatoun's voice is like a whisper in my ear.

Grandmum Alice has so many lines on her face, I can't imagine her ever having been a little girl or a daughter, but I know she must have been, once. That's the way of the world. We're born wrinkly and then we go smooth for a while and then we go wrinkly again and our heart – which is really a clock – stops and we're dead.

After some cheek pinching Grandmum Alice lets go of my face, pokes around in her pocket and hands me some toffees. She leans down to kiss me and when she pulls away we're attached by a curtain of hair – mine – caught in the row of needles pinned under her collar. She gently unpicks me then pushes me back so she can see the travelling outfit Mummy made me for this trip.

This is the grooviest thing my mother ever sewed. A lime-green mini with stars and moons and planets on it. I'm still wearing the matching coat on top even though I'm boiling. The coat is not fastened with buttons, nor with hooks, but by a chunky zip with a huge Go-Go-girl ring on the end.

I strike a pose then do my special 'Top of The Pops' dance for them. They clap as I dance, Grandmum Alice and Auntie Verginia, who is now doing the squashy face thing to me and singing her "I'm going to eat your eyes and nose!" song again. When I finish, they drag me towards the sofa. Towards the old man in the crocheted hat. I stare at his feet in blue flip-flops. His toenails are yellow and the big toes are hairy.

"This is your Grandad Haygaz." Nene Khatoun's voice, Mummy's lips. "An orphan with no ties to bind him. We became his family and he carried us here." When I look up at his hands I see that he could easily carry me in just one of them. Mum tells me to do the dance again.

When you're alone and life is making you lonely,
You can always go – downtown!
I sing as I shimmy and twist.
Forget all your troubles! Forget all your cares! And go
Downtown! Lala lala lala, Downtown! Lala lala lala laaaaaaah![1]

I sing as loud as I can, hoping that Grandad Haygaz will stop

---

1 *Downtown*, Petula Clark, 1964.

crying. Instead, he lunges at me and buries me in his arms. Old Spice. I know that smell.

"Downtown, downtown," he croaks, "Downtown!"

Mummy sits next to him on the sofa and perches me on his knee. He inhales my hair and we sit facing the door opposite as he sobs down my back. I've never seen a grown man cry so much – usually they shout.

"He's happy," Mummy whispers. "He's crying because he's happy." I'm not sure I believe her. Parents lie sometimes, and I already know he's an orphan and they're always sad, even if they get given another spoonful of gruel. Anyway, I move away as soon as I can, thankful that it's Robert's turn to display his travel outfit now. Maybe he can use the hanky he wasn't allowed to blow his nose on to dry Grandad's tears.

I look away and there, in the doorway, is another person I've never seen before, her long face watching me. Where do they all come from, this family of mine? Nene Khatoun's voice follows me.

"That's Umme Ferida, my sister-in-law. Your great-great-aunt. Eat her food and watch the slippers on her feet. They'll fly off and bite you if you behave badly."

Umme Ferida tuts and disappears back into the shadows. I can hear kitchen noises and then someone pokes me in the back with a gun, just where they should be careful because it's my kidney and that's a delicate organ.

"*Dungulugh!*" Auntie Verginia says, slapping Billy across the head in a waft of perfume.

"Your cousin. Billy. Almost your brother. Never fight amongst yourselves. Blood and water, blood and water, remember that." Nene Khatoun looks at me as if what she's saying (or really, the voice in my head) makes any sense. Does it? Billy aims at my skull, blows it apart and kicks my brains under the table.

"Oi! Behave!" Uncle Jack yells from the balcony. He's Billy's daddy who picked us up at the airport when we arrived. He's got ginger hair and a moustache and is wearing nothing but shorts.

"Seaside tomorrow?" he asks. I nod eagerly. He blows a smoke ring at me and turns back to watch the telly which is on the other side of the balcony. That's possible because it never rains in Cyprus – Mummy told me – so no problems like getting electrocuted and dying in the middle of *I Love Lucy*. Billy whoops like an Indian and runs off. A gentle hand lands on my shoulder.

"And this, of course, is Nene Khatoun," Mummy says.

"That's me," says my great-grandma, smiling her pink smile. "Open your eyes and you'll always be able to hear me. I have many stories to tell."

Mummy is looking at me and Nene suspiciously, so I salute like a Brownie and Nene winks again before disappearing slip-slop, slip-slop into another room, her head bobbing like one of those toy dogs in a car.

As she leaves, Umme Ferida comes in with a tray. They almost collide in the doorway and Umme Ferida hisses. She's got funny legs that poke out the bottom of her skirt, very wide apart. She's wearing her slippers and I can see they are good for smacking. The back is folded down and the heel is slim enough to fit the palm of her hand. She's bringing us drinks in bottles. There are pretty glasses on the tray and a plate of powdery biscuits. Umme Ferida puts the tray on a little wooden table that has holes carved in the legs like lace and pearly white flowers set in the wood. She pulls up a string that's tied around her waist and separates a large key from the bunch. She uses this to open the bottle caps. I've never seen this before. She does it like flicking a coin, dropping the caps in the tray afterwards. I pick one up. The edges are pretty zigzags and inside there's a bit of cork which smells sweet. The top has a dent in it, where the key bent it back. I put it in my pocket. Umme Ferida sees me and raises one eyebrow. I'm sure I see her slipper itching to fly off her foot but instead she hands me the other two caps and tries a smile. She picks up a glass and pours a drink in it. Sideways. 'Coca-Cola' the bottle says in loopy writing. We drink lemon squash at home and Lucozade when we're ill. This is different. This is black velvet lit with sparkler fire. I watch the Coca-Cola fill up behind a hula-hula dancer on a Hawaiian beach. Umme Ferida hands me the glass. I look over at Mummy to see if it's all right to accept this gift, but she's too busy with Auntie Verginia, so I take it. I don't know whether to drink it or save it forever in its lovely glass, so I sip it two bubbles at a time.

I'm getting tired. I don't want to meet family any more – they are too many, too much. I feel a bit sick. Homesick. Time to become invisible. I slip off my coat and let my hair fall over my face. Now that I can't be seen, I feel better. I wonder how Daddy is, all alone back in England holding the fork. He's probably asleep. Is it late there like it is here? I can smell mothballs. Nene Khatoun is back, followed by Billy. She's holding something behind her dress.

"It's a bed!" Billy shouts, ignoring the fact that I am invisible.

"We made it together!" They place a small wooden doll's bed in my hands. It is the most beautiful thing I have ever seen.

"I banged it in with a hammer. Look." Billy shows me the nails underneath. The headboard has a pattern drawn in pencil then traced over with something sharp. A milky blue marble is glued on each corner.

"China blues. They're rare," Billy says. "I had three and I won the other one yesterday. Piyoong!" He flicks his finger and thumb with one eye shut and runs off to get his collection.

My legs are beginning to feel wobbly. Nene Khatoun sits me on the floor and crouches down next to me so we can explore the bed together. There are little sheets tucked in, the top one embroidered at the edge with blue and yellow flowers. The same embroidery is on the pillowcase and in the middle of the pale blue blanket. The mattress is covered in stripes the same as the pillow. Nene Khatoun says it is stuffed with real hair.

"Our hair," she says, pointing her finger around the room.

Everyone is still wandering around us, legs and feet, legs and feet. Their voices come and go. The television laughs. At least Grandad has stopped crying. He's playing with beads now. Click-clickclick. He counts them on their string, sitting on the sofa, looking exhausted. My eyes are itching so I rub at them like I know I shouldn't.

Nene Khatoun reaches out and strokes my face, "Go to sleep," she says. "Don't worry about us. We'll all be here in the morning." She puts her arm around my shoulder. "And the next day, and the next, and the next. And always."

And then she crumples me up, gently, like a tissue until I am small enough to fit in my new bed. She tucks me in, singing a lullaby, and I can smell the fresh cut wood as the sheets cover me in a cobweb of sleep. I am falling. Falling, falling, falling.

The night is black velvet lit with sparkler fire. My family are old – ancient as angels – and they live near the sea and smell of onions and mothballs and cry when they're happy. They wear keys and loose slippers, smoke cigarettes and drink Coca-Cola and pin us to their hearts with our hair.

My family, my family, my family and me.

Khatoun Khouri

Ourfa, The Ottoman Empire, April 1895
Khatoun

Two figures appear at the crest of the hill. Two strokes shimmering against the flat glare of sky. A mother and her son, walking side by side, their feet throwing up dust as they go.

It is a beautiful spring morning, the kind that takes your breath away and makes you love your neighbour. The sky an ever-reaching cerulean heaven. Bright, startling, without cloud. The air is alive with the hum of insects and in the distance a dozen boys whistle and call to each other over a ball. The mother, a graceful woman of fifty, walks tall. Her son, late twenties, follows a pace behind; bent, brooding, melancholy. He's wearing formal dress in dark colours as if his purpose were serious – marriage perhaps, possibly death.

Whatever it is, Iskender Agha Boghos has his eye fixed on one thing – the tin flask swinging at his mother's hip. It contains nothing special, just water, but his doleful eyes tell how desperate he is to stop and rest under the eucalyptus – to let his collar go, take off his shoes – go anywhere but forward. If only he dared ask.

She strolls beside him, his mother. Seyda Agha Boghos; wife of Abraham; mother of four. Pale skin, a dusting of freckles, grey eyes narrowed against the sun. Seyda has covered her hair with a scarf as always; nevertheless her fingers constantly seek loose strands, peeling them from her forehead and poking them back under the muslin. She's ignoring Iskender, pushing forward through the heat, her gaze steady.

She can see it. There she sits at the head of the table, a streak of white sweeping through her glorious red hair. A large, straight-backed chair, fine white linen, crystal glasses, the wine from abroad. And family. A *large* family with *lots* of grandchildren. Hacme the fortune-teller had seen it. So had her friends. So why were her children spoiling her plan? Yes, Loucia and Sophia, her other two daughters were already married with children but they lived miles away. Baghshish and Damascus. Hardly ever visited. So what had happened to Ferida and Iskender, the two still at home? Ferida — skinny as a stick with vile language and that horrible habit of squashing down the backs of her shoes. Who would marry her? Or Iskender? Who wanted a husband who read books all day? *Dungulugh*. Idiot. She shifts her eyes sideways and watches him as he walks.

He has her nose and teeth and her husband's smile. That's good. Not much hair up top but a thick moustache to compensate. (If he could just keep his fingers out of it — that nervous tic.) Dark eyes, the colour of olives. Maybe set too close together. Maybe not.

"He's too handsome," her friends tut-tutted, "it scares the girls away."

"Pah!" Seyda snorts. She blames education not beauty for Iskender's predicament. If Pastor Tovmasian hadn't persuaded them to send him to college, he wouldn't have learnt how to think too much. Iskender can cut a mean deal in Farsi, write accounts up in French, read the papers in Turkish and recite sonnets in English. And that's where it ends. When it comes to holding a simple conversation in his own language with the opposite sex he's as dumb as a mule. Handsome, poetic, an expert on world politics but no wife and no child and what use was that to anyone?

Seyda tucks back that annoying wire of hair again. Iskender is carrying, of all things, a book under his arm — as if he thinks he'll have time to read somewhere, somehow on this busy morning. Surely he must know the true purpose of their visit? She looks down at his feet. The right foot pointed inwards, dragging like a child's.

"Turn back! Go home!" his boots cry out step by step. Seyda sighs. Poor Iskender. How much happier he'd have been left at home with his books.

Iskender — and yes, he does know the true purpose of their visit — feels the same way. It's not that he's averse to the idea of marriage; in fact, he thinks he might like it. But the thought of sitting in a stranger's parlour being served lemonade and sweetmeats by a girl he's supposed to look over and appraise. To him that's barbaric. Everyone watching, breath sucked in, nudge-nudge. His every tic and awkward manner discussed later over dinner with another dozen people. On top of this, he'd actually have to start a conversation with the girl. Appalling! So much simpler to stay single and have his sister Ferida cook his food until he dies. He looks down at his gleaming boots.

"Turn back! Go home," they squeal.

"I would," he mutters into the dust, "I would if I could."

"What did you say?"

"Nothing, *Mayrig*, nothing."

"Hmph. Now it's back to nothing is it?" Seyda rolls her eyes. Her son. Like a lamb to slaughter. And her dragging the poor beast by the neck, skittering over the stones to the public drain. Everything would have been fine; things would have stayed the same if it hadn't been for The Ourfa Ladies Sewing Union and her meddling friends.

"She's a little young to rush straight into marriage…" *Digin* Tamar, head of the Union and self-appointed matchmaker, had pronounced at the 'emergency meeting' several months ago.

"But young enough to learn the proper way to love your son!" Beatrice had added, making a lewd gesture with her fingers. *Digin* Tamar had shot her a dangerous look before continuing.

"The girl's name is Khatoun Khouri. Father is Palestinian from Jerusalem. Mother an Assyrian from Mosul. They all speak Armenian. Girl is thirteen. Pale skin. Thick hair. Good eyes. All of her teeth. She cooks, helps around the house and is good with animals. Two sisters. Married. Father and two brothers are goldsmiths. Another brother, a student. They have a farm inherited from the mother's side. Sheep, wheat, olive groves. They're up to here with stuff." She sliced her hand across her neck. "It'll be a good dowry, land in Garmuj, just outside the city. Never mind they're not Armenian. They've assimilated." She winked at Seyda, put her hand out for more nuts and the room murmured in assent, the fire crackling, the coals shifting in the *tonir*.

"Good!" Seyda nodded pensively. She understood land. Land meant a future as far as the horizon. She looked up from the fire. "She sounds ideal. But my son — he's a funny one you know — he likes books. Does she read, this Khatoun?"

"Of course! She's rewriting the Bible as we speak!" Beatrice quipped.

"Ouf! Shut up!" *Digin* Tamar spat a husk into her palm. "Give

you wine, you turn it into vinegar. Ignore Beatrice, *Digin* Seyda.
And no, Khatoun doesn't read but one of her sisters does – she's
a teacher in the provincial school. And the other brother is at
university in Damascus. I've seen him at the train station with
his books."

"Ah, that's good," Seyda smiled. "The brother reads."

"Oh yes, the brother reads. All of them do."

"That'll do. That's good. Brothers that read are good."

"What more could Iskender ask for?"

"Nothing."

"No."

"Perfect."

"*Insha'Allah.*"

The women huddled closer, their feet tucked under the blanket around the warm *tonir*. The dishes of treats were shuffled,
emptied, refilled. Beatrice shoved a handful of raisins into her
mouth, swallowed and belched.

"Well. I'm ahead in the game. I took the trouble of finding out
when she would be at the baths and went to have a look."

"No!"

"Yes."

"No!"

"And?"

"Small." Beatrice giggled. "No hair. Slim in the hips. Not quite
a woman yet…"

An impatient flap of skirt stopped her short. The Elder Shoshan, tucked like a crow into the darkness. "You stupid gossip!"
the old woman snapped from her bed. "None of this matters.
The girl comes from good family. *I* knew the grandparents –
that's what matters. Her grandfather was a priest, his brother a
doctor. That's all you need to know. The rest is gossip."

"Well, I thought it was important," Beatrice said. "I'm not
ashamed I went to look her over." She ignored The Elder Shoshan's eyes boring into the back of her neck, grabbed another
handful of walnuts and proclaimed, "There's no doubt she's a
virgin. Her *boutz* was smooth as a peach!"

"*Asdvadz!* Of course she's a virgin!" Seyda cried out, outraged.
"How could she not be? She's a child!" Sadly, before she could
reach Beatrice with the back of her hand, *Digin* Tamar had intervened.

"Calm down, Seyda! You know better than to listen to Beatrice. Frivolous girl. Always causing trouble. I have to admit, though, she has a point — tastelessly put, of course. In a situation like marriage, *all* things must be considered." She silenced Seyda with a raised hand. "Ah, ah, ah! You wouldn't buy a bolt of cloth without checking it for imperfections first, would you?"

"Ha!" Beatrice stopped poking at her teeth with a stick. "I remember the day *Digin* Seyda refused to buy cloth from us because she saw a moth in the shop. Can you imagine? One little moth woken up from its sleep and she got all high and mighty!" She winked and dug the stick back in.

"That isn't true!" Seyda jumped up. "I didn't like the weight for a dress. And you, would you buy flour from a shop where you saw mice?"

And then, just as Beatrice stood up, a shriek. "You women are soft!" The Elder Shoshan hit the floor with her stick, overturning the bowl of empty shells with a clatter. "Talk about the girl — not your own vanities!"

The two women sat down again. Silence settled over the room and Beatrice, still unable to control her childish urges, crossed her eyes at Seyda who sat glaring at her across the *tonir*. The coals fell. Settled.

"Well, there you have it," *Digin* Tamar concluded, taking the walnuts from Beatrice and handing them round. "Good background, good family, educated brothers and an excellent dowry. It's a match. Our only problem is getting that mute son of yours to open his mouth and propose. Remember, love enters women through the ears not the eyes."

"You do it the right way," the Elder Shoshan yelled from her corner. "The old way. You take him to the house and she brings him a lemonade. Let him take a look. Then you arrange it — the parents. Never mind that he's twenty-eight. All men are children. They need help. *Digin* Tamar will make the introductions. I will give my approval, and that's it. Enough. And enough of this chitter-chatter. Go away, I need sleep. Beatrice, show the ladies out." She waved her stick at the door and sat clutching her shawl to her chest, her face lifted at an austere angle for the women to kiss as they filed past.

And so it had been arranged. *Digin* Tamar had spoken to Khatoun's mother, Mertha. Genteel nods had been exchanged at the baths, introductions made, coffee drunk, oranges peeled, relatives consulted and, finally, *Park Asdoudzo!*, the first visit set for this beautiful blue morning, clear as a church bell. Seyda had said nothing about the true nature of their visit, telling Iskender that she had business with the Khouri family that went back years. She had to go and see them and their farm was almost two hours' walk from home. Of course Iskender would have to accompany her. It was not safe to travel anywhere alone these days.

No one had mentioned the word marriage but as they'd left home this morning, several ladies had stopped their sweeping to wave and nod like conspirators as mother and son passed. Iskender had laughed.

"Moses walking through the Red Sea, the whispering waves closing in behind him," he'd muttered. He waved at the neighbours, called out "Good morning!" cheerily and irritated Seyda. Oh, he looked like a suitor all right – tall and imperious in his suit jacket and fez – but looks and smiles would not be enough.

Seyda knew Iskender would never be able to break the ice even with a girl less than half his age. He would scare her off with his silence and these days, brides had some say. Seyda had to get Iskender talking before they got to their destination and so far she'd had no luck.

They'd set off early this morning, leaving home via the cool winding streets of the Armenian Quarter, their steady breath the only sound between them. That and the sigh of new shoes. The minutes had passed, Seyda casting her eye around for inspiration. But beyond their neighbourhood with its inquisitive sweepers, the town was still asleep. Eventually, in desperation, she'd flung her hand in the direction of a small courtyard thick with flowers.

"How beautiful," she'd sighed. "What kind of plant is that?"

"Oleander."

"Oleander?"

"Oleander. Poisonous."

"And that – what's that?"

"Pomegranate."

"Pomegranate?"

"Yes. Very young."

"Oh. That's why I didn't recognise it," Seyda had laughed. "No fruit."

"No. Too young."

And then Seyda had chattered away about everything. The plants, the trees, the cloudless sky, the early morning vendors and their wares, their strange hair and odd fabrics. She conjured up the lives of the people who lived behind the peeling shutters and cracked doors they passed. What were their names? And who could have lost such a fine shoe in the gutter? She talked as if she had never been down these streets before and needed her son to guide her. She prodded and questioned and he replied monosyllabically until the rising heat got the better of her and she too fell quiet, her mouth full of dust.

The journey had continued in silence. Past the busying market place and on through the leafy neighbourhood of larger houses to the outskirts of town. The sun rose. The air grew stale. They walked past barking dogs and startled children, out into the surrounding farmlands and on until now, when finally exhausted by the heat and silence, Seyda has come to a stop in the shadowy eucalyptus grove at the crest of a hill. She relieves the tin flask from her hip, opens it and takes a slug of water.

"Here," she says, handing Iskender the flask and watching him guzzle. "Let's catch our breath." She lowers herself down and leans back against a tree trunk, shedding its bark in elegant papery strips. Iskender sighs. He finds a stone big enough to sit on, rolls it next to his mother and perches over it like a bird. He digs his finger into his collar, pulls it away from his neck and lets the heat escape. Seyda wipes her mouth with the back of her hand and points to a distant palm grove in the valley below. A handful of buildings with whitewashed walls glare back in the sun.

"That's it. The Khouris'," Seyda says. She stretches her feet out in front of her and rolls them around. "Won't take much longer."

"Hm," Iskender replies, already lost in the pages of his book.

They'd whispered for a while that he was deaf. Or stupid. Tore their hair out at nights, not daring to voice their fears lest they come true. When he finally began to speak, Iskender's voice had slipped through cracked lips like thin parchment. He was four years old. His dreams populated with heavenly creatures, his speech sparse and often unintelligible. Not for him the cacophonous games of children and the tralala of song. Iskender preferred silence and the musty pages of his father's books.

Seyda looks up at the majestic trees, wondering how she will bring him back to earth. He's closed his eyes and is breathing evenly, one finger suspended in the pages of his book, the other hooked in his collar. His lips are moving, his face changing with his thoughts.

"Gabon," he says in that startling way of his.

"Gabon?"

"Oh. It's a place. Just thinking," Iskender smiles at his mother.

"Well stop it!" she snaps back at him. "Stop thinking!"

The trees droop. Seyda closes her eyes. Her armpits are soggy, her crisp cotton dress wilted. She can hear them already – 'That mute crane? What *was* she thinking? He should join a cloister. More luck there.' She craves the cool of her room, the smell of Ferida's cooking. This ridiculous failed mission behind her, not still ahead. She struggles to her feet with a groan, slapping Iskender's outstretched hand away.

"*Hayde*. Come on," she snaps. "Let's go."

They set off down the hill, happy to be in shade for a while. Iskender hangs back, watching his mother. When they'd set off this morning she was indomitable. Strong and beautiful with only her son's interests at heart. Now she looks older, her shoulders soft, her footsteps less sure. Her headscarf has slipped and there's a smudge across her temple where she keeps worrying her hair. Iskender would gladly give her his handkerchief but knows she'll wave it away, annoyed.

It's his fault. He's been sullen this morning – the way he is with most people. His shoes hurt. He wants to kick them off, walk back to the trees barefoot and finish his book. But more than this, more than anything in the world, he wants to make his mother happy. And the answer, there in the steady pace of her foot, is suddenly, stunningly simple. All he has to do is say *yes*. Yes to anything she wants. He mouths it silently behind her back. "Yes, *Mayrig*. *Uyo*. Yes." She looks back, eyes narrowed. Turns away again. She didn't hear him.

They pass through the grove into the baking sun. The air a mix of sage and goat. Iskender drops his book, trips over it, yelps and picks it up. He tucks it under his arm again, a ghost of dust ruining the side of his jacket. Seyda scowls. In the old days...books... words...words in books...never mind. She'll try one last time.

"I'm worried," she starts.

"Yes?"

"Your father. His heart."

"Yes, of course." Iskender pauses for a moment and then, "Why? What's wrong with his heart?"

"It's breaking."

"Breaking?"

"Yes," Seyda snaps. "He wants to see his grandchildren. It's breaking his heart. The few he has are scattered here and there, meanwhile he's getting older and sicker. And so are we all."

"Yes, we are," Iskender smiles. "We are all getting older."

"Time passes. You can't turn back a clock..." Seyda turns back to emphasise her point and breaks off to stare at her son. He has stopped walking and is standing in the bright sun, one hand clasped over his heart the other held out towards her. Smiling.

Is it for fear to wet a widow's eye,
That thou consum'st thy self in single life?
Ah! If thou issueless shalt hap to die,
The world will wail thee like a makeless wife[2]

He bows elaborately then stands, grinning.

Seyda glares back. She stretches out her hand and slaps her cheek hard. "What did I do? What did I do to deserve you as a son?" she wails. "I despair of you — an old man and still acting like a child!"

And then, instead of the apology Seyda expects, Iskender bends over and begins to shake. His shoulders shake, his head shakes, the tassles on his fez — everything shakes, but not a sound comes out of his mouth. Finally, with a whoop, he throws his head back for air and his fez topples into the dirt.

"What?" Seyda yells at him. "What is *wrong* with you?"

Iskender crouches down to retrieve his hat and spits into the earth, still laughing. He reaches out, slips his mother's hip flask from her belt and splashes water all over his face.

"Mother," he says, straightening up and kissing her on the forehead, "I shall bend to thy will gladly."

"That's it," Seyda says crossing herself. "You have finally lost your mind. Inglis? *Inglis?* Now? You know I don't understand. This is not a good time to go cuckoo my son."

---

2 *Sonnet 9,* William Shakespeare.

"I know and I apologize," Iskender says with mock gravity, "but in my madness I have seen the light." He begins to chuckle. "Why don't we banish heartbreak and longing and gather all the family home for my wedding?" He removes the spotless handkerchief from his jacket pocket and wipes his face, chortling.

"Who said anything about your wedding?"

"The whole neighbourhood knows."

"The whole neighbourhood?"

"As far south as Harran."

"Pah!"

"Well."

"Well."

Seyda snatches the flask back from her son and takes a sip. Stares at him. "So, the whole neighbourhood is talking, eh? See what you've done to me! Now I'm the subject of idle gossip." She purses her lips but there's a light in her eyes. She hasn't seen her son laugh for months. She hangs the flask back on the cord around her waist and sets off again. "Let's keep moving. We don't want these people to be waiting for us. Not with the whole neighbourhood gossiping. And, since the whole of the Ourfa district is already discussing your marriage, let me speak *my* mind."

"Please do."

"You're an old man and a stubborn fool. You should be a father by now."

Iskender winces, bends down to adjust one of his laces.

"Don't stop. Iskender. Son. Look at me," Seyda softens her voice as he squints up at her, one knee in the dust. "Tie your shoe and keep walking. Good, make it tight. This woman we're going to see, Mertha Khouri — she has a daughter, Khatoun. She's pretty, she cooks, she cleans, she's artistic, her brothers read and..."

"She's thirteen years old," Iskender puts his hand up, stemming the flow of information. "I've already heard all about her. She's a child, Mother. I'm more than twice her age."

"Then you're old enough to be married. You're *more* than old enough to be married. And thirteen is no longer a child. In my day we were already promised at nine, ten years old!"

"I know, *Mayrig.* But times change. I can't marry a stranger. I have to know the girl first. And..." he pauses, looking for strength before adding the remark he knows will infuriate his mother the most, "I must be in love."

"Love! Pah!" scoffs Seyda. "Don't start that rubbish about love again! What do you youngsters know about love? It grows like a plant. It's not something that hits you in the face. Oh yes, here I go, I walk around the corner and there you are and suddenly-suddenly I'm in love? Rubbish! And how long does love last? Eh? Until your first child is born and then you have no time!"

"Perhaps we should continue this conversation later," Iskender suggests, nodding ahead of them. Seyda's last invective has propelled them towards the farm and a dog leaps snapping out of its sleep under the palms and runs off to announce their arrival.

"*Asdvadz*," Seyda sighs, her busy fingers working her headscarf.

"Forget God. Forget you. How do *I* look?"

"Dusty!" Seyda says, slapping at Iskender's jacket with her hands. "And far too beautiful. Don't forget, *'Love enters men through their eyes but women through their ears.'* It doesn't matter what you *look* like as long as you *talk* to her. Try, if possible, to stick to Armenian. And make her laugh." She reaches up and smoothes his eyebrows with her middle finger, anointing him with motherly spit. She takes a breath, turns and sails across the stone threshold of the courtyard.

"*Parev, Parev!*" she cries, arms flung up to the sky, mirroring the bride's mother, *Digin* Mertha, who stands with arms similarly outstretched on the opposite side of the yard. Iskender ducks under the door frame and follows his mother into the compound, one hand waving a meek hello at his hip.

The air is thick with the smell of baked bread, the ground covered in colourful sheets littered with peppers and tomatoes spread out to dry. To the right, the kitchen spills out into the yard in a happy tumble of pots and pans, their polished faces upturned to the sun. Next to this an old woman sits with her back to Iskender. She holds a large silver sieve between her hands and as she shakes, great white clouds emanate, covering her from head to foot.

As his mother is ushered indoors, Iskender stands back, transfixed. The clouds of flour billow and settle into a perfectly symmetrical cone under the sieve. The nature of light and air, the forces of balance and gravity — the old woman is master of them all. She sifts again and Iskender sees — just for a fleeting moment — two outstretched wings of pale light surrounding her. It must be the heat. A trickle of sweat slips down his shirt and strokes his side. He can't help noticing how long the woman's fingers are, how rhythmic her hips. Her hair is thick, luxuriant, plaited in two healthy braids that drop to her waist; the ends curling back like unanswered questions. He is mesmerised. The more she shakes, the more her hair comes to life. He takes a step forward and a sudden cry shatters his dreams.

"Khatoun!" *Digin* Khouri calls from the doorway, "Clean up, and bring some refreshments for our guests."

The flour sifter stands up and turns to face the visitors and Iskender yelps. The long plaits belong to a beautiful girl. Of course! They are white with flour not age. The young woman facing him only reaches his third rib. She has slanted, Assyrian eyes, the softest blush of pink to her cheeks. If she held out her hand she would surely be holding an apple. And that hair...She smiles at him, lowers her eyes in the customary way and disappears into the kitchen.

A deafening silence envelops him and Iskender turns to face the two women causing it. They stand in the doorway, gleaming with delight. Not a single moment of his rapture has gone unnoticed. Mother and mother-in-law are fluffy and plump, exchanging that nod, that sly, almost imperceptible comma drawn with the point of a chin, one eyebrow raised. He is too shaken to feel embarrassed.

Love has entered through his eyes.

Khatoun and Iskender Agha Boghos

Ourfa, The Ottoman Empire, Spring 1897
Ferida, Iskender's sister

She's sitting there, this little bird, so small you could slip her into your pocket or wear her like a jewel on a chain. A single pearl suspended from your ear. She's so delicate you could snap her with words or bruise her with a sneeze. And she's pretty, oh yes; your girl shines beneath that wedding veil. Glows like a shepherd's lamp up in the caves. You want to reach out and touch her. To stop her trembling at the altar, but it's too late, *Digin* Mertha. You gave her away; the bride belongs to her man now. Only your memories are yours to keep.

Remember the day she was born? A screaming white angel, her wings folded in as she slipped your waters and landed on earth. The whole town heard the story. Even I. How the crops yielded double that year and people came to touch the hem of your child. You fed her on apricots and pomegranate seed and she never grew bigger than a wingspan could carry. You were right to keep her sheltered at home. Out of the wind. Out of the sun. The sun would have burnt her, the wind carried her away. And her heart? Her heart would have been stolen, fried with wild sage and eaten by now.

You secured her to earth with thick apron strings but a bird flew by and with its purple beak severed that rope. Took your girl with him. And now she sits there, your pearl. Trembling, trembling home from the baths despite burning *arak* poured down her throat and the heady song of the *zurna* and the beat of a tambourine. We stripped her naked of hair with sugar wax, painted his name into her hands and her feet, and still she shook until we paid the dancer more money and finally, when the dance got so wild even I was afraid, finally, her face split open and smiled.

And look at him, standing next to her, his skinny leg bent. My brother, Iskender. Doesn't he look the happy one? He's always dreamt of angels and now look at him; caught one of his own.

Look. Look at the space between them — just a finger apart —
burning. Look at her with mother's eyes one last time, *Digin*
Mertha. As soon as the prayers are over and the blessings are
done, she'll part the *douvagh* and show him her face and the child
Khatoun will be gone. We, her new family, we stole your cup
and spoon. She'll follow his footsteps now. Sleep in his bed. And
how will *your* mornings be?

You'll be picking stones from the lentils alone. The lamb and
the goose bleating her name as you feed them.

And in my kitchen the water will boil too many times.

A bride. Somebody's loss, somebody's gain.

So come now, mother Mertha, throw open the doors and let
the steam curl our hair. Let's drink rivers of *arak* and fill our
bellies like drums. Take out our kerchiefs and kick off our shoes
as we eye up the men. And we'll know we've had a good party
when glass shatters on wall. And tomorrow I'll bring you white
muslin stained red with blood and you'll know. She's no longer
a girl but a woman, her wings folded away. Now she is ours to
keep. So feast your eyes on her *Digin* Mertha, while you still can.
Your jewel is soon married and hung with our gold.

Sisters-in-Law

Baghshish, Between Ourfa and Aleppo, September 1898
Khatoun

If only he could bend down and whisper a word in her ear.

But what to say?

"Look at the distant hills scattered like discarded linen across the horizon." If he mouthed that to her what would she say back?

His wife.

Iskender pulls the horse to a stop. It's almost dusk and they've been on the road since dawn, travelling through endless plains bleached flat and colourless by the relentless sun. Finally the heat has broken and the parched landscape has given way to ripe wheat fields lit with gold. In the distance a boy pushes his fat-tailed sheep across the pasture so slowly it's only possible to tell he's moving by the clunk-tink of bells in the air. Further to the south, low hills do punctuate the horizon like discarded linen. Majestic purple shadows against a light-streaked sky.

Iskender takes a breath. Poetry leaves him, practicality lands. "Baghshish," he says, jabbing his chin towards a group of buildings under the trees ahead of them, "Everything you see belongs to my sister, Sophia, and her family. The farm, the fields, those sheep. There's a village further on — around that bend — Baghshish proper — that belongs to them too." He fiddles with the reins, waiting for her to reply but Khatoun's eyes remain closed, her hands clasped around the bundle in her lap. "Anyway, they're expecting us, so..." Iskender flicks his wrist and the horse sets off in the direction of the ranch, the dust powdering the vines at the side of the road a pale yellow.

His wife.

He'd planned a honeymoon by the sea. Beirut. He wanted to hold her like a shell to his ear, to smell the salt in her hair. To take morsels straight from her mouth and put them in his. He'd bought a new suitcase — tan leather with a scarlet interior — but the very day Kashioglu The Leatherman came to deliver it,

Iskender's father, who'd jumped out of bed and asked for his paper in his office with coffee, had died on page four. The suitcase
sat by the door all through the period of mourning, Iskender
suddenly too busy to notice.

He was conscious of the child bride that sat next to his mother at meals. Who hid behind his sister's skirts, skewering meat
and wiping homesick like rain from her cheeks. But the ledgers
and books narrowed his attention to a small pool of lamplight in
front of him, and at night he found himself removing his shoes
and entering a room already thick with her dreams.

And now?

Now it was too late for honeymoons. More than nine months
had passed and the women were whispering and giving those
sidelong glances. Those looks with the eyebrow involved. And
out of the blue a letter had arrived from his oldest sister, Sophia,
inviting them to harvest at her farm, and Ferida had had the suitcase packed and on the wagon before anyone could open their
mouth to object.

"Take Khatoun to Sophia's farm and give her a holiday, Asdvadz! Pale, skinny creature. And whatever you do, keep her
warm. Don't let her get cold. And when the harvest moon is
full, sleep with your window open and let the moon see you.
Then do what a good husband does." She'd spat into the air three
times, stuffed a warm bundle of eggs and freshly baked simit
into Khatoun's lap and disappeared indoors.

Iskender's mouth begins to water. They are so close, he can
smell the farm ahead. Slow-cooked lamb, stored apples, horse
dung and smoke. A large, two-storey building sits in the middle of a compound encircled by a stone wall. A gravel driveway
leads up to the porch where the front door, painted the same
deep blue as the Euphrates in summer, has almost disappeared
with the fading light. A handful of outbuildings scatter amongst
the trees to the right. A line of washing hurriedly being pulled
down under the sycamores. As soon as their wagon hits gravel, a
dog begins to bark and the deep blue door bursts open scattering
children and pets out like pebbles.

"UncleAuntieUncleAuntieHellohellohello!" they screech,
crushing each other in a scramble of paws and tails until the tall-
est of them — a girl in boy's britches — climbs up onto the wagon

and screams, "Enough!" Even then, the dogs keep yowling. As soon as there is a semblance of quiet the girl in britches turns to Khatoun and salutes.

"Hello Uncle, sorry Auntie – only three of us were supposed to come and greet you," she gestures towards the two lanky boys nuzzling the horse, "but the little ones do what they like – they don't listen – just like the dogs."

Iskender can count at least ten tousled heads and almost as many dogs circling the wagon and spooking the horse. All of the dogs are wearing iron wolf-collars which clang and batter like bells as they circumnavigate the crowd.

"I'm Mariam," the girl smiles, "that's George, that's Basil and the little ones are The Pests." She grabs a few bags from the cart and starts tossing them down to the other children who deftly avoid them. The tidy parcels thud to the ground and Iskender scrambles for his good suitcase as Mariam turns her attention to Khatoun's bundle. "Sorry about the noise, Auntie. Give me that. What, fragile? Yes, you keep it then. Come, I'll show you inside." She leaps down, helps Khatoun disembark and leads her by the arm, herding the gaggle of children in front of her.

"Basil! George! Wake up! Leave the horse alone and take Uncle Iskender to the stables!" she waves her arms at her brothers and they stare back at her goggle-eyed. "Boys," she says with a shrug. She pushes the little ones towards the front door, all of them pulling and plucking at Khatoun's fine travel dress.

"What is it?"

"Silk."

"Your mother made it for you?"

"Yes."

"And now you're married you'll be making little dresses too?"

Mariam yanks the chatty girl's plait. "Who said you could ask questions Rachel? Go on, take this box inside and keep quiet."

She is just a finger younger than Khatoun and rolls her eyes at talk of babies. Life to her is tearing across the plains on her horse. She knows she thinks differently; she's had enough lectures on ladylike behaviour and what is expected of her; but a woman stuck with a baby on her breast can't run, can't fight, can't survive. One day, she knows, that will be the difference between those that live and those that don't. Defiantly, she grabs Iskender's valise and hoists it up onto her shoulder, startling

Khatoun. She points to the door with her free hand, "And that's my mother."

Sophia waits for them on the porch, her eyes lively, one eyebrow – the right one – raised in a permanent question mark. She has inherited Seyda's pale milky skin and sprinkling of freckles and she smiles easily, finding life itself amusing in her European dress, buttoned high at the neck. She buries Khatoun in her ample bosom and with a quick flick of fingers, scatters the children away.

"The men will be in shortly," she says, leading Khatoun down the hall into a large sitting room. "Abdanour is in the stables showing off the horses to Iskender," she rolls her eyes. "Horses come first in this family. I've warned him not to take too long. Here, sit opposite me so I can see your lovely face. So, how was the journey? How are the family? Are you hungry?"

Before Khatoun can answer even one of the questions the door opens and four of the children file in again, this time with slick hair and scrubbed skin.

"Mariam."

"Sara."

"Bahie."

"Rachel."

They bob politely as they call out their names. Mariam is now in a dress matching her sisters but her shoes are scuffed and the ends of her braids loose, not beribboned like the others. Khatoun wishes she knew where her bags went. In one of them lay several stuffed dollies, a carved mirror and an olivewood comb she'd brought as gifts. She glances anxiously towards the door and Sophia laughs.

"Don't worry. There's no more. The Pests are being put to bed already – it's long past their bedtime. We told them they could say a quick hello if you arrived before dark. They're Anni's."

"Anni?"

"Yes. My other sister-in-law, Sammi's wife. Anni and Sammi. Yes, I know, it rhymes. They are a poem. She wanted to say hello but she has to stay in bed – doctor's orders. She's got another one on the way. You can meet her tomorrow." She's about to say more when the door flies open. Two men, dressed entirely in animal skins, slide across the flagstones, skid to a halt in the middle of the room and burst into song.

"Tomorrow! You can meet her tomorrow!" they harmonise. The shorter of the two, the one with black hair, bows effusively and the other, taller, more handsome, sweeps round the room scattering children and cushions perilously close to the fire. When he gets to Khatoun he hoists her into the air, arms pinned to her sides and kisses her numerous times on each cheek, stamping his foot and whooping after each kiss. Iskender watches from the doorway, his fingers busy in his moustache.

"Still as small as a dolly!" Abdanour laughs as he sets Khatoun back down and pinches her cheek. He bends his elbow and pretends to lean on her head making his daughters squeal, then stretches up, exposing his tight hairy belly as he smells his armpit. "Oh dear. That'll have to wait," he says, "I'm starving. I need food. Or maybe I'll just eat someone here. Which one of you looks tasty?" he skims the room and the young girls screech and jostle behind each other. "Skin and bones, all of you," he yells. "Come on, we need *real* food. It's eat or be eaten. Follow me!" He marches past Iskender, trailed first by the children then Sammi, who backs out of the room bowing, furry hat in hand.

"My husband, Abdanour, always in high spirits, and his brother, Sammi, not much better," Sophia laughs. "Come, I'll show you where you can clean up and then let's eat or Abdanour will come looking for us. One day he really will pick you up and carry you off under his arm, don't doubt it!" She pushes them out into the corridor, Iskender muttering into his moustache, a hooked finger snaking towards Khatoun's shoulder.

"Oops, your fez!" Sophia says, knocking the hat off his head and catching it with her foot before it hits the floor. "Just in case you're too stiff to get it back." She plops it on her head and steps past the couple into the hallway. "Come on. It's eat or be eaten, remember?"

Dinner is set in a cavernous room with thick walls and heavy rafters. A fireplace crackles at one end, at the other, French doors open onto a beautiful tree-filled courtyard. As they file in, the doors to the courtyard are shut and the fireplace leaps to life. The wall lamps are lit, the one from the other. Tall candles illuminate the table which is already set with steaming platters of *pilaff* and lamb, pots of yoghurt, olives and pickles. The children arrange themselves around the table, boy, girl, boy, girl and at the head — his eyes faded to a milky blue — sits Old Glore Boghos, the head of the household.

His teeth have gone, his features have withered but he still has broad shoulders and a solid chest you could thump. He smiles at Khatoun and beckons her over. He takes her hand in his and holds it to his cheek for a moment and then to his lips. He reaches past her for Iskender and allows the younger man to droop over him as he kisses both eyes and then, with a smile, urges everyone to start.

"Eat, eat," Old Glore says, releasing his hold. He waves his hand across the table and the chairs fly out, squeezing Khatoun between Abdanour and Sammi who pile food on her plate faster than she can eat it. There is a constant stream of stuff coming from the kitchen. Flat loaves of bread. Vegetables. Jugs of wine. The plates are passed around. The bread stuffed into each other's mouths dripping with gravy. The searing hot pickles chased down with wine.

And all the while, Khatoun is transfixed by Old Glore. His face is in perpetual motion, nodding constantly as if in private conversation. His eyebrows furrow and his lips tremble — sometimes so much he has to abandon his spoonful and reach for a napkin instead. Every once in a while he barks out a laugh which every one at the table ignores. His eyes have faded to a milky blue but when he turns to face whoever is speaking they light up silver. He listens with a smile, as if he already knows everything and is just humouring a child. On his right there is an empty space — not laid for dinner but vacant, nevertheless, throughout the meal — as if someone were expected. There are at least five conversations going on at once. If she could just clear the space in front of her, Khatoun would lay down her head. Maybe listen with her eyes shut. Perhaps just one of them. She pushes her plate forward an inch and catches Old Glore staring in her direction, his face finally still.

"Tired?" he asks.

Khatoun nods. The table seems suddenly quiet.

"How long is it taking these days, in a wagon?"

"We set off before dawn," Khatoun says, looking across at Iskender before adding, "The journey was fine, thank you."

"And now you're ready for sleep, I can sense that. Tomorrow night you will join us for conversation and games after supper, but tonight your wings may carry you where they will. To infinite heavens, *Insha'Allah*." And with this he nods at Sophia who stands expectantly, ready to show Khatoun to her room.

"I'll be back with coffee," Sophia says, pushing Iskender back down into his seat. "Cards. You and me against Abdanour and Sammi. We'd better win or you'll lose your fez once and for all." She grabs a lamp from the wall and leads Khatoun out of the room, the row of children calling "good night" as they go.

Down the corridor and into the dark stairwell. Khatoun is exhausted. Her bones are heavy and the wine is making her head loose at the neck. She trips on the hem of her skirt going up the stairs and Sophia giggles, reaching a hand out to steady her.

"Our home-made wine," she laughs, "it'll get you every time. We always sleep up in the summer, that way we can have the windows open for air. Downstairs is for the colder nights. Here," she guides them to the top of the stairs and into the first door on their right, "this room is yours." She walks over to the dresser and lights a lamp and the warm tones of the kilims scattered across the floor jump to life. "This is where I used to sleep when I came here…oh…forever ago. Come, look at this." She crosses the room and throws the shutters open onto a wide stone balcony. A cool breeze, sweet as the scent of apples invades the room. A million stars light up the sky, a pale wash of milk against the inky black.

"I used to spend hours out here counting them until I fell asleep," Sophia says. "I always woke up back in bed with no idea how I got there. In the morning, over tea, Old Glore would talk to me about the planets. Which stars were visible at what times. He was the one that taught me to look up when I felt sad. 'A different perspective always helps,' he'd say. That and, 'How many is in infinity? If you can answer that, you'll rule the world.' Of course I tried! 'Infinity is infinite,' I'd tell him and Old Glore would laugh. 'And what about infinity plus *one*?' Imagine – these stars are millions of years old. We're just specks of dust compared to them…our lives already over before their light even reaches us."

Khatoun looks up at the stars wondering who might be mad

enough to try counting them. Right now she can hardly focus on anything. She yawns.

"Sleep for you," Sophia smiles, "I'll see you in the morning. Someone will come and get you. Good night," and with a swift kiss she is gone.

The bed smells of lavender and as soon as she slips under the sheets Khatoun is asleep. She's aware of Iskender joining her later; the sliver of light sliding across her cheek as he throws open the window, the soft pad of his feet across the floor, the scent of brandy as he breathes warmth into her neck and strokes her thigh.

In her dreams, a woman smiles at her with stars in her eyes. She is seated to the right of Glore Boghos in that empty chair, embroidering a piece of linen as she listens to her family. She looks at Khatoun and the light from her smile is a million years old and stretches into infinity. Khatoun is welcome she is told and the stars will be her children. First, though, she must sew them into the world.

"Find your silver thread," the woman says, "and keep your needles shining. Like the moon."

The next morning there are even more faces at breakfast, the Pests included. A stream of girls bring in tea and jam, eggs and cheese from the kitchen. The doors are open, the birds pecking at crumbs in the courtyard. Unlike dinner the night before, breakfast is a hasty affair. As soon as they've eaten, everyone scatters; the young girls to the kitchen to help with the bread, the boys to their tutor — a skinny woman with acne in an unfortunate lemon-yellow dress. Even Old Glore waves *adieu* and takes to his horse, the age melting from his limbs as he slips easily into the saddle and heads out to the fields. And before Iskender can hide with a book and another pot of coffee, Abdanour and Sammi have dragged him off, bustling his immaculately dressed torso out into the warm sunshine.

"Don't worry — he'll look great in goatskins!" they threaten, flicking each other with whips as they go. "On Jermug — the mare who doesn't know 'No'."

"You wouldn't do that to him…"

"Why not? She loves strangers…"

"Oh, Lord!"

Sophia laughs and takes Khatoun's arm, "Ignore them. Your husband will be back in one piece, you'll see. Come with me. We'll take tea to Anni, and then you can see the rest of the house."

"Is Anni all right?" Khatoun asks, "We won't be disturbing her will we?"

"Oh no! She's demanded a visit. If she had her way she'd be up and giving the girls hell in the kitchen. It's doctor's orders — she has to lie down for the next few weeks and it's driving her mad. She'll love the company. Come, you carry this," she hands Khatoun a steaming tray of glasses that has arrived, "and I'll bring these." She plucks a linen covered plate from the table and leans into Khatoun. "And don't tell her husband — she's not supposed to be eating sweets."

Together they creak up the stairs and down the corridor to the end, turning at the window into an annexe where a young girl sits by the door, sewing. She puts down her work and stands up to open it as they approach.

"Zeta stop, have a rest," Sophia says dismissing the girl, "Go outside and get some air. Sammi," she tuts, "has someone sit here all day *in case* Anni needs anything. As if we don't all have better things to do. Husbands! Too nosy. And he's getting worse."

She pushes the door open onto a beautiful sun splattered room, a huge bed sailing in the middle, a mess of pillows and blankets. Propped up amongst the cushions is a pregnant woman — her blue silk gown thrown open for air, her hair loose around her shoulders. She's clutching a book in one hand and kicking a patterned eiderdown onto the floor as they enter.

"*Pari louys!* You must be Khatoun, come, come!" she says, dropping her book and patting the bed.

Sophia sets the plate of goodies on the nightstand and swoops in for a kiss. "Khatoun, meet Anni — mother of The Pests. Anni, this is Khatoun — the girl who *finally* captured my brother's heart." She snuggles up to her sister-in-law on the bed and reaches back for the plate.

"Khatooooooooun!" a wide smile splits Anni's face, "I've heard *so* much about you and now I see it's all *true*. You *are* a little dolly!" she starts to giggle and Sophia joins in. They clap their hands with glee as Khatoun stands there with the tea tray, steam rising from the thin patterned glasses.

"Put the tray down," Sophia laughs, "sit with us."

"Yes, *sit*," Anni says, "but first, promise me something. Don't *ever* take anything said in this house seriously." She kicks a bolster onto the floor and pats the edge of the bed again. "Now sit *down*."

Khatoun clears a space on the nightstand with her elbow and gets rid of the tray. She slips off her shoes, smoothes down her skirt and settles next to the women in their sea of pillows. Sophia leans over to the window, grabs an old walking stick that had been resting against it and pushes the shutters open. The view across the plains streams into the room.

"There they are," she says pointing to three figures on horseback, "our husbands."

Khatoun sips her tea and watches the riders as her sisters-in-law catch up on yesterday's gossip. Lessons, food, who ate what. The colour of whose movements. The girls' monthly swings. In the distance the men shrink to dots and disappear into the haze.

"Mmm, *kurabia*," Anni says reaching for another pastry. "I'm supposed to be on a diet. Can you imagine? A pregnant woman on a diet? That doctor of mine is full of modern ideas. I'm not doing this again."

"*Again?*" Khatoun asks, setting the women off into laughter again.

"Why? Do you think there's too many already?"

"I...no...I don't know...how many...How many *are* there?"

"Fourteen between us," Sophia laughs.

"Don't! It's still thirteen until...you know..."Anni rubs her belly.

"One a year, every year since I got married," Sophia says. "First six are mine, the seven little ones are Anni's. The Pests. And that one on the way. Definitely another pest."

"The men make horses and we make children," Anni sighs. "Thank God we have the land to sustain them."

"*Park Asdoudzo.*"

Anni turns back to the window with a yawn. "And where are they now?"

"There," Sophia says pointing her stick lazily towards the horizon. A flicker of dots in a dust cloud.

"Time to shut my eyes I think," Anni sighs. "No blankets, no more pillows," she murmurs as Sophia picks up the discarded linen from the floor, "it's too much. I'm too hot."

Khatoun finishes her tea and since the lightly powdered biscuits have all been devoured, the shutters are pulled and they leave the ripe Anni to her nap.

They drop off the trays with Zeta, who is back in her corner feverishly attacking her embroidery, and continue down the corridor, the floorboards creaking as they pass. Sophia pauses at the top of the staircase that curves down to the hallway at the back of the house. A framed photograph of her family hangs above a small wooden table on the landing. Her children posing with her in a studio mock-up of a grand sitting room filled with potted plants. Abdanour stands behind her, slightly to the left, one hand resting on her shoulder, his eyes suppressing a grin and Old Glore Boghos sits next to her on the little striped *divan*, his pale eyes staring straight through the lens of the camera. Behind them, a backdrop of billowing clouds looks odd – as if one whole wall of their house had simply fallen away, leaving them both comfortable but exposed to the elements.

Sophia is quiet. She leans in to the photograph and traces her finger over the faces of her children.

"I notice you're still slim after a year of marriage," she says, her voice so low, Khatoun is not sure whether she just imagined it. She'd been thinking the same thing. Anni, she's calculated, has been continuously pregnant for the last eight years. Almost half of Khatoun's life. She can't imagine what it will be like to sit amongst family in some draughty studio and have her photograph taken. Standing at the top of the creaking staircase staring at the strange, distant expressions in the photo, Khatoun feels homesick. Not for a place, but for a time when nothing was asked of her, nothing expected other than that she complete her chores. Childhood. So simple and gone so soon.

"Let's go and sit for a moment," Sophia says, leading Khatoun down the stairs. As they enter the courtyard a woman appears noiselessly from the kitchens and asks what they'd like.

"Coffee, some grapes. Not too much, we've just had tea, thank you." Sophia eases herself into a chair under the trees and kicks off her shoes. "So," she says, smiling.

"So," Khatoun smiles back.

"How old are you now?"

"Sixteen."

"That's young. And in this life, youth is on your side. Your whole life is still ahead of you."

"*Insha'Allah.*"

"And you and Iskender...he is...you are...you know...everything is...*good* between you?"

Khatoun stares at Sophia blankly.

"When you're alone together...you...enjoy each other's company?" her eyebrow hovers.

"Of course."

"Good," Sophia smiles.

"Although..."

"Yes?"

"Sometimes he's too quiet."

"*Quiet?*"

"He doesn't say anything."

"What do you want him to *say?*"

"I don't know. He could talk to me."

"Talk to you?"

"Yes. To make our time alone more interesting."

"*Interesting?*"

Somewhere a door slams and a child begins to wail. Sophia shifts in her seat and leans forward.

"Listen, Khatoun, woman to woman, tell me straight. Is everything the way it should be, sweet-talking in your ear or no talking, you know, at *that* time, between a *man* and his *wife?*"

Khatoun frowns for a moment and then, hand to her face, "Yes, *Asdvadz*, yes!"

"Well, thank the Lord for *that!*" Sophia plucks at the high collar of her dress. "I'm so sorry. I had to ask. It's none of my business...but family is family and Iskender can be a little different and everyone thought I should ask because I'm the eldest..."

"*Everyone?*"

"Yes. I mean no! Just family. Not *everyone*. No one in fact. No one else is gossiping, no one at all. Just...us..." she stops and looks around frantically. "Where *is* that girl with the coffee?" The two sisters-in-law stare at each other for a minute and then burst into laughter.

"Family business," Sophia says, wiping her eyes, "it's the worst! You'll be fine. You *will* have children, *Insha'Allah,* but it may take time. I hear you were a late bloomer. And don't blush again, you're family now. Women talk."

Khatoun nods, "I know. I'm learning. They say I started late, that's why we had such a long engagement. I think your mother wanted to make sure I could have children first. I know they all looked at me differently after I changed into long skirts. And now they look at me in a different way altogether."

"And I know *that* feeling," Sophia sighs, "eyes always on you. Whisper, whisper behind your back. Don't be surprised. You thought you were the only one? I'm just the same as you. You see me as this older woman with her life in control – but let me tell you, it wasn't always that way. I know how you feel. I've been through exactly what you're going through. I was twelve years old when I was promised to Abdanour and sent to live here. They'd only just buried their mother, Nairi. She was my mother's best friend and she died suddenly with no warning, poof, just like that. Abdanour was at school in Aintab so he was away for long periods of time and I was left alone in this house with his little brother Sammi and Old Glore who terrified me. All I could think about was my life back in Ourfa, my friends, my sisters. I'd hated them at home – always squabbling about ribbons and hair. Ferida and her moods. I even missed Iskender and his stupid jokes. There were no jokes in this house. The whole place was covered in sheets, the mirrors turned to the wall. I kept thinking, 'Why me?' Abdanour's mother could read and write. She spoke French, English, Arabic – who was *I* to step into her shoes? I cried myself to sleep every night and when I walked into the kitchens in the morning the cooks would be ruining the food with *their* wailing. That empty chair at the table? It's Nairi's. Empty, except to Old Glore. Some days I could smell her. Once, her footsteps followed me through the house and she sat at the edge of my bed and watched me sleep. But I was never scared. Lonely, yes, but never scared. You see, this house loves women. These stones were laid thousands of years ago for families to be born into, to have a heartbeat that would nourish the fields. When there's harmony in the kitchens, the crops do well. When there's love at night, the horses breed. My mother knew this and as soon as Nairi died she brought me here, promised to Abdanour, the eldest son."

Sophia pauses, accepting the tray of thimble sized coffee cups and water from the maid. She takes a sip and nods at Khatoun to do the same.

"Drink it down. Don't let it get cold. See, Old Glore didn't want a new mother for his sons, but a new *daughter* – that was something else. I lived here as brother-sister with Abdanour for four years until I was ready for marriage. I was lucky. I had all that time to get to know my husband and family before we married." She takes another sip of coffee and giggles. "As a matter of fact, I liked Abdanour from the beginning, I just never showed it. We'd started talking and I began to miss him whenever he went back to college. I was happy to marry him and I still am. Finished your coffee? Good. Turn the cup upside down. I'll read it in a minute."

Khatoun watches a leaf spiral slowly to her feet. She picks it up and twists it around in her hand, watching the curled edges change colour.

"My favourite tree," she says looking up. "I like the smell after it rains."

"Sycamore. Yes, sweet like apples. Reminds me of the mountains."

"I liked Iskender when I met him, too," Khatoun says. "He spoke to me. When I brought the lemonade."

"He *spoke* to you? That first day? Iskender? What did he say?"

"He asked me if I had ever cut my hair."

"He asked you *what?*"

"He asked me if I'd ever cut my hair."

"And what did you say?"

"I shook my head, no. Then he spoke again and your mother gave him a terrible look."

"Why? What did he say?" Sophia shoves the platter of grapes towards Khatoun.

"He said he hoped I wouldn't cut my hair until the day I died. He said if I let it loose, it would surely carry me to heaven like angel's wings."

Sophia stares at Khatoun, a purple grape just inches from her lips. She pops the grape into her mouth and begins to chuckle. "Oh my! I heard there was a scandal but no one would repeat it. Normally he's completely tongue-tied but sometimes...there's definitely a poet in there somewhere. *Agh*, Iskender! And what did you do after he said that?"

"My mother sent me to get the preserves we had made the year before. All the way to the cellar. When I got back it was as if nothing had happened. Iskender didn't speak to me again. He was looking down at his shoes. Moving his feet in them and they were creaking. He was completely lost in his shoes. That's when I knew I liked him. I dreamt of him that night."

"You dreamt of Iskender?" Sophia is astonished. They'd only met formally before – once at Khatoun's wedding and then at Sophia's father's funeral – and on both occasions their only exchanges had been the usual pleasantries made between sisters-in-law. In fact, at her wedding, Khatoun had been so quiet and had trembled so much, Sophia had had to slip her a drink to calm her nerves. And now here she is, sharing her intimate secrets over coffee.

"Yes. I dreamt of him many times but that night was the first. I dreamt he came to me and undid my hair. It fanned out like wings and carried me up into the sky, just as he'd said it would. The sky was pale blue with clouds edged in gold. I floated up and up and when I looked down there was everything I was leaving, far away on the ground. My family, my house, my pet lamb. I heard a voice nearby which calmed me. It was Iskender – he was singing and I started to sing with him. And time passed while we flew in the sky and the next thing I was singing to him and he was an old man, and then he was dying but it wasn't sad. On the contrary, he was happy because I'd never cut my hair and I would always be able to find him in the afterlife by undoing it and floating up to heaven."

Sophia looks at her sister-in-law and realises two things. First, Khatoun had obviously been starved of conversation for the last year (*Idiot Iskender! Useless Ferida!*) and secondly, her brother had finally met his soul mate. Here was someone that not only entertained Iskender's thoughts but took them and embroidered them with her own. She bends to kiss Khatoun's hand.

"You two will be fine," she says. "I can see that without even looking into your coffee cup. Which reminds me, hand it over so that I can see what else is in store."

Khatoun pushes the saucer across the table and Sophia picks up the cup and peers into it.

"Aha, three...no...four children...but not for a while...you have business to take care of first. Look here...see, life sends

you back and forth, back and forth, some of it difficult...but...
all the pieces of your life come together with stitches. Your life,
your children's and theirs, everything comes through this needle
here. Look."

Khatoun peers into the cup. "You see all that in *there?*"

"Yes."

"And the difficult times?" Khatoun twists the cup from side
to side trying to make sense out of the swirling brown lines in
front of her.

"Don't worry," Sophia is emphatic. "The troubles will slip beneath you like silk on a sewing machine, see," she points to a
splatter near the handle, "and look, you *are* carried on wings. You
will move and move again. All your life. Interesting." She puts
the cup down. "Do you sew?"

"I used to. My embroidery is good but I'm more in the kitch-
en."

"Ha! No wonder my sister has it in for you!" Sophia slaps
her thigh and chuckles. "You need to get out of the kitchen,
fast. That's Ferida's domain. Let me see your hands." She takes
Khatoun's fingers and holds them up to the sky, "Look! Perfect.
Well, that's you organised. I see gold, fabrics, jewels, pearls,
many many servants, a cavernous house – oh yes, and a husband
with shirts that are *finally* loose enough around the collar!"

Khatoun laughs. "I would love a big house," she says, eyeing up
the stone walls that had seemed so imposing the evening before.

"And you'll have one bigger than this, trust me. Come, I'll
show you around." Sophia pulls her chair back to stand and the
same silent maid appears, gathers up their cups and follows
them into the kitchens.

Khatoun has no idea what to expect. In Ourfa the houses have
dirt floors covered in rugs that are impossible to sweep. This
house has stone everywhere, even in the kitchens. Even across
the floors.

She follows Sophia into the first of several high-ceilinged
rooms that interconnect through a series of doorways. The first
room is empty. The next, hung solely with saucepans; copper,
bronze, tin, arranged neatly by size. The following room is lined
with glass cabinets, delicate flowers and vines crawling all over
the European porcelain displayed within. Before she got married Khatoun had eaten from a communal plate at home. Sitting

on the floor. With fingers. Never from anything painted with flowers.

And now into the largest room with its high-vaulted ceiling and crescent shaped skylights. Charcoal burners bubble along the length of one wall and a stone slab the size of a door serves as a table in the middle of the room where a team of girls are busy packing stuffed vegetables down into saucepans with stone weights.

"*Digin, Digin, Digin*," they bob as they see Sophia, "*dolma* tonight."

Through the kitchen into a side room, the air powdered white. Ghostly figures moving about in a flurry.

"Anoush?" Sophia calls.

"*Digin* Sophia!" Anoush says, stepping forward and pushing her hair back with her wrist, "I didn't see you come in!" Behind her, at a low table the Pests are busy at work. One is sifting vast mountains of flour, the other is spreading it across the table thin as a sheet, and the littlest is elbow-deep in dough. Their whole corner is powdered white. As soon as they see them, the girls hurtle over, their clammy hands looking for love. Quicker than them, Sophia does a swift sidestep and with a pirouette, leads them to the sink.

"Where's Mariam?" she asks.

"Finding eyes."

"And Bahie?"

"Teeth."

"And Baby Lousaper?"

"They were all here a minute ago," Anoush shrugs, "right under my feet. We're baking harvest dolls."

"Of course," Sophia smiles. She gestures for Khatoun to follow her, crossing the kitchen in a few strides, a cautionary finger at her lips. She chooses a heavy door and leans in, pressing her cheek to the wood and listening. Suddenly, without a sound, she yanks it open. Mariam, the eldest, is balanced precariously on a stool, rummaging amongst the jars normally out of reach on the upper shelves. Below her, Sara, Bahie and Rachel sit around Baby Lousaper feeding her treats like a pet. Baby Lousaper is making her way through fistfuls of *rojig* and *halvah*, the front of her starched pinafore slick with spittle and juice. She belches, sicks up brown jelly, pushes more into her mouth and wails.

The kitchen falls quiet; Mariam suspended on the stool, the pots bubbling, Sophia's right eyebrow – the one like a whip – rising. Just before it hits heaven, Sophia turns to Khatoun with a smile.

"And this is the pantry," she says, "This is where we keep all our preserves; the cherry and quince jams, the grapes in molasses. Dried meats hang up there. Mariam? Thank you. *Bastourma* and *soujouk*. Pickles on the lower shelves and sweets like *lokhoum* and sugared almonds up on the highest shelves away from mice and vermin. As you can see, it's a wonderful place. The sort of room I used to hide in when I was little. The smell is quite intoxicating. We keep all our spices in here that we import from India. That's part of the business. We send them wool and bring in delicious spices to sell in neighbouring towns. Of course, it's part of the job that we sample everything. That way we know the quality of what we are dealing with." She gently pushes the pantry door closed on her incredulous daughters, leaving them to scuttle out behind her back moments later with the wailing Baby Lousaper.

"I think the girls have had enough of cooking for one day," Sophia tells Anoush. "Please make sure they're all clean before lunch." She steps out into the hall, dragging Khatoun behind her and only stops when she is sure no one can see them. She leans back against the wall, laughing. "God's gift and a mother's nightmare! And you say you want children? Let's go, there's more."

As they head down the corridor Khatoun can hear voices. The singing gets louder until they reach their last stop – the laundry – set in a wide alcove running along the back wall of the kitchens. The far corner is dominated by a huge copper boiler where the household water is heated to scalding every morning. The room is filled with steam and four rosy-cheeked girls are busy over their stone tubs, scrubbing away at sheets and clothing. The room smells of pine and their singing reaches up to the domed ceiling, turning the room into a mini cathedral.

"Washing day," explains Sophia, "we do it once a week – and the girls practice their church songs in here. The moisture is good for the throat. Beautiful isn't it?"

"It's so peaceful," Khatoun agrees, "I feel I want to stay and join them."

"You can join them in Church on Sunday," Sophia laughs. "What would my brother say if he came back and saw you up to your elbows in our washing? He'd never forgive me. Anyway," she glances at the gold watch hanging around her neck, "it's time we took a break and got ready for lunch. Why don't you go up to your room and relax for a while? The men will be back soon with their tales of gore from the outside world. We'll need to be rested just to get through their stories."

Khatoun finds her way back to her room. The bed has been made and the shutters closed but instead of lying down on the fragrant bed she walks over to the French windows and steps out onto the balcony. White heat. The scalding silence of noon. Something about the heat calms her. The house with its many rooms and beautiful things has made her feel small. How can she satisfy her husband when the rest of his family are so worldly and outgoing? Some evenings pass when hardly a word is said between them. She always thought this was normal for new husbands and wives but now she's no longer sure.

She squints into the distance. That is how far away she is from being where she should be. Out there in that shimmering horizon, that is where she is, and this is where she needs to get to. She wants noise. Sticky fingers and tears. Floury footprints and spittle to clean. Not dust to sweep from one room to the next. A trickle of sweat runs down her forehead into her eye and she reaches up with the hem of her skirt to wipe it away. When she looks out again she can distinguish three small figures making their way home. Soon they are close enough to make out the one from the other, but there is something different about them. Something odd.

It's only when the men turn to ride alongside the low wall circling the house that Khatoun figures out what it is. Sammi is now wearing Iskender's fez pushed high on his forehead like a unicorn's horn and Iskender is wearing Sammi's wide-brimmed fur hat – like a farmhand. And he's laughing. Khatoun has seen him smile before but never laugh and right now he's laughing so much he's in danger of falling off his horse.

At this moment Sammi spies her on the balcony and pulls his horse up into a majestic rear. "Oh beauteous one!" he calls out before she can turn and hide. "Which one of us poor suitors will you choose?"

"*Me!* Take *me*," Abdanour yells, "I'm the best horseman!"

"Liar! I'm best and I can prove it."

"In your *dreams!*" Abdanour yelps, taking off at a full gallop, a whooping Sammi leaping the wall after him.

The dust settles around Iskender who sits on his horse facing his wife, a wide grin still on his face. "So," he asks, "which one of us *do* you choose, oh Beauteous One?"

A blush rises to her cheeks burning deeper than the sun. A voice sings lullabies in her ears and her wings spread out, spread out around her. The house creaks with delight and she takes flight, drifting high, high, higher into the pale blue sky, her silver needle in hand.

"You. I choose you," she sings in harmony as she embroiders the edges of clouds a rich gold. "You are the one."

The Singer

Ourfa, Summer 1900
Khatoun

Early morning. The heat is quietly seeping into the dusty streets that wind through the Armenian Quarter as Khatoun and Ferida quickstep towards *Digin* Aghavni's house. They're late for their lesson – something the pinch-faced Aghavni has already warned she *will not tolerate!* It's not their fault – they were already at the door ready to leave when Grundug had turned up, limping and bloody-pawed. A quick examination had revealed a long sliver of metal embedded in the soft pad of his forepaw.

"Stupid animal!" Ferida had screeched, dragging the slipper off her foot. "He's been at the silversmith's again!" At the sight of worn leather Grundug had set off around the house, bloodying nearly all of the rugs before Khatoun had been able to catch him and remove the splinter. It had taken both of them to bind the wound with rags which Grundug had immediately gnawed off under the table. Then they'd had to mop up the blood before it set into the kilims and ruined them forever. Finally, with a woe-begone Grundug tethered to the back door, they'd set off for their sewing class, Khatoun unable to shut out Ferida's invective about the dog.

"He licks my face with stinky breath…always under my feet when I'm cooking…pisses in the doorway…he even wants to sleep with me…as if I want his fleas! Stupid animal."

Grundug was Ferida's dog – her surrogate child and the love of her life. Discovered as a pup in the gutter, he'd been attached to her heel ever since. Khatoun smiles at Ferida's complaints, unwilling to accuse her of jealousy, even though that is obviously what is wrong this morning. Grundug may love his mistress, but he has other feelings entirely for the curly-haired little bitch that sleeps in the doorway of the silversmith's every night. Feelings that enrage Ferida who expects to wake and find Grundug at the end of her bed with looks of love solely for her.

"Stop laughing at me and go faster!" Ferida yells, "We're going to get an earful for this!" They break into a gallop for the last stretch, reach the heavy panelled door set in the wall of Aghavni's house and push hard against it. It is locked. Ouf! One of them must now take the bronze hand that serves as a knocker, bang it down on the plate ("Not too hard — women are never strident!") and announce their arrival. They look at each other. A lecture is inevitable. Tardiness. The value of time. Ladylike manners. Khatoun shrugs, reaches for the knocker and gives it a hefty bang.

The door springs open and *Digin* Aghavni stands smiling in the well of cool air in the hallway.

"Oh!" she says graciously, "What a lovely surprise. How delightful to have your company. Please, *do* come in."

Khatoun and Ferida step inside but before either of them can begin to explain, they are pinned to the wall, shoulder to shoulder and the front door bolted shut.

"Ladies never run," Aghavni says, "especially in public. As a married woman, you should know better," she admonishes Khatoun. "And as for you," she plants her face inches from Ferida's and lowers her voice, "please remember never to run until you are married. People may think you are a loose woman otherwise. Now," she steps back smiling again, "since this is the first time you are late, I shall forgive you. By God's grace, it is in my heart to do so. The next time, however, you will have to do as the other girls, and stay late, unpicking seams as punishment."

"Yes, *Digin* Aghavni. Thank you," the girls nod, bob a brief curtsey.

"Unpicking? Me? *Kaknem*," Ferida mutters into her armpit.

"Ferida?"

"Nothing."

"May the good Lord bless you."

"And you."

"And now, let us wash our hands and begin." Aghavni sets off down the hall to the alcove where an ornate washbasin stands. She lifts the jug and pours water over their hands, handing them each a small linen towel embroidered with their name when they are clean.

She's a good woman, *Digin* Aghavni. An orphan brought up by Scottish missionaries in Marash, who'd nurtured in her a devotion to both God and the great Queen Victoria. She was once a pretty girl but her face had changed when her one, brief engagement had ended with the massacres of eighteen-ninety-five. Her fiancé, a goldsmith, had been at work, bent over his latest piece – a wedding bracelet he was setting with emeralds for her. Oblivious to the commotion outside in the street, he had looked up in surprise when the door burst open only to receive a bullet in his left eye that left the workshop wall spattered with brains.

Her heart broken beyond repair, Aghavni had fled the city she'd once loved and moved to Ourfa. She set up business – a small trade school teaching dressmaking – and dedicated her life to bringing the love of Jesus and the morals of Queen Victoria to the girls she taught. A brilliant seamstress, she took in just half a dozen students at a time, working them hard. She showed them how to cut patterns, manage a machine and perfect their needlework, quoting either the Bible or her antiquated Scottish book on etiquette as she drifted beatifically amongst them.

Khatoun and Ferida were her newest students and although Khatoun showed great promise, Ferida was a thorn in the side with her uneven stitches and hasty cutting. She'd be far better off in the kitchen, Aghavni thought, although it was doubtful she'd ever marry with her quick temper and sour looks. Maybe that was the cause of her bitterness. Who could tell? An unmarried woman with vile language, a cack-hand and a plain face. Still, every woman had her place in society, just like herself. God bless the spinsters of the world. Amen. And now to work.

"Inside," she says, opening the door to the workroom and ushering them in. Four other girls are already bent over their sewing.

"Good morning, Ferida. Good morning, *Digin* Khatoun," they chime, looking up only when their next stitch is done.

"Good morning, everyone. We apologise for being late," Khatoun says.

"Yes," Ferida mumbles, "sorry."

"We forgive you. It's nothing at all," the girl on the far right smiles. "Do please join us," she indicates two covered tables at the front of the room and returns to her embroidery. Khatoun sits cross-legged at one of the low tables and pulls the flower-sprigged dust-cloth away.

The little machine smiles back at its proud owner. Khatoun reaches out and strokes the shiny black metal, tracing the ten-

drils of gold vine that decorate its sides. It had been her mother's
– passed down as a gift to celebrate her eighteenth birthday. And
now she's learning how to use it. Khatoun eases the handle forward and the needle lifts up.

"It says 'Singer' in English," *Digin* Aghavni says, extending a
finger over Khatoun's shoulder and underlining the word, "*Ye-
rkchouhi*. And if you treat her well, she will sing for you all your
life and bring your gift to fruition."

Khatoun laughs. "I'm not sure I have a gift, *Digin* Aghavni,
rather a good teacher."

"Hmm, flattery," Aghavni looks stern, "Unfortunately, it will
get you everywhere in this world." She lets in the glimmer of
a smile before moving on to the next girl, "Keep up the good
work, and the Lord will praise you."

Khatoun reaches under the table for her sewing. Folded neatly
into a pile are the pieces she has already cut out and tacked together. An overcoat in European style. The cloth, a soft gabar-
dine from Germany – a sample from one of the manufacturers
her husband supplies. Iskender had brought the bolt home just
the other day and Khatoun had calculated enough material for
five coats; something small and fitted for herself, an overcoat for
her mother, a jerkin for Seyda, a jacket for Ferida. The coat she
is working on now is for Sophia, her sister-in-law in Baghshish.
Sophia who'd looked in her coffee cup under the plane trees and
said sew, sew, sew, even before Mertha had thought to pass down
her machine. Khatoun fingers the soft indigo wool. Once the
coat is complete with round collar and velvet trim at the cuff,
she will decorate the bottom with a galaxy of silver stars, inside
and out, so that when Sophia walks, the solar system will spill
from her hem and catch the gaze of all she passes.

Khatoun would like to build her life with this machine. As she
feeds the dark blue thread through the intricate pattern of hooks
she feels strangely at home, as if she'd been searching for something all her life and hadn't known what until now. Carefully,
she lines up two matching pieces of material under the needle
and snaps the lever down, pinning them into place. Slowly, she
strokes life through the smooth wheel and into the machine.

Tac-atac-atac-atac, it murmurs under her hand. The dark blue
cloth flies away in front of her, endless, like the night sky. Ef-

fortless. Easy. Khatoun could shut her eyes or sew blindfold it goes so easily. Some things do. And others. Others do not. A bird catches in her throat, unable to fly. She's been married for three years now and still nothing has happened. Her slim waistline – once the envy of girls – is now the object of gross speculation and gossip. Even in this room. The only married woman amongst them. Barren, just the same. Once, the thought of being a mother terrified her, but now the idea that she may never be…the bird flutters. She coughs.

"Dust in your eye?" *Digin* Aghavni murmurs right next to her ear, "Be careful." She bends in close, watching Khatoun's stitches snake through the cloth. "A good seamstress needs nimble fingers and sharp eyesight. Take care of both and you'll do well – you're already one of my best students. I see an infinity of stitches in this machine. As infinite as the stars."

Khatoun turns to look up at Aghavni and the cloth runs away with her, her fingers narrowly missing the bite of the needle.

Aghavni tuts gently, "You see, never take your eye away from what is in front of you. That is what is most important. When something is hard, the breath goes. When something is easy, the mind goes. What is the time? Now. Where is the place? Here. Don't live in your dreams, bring them home and make them reality. Now pay attention." She moves on again, over to Ferida who is standing awkwardly over the cutting table slapping down some slippery fabric and trying to pin it into place.

Khatoun reorganises the cloth under the needle. The machine trundles along, shaping the coat she will give as a gift. The stitches bite into the wool, creating a smooth valley that runs on forever. *Never take your eye away from what is in front of you.* Soon the coat will be finished and the embroidery will sparkle from the hem. *Find your silver thread. Keep your needles sharp, shiny.* She will pack it in vetyver and send it by mule to Baghshish. *Bring them home. Make them reality.*

She tries to concentrate on what is in front of her, but it is sucking her in. She sews into the centre of her being, a dark night sky of inky fabric enveloping her. She drifts high into the solar system and hangs, suspended above the world. Weightless, timeless, a lustrous spill of stars swirling around her within a dense, moving cloud. Voices far away, too distant to distinguish. She searches and sees no one but can hear them call out her name. A name she doesn't recognise. She must drift closer to earth through time. And then, there in the wind, Iskender singing his lullabies. The cloud around her collapsing, spinning, the other voices joining in harmony. And finally they're there. Right in front of her. Her family. Her children. And theirs. And theirs. And theirs. And the fabric flows beneath her fingers and the needle is sharp, and her eyes are bright and the machine, warm from her touch, glows and purrs.

Now she has heard them. Now she has seen them. And soon, once she has stitched them into her life, one by one they will come. And the needle flies, sending sparks across the dark, lush fabric in front of her as she moves forward, forward always forward in time.

Leaving Home

Iskender's House, Ourfa, November 1903
Iskender

Iskender lies on his side, listening. He can hear her up on the roof. One, two, three, pause. Four, five, six. The footsteps stop. The skylight creaks open and the room lights up in angular shafts as Khatoun steps inside. She slides the bolt into place and sits on the fourth stair from the top – the one that always complains when anyone steps on it. He wouldn't have to fix that now. The stairs could rot and drop away like old flesh for all he cared.

He strains his ears. Khatoun is quiet, watching the room from her perch. Listening, as he is, to the huddle of people sleeping on their floor. The smoker's rumble from his own chest. Stale scraps of lullaby escaping Ferida's lips. Mertha snoring. Something, somewhere, dripping. But the room? The room itself is mercifully silent. For years the walls had echoed with whispers that seeped through the plaster like poison.

"She's too small in the hips."

"Still a child."

"Must live like brother and sister." An angled brow and pursed lips.

The stories had oozed through the cracks until their clothes were damp, the fires smoky. It was only when the gypsy with one arm put a curse on the Mgrdichjians that the attention had turned elsewhere and the gossips assumed that that was it. Khatoun and Iskender Agha Boghos were, and would always remain, childless.

Which explains why, after six years of marriage, Iskender had been convinced Khatoun was dying. Dying the same way as the silversmith's wife. Exhausted. Headaches. Gone. It had started one morning at the machine. He'd been watching his young wife at work, his book lowered, his coffee gone cold. She was busy attaching a bodice to a dress when she'd had to lie down for a sudden and immediate nap, one arm draped over the Singer.

When she woke up again she found Iskender crouched by her side, a look of panic in his eyes.

"My dreams were filled with sunlit shafts of water," she told him, "and now I'd like to eat meat grilled on the bone with lemon and salt."

Contrary to his fears, Khatoun was not dying, but it took his wife several weeks to figure out what *was* happening, by which time she was so confounded by the realisation, so enthralled with her blossoming breasts, that yet another week passed before she thought to share the news with him.

They'd eaten a huge dinner she'd had to force down, causing Ferida to hook a dripping okra under her nose, sniff it, roll it around in her mouth and swallow it with a scowl. Iskender had piled more onto his plate, complimenting his sister on her delicious stew and Khatoun had taken the opportunity to slip away from the table.

When he followed her into their room he found the contents of her pockets emptied onto a tray next to the mattress – a balled handful of *pilaff*, a hunk of bread, two peppers and a pickle. She lay face down, buried in the cool eiderdown, turning over only when Iskender let out a long wheeze and perched at the end of the bed, shifting from side to side with indigestion.

"Don't," he grunted as she stretched out her foot and nudged him in the small of the back, "I ate too much. It hurts."

She did it again.

"What?" he turned to look at her over his shoulder. She stared back at him.

"What is it?" he asked. She raised her eyebrow in response.

"Are you alright?" he asked nervously. "Is it another headache?"

"No. No headache. Just tired."

"Good. Rest," he patted her foot and turned away with a sigh, loosening his collar with one hand before bending back to his shoes. Ouf, his belly hurt. Khatoun pushed the end of her foot further under his bottom and wriggled her toes.

"What?" he turned back, irritated this time, "Why do you keep poking me?"

She slid her eyes down to her belly then up to his face. Back to her belly. Back to his face. He watched, confused and then, "Oh!" his fingers flew like a girl's to his lips.

"Yes," Khatoun nodded. She shimmied off the bed and stood in front of him. Peeled the fingers from his startled face and placed them around her hips, kissing the bald spot on his head as he buried his face in her skirt and inhaled. When he looked up she saw he was crying which made her laugh as she sank into his lap. They slept that night curled up in a tight ball, his hands cupping her like a fragile egg. The next morning he was gone and it was the sound of his sister's raging that woke Khatoun.

"You stupid *dungulugh*!" Ferida yelled as she kicked the door open and entered backwards with a tray in her hand, "Why didn't you tell anyone? What if you'd lost it! *Asdvadz bahe!*" She passed a bowl of soup under Khatoun's nose and set it down on the table. "*Tanabour*. Eat that and stay in bed until the midwife has been...wait...what?...what is this? *Asdvadz*, you'll strangle our baby before it's even born!" She pulled Khatoun into a sitting position, slopping soup all over the sheets as she yanked feverishly at Khatoun's buttons.

"Our baby?" Khatoun laughed, realising she had fallen asleep still fully dressed, "I thought it was mine!"

"Yours? *Kaknem!* Who's going to feed it and bathe it? Who's going to wipe its *kaka-vorig* while you daydream and sew nonsense? *Me!*"

Ferida grabbed Khatoun's clothes and spun out of the room, the door slamming a shower of plaster loose from the ceiling. Iskender, who'd been standing in the hallway throughout the whole exchange, reached for the door, opened it tentatively and stuck his head in the room.

"Sorry, *jan...*" was as far as he got before Ferida pushed him aside and marched back in wiping her face with the back of her hand.

"Here, let me help you," she said, suddenly uncharacteristically calm, "you need to eat if your son is to grow." She sat at Khatoun's side, spooning barley gruel into her mouth, a single tear suspended from her nose the whole time.

The summer blazed by and on a scalding afternoon in August the baby came, slithering into the fat meaty hands of the midwife who hoisted it up by the feet and slapped it hard on the bottom.

"It's a girl! A real fatty! *Park Asdoudzo!* Praise God!"

And thus Alice was born.

Iskender was delighted. The women had convinced him the baby would be a boy, mapping out his glorious future over the kitchen table — Goldsmith! Scholar! Engineer! — but secretly Iskender had prayed for a girl. Something small and manageable. A little *boubrig* like his wife.

Every evening, as soon as he finished with the books, he'd hold Baby Alice to his chest and sing, drowning in the soft, fat folds of her flesh, addicted to her velvety blue-veined skin. He smiled those days. Clapped everyone on the back, tipped waiters outrageously and whistled all the way home. And as soon as he knew everyone else was asleep he'd open another bottle, drink himself into a stupor and cry inconsolably into his dreams.

You see, life had always seemed extraordinary to Iskender. There appeared to be a universal law that not everything could be perfect at the same time. God gave gifts of love at the most unexpected moments but Fate dictated that life itself become more fragile with each shift of the heart. These thoughts, previously just late night ruminations over a game of chess, had become concrete shortly after he first met Khatoun, when he realised without a doubt that he had fallen in love with her.

It was on one of his first visits to her farm, chaperoned by his mother. The early days of courtship. He'd been racking his brain for words to impress her with as she slid by with coffee when a sudden cacophony outside had startled them. Horses, dogs, even the pet lamb bleating. They'd thrown open the gates and a neighbour had run into their compound, dragging them all up onto the roof to see. Thick yellow smoke billowed in ugly clouds above Ourfa, the city Iskender and his mother had ambled out of just hours ago. Their home.

Iskender stood so close to Khatoun he could smell the warmth from her neck and could have (if only he were bold enough!) reached out to still the gold acorn that trembled from her ear. They spent that night pacing the roof, watching the poisonous sky. As soon as it was light, his mother (his *chaperone!*) insisted on setting off home again, despite the pleas from Khatoun's parents to stay. Nothing could dissuade her. Seyda had a sick husband at home and — according to Hacme the Fortune Teller — a peaceful death in bed with streaks of grey in her hair. This was not her time. This was their petulant Sultan, Abdul Hamid punishing the *giavour* minority for daring to protest mistreatment. All summer he'd been playing this game, despite the outrage of the European powers. Blindfold, stick a finger on the map, order the infidels dead. Eat another *lokum*.

Seyda hovered impatiently in the courtyard as the lovers stood trying to say goodbye. "Come on, I need to see what's happened to our home!" she barked, "*Menug parov* and let's go."

Khatoun pushed a small piece of cloth into Iskender's hand and he pressed down with his thumb, trapping her fingers for a second. Her eyes flew up to his, startled birds, and then she pulled away and fled indoors. Seyda was already off down the road and Iskender had to run to catch up with her. He trudged by her side, fingering the fabric in his pocket and discovered it was wrapped around something hard. He pulled it out and there, in his hand, was a single earring – a perfect gold acorn. It made his heart race and his armpits flood with sweat. His guts almost gave way and for a moment he forgot his name and couldn't fathom why he was following the retreating figure of his mother away from love and towards certain death.

They crept into the Armenian Quarter the long way round; following the stream to the south, turning north at the Dergah gardens and ducking through the back door of Bakladjian's Bakery, from where they were able to leap their way home across the roofs. It was deathly quiet, as if a swarm of locusts had come and gone. When they finally reached home, Ferida's bony fingers spirited them in through the skylight as if she'd been expecting them.

The city was in turmoil, she told them, it was a miracle they had arrived in one piece. Six thousand Armenians were dead, three thousand sent soaring to heaven in the flames of the great Apostolic church that had been set on fire the previous night. Oh, Holy Virgin!

A rapid, violent round of slaughter followed. The Armenian Quarter was curfewed, its shops looted. Outlying villages were burned and whole herds of sheep taken. Farmers started locking their tools away at night, sleeping with their scythes and pitchforks ready, their families curled up with the mules. And then, just as suddenly as it had started, it stopped. The Sultan's attention had moved elsewhere. Both Iskender's and Khatoun's families were intact but nearly all of their livestock was gone.

Travel outside the city centre became impossible. Iskender had discovered his angel but was now unable to see her. He became sick with terror, his bowel movements rare. The walls of the city seemed to offer some kind of security – at least their doors could be bolted and the shutters clamped down. Khatoun, though, lived in an unprotected home in the middle of nowhere. Her father and brothers worked in the jewellery district inside the city and were stuck by the curfew. Locked up in their workshop with the gold, leaving the women in Garmuj protected only by farm hands. And how loyal were they? It was only after Mertha received that visit from one of their neighbours – an oily man with two wives and a dozen children – that they got a bigger dog to stay in the house with them.

"Mertha *Hanum*," the neighbour had whined, "as a loyal citizen obeying our Sultan, I took some of your sheep which I now have safe at my farm. As a neighbour, please bless me so I may enjoy the flock with a clear conscience."

Mertha had handed him a loaf of freshly baked bread. "As a neighbour, please take this to your family and wish them well," she'd replied, "but as a lowly *giavour* I do not possess the power of forgiveness. Perhaps you should ask the sheep." And with a smile she'd stepped him away from the kitchen and closed the door in his face.

Despite the big dog sleeping by the door Iskender hated the thought of Khatoun out there. Her and her sisters who still called their geese by pet names. As soon as he deemed it safe to walk the city again, he began trekking out to the eucalyptus groves overlooking the plains of Garmuj. He'd set off at dawn, before anyone could stop him, and sit the whole day watching a finger of smoke curl to the skies – letting him know that life within that precious courtyard continued as normal.

He notched the days off impatiently, digging into the trunk of a tree with a sharp stone, mulling over news of the latest atrocities elsewhere. Knives, hoes, axes; all things used to facilitate daily life were now turned into cruel instruments of death against their owners. Van, Khizan, Constantinople. Armenians in every city, every village under attack until a group of Dashnaks occupied the Ottoman Bank, held the employees hostage and pushed the plight of the Armenians home to the Great Powers. Finally, European diplomacy prevailed and the Sultan, after a last few petulant rounds, let the *giavour* minority rest.

With the curfew finally lifted, Iskender's courtship of Khatoun resumed and as soon as she'd changed into long skirts, he married his child bride and brought her home in a flood of relief. She slept tucked up in the sweat of his arms and he instructed his sister Ferida never to leave her side – a difficult task as she managed to slip away constantly. She was always to be found up on the roof looking out towards the fields. Towards Garmuj.

And then, once again, Fate dealt her hand. It had long been Iskender's dream to present his father with a grandchild, but Abram, having waited patiently for Iskender to get married, closed his eyes at his desk one morning, sighed into his newspaper and was gone. Those long, languid evenings around the *tonir* listening to the mournful twang of his *saz* were now filled with bookkeeping as the family business fell into Iskender's hands. His days were spent in cotton fields, overseeing the wheat harvest or fixing a mill. He often found himself travelling as far as Aleppo, leaving his most valuable commodity at home.

"'*Her husband's to Aleppo gone, master o'the Tiger!*[3]'...It's Macbeth – Shakespeare. He writes plays and...never mind..."

His head ached with constant thoughts of mortality and his daydreams were no longer of seraphim but of angels of death. How dare love bring so much fear? He completely lost the art of laughter and once, when a merchant's bawdy joke made him smile, he felt his lips crack open and bleed with surprise.

Meanwhile, Khatoun kept busy. On her eighteenth birthday, her mother had turned up with a bundle in arms.

"My sewing machine. You'd better have it," she'd said, handing it over. "It's time you learnt a craft. Time you started creating things."

And so poor Ferida, who preferred life over the stove, was forced to cut and bend cloth for two years simply so she could walk Khatoun to *Digin* Aghavni's dressmaking classes, complaining vociferously about it the whole time.

"All this getting a 'craft' is nonsense," she'd whine to Iskender. "If your wife stopped running around and took fewer baths maybe she'd start a family and we could all stay at home."

By now Iskender's thoughts had become so bleak he was not sure he wanted a family. Women died in childbirth all the time and he no longer trusted Fate. If they had a girl she'd be too pretty and someone – the wrong someone – would want her. And if they had a boy, he would be rounded up one day and never seen of again. And where would they put a baby anyway? Their

---

3 *Act I, Scene III, Macbeth,* William Shakespeare.

house was tightly packed as it was. Mother, daughter, brother, wife. It was enough. And how would he support a larger family?

And who already suspected the truth?

That everything – the cotton, the wheat, the import-export, everything his father had handed down with pride – was spiralling out of Iskender's control? That despite hours spent over the accounts, their money was slipping through his fingers. He had no idea how his father, God rest his soul, had done it. The taxes alone were crippling; the property tax, the cotton tax, the construction tax on every brick they fixed on an old building. The window tax, the sanitation tax, the money taken for education that never found its way to Armenian schools. The police raids every few months that left them light of donkeys. And the thuggish gendarmes who accompanied the tax collectors who, despite their oiled hair and bespectacled faces, were the worst thieves of all. The family had farmed the same lands for more generations than were in the Bible and they still had to pay rent and hand over a tenth of their crops straight to the government.

By the time Khatoun had fallen pregnant Iskender knew that, no matter how hard he pored over the books each night, the figures would never add up. Somewhere, somehow, there was a leak. Someone loyal to his father perhaps, but not to him. He searched the blank faces of his foremen and employees but the same fractured smile came back from all of them.

"Sorry, *Efendi*, yes, *Efendi* – I'll keep my eyes open."

Every night Iskender drank more and slept soundly enough, but as dawn broke over the slow rise and fall of his wife's chest he could feel the apprehension creep back. And then, as he sat on the edge of his bed one night wondering where he'd gone wrong, his wife had nudged his hip with her foot, smiling at him as she placed his disbelieving hands over her stomach. And, as he bent in towards the life growing there, his panic had subsided for just one second before the familiar rush of bile, the acrid stench of fear hit. And she'd laughed at him in that way of hers and he knew. Knew that he held existence in his hands and had to protect it. It was time to go.

He'd started with the family. As they sat around the fireplace one evening, a few months into the pregnancy, he stood, cleared his throat and spat into a handkerchief.

"What do you need, son?" Seyda asked, kicking Ferida's leg under the blanket.

"Nothing. Just sit." He rarely spoke out and Ferida hung on her haunches for a moment ready to go fetch, before settling back down. The women looked up at him as Iskender sketched out his plan. The fields would be bartered, the business closed down, the house packed up and sold. It was the end of an era. Sultan Hamid was not to be trusted; it was time they all realised that. Uprisings were brewing in all of the provinces (the taxes, the army conscriptions, the ability to travel freely and just about everything else) which meant reprisals were just down the road. In the next round of slaughter they may not be so lucky. Each woman should shut down her life, say goodbye to her friends, and gather whatever would fit in a wagon. They were going to Aleppo in the south where he had business contacts and life was safer. Aleppo still had a decent economy and plenty of business opportunities. It was a cosmopolitan city, which was a good thing. Too many foreigners around for the Armenians to be publicly harassed. In a few months he hoped to have everything settled. That was all.

The women were silent. Grundug, startled by the sudden quiet, began to whine and scratch at the door and Iskender let Ferida's dog into the salon for the first time without complaint. Which is when they knew he was serious.

The months swept by. Each day Iskender taking trips to the outlying fields. He stopped the red-cheeked boys as they ploughed grooves in the earth with their oxen, explaining that next years' crop would belong to someone else. He visited the threshers, the winnowers, the wholesale merchants, the workmen who sharpened his scythes. He went to see his spinners, telling them to dry their tears and compensating them with dresses. Letting those that didn't own their wheels keep them. He watched yards of blue cloth spill like endless skies from their vats of dye for the last time. Stood patiently as the weavers wound cloth onto bolts for shipping, trailing his fingers along the smooth spine, telling them all, "Come spring, this will no longer be mine."

His foremen were shocked. Had they done something wrong, they wanted to know. "Sorry, *Efendi*. Sorry." He haggled and fought and gave up struggling for good prices, just wanting to be rid of everything and then stood staring at fields that were no longer his, etching them into his memory. Knowing what his father would have said. Avoiding his mother's eyes. The bank swelled with his money and he went over the figures in detail, carefully extracting an amount for travel, their new home and their next business — whatever that may be. And finally, he sent telegrams to Aleppo, telling his friends they were on their way.

Seyda was distraught. Ourfa was the only home she'd ever known. She'd been born two streets away, had circled this neighbourhood on her wedding day and again with her husband's remains. Her four children had been conceived within these walls. She could trace all their lives in the neatly folded blankets and tablecloths buried in cedar. It was impossible to decide what to get rid of. Which carpets to keep and which should be thrown. The newest? The most expensive? Or those that told a story with every patch and hole? She began to see things in the spaces left behind. The faded square on the wall where her husband's photograph had hung. The emptiness that slapped her each time a piece of furniture exposed the bare floors. She took to the rooftop for air, spending hours overlooking the city.

On the hill in the distance was Nimrod's Throne, its two slender columns silhouetted against the sky. Abraham's pool with its precious carp shimmered below. Each of her children had sat at the edge there trying to name the fish when they were little, watching the larger ones shadow the small. Far in the horizon, beyond the flat roofs, the fertile plains that her husband had farmed stretched as far as she could see. When her husband was alive they'd had wealth beyond their dreams. Now Abram was dead and she was preparing to slip away with a few belongings in a wagon. She tried to think of one precious thing apart from her Bible to take with her and all she could come up with was his image. His belongings were gone, his businesses sold and now she was deserting his bones. Watching the city fold into the night, she knew she would end up taking practically nothing in hand but much in mind. And thankfully that would fade with age.

Ferida became practical. She organised saucepans and pots into piles, discarding the oldest except for her battered *pilaff* pan. She inspected the bedding, spent nights stitching up moth holes and restuffing quilts, ruining her eyes in the dark. Her wardrobe shrank to a handful of dresses. All the fancy things she'd once saved for another life were given to the Protestant orphanage. She'd all but given up on marriage and knew what her life would be. She had few friends and her flirtations were all in her mind and so easily transported. In fact, the idea of having another go at life cheered her immensely. She toyed with the idea of reverting to her original name, Vartere, the name she'd used before her Turkish friends changed it; but as she tried whispering it to herself in front of the mirror she felt silly. Perhaps it was the side parting in her hair. She brushed it straight back. Still no good. Possibly it would fit once in Aleppo. Maybe, just maybe, life somewhere else would be different. The image in front of her smiled.

Khatoun spent the last months of her pregnancy stitching. She sewed as if that were all she had ever done in her life. The piles of scraps she'd collected over the years were transformed into quilts in intricate designs. The closets and chests were thrown open, their clothes dragged out to air in the sun. Nothing went untouched. Hems were dropped, sleeves lengthened, coats turned into jackets, dresses into bags. She had to be dragged from the machine at night in order to eat. Eventually, shortly before they were due to depart, and with a newborn at her breast she declared herself done. Every member of her family had something. Those that were staying behind had keepsakes and comforters and those that were going forward had new wardrobes for their new life.

In their last few days she spent as much time as possible with her parents, worrying Iskender. Maybe, he fretted, she wouldn't want to go. Maybe she'd put her foot down and stay. Modern wives did things their own way these days. Her sisters, Bahie and Lativa, dangled Baby Alice in their arms, kissing her over and over and fattening her with love and slipped treats whenever Khatoun's back was turned. On the last day, her father took her aside and hung a heavy gold chain round her neck.

"Time to go. Time to follow your man. And always time to remember your family." He tapped the intricate watch dangling from the chain, cigarette in hand, "Always time."

Mertha gave up the Bible inscribed with the names of her family from as far back as Mosul. She'd added 'Alice' to the bottom and placed her finger in the empty space beneath, stroking it with a sly grin before closing the fat book and handing it over. And so it was done.

Iskender stretches out on the floor, lets out some gas and pulls Baby Alice in closer. There are just hours of darkness between them and dawn, which will see them loaded up and on the road to Aleppo. The stairs creak and Khatoun gets up from her perch and descends. She removes her slippers and steps past her sleeping family. All of them gathered to say goodbye except for her brothers. Mother, father, sisters. All dreaming. She lies down behind Iskender and threads her arm through his, her breath warm against his neck.

Iskender smiles. There had been a time when all things spoke to him – the sky, the wind, the rain, the sun, the moon. The walls were once wood accustomed to the crawl of insects, the song of birds. They told of fat veiny hands hoisting them into place, of cool, wet plaster dressing them. They echoed with vile gossip and hid fearful shadows but now...now they were just walls. Walls that held up a house that would be empty in hours. The shadows are silent, the night stirred only by the expectation of what is to come. Iskender is surrounded by family and there is no leaving home. Home lies within.

Work Horse

Ourfa, Winter 1903
Ferida

Morning. An empty room. The little machine sits forlornly in the middle of a table scattered with plaster dust.

Bang! The door flies open and Ferida comes running in carrying a large piece of cloth. She throws it over the machine, trusses it up into a bundle and carries it outside, elbowing her way past the neighbours and setting it down on the road next to the wagon with an "Ouf!"

Iskender and Khatoun are already seated up front under a blanket with Baby Alice. She's just three months old and sucking so noisily at the teat, Ferida feels sick.

"Thank you, *jan*," Khatoun says smiling down at Ferida over the baby's snuffling head. "I can't believe I almost forgot it."

"*Ugheg*. It's alright," Ferida mutters as she grabs the machine and heaves it up into the cart. "*Ugheg, ugheg, ugheg, ugheg, ugheg!*" She slaps the helping hands away and clambers up herself, perching awkwardly on a pile of belongings next to her mother. Seyda pats the floor next to her.

"Sit," she tells her daughter.

"I'm comfortable up here," Ferida snaps back. She tightens her headscarf and tries to drown out the sound of Grundug's whining.

Everyone is taking their prized belongings with them but not her. No, *she* has to leave her beloved dog behind. For a start, she's been told, there's no room for him on the cart and secondly, Khatoun's parents want Grundug on their farm for extra security. So that's it. She bites her lip and ignores his howls. One of her bootlaces is fraying and she bends down, snaps off the end and reties it, ignoring the friendly faces swarming round the cart with their goodbyes. Eventually, with a "Ho!" from Iskender, they set off, leaving Grundug yelping her name into the dust.

Ferida sits back and watches the well-wishers recede into the distance. There go the neighbours, now the proud owners of half the carpets that lit up their dust floors for generations. And there's the shopkeeper from down the road, sad to see his bartering women leave. Ferida had loved her daily fight with him. It was almost as if…but no…they were both too old for that. Next to him, bent over his stick like a river crane, the wrinkled old foreman from their cotton-mill snivels into his handkerchief. He'd been with the family since before Ferida was born and was hoping they'd see him to his grave. Sorry old man. And that's goodbye to Lativa and Bahie, Khatoun's sisters who are frantically waving and pointing to one of the parcels in which they've hidden gifts. And lastly, there, clutching Grundug, *her* Grundug, by a greasy length of rope stand Khatoun's parents, weeping as their little darling heads south on the Aleppo road with her fat-faced baby in arms. A dream finally realized and then cruelly snatched away. It had taken Khatoun so long to conceive that when Alice had finally arrived, everything else in their lives had been eclipsed. It was as if no one had ever had a baby before. One simple gummy smile from the chubby infant and everything else had been wiped from memory.

The wagon turns a corner throwing up a cloud of dust that showers Ferida and her mother in grit. They flap at each other with cloths and when they look back, the people waving goodbye are gone. Only the houses stand out. A steeple. A minaret. A weathervane. Ridiculous thing.

Next to Ferida, Seyda sits straight-backed against their pile of belongings, her face placid. Their home has been sold. Their business is dead. Life as she knew it has disintegrated into a fragile bank paper held in her son's hands. She trusts Iskender will keep it together, and this is what gives her the strength to sit in the back of this cart and start life over. At her age. *Asdvadz!* She closes her eyes. While it's still cool, she may as well try and nap. Catch up on lost sleep. She drops her chin to her chest and within minutes her head is bouncing gently to the churn of wooden wheels over potholed earth.

Ferida watches her. She hates how some people sleep so easily. So comfortable anywhere. The last bundle to end up on the wagon was the little Singer and as they'd turned the corner it had fallen and is now lodged uncomfortably in the small of Ferida's back. She shoves it with her hip but it won't budge. She has to swivel round and rearrange everything before she can drag the machine in front of her. She doesn't want to lose it off the open end of the cart so she keeps it within arm's reach and settles back, muttering.

She'd sat and stared at this machine for a long time. Sat and tried to turn fabric into clothing. To fashion flat, inanimate fabric into shapely waists and flirtatious hems, her hands thick, her fingers bent in all the wrong directions. When Khatoun had an idea, she turned it into paper and then into cloth and soon a beautiful dress was gracing her ankles. She could sit with Alice sucking at her breast while the machine churned out blankets and frocks all of its own accord. Now look at it. Draped in an old piece of sacking. Ferida felt like kicking the machine. Whipping it like a dog.

When her father had been alive she knew what gave her purpose. To make him happy. She was mistress of his belly and could turn the most meagre of ingredients into a feast. Her father had adored her and she'd never wanted the love of another man. And then he'd died and it was too late. The years had already gone, taking her youthful complexion with them. Who would love her now? She was little more than a maid to her brother and his family and plain in the face. With each lurch forward she is leaving all that is familiar behind and going to God knows where with who the *eshou botch* knows who.

"Whoa!" Iskender yells, pulling hard on the reins. They have reached the river and the horse spooks at the water, executing a sideways jump. The cart seesaws from side to side and skids to a halt, upsetting all the luggage and knocking Ferida off her perch.

"*Hayde* Fundug! *Masha'Allah. Hayde, hayde!* Ho!" Iskender cries. He cracks the whip and the cart lunges forward onto the sagging bridge and everything slides towards the front, the hateful machine now slamming into Ferida's rickety knees.

"*Kaknem!*" she snarls, kicking it away again. She wants to grab it by the neck, throw it into the river like a sick dog and watch it drown. It would be an accident — who'd know? She glances across at Seyda. Miraculously still asleep. Ferida inches herself towards the back of the cart, dragging the machine with her. She hangs her head over the edge, a rag doll in the spray. The river, swollen by recent rains swirls past, caressing large boulders. Ferida pulls the machine closer and balances it on the edge. The river spits in her face.

"Careful in the back there!" Iskender calls out. Khatoun looks over her shoulder at Ferida, a worried look on her face.

"Are you all right? *Ugheg es?*" she mouths. "Do you feel sick? Want to sit up front?"

"She's fine!" Seyda calls back, one eye open, staring straight at Ferida. "We're both fine, aren't we?" her keen eye remains on her daughter hunched at the back of the wagon, one fist tight around the neck of the sewing machine. And then she snores. Her eye rolls back in its socket, her chin drops to her chest and she is asleep once more.

Ferida abandons the back of the cart and wipes her face clean with her skirt. She lies back, arms open to the sky. The air is calm. The sky a pearl grey shroud darkening to indigo just above them where the last few stars shine. The sun has arrived in the east, fringing the edges of night with gold. A cool river breeze lifts, Seyda snores and Ferida starts to cry.

Tears roll down her neck and pool in the hollow at the base of her throat. She's going to soak the front of her dress and make herself ill. If she had the strength she'd wipe the tears away and gather her shawl around her but her hands lie limp at her sides. She looks at the beautiful sky and wishes she was up there, a bird, not down here on the bare wooden floor of a second-hand cart. Something familiar nudges her hip. She automatically stretches out her fingers to stroke Grundug's nose only it is hard, metallic. The little Singer has burst free of its sack and is trying to climb into her lap.

She starts to laugh and reaches down to pet it. Moments earlier she'd tried to drown it. *A machine.* She's definitely going crazy – maybe the lack of spinach and irregularity of her moon. She picks up the machine and holds it close. Drapes it again in its cloak of linen. It purrs against her chest, the warm, oily fragrance seeping through the bundle, infusing her with home. How many nights had she spent asleep at the sewing table, inhaling this very smell? Her fingers worn with the effort of trying to do something that was beyond her – the tattered remnants of her sewing strewn across the floor. How many times had she woken up with the imprint of cloth pressed into her cheek as she started water for breakfast? It was part of her life.

She can hear *Digin* Aghavni their old sewing teacher moaning at her. Another lecture on how to place one's legs and yes, she *did* mind the stitching, an apron was still an apron! And Seyda heaping praise on each misshapen potholder she presented. And Khatoun swallowing hard at the crooked-hemmed dress Ferida made for Baby Alice that straightened out all on its own a week later. Their voices were held together in the hum and murmur of the machine now clutched to her heart. Ferida reaches into her pocket for a length of rope – a Grundug piece of rope – and ties it gently around the machine, securing the other end around her wrist. She holds the Singer close and rests her forehead against its spine, her tears dried by the soft linen sacking. Sleep drags at her bones and she succumbs, listening to the voices, holding a precious piece of home next to her heart. And they go forward, all of them, together. Forward into their new life.

Aleppo

A poem, 1st draft, Summer 1904
Iskender Agha Boghos

Halab. Alep. Aleppo. City of Song.
Above a citadel
High in light
A mote flies
On zephyrous...song.

Iskender puts the pen down and reaches for his coffee. Cold. And perfumed with cardamom as they do here. He prefers it without but still forgets to tell anyone. Next time. He reaches for another cigarette, lights it and starts again:

Above a citadel, high in light,
A mote flies in on zephyrous song.

The warm sun floats it, and lilted song.
The flame of cooking, the languid wave...
no...
a languid wave...of hand...

Hand? Hand? *Agh!* So...pedestrian. Hands and feet have no place in poetry, Iskender thinks. He takes another drag and surveys his work. And there's 'song' twice in two lines. He's bad at this. A rotten poet. A rotten poet with a shaky hand. Perhaps it's too much coffee. Maybe not enough. He drinks the swill down to the grounds, grimaces and scrawls:

A mote flies in on zephyrous...throng.

Not bad. It could work. There were lots of them and they were singing. It made sense. He blew out a smoke ring and stabbed the hole in the middle with his pen.

Outside, someone had hung a bell from one of the shutter dogs and it chimed softly as the wind blew. It was pleasant being upstairs for a change. There was a window to fling open. There was a breeze. And the view! Rooftops dancing shoulder to shoulder with a million church spires. Minarets pointing to God in a pink streaked sky. Doves flying and settling under the eaves. Swallows diving, searching out insects to feed. And that majestic citadel crowning a hill. No wonder they called Aleppo the 'City of Song'. Music played from every balcony. And the local tobacco was excellent. Lung-searing and rich like chocolate. Iskender liked the fact that he could write at *his* desk by *his* window in *his* study. Never mind the room was little bigger than a closet. It had previously been a storeroom and the women had raided it when they'd moved in; reassigning the lumpy furniture to the various small rooms crammed together into an apartment over the restaurant below. Yes, a restaurant! A new and unexpected business that had landed in their laps.

And it was such fun, entertaining all those nightly wags. The writers, the French expatriates, the travelling merchants, the relic seekers, the English and American antiquarians, the Jews, Assyrians, Yazidi, Sunni, Shi'a, Kurds. Aleppo held them all, the silk-road spilling books and wares and people all over the city; each of them needing shelter and food and a place to vent the intricate lunacy of their artistically gifted minds. And Iskender had just the place for them. A soirée house. *Zankagadoun*. The Belfry. Food, wine, poetry and song. His muse was with him at last. Now was the time to write and this would be the first of many poems he would compose for her. His lover. His wife. He picks up his pen once more, and with a flourish, dashes off another line:

The warm sun floats it, and lilted song,
The flame of cooking, a petalled kiss on hand...

"Iskender!"

"What?" Iskender jumps, midway to pressing his lips into his palm.

"What are you doing cooped up in here alone?" Seyda says from the doorway, one hand on her hip, the other clutching a sheaf of pale blue paper.

"Nothing, *Mayrig*. I was just working on..."

"I know, I know," she says, shaking her head, "one of your poems. Put it away now, son. Some letters have arrived from Ourfa. We need you to read them. Downstairs in the kitchen." She turns to leave and pauses in the hall. She looks back at her son, "And who are the poems for?"

Iskender blushes. "My wife, of course! Who else would I write for?"

"Then you are even more of an idiot than I thought you were. *Dungulugh!* Love poems to a woman who can't read? Who's going to read them to her? Hm? You? So then, what's the point of writing them? Put them in your head and keep them there, son, where no one can mess with them. *Hayde*. We're waiting for you in the kitchen. I have *arak*. And wash your fingers before you come down. They're covered in ink." She waves the sheaf of paper in the air and leaves, the door shutting behind her with a click.

Iskender studies the page on his desk one last time. He picks up his pen, sticks it in the inkwell and continues where he left off:

Above a citadel, high in light,
A mote flies in on zephyrous throng.

The warm sun floats it, and lilted song,
The flame of cooking, a petalled kiss on hand!

And the mote
just wants
to float
down
to
earth
and
smudge the fat pink cheek of a mother.

He puts the pen down onto the page, a bloom of ink immediately spreading across the ivory vellum. He stands watching it for a minute, wipes his fingers on his trouser leg and steps out of the room.

October Skies

On the road from Aleppo to Ourfa, October 1904
Khatoun

The road curves up around the hill at a shallow incline until it reaches a ridge near the top. Here it levels off and the walk is easy. On one side it hugs the warm rock-face scattered with sagebrush and leafless trees. On the other, feathery clumps of purple grass soften the view over the arid plain below. The road dips in and out of the shade as it rounds each bend – the cool inlets cloaked in mauve while the gentle curves that protrude over the valley remain lit with gold.

They're on the move again, Seyda, Ferida and Khatoun. Heading north this time through the limestone massif to the dry, flat lands that stretch east to the Euphrates and on.

"How far can a dog walk into a wood?"

"Half way," Khatoun groans, "because then he's on his way out again. We've heard that one a hundred times before."

"Runs around all day. Sleeps with his mouth open?"

"A shoe."

"No. Your husband. I win!" Ferida slaps Fundug across the haunch and the horse skitters across the dirt track, the wagon lurching dangerously behind her.

"The edge!" Seyda screams and Ferida leaps for Fundug's reins, pulling the horse to a stop just before the drop.

"That would have been nasty," she grins, looking over the edge in mock horror.

They're going back to Ourfa, the women, and have been trekking all day – climbing steadily to this ridge. Stretched across the plateau beneath them sits Aleppo, the ramparts of the old city wall grinning a gap-toothed smile where they can be seen, the city's hundred million spires and minarets miniscule from this distance. Any minute now the first *muezzin* will float the *azan* and his voice will reach them, insect thin on the wind.

It had been Ferida's idea to have a competition. Having finally finished her repertoire of disgusting songs, she'd demanded to know who knew the most riddles. Since none of them could remember the same one in quite the same way, there was no clear winner and an argument had ensued about who was fit to judge anyway. Fundug, they'd decided. *Masha'Allah,* Fundug, their almond-eyed mare.

Ferida eases the horse away from the edge and back onto the path. "No need to kill us now, Fundug. Two more days and we'll be with Khatoun's parents. Then they can kill us with their village cooking."

"If we ever get there."

"*Insha'Allah.*"

"*Park Asdoudzo.*"

The letters from Ourfa had been coming regularly since they'd moved to Aleppo. At least once a week, a fat missive in Thooma's myopic scrawl arrived.

'*Our Baby Alice jan, granddaughter from heaven, is probably walking-eatingdancing by now and we're missing it.*'

He never suggested that Khatoun go home for a visit, insisting instead that he was proud of her for following her husband '*so far away!*' But it was an obvious plea that swam from every page.

Khatoun had watched Iskender's face as he read the last letter. A sentence to himself, pause, his reply out loud. A backwards sort of letter-reading from which Khatoun had learned what her father wanted of her by what her husband obviously did *not.* Iskender had looked anxious even as he nodded encouragement in-between paragraphs. It was another twelve page opus, full of stories about the geese, the rosewater batch and how Khatoun's imagined life must be '*across the desert and a long way from home.*'

Khatoun knew it would be a blow to Iskender ("Business is *good,* we all *love* Aleppo, city of a million churches! Yes, yes, life is *grand!*") if all his women wanted to go back home. And that is exactly what would happen if she floated the idea. There was no way Ferida would let her travel alone and if Khatoun took Baby Alice and Ferida with her, what about Seyda? Not a day passed without Seyda mentioning her husband's grave; who was visiting, praying, plucking the weeds from Abram's face? As Iskender folded the letter and slid it back across the table to Khatoun it was Seyda who spoke.

"Did you know it takes a human body as long to decompose in the earth as it does to grow a baby in your belly?"

"Have another drink, *Mayrig*," Iskender said sucking on the corner of his moustache. Seyda ignored him.

"If I died tomorrow and you buried me, I would be bones by the time your next baby is born."

Khatoun tucked the letter into her pocket and looked up. It had only been that morning that a familiar knot in her gut had sent her retching into the yard. She hadn't said a word but now all eyes were fixed on her. She shrugged.

"I was going to say something..."

"She shouldn't travel when she's too far gone," Seyda said shaking her head. "Khatoun's father desperately wants to see her. There's another baby on the way. So?"

"So?"

"It'd better be sooner than later."

Iskender had dragged the scarlet-lined suitcase out from under his bed that night. He'd emptied it of books, polished the key and handed it to his wife. A flurry of packing had followed, busyness masking delight. Bundles of clothing and gifts grew in a pile by the door until earlier today, when, with the sky still a shade between pink and grey, Iskender had loaded them up onto the wagon and the women had set off, leaving their neighbours huddled in a knot.

"Look out for bandits!"

"Mountain lions!"

"Wolves!"

"Come back soon."

"Of course."

"*Insha'Allah.*"

And they were off.

Khatoun and Baby Alice are sprawled out comfortably in the back of the wagon using the luggage as pillows. Above them the sky is a dome of blue, a few fat clouds scudding lazily by. Ferida and Seyda sit up front, mostly allowing Fundug free rein.

"If you reach up you can grab them," Khatoun says pointing to the rolling clouds. Baby Alice chuckles, her fat hands grasping at the air.

"*Hrshdugig! Hrshdugig*," she calls out, making everyone laugh.

"Hello angels!" they wave up at the sky, "Hello *hrshdugigs!*"

The hurrying clouds are gathering just over the ridge in the direction they're headed. Bulbous-silver, iron-grey. Down the slope on the other side, still several hours away, lies Baghshish, their first port of call. The Glore Boghos household. Family, food and respite from the dust. Sophia's confident smile welcoming them. The air is warm, the plateau below still bathed in gold although here and there, the first pinpricks of lamplight can be seen. It'll be dark soon and the women want to be on the other side of the hill, already descending, before then.

"Come on, Fundug," Ferida urges, "all the hay you can eat when we get there." The horse quickens pace and Khatoun closes her eyes and tries to tune out Ferida's voice. She loves her sister-in-law but the better the mood, the more disgusting the jokes. The last one, about a flea and a moustache and a hapless woman's private parts was too much. Khatoun leans back and moves a shoe from under her shoulder blade. Alice is breathing heavily, her eyes closing. Here and there tall fennel bushes line the dirt road, their fragile limbs delicate skeletons after the heat of summer. A bird flits amongst the bushes. A dragonfly skims by in search of water. Something cries out and Khatoun follows Ferida's finger up into the sky. Above them, to the left, two hawks circle in wide, lazy arcs. One calls, the other follows.

"Must have found food," Seyda says, pulling Ferida's hand out of the air and back onto the reins.

"Or guarding their nest."

"No, they're after carrion. I can smell it. That means wolves will be coming. Ai! What's that?" she startles as a handful of pebbles trickle down the slope and scatter in front of them. "Keep moving."

"Most likely a bird we startled," Ferida snorts. "And there is no mountain lion. And there aren't any wolves. That's just a story cooked up by jealous husbands to scare their wives into staying at home."

"Maybe there aren't any wolves. Maybe there are," Seyda says. "But there are *definitely* snakes. They love the smell of babies, that's why I want her kept up off the ground," Seyda gestures towards the back of the wagon.

Ferida laughs – a short, sharp bark, "*Mayrig*, stop! It's not the season for snakes. There are no wolves. The birds are just stupid things in the sky. Everything is scared off this path anyway, what with all the horses and people coming and going."

"What people? What horses?" Seyda asks. "There's no one else for miles, just us and them." She looks back up at the birds.

"Yes. And if we watch them for too long we'll lose our balance, fall over the edge and break our necks and die," Ferida jokes. She can't tell whether Seyda is serious or not and in a way she doesn't care. She's going to see her dog Grundug again and that's all that matters. Not even her mother's odd mood can bring her down. Fundug, Grundug and their recent acquisition, the grey kitten, Mundug. Animals. So much simpler than people. As far as Ferida knows, no one has ever come to harm along this road. Still, she slaps Fundug's rump again. They should keep going. Trouble never catches a speedy foot.

"Stop," Seyda announces suddenly, "I want to stop."

"*Stop?* Now?"

"Yes. Stop the cart."

"You just said to keep moving," Ferida snaps. Old ladies, pregnant women and infants. She makes a mental note never to travel with them again.

"Stop the cart!" Seyda insists, "I'm hungry."

"Oh, food. Why didn't you say?" A quick bite to eat would make them all feel better, Ferida decides. "I'll stop at the bend."

A short distance ahead, a flat, sandy outcrop wide enough for several wagons hangs over the valley. The rock's surface has been carved with names and love letters, and here and there, little piles of stone clamber in impromptu sculptures. Ferida guides the horse to a rest, jumps down and stretches out, rolling her head first around one way and then the other. Aleppo shimmers beneath them, her ancient Citadel crowning one hill, her skirts spreading to the surrounding moat below, the *souq* opposite hemming her in. Ferida interlaces her stringy fingers and presses them to the sky, making them crack. She likes the *souq*.

It didn't matter where you ended up in the world if you could find the *souq*. And Aleppo's rivalled all those in existence. Ferida was at home in those narrow alleys filled with carpets and textiles and hair dye. The jewellery sparked vivid daydreams and the beautiful inlaid woodwork intrigued her. Who, she wondered, would be lucky enough to receive such wonderful stuff? The silver trays and lapis beads? The perfumed vials and floating silks?

On her solitary treks she most often found herself in the alleyways, watching her face distort in the beaten copper cooking pots. Nothing could compare to this colour — not silver, not gold. Love for Ferida was food. Perfume, not frankincense, but the pungent aroma from one of the huge mounds of spices piled at her feet. Touch, a hand deep in a sack of red lentils, a twig of cinnamon curled around itself. Up on this ridge, in this silence, it is hard to imagine the noise and smell of the city below. The *orospou* women giggling around café doors, the street kids picking through choked gutters. The delicious aroma of skewered meat spitting over charcoal.

"Do you think he's eaten already?" she asks, leaning into the wagon for a bundle. She unwraps it and starts pulling cheese and olives out of an earthenware crock.

"Iskender? No," Khatoun pushes another pot towards Ferida with her foot, "Here. The bread. He'll forget, of course." She slides off the back of the wagon, trying not to disturb Baby Alice who is still fast asleep. Seyda spreads a cloth over the floor of the wagon, throwing one end over Alice as a blanket and Ferida hands out large sheets of flat bread filled with cheese and olives.

"I must have dozed off," Khatoun says, rolling her bread up tight. "Look at the sky now." The sun is low, the rays slanting towards them in luminous sheets through the gaps in the clouds.

"Never mind the sky," Seyda snaps, "we were talking about your husband. He's probably starving by now." She slams the lid of the bread pot down, her nostrils flaring.

Ferida widens her eyes at Khatoun, snipping the air in front of her mouth with an imaginary pair of scissors. "Keep quiet," she mouths. And then, out loud, "Iskender will be fine," she tells Seyda, "If he goes hungry he's an idiot."

"An idiot? You think it's funny to starve? You make jokes about your brother like he's some idiot? What is he doing back there all alone? And what are we doing in the middle of nowhere? Not here. Not there!" Seyda gestures around her with her hands.

"We're on our way to see family," Khatoun says gently.

"On our way? In your mind. In my mind we're leaving family behind."

"Enough, *Mayrig*!" Ferida barks. "Iskender will be fine. I left enough provisions to feed a city. *Digin* Iskuhi is going to cook for him. No one is going to starve."

Seyda glares at Ferida. She dusts her hands on her skirt and starts back in the direction they came from. "Maybe it's me then. Maybe *I'm* the one who'll starve. I will never see Iskender again, that much I do know."

"Don't be stupid, of course you will. Wait! Where are you going?"

"It used to be we all stayed together under one roof," Seyda shouts over her shoulder. "Now we spend our lives scattered, shuttling between who we were and who we have become."

"I thought you were looking forward to travelling!" Ferida explodes, her voice shrill with agitation.

"It's too confusing. Backward, forwards. All this travel just deepens the need for one place. *And stop following me!* I'm only going to relieve myself. I need privacy, ouf! Just pray the wolves don't get me."

Seyda disappears around the bend and Ferida throws her hands up in the air and walks back to Khatoun. "Don't ask me," she says, shaking her head. "She was fine and suddenly her mood changed. No idea why."

"What does she mean, she'll never see Iskender again?" Khatoun asks.

"Nothing. It's just her talk. She's worried he'll go to pieces. You know what he's like, writing – what is it he calls it – haiku? Sleeping in his clothes with nobody to watch over him except friends. And what friends? Those two with the automobile – the so-called artists? I've never seen so much *barab glir* in my life as their paintings!"

Khatoun laughs, "Maybe we should keep going. I'm sure she'll feel better in Baghshish. Shall I wake Alice to feed or let her sleep through?"

"Let her sleep. But you're right. Let's go. It would be nice if we'd turned the hill before sun down... What? What have I just said? *Asdvadz!* What's wrong with everyone today? You're looking at me as if I just said something wrong," Ferida steps back, exasperated.

"Iskender," Khatoun says. "I just remembered. I promised Iskender I'd watch the sun set over Aleppo. He said he'd stand on our roof and do the same. Then we'd know we were thinking of each other at the same time."

"Of course," Ferida smirks, "let's hang around until it's too dark to put one foot in front of the other, just for him. No wonder he forgets to eat. Both of you have your heads up in the clouds. Come on – if we sit here much longer you'll be waving to your husband from right here – we've got less than an hour of light left. Look at the sky."

As Khatoun packs up the wagon, Seyda drifts back, walking straight up to her and kissing her lightly on the forehead.

"I'm sorry," she says with a shrug, "I have no idea what is wrong with me. These strange thoughts keep taking over my brain. My heart feels heavier with each footstep – I have no idea why."

"Maybe you're tired, *Mayrig*," Ferida says, "Why don't you rest in the back while we continue?"

"Yes, I think I will," Seyda says, "I'm getting old suddenly." She climbs up into the wagon and huddles next to Alice under the blanket. "Wake me up before we get there so I can fix my hair. I don't like any of the grey to show."

Ferida gives Khatoun a hand up onto the seat next to her and Fundug sets off. The hills ahead are still bathed in warmth and the air is calm.

"Not long before be sunset," Ferida says. "I'm not promising anything but if we make good time, maybe I'll stop at the top for a moment, before we turn the hill. Then you can do your goodbyes." She's used to Khatoun and her brother now and although she'd never admit to enjoying their love games, she likes the look she catches on Iskender's face as he pokes at his dinner with a fork across the table from his wife. The only men that ever look at her are tradesmen and most of them keep their gaze low in the vain hope that she won't harass them for too long over the poor state of their meat or their sorry looking vegetables.

"I'm sure Iskender will be fine without us," Khatoun whispers turning to look at her. "Maybe your mother is worried he'll miss us so much he won't get anything done."

"Of course she's worried and do you blame her? What other man do you know that likes poetry – especially in foreign languages? And don't say his friends from the club – they're just as odd. And if he wasn't so generous with those same useless friends we'd all be doing better. What use is a restaurant if everyone eats for free? I can't tell you how many times I've stood over tables waiting for them to pay. They look up at me, then glance over at him and then start with that story about how they just popped in and Iskender 'invited' them to dinner. I smile like an idiot and wait till they dig in their pockets. I can see them seething but I don't move a single muscle until the money's in my hand. *Vordevans*, all of them," she spits into the ground. "I frighten them."

"That's not hard. You used to scare me when I first met you."

"Don't be ridiculous!" Ferida snorts. "You're the scary one with all those disappearing acts and silent treatment. We thought you might crack at any minute and do something like the leather-man's wife. Remember what she ended up wearing? What a disgrace."

"Be serious," Khatoun laughs, "you frightened me. You're so big."

"Yes, and look at you. Even a small fire can burn down a big house."

"Iskender will be fine," Khatoun pronounces, more to herself than Ferida. "Without all of us to worry about he'll do much better. I hope so. He's usually more of a book person."

"A 'book person.' I'm going to tell him you said that when I see him. 'Your wife thinks you're bookish.'"

"You know what I mean," Khatoun sighs. "He's good with numbers and languages but not with having to talk to all those people every night."

"What are you saying? He doesn't speak to the patrons at all — just hovers like a bat in the corner, twiddling his moustache. I'm telling you, he may be my brother but we're definitely not cut from the same cloth."

Before Khatoun can reply, a plaintive wail from a goat reaches their ears followed by the gentle whinny of horses. As if in response, Fundug quickens her pace, blowing softly through her lips. Around the curve, nestling in the throat of the hill just below them they can see a small farmstead. The pungent smell of dung and chickens drifts up and Fundug snorts with pleasure.

"Our last look at civilisation," Khatoun muses. "One day, when we travel this road, I'm going to go down and meet the people who live there."

As if by answer there is a sudden thud of hooves then a billow of dust and a beautiful stallion appears, blocking their way forward. Fundug stutters to a halt, the cart clattering behind her. The stallion has a rider — an imposing, hatchet-faced stranger towering above them — his lambskin hat making him appear even taller. He has deep-set eyes, a craggy mountain face and a smile littered with gold. He nods politely, lights the cigarette dangling from his lip and squints against the smoke.

"Good evening, ladies."

"Evening."

"Going far?"

"Maybe," Ferida answers tersely.

The man points across the sky to the lowering sun. "It'll be dark soon," he says.

"We know what time of day it is," Ferida snaps back. "That's why we're in a hurry." She flicks the reins across Fundug's back but the mare is far too interested in her handsome new friend and digs her heels in, whinnying softly at the stallion. Embarrassed at the disobedience, Ferida stares the man down and barks, "So. What do you want?"

"Nothing," he smiles back, toying with his cigarette. "Just greeting strangers on the road."

"We're stopping at Baghshish, ouch!" Khatoun answers, pushing Ferida's fingers away with her elbow. "That's not too far is it?"

"Not far," he nods. "The Glore Boghos farm. Good people. Any relation?"

"No!" Ferida jabs Khatoun again. "We're the maids."

The man throws his head back and looks down at their neatly hemmed dresses and soft leather shoes. "You don't dress like maids," he says.

"How would you know?" Ferida asks. "Got any maids yourself?"

"Ferida!" Seyda snaps, clambering out the back of the wagon. She glares at her daughter as she walks up to the man's horse and rubs it gently on the nose.

"Good evening. Seyda Agha Boghos. Please ignore my daughter; her bark is sharp but her bite is toothless."

The man laughs and points to the small farmstead tucked into a fold below. "They call me Hamzah. That's my farm down there. I'm off to see a friend for the evening. It's not very often I meet any one else up here, especially a gaggle of women. Unaccompanied women, at that."

"Well," Seyda smiles, "we're not unaccompanied. We have each other."

"Most women are afraid to travel alone. They're scared of meeting bandits."

"Should we be scared?" Ferida asks.

"No. There are no bandits," Hamzah grins. "Nothing to fear along this route. Nothing tangible anyway."

"What does that mean?" Ferida snaps.

"Nothing," Hamzah flicks his cigarette to the ground and his horse steps on it, extinguishing it expertly.

"What do you mean?" Ferida presses. "*Nothing tangible?* What does that even mean? I don't like word games. Is this road safe or not?"

"Yes, it's perfectly safe," Hamzah says. "You ladies will have a pleasant trip."

"But?" Ferida insists, "I can hear a 'but' in there. Just spit it out – whatever it is you want to say. I'm in no mood for this!"

Khatoun looks at the horseman uncomfortably. Her sister-in-law can be brusque at times but her behaviour right now is verging on rudeness. "I'm sorry," she mouths and he smiles back, his teeth sparkling momentarily before they disappear under the curl of his lip. He lights another cigarette and stares at the women as the horses sniff the air between them.

"My wife," he says eventually, behind a cloud of smoke, "she hears voices. Coming from these hills. They disturb her. Some people say it's voices from the Dead Cities, but they're far from here. In that direction. It doesn't make sense to me."

"Dead Cities?"

"*Asdvadz!*"

"Now you've scared her. Thanks," Ferida says, fanning her mother irritably.

"What's to be scared of?" Hamzah chuckles. "People who are alive are much scarier than people who are dead. The dead cities are just abandoned towns. The hills are full of them. Huge, stone houses. Rich. Empty. No one knows who lived there or why everyone left. Even the graves are empty. So, where could the voices be coming from? The friend I'm going to see tonight – he's a doctor. My wife's been bad recently. I'm hoping he can give me something to make her sleep."

"What do the voices say?"

Hamzah shakes his head, "She doesn't understand them. They don't speak our language. Women, she says. Mostly women and children." He pushes his hat back and wipes his forehead with his sleeve. "I used to laugh at her but whenever the wind is high, she has these dreams and it upsets her and now it's getting to the animals. And me. Some nights, none of us sleep."

Seyda looks up at him intently, "Your wife's name?"

"Asiya."

"Tell Asiya to wrap bread in a cloth, put milk in a glass and give it up to the voices when she hears them."

"Bread and milk?"

"Yes."

"Bread and milk. That's it?"

"Yes."

"I'll tell her."

"And this," Ferida says, rummaging in the wagon. She pulls out some herbs, wraps them in a handkerchief and throws them to Hamzah. "Boil them until the water goes green and drink it hot. It will help bring sleep and cut the dreams."

Hamzah lifts his hand to his chest and bows graciously, "Thank you, ladies. And now, before it is too late I must be gone." He presses his knees into his horse and is about to leave when the air splits open with a cry. The stallion spooks and Hamzah leans back, sitting hard and heavy, hands firm and low, to settle it.

"That gave me a fright!" he laughs. By now Baby Alice is at full pelt and Khatoun is clambering into the back of the wagon to pick her up. "I had no idea you had a baby with you. What a pair of lungs!"

"Maybe that's what your wife hears," Khatoun suggests, picking up the infant. "Maybe it's just other travellers along this road. I'm sure voices carry. She can probably hear us now."

"With a cry like that you're surely right!" Hamzah grins. "Well, ladies, it has been pleasant but my friend is waiting for me. Have a safe journey." He winks at Ferida, tucks the herbs into his waistband and with a "Ho!" springs his horse forward.

"Wait! What about wolves?" Seyda shouts as he turns and heads up some hidden trail, "Or snakes? And mountain lions? Should we be worried? Have you ever seen one?"

"Mountain lions?" Hamzah chuckles over his shoulder, "That's an old woman's tale. I've lived here all my life and never seen one. Only its paw prints." And with a roar of laughter he spurs his horse into a gallop up a path invisible to the women in the fading light.

"Get in, we're moving," Ferida says, helping her mother climb up and pushing Fundug on again. Before long they reach the crest of the hill which is where they will turn, slipping into shadow as they descend into the valley on the other side. Ferida halts the horse and they all turn to look at Aleppo as the sun sets.

The clouds have turned grey in a luminous sky of mother-of-pearl. As the firmament slowly lights up with magenta, the clouds bruise and darken and soon the whole sky is a wash of purple and blue. A bird sweeps out of the shadow, dropping silently into the valley below. In the distance, Aleppo sits like a shimmering island in a darkening sea. The horizon fades into sky and it becomes impossible to judge distance as the light is sucked away from in front of them.

"Goodnight, son," Seyda mutters, "Goodbye." She touches her heart, her lips and her forehead with a shaky hand.

"Goodnight, Iskender," Ferida whispers, "don't forget to eat! And make the *vordevans* pay."

Khatoun remains silent, her eyes capturing the last moment before the sun slips away. Earth and sky merge as the light fades. And now it is gone. They turn from the spectacle and urge Fundug on.

As soon as they turn the hill, a cool breeze rushes upslope to greet them. The sky above is a watercolour of shifting hues, the clouds still visible against a darker sky. The wind bundles the clouds towards one another into a blanket of grey and it is not long before the first raindrop hits.

"*Kaknem,*" Ferida spits, "I *knew* it. I could feel it in my knees. If we hadn't stopped to chitter-chatter with that imbecile and watch the sun set we'd be half way down the hill by now."

"I'm sorry," Khatoun says pulling her shawl over her head and handing Ferida a blanket.

"*Asdvadz,* a little shower never killed anyone," Seyda smiles, her face turned up to the sky, "I haven't felt rain for months now."

The first drops are sparse. Big, heavy globules that bomb the earth like summer plums. In the distance, the faint glimmer of lights from Baghshish beckon. Hopefully, since it's downhill, they'll be wrapped around the *tonir* with soup in their bellies before too long. If only the rain will stay as it is.

They sway along for a while, sheltering under their shawls and blankets, focused on the distant rumble of thunder. Every now and then the entire valley lights up ahead of them. Light. Dark. Light. Dark. The thunder moves closer, the rain gets heavier and it is not long before their covers are soaked. Ferida urges Fundug on and the poor horse tries to quicken her pace but the road is already treacherously slippery.

The women are silent, intent now on reaching their destination as soon as possible. The wind picks up and licks past with a knife-edge. Khatoun huddles over Baby Alice, holding her close to stop her grizzling. The infant's piteous cries swirl around them, splitting the air and echoing in the wind. The wind howls back. The rain drums harder on the earth.

Which one of them notices first, is hard to tell. It's not just Baby Alice that they hear now. A million voices carry with the wind. Women and children. *Hanuuuum hanuuum!* The wind howls. The valley sheets with fire and a thunderous clap cracks the sky open directly overhead. Fundug balks, almost tipping the wagon over and refuses to take another step forward.

"*Hayde,* Fundug. *Masha'Allah!* Keep moving, come on!"

Ferida and Seyda disembark to try and persuade the horse, their feet sliding in the mud as they attempt to drag Fundug down the slope. Khatoun straps Alice to her back, clambering down into the sludge and pushing Fundug from behind. The squall whips past them, the rain stinging their eyes. Bony fingers poke at their chests. Gnarled hands reach out, take frantic hold then slip past. Each time they turn towards their destination the wind spins them, spins the women back round. The only way they can continue is to turn away from the gale and walk backwards, their breath dragged from their bodies with the wind. The water is up to their ankles and all three women lift up their voices and begin to weep with the wind.

Khatoun wants to stop. To sleep in the warm embrace of sweet smelling earth. She throws her head back and the rain pours a river down her throat. Up in the turbulent sky a lone star is visible to the north. She concentrates on this through the lashing rain. The child in her belly complains. He is too small to feel, but his cries can be heard in the creak of her joints, the sway of her hips. He is headed back to Ourfa to be born in his homeland. The lightning flashes and the heavens weep and the deep rumble of discord sends them down the mountainside.

In years to come this road will seep blood. The sun will rise and set and a nation will be extinguished with the light. Dusk and dawn will merge, sucked together into night. People will eat. People will sleep. The cities will shimmer with lamplight. The crickets will continue to sing. The clouds in the sky will scud by, the angels drifting apart and together again. And in the burning hot sun of the Syrian Desert the birds will find their prey.

Small Stitches Will Keep Us Together

Garmuj, Ourfa District, Autumn 1905
Khatoun

The little pocket of sky outside the window is turning dark. Khatoun puts down her sewing and listens. There it is again. The first cricket. She stands up, tiptoes over to the sleeping mats and pulls the thin muslin curtain aside. Alice is finally asleep, one arm folded in under her chin, the other abandoned across the patchwork, palm up. Years ago, when this was her room, Khatoun had lain in exactly the same spot watching the sky change from turquoise to indigo in that same window. A star or a cricket. Which would send her to sleep first? Tonight, the cricket. She rests the back of her hand on Baby Alice's forehead and pulls the quilt away. The past few nights had been warm even though they are weeks past the harvest moon and the trees have already changed colour.

The small oblong window is set high in the wall. On the wide ledge there is a carefully placed collection of broken glass, polished by the waves and picked up at the seaside by her brother on one of his many excursions before the train carrying him back to University crashed on the Damascus line, ending his brief and spectacular life. Khatoun's sewing machine is set up under the ledge on a low table in front of a worn cushion. She's usually happiest on the floor at her machine but tonight had been difficult with a complicated bodice no other seamstress would touch. She sighs. It's late. Iskender is late. Khatoun grabs the dress and holds it up to the light. Small, neat stitches which are good enough, but a heart shaped corset with killer boning that was impossible to replicate, despite the yellowing *Petit Echo de la Mode* that had accompanied it. She'd have to bring *Digin* Mkhtchian with all her endless chatter in for another fitting. The dress smells of cloves – packed in the chest to keep the fabric fresh until the sallow Mkhtchian girl had finally accepted one of the trembling suitors her mother had paraded in front of her. The smell reminds Khatoun of sickness. Sugared tea and childhood stories. She shakes out the dress and goes to hang it under a sheet near the window, startling Afrem in his crib. He's lying flat on his back, both arms stretched above his head, his face turned to the side, those long, jet eyelashes skimming his cheeks. Khatoun bends down and kisses him, resting her face inches from his, counting his breath rise and fall, rise and fall ten times.

He'd come early, this second child, Khatoun's waters breaking in the middle of the night as she'd walked the rooms, unable to sleep. She'd been lying on her side listening to something scratch its way behind the plaster, eventually getting up and following it from room to room, a slipper in hand. It was time, she'd thought, to make a net to cover them all while they slept to keep the insects out. With cold feet and no sign of her nocturnal visitor Khatoun had returned to her room and lain down again. A trickle of liquid dripped down her leg and stopped the moment she stood up again. A sweet odour followed her as she crept into the family room and shook Ferida awake.

"My waters," she mouthed.

"*Kaknem*! My knees!" Ferida hissed as she sprang up too quickly and pushed Khatoun out the door and back to her room. "Lie down. Give me Baby Alice. *Asdvadz*, my knees!" She scattered cushions about, scooped Baby Alice up and carried her away, still sleeping. Khatoun stretched out on the mat, her palm resting in the warm indentation her daughter had just lain in. She smiled. Soon there'd be another one. Ferida stuck her head back in the door and told her to yell when she needed her, that she would be in the kitchen and not to dare wake anyone else, she would deal with everything. Khatoun waved her away and closed her eyes, waiting for the contractions to start, hoping they would be fast and easy. Sleep came first and she dozed comfortably. An hour later she woke up. Still no pain. A cup of tea sat on the floor next to her, a cold film scurfing the surface. She lay there looking out of the window, waiting to feel a kick but the baby was still.

"Wake up," she urged, giving her belly a vigorous shake, "come on, little one, wake up." She missed the constant movement of the last few weeks. He'd been an active baby sticking out straight in front and low, prompting the chorus of "It's a boy!" as she passed; her friends throwing down imaginary bets in front of her. She knew they were right by the way he pummelled her from inside. He enjoyed a good fight, vigorously defending his space. Khatoun could grab his foot and guide it across her belly only to have him shove it back under her ribs with a kick. But now he was quiet.

"Come on," she urged, patting her stomach. She paused, waiting for his reply. Nothing.

It was still early, not yet light, and the house was quiet. She could smell bread baking as she stood up and went to the door. She called out to Ferida and within seconds heard her slippers slap-slapping across the yard.

"Is it time?" Ferida shouted, dusting the flour from her hands into her hair. "What are you doing out of bed? Will you lie down like a normal woman? I was just coming to see you."

"Wait," Khatoun said, struggling to keep Ferida from pushing her back down, "I want you to fetch *Digin* Azniv. Tell her I haven't felt him move for a while."

"What do you mean 'for a while'?"

"Since I've been sleeping."

For a woman with pains in every joint Ferida could move fast. She turned on her heel and disappeared.

Soon another pair of slippers came scurrying across the yard and then another. Mertha and Seyda, mother and mother-in-law, their shawls flapping, their hair in a mess. They bundled in through the door and stopped several feet in front of Khatoun, hovering, afraid to touch her, elbowing each other instead.

"Ferida woke us," Mertha said. "She's gone for the midwife. What can we do? Have the pains started?"

"Not yet. Only the waters."

"Sooner than we thought, eh?"

"*Masha'Allah* boy! You're on your way!" Seyda clapped her hands and the pair set to the room, tidying and untidying it, hissing at each other until Ferida returned, the midwife in tow.

With loose jowls, yellow skin and scant hair, Azniv the Deliverer was not pretty. Her eyes were her feature. Frank, honest, amused. She wore a flax apron over a dress deep with pockets. Clank-clank she walked. Behind her, a daughter; a skinny girl with wide hips and flat chest who shadowed her mother with an intent expression and no words.

Azniv the Deliverer bent down, pressed her ear to Khatoun's

pregnant belly and listened for what seemed an eternity. Her nose flared, her eyebrows knit together, her eyes shut and then opened again.

"He's fine," she pronounced finally, standing up, "just sleeping." She dug into the folds of her dress and handed a long iron poker to her daughter. "Go burn the *sis* in the fire, girl. Ferida *jan*, warm two large stones, wrap them in cloth and bring me hot water and clean rags. And you two..." she turned to Mertha and Seyda who were still fussing over a broom in the corner in their own dust cloud. "Why don't you ladies get washed, dressed and come back in a while? That way you'll be fresh when I need you."

Ferida glared back at Azniv, "Stones are in the fire, water's boiled twice already. I'll go fetch for you." She left the room, shooing the midwife's daughter in front of her like a spider.

"Sorry about Ferida," Khatoun started but *Digin* Azniv waved her hand in the air.

"I know her ways." She leaned in close and dropped to a whisper, "Thinks she's a midwife, your sister-in-law! And how many has she delivered, eh? Maybe a dozen cats and that dog of hers!" She chuckled. Sat back on her haunches. "And you – the fact that you're sitting up laughing makes me think we're a long way off. Ferida says you've had no pain?"

"Nothing," Khatoun shook her head, "not even the slightest."

At that moment a loud scream pierced the walls. Alice had woken up on Ferida's mat just inches from the tortured picture of Christ propped up against the wall. Casting around for something familiar she found the room dark, the smell wrong and the man by her pillow bleeding from his crown of thorns.

"Waaaaa!" Baby Alice wailed into the darkness, "Waaaaa!"

Back in her room, Khatoun got a hefty kick in the belly and yelped.

"There he is," Azniv the Deliverer smiled. "Already knows his sister's call. Now we can get on with business. Either we wait for him or I can make tea which brings on the pains, makes things move faster." She sat on her heels and cracked her fleshy fingers. "So, what's it to be?"

Khatoun looked at her. Iskender was still in Aleppo. In his last letter he'd written a poem *'Catching my Son as he Falls from the Womb,'* which had brought them all to tears as Thooma read it out loud, but even if they sent Iskender a telegram right now, he'd never make it in time. The journey took a good two days and nights if you travelled flat out and Khatoun couldn't imagine being in labour for that long. "I don't know," she grimaced, "I've heard the tea makes the pain worse."

"Pain is pain. Without pain we don't appreciate what we end up with. Anyway," Azniv the Deliverer tapped the bag at her waist, "I have plenty for pain."

By now Ferida and the voiceless daughter were back, busying themselves with a large bowl and a pitcher of steaming water.

"Why don't you let me take a look," Azniv the Deliverer said. "Lie back and bend your legs; maybe there's something else I can do. The bowl, please." She washed her hands, lifted Khatoun's nightdress and immersed her arm up to the elbow. A sharp pain ripped through Khatoun's body and a sudden gush of water soaked the bed. "There we go," Azniv smiled, exposing her sharp, evenly spaced teeth as she washed her hands again. "Now he knows we're here."

"What did you do?" Ferida asked, suspiciously.

"Tickled him on the head. Got the sack out the way. Won't be long now. By the way, the water was the perfect temperature, Ferida *jan*, thank you." She stood up and took the blackened poker from her daughter. "Soon as the head comes out, the Devil's ready to jump. This will confound him." Azniv the Deliverer walked the perimeter of the room, drawing a cross on each wall with the sooty tip of the *sis*. "God is the deliverer. I am but his medium. God bless this child." Her daughter followed her, sprinkling salt at her feet and spitting freely into the air.

As she attended to God and the Devil, the house waited in a haze of bread and fennel tea. Everyone spoke in a murmur, even Baby Alice who sat in the kitchen watching the pots boil with Mertha. Ferida shuffled around the edges of the room, following the midwife, tut-tutting non-stop at the spider-like daughter. Thooma appeared at the door for a moment before retreating with a wave to smoke outside the kitchen and Seyda reappeared, fully dressed, her hair pulled back in a clean, starched head kerchief. She settled down next to Khatoun. The scent of soap and roses.

"Are you cold?" she asked.

"*Ohhhhh,*" Khatoun moaned. "*Ahhhh.*"

"She's shivering."

"Told you it would be quick," Azniv said, putting the poker down, and rolling up her sleeves. "Come on, girl, let him slip into the world like a big fish!"

The first five pushes were silent. The sixth pierced the walls and the head was out, the cord wrapped twice around the baby's neck. Azniv the Deliverer speedily unwound it, showing her daughter how to make a hook of her finger and follow the cord around. With his body still yet to slip the stream, the baby let out a little mewl and a final push sent him skidding into Azniv's arms. With her thumbs she rubbed the blood into his cheeks and laid him onto Khatoun's chest where he yawned, snagged a nipple and sucked.

"Not two breaths into the world and he's hungry," Mertha cried from the doorway. "*Masha'Allah*, Grandson!"

After he had suckled, Ferida took the baby aside and bathed him in egg froth and rosewater. She took a small cube of fat, melted it in her fist and rubbed it all over his body before swaddling him tight. Miraculously, the baby dozed peacefully through everything. Azniv inspected the afterbirth, deemed it full of good tidings and wrapped it in cloth for burial instead of the fire. Barely two hours had passed since her arrival, but the news had already travelled and a small crowd was gathering at the walls of the compound. A healthy baby was always good news and a stream of mothers came by to drop off baskets of fruit and pastries. The huddle of men smoking under the palm trees pushed and slapped Thooma, getting overly boisterous when they heard it was a boy. At the baby's first cry a cheer had gone up and now Ferida went out to see them. She handed sweets out to the children and almost broke into a smile as she pinched the littlest on the cheek.

Back in Aleppo, Iskender had no idea he had a son tucked up safely in bed until the telegram arrived the next day.

'IT WAS EARLY STOP IT'S A BOY STOP HE MISSES HIS BABA STOP.'

That night the *raki* flowed and everyone ate for free at *Zankagadoun*, Iskender's family diner.

"You must go immediately!" *Digin* Iskuhi (landlady, restaurant help, mothersisterwife substitute) cried. "Your first son! God bless him," she spat in between her words, burst into tears and ran from the room. An hour later, just in time for the supper crowd, she returned, pulled Iskender down from one of the tables where he stood reciting foreign nonsense and pressed a plain paper package into his hand. When he opened it a pair of sky blue jackets crocheted in fine wool fell into his hands.

"It's the softest wool from India," *Digin* Iskuhi wept. "They comb it bit by bit from the neck of a living goat. I kept them twenty years. Ever since the twins...God bless their souls. They only got to wear them one time. Take them before the moths do. And listen to me; don't waste your time here. Go back to your homeland. Back to your family. That is the most precious gift God can give." She patted his shoulder and was about to plant a kiss on his lips but was stopped by the loud cheer from the other diners. "Leave us alone!" she laughed, one arm wrapped around Iskender's skinny neck. "He's young enough to be my son!" Then she kissed him with passion.

When the last customer had been dragged out from under the tables and sent singing into the street, Iskender wandered upstairs to the apartment. The rooms were empty. Nothing superfluous about. There were no clothes to put away, no dishes to clean; only towers of books and that sea of paper drowning his desk. He dropped into his seat and stared at the open pages in front of him. Figures and numbers jumbled together and swept apart again. What had *happened* to numbers, he thought. They used to be his friends. Now, whatever he did with them, however he stacked them, they never added up. With or without a drink. It was a disease he'd picked up and couldn't shake. Losing money. It stank.

He was up to his neck in loans, the money that came in was never enough and the young girl he'd hired to replace Ferida in the kitchen spent more time in tears than cooking. "It's just my way," she sobbed into the sink, "I have inherited loneliness."

Iskender unlaced his shoes, kicked them off and spread out his toes. He lit a cigarette and patted the pile of papers covering the table in front of him, searching for an ashtray. None to be found. He dragged one of the ledgers over, tore a page from its string and crumpled it into a ball. Gently he tapped his cigarette into the jumble of numbers in his lap. His head throbbed, his feet smelled and he had terrible gas. As the moon sank outside the window, Iskender smoked himself to sleep in the chair.

The next morning he composed his reply.

'STAY THERE STOP I WILL COME TO YOU STOP.'

Thooma was delighted when he read the news. Another man in the house! With Iskender installed he'd have someone to share a smoke with other than Ferida and they could drink together without one of the women slipping the bottle away and jamming the cork in under the table.

"The sooner he comes the better," he smiled. "A son needs his father. I'll send him a letter."

No one knew exactly when Iskender would arrive ("I have business to settle – it will take time") but the smell of baking greeted each day. Mutton was cured, tomatoes were dug out of the sand pit, pastry supplies doubled. Mertha even took the large key from the nail in the kitchen and introduced Ferida to the cellar under the foundations.

"Take anything you like," she told her, "you cook. Let's celebrate." Iskender's arrival was to be treated as a new beginning, everyone together again, fat and delicious, it was agreed.

And then Seyda died.

It came as a surprise to everyone but herself. She'd caught a chill the night they'd departed from Aleppo and it had never left her. The frantic rains that howled around them that night had seeped into her bones, slowly working their way into her heart, saturating it. Making it rot inside her ribcage.

Her dreams pressed down on her chest as she slept and she woke in a sweat, her clothes drenched, her bones brittle, her tongue thick with fur. Voices whispered in the shadows and followed her everywhere. Seyda was tired. Sick of wandering. She no longer knew where her home was. Even though they were back in Ourfa they were stuck at Khatoun's family farm, far from town and the stone walls of the Armenian Quarter and her old house. It had all seemed much richer in her imagination. On arrival the fields were not quite as green, the skies never as blue. Even the hospitality of Thooma and Mertha failed to hide the shabbiness of their home. The earthen floors, the communal plates, the pervasive smell of dung.

She knew she was dying but kept it to herself. Not even Ferida, who slept beside her mother each night, knew how ill Seyda was. She still stood tall, wore her sleeves long and kept herself shaded from the sun like a youngster. Her thick auburn hair, worn in a loose knot, was streaked with grey but nothing had dented her patrician gaze. Not for Seyda the fiery temper and broken pots of kitchen wives. She was as still and placid as the surface of Lake Van. Her rhythm, the even tick of a clock. No wonder then that her death came as a surprise.

She had visited Khatoun the previous night, after supper.

"All the way from Van," she said, piling walnuts into a basin and watching Khatoun devour a handful. "Walnuts and raw on-ions – the best for mother's milk."

"The walnuts I agree with," Khatoun laughed. "The onions..."

"You eat your onions and you'll live to be a hundred, trust me. And how's *he* feeding?" She smiled at the newborn in Khatoun's arms.

"Non-stop," Khatoun sighed, "I put him down for a moment and he's hungry again. It's exhausting." She finished rubbing Afrem's back and held him out to Seyda who took the infant and cradled him in her lap. He snuffled a moment, gave a little yawn and punched the air before settling down.

"Just like his father," Seyda smiled, touching the small beauty spot on the cheek below his left eye.

"Yes. The image of his father." Khatoun's fingers were busy undoing the strip of cloth that laced through the bottom inch of her braid. "He'll be here soon. The way days and nights blend into one, it will seem like tomorrow."

"And what does tomorrow look like?" Seyda asked. She watched Khatoun unbraid her hair. "He had such a hunger you know, Iskender, when he was a child. And if he didn't eat, he had the dreams. Strange dreams I couldn't fathom. We were worried something was wrong with him. Did he tell you that?"

"No," Khatoun slid a comb out from under the mattress and began to work her way through her hair from the bottom.

"Oh yes," Seyda continued, "he didn't speak. I tried to teach him; I sang, I laughed, I shouted at him. Nothing. He was four years old before he said anything, and then, suddenly, out of no-where, a voice like a page ripped from a book: '*Mayrig*, do you know who they are that have golden wings and kiss me when I'm asleep?' I nearly jumped out of my skin. *Asdvadz!* 'No idea,' I said trying to stay calm. 'And why haven't you said anything until now, son?' He thought for a second. 'Until now I had no ques-tions,' he replied. 'Everything was quite satisfactory.' Four years old. *Agh*, Iskender!" Seyda laughed. "It was Ferida who figured it out. He was dreaming of the illuminations in the books Pastor Tovmasian showed him. The pastor was a collector. He had a small library at the seminary and Iskender loved visiting."

Khatoun coiled her hair around her hand and let it drop. "The only thing Iskender told me was that he wanted to be an artist. If he hadn't had to work for his father, he said he would have studied art. Or become a writer. A poet."

"Oh yes. Writing. That was Iskender's talent. And if he wasn't the only boy maybe we could have indulged him. But poetry? Literature? Art? They don't build roofs and feed bellies. We needed him to work. We still do." A moment passed in silence, Seyda watching Afrem sleep before she offered the baby back. As their hands met, she grabbed Khatoun's wrist.

"Promise me something," she whispered with sudden urgency, her fingers digging into Khatoun's flesh. "Whatever Afrem wants to do, wherever he wants to go, you let him. Don't be like me. Indulge him. Let him be who he is. One day we're born and then the next..." she paused, her hand suspended in the air, "the next, who knows. Who knows what God has in store for any of us other than birth and death." She stood up, the empty walnut shells secured in her apron. "Amen."

"Amen," Khatoun echoed. She placed Afrem on his back in the crib and was about to stand.

"No. You too," Seyda smiled. "Now you indulge me. Lie down. I'm going to sing you a lullaby." She threw a quilt to Khatoun, stood in the doorway and sang. The air turned thick, the walls closed in, people came in and out of the room, their kisses suspended on air. The songs faded, the moon slipped away, the earth turned and the sun rose.

It was dawn. Khatoun lay tangled in the blankets, still dressed, the early morning sun slanting through the window. She couldn't remember falling asleep, only the expression on Seyda's face before it had blurred into oblivion. And then she heard the scream.

It was poor Ferida who discovered her mother was no longer alive. Seyda lay flat on her back, arms at her side, her hair spread out around her in a sea of flame. She had dressed in clean underwear, crisp from the washing line. Around her neck, a simple gold cross and by her side that old Bible she carried everywhere wrapped in a shroud. Her skin shone and a smile lit up her face.

The lines around her eyes had faded and the dusting of freckles across her nose made her look young again.

Ferida had been sleeping next to her dreaming of food – peeling an onion slowly, taking one layer off at a time. Her mother had come to her in her dream and laughed at her tears.

"This is how to stuff an onion," she'd said, pushing Ferida aside, "First you flake the golden skin off and then, with a sharp knife, make a slit in the top. Boil a pan of water, drop the onion in and let it cook for one minute. When it has cooled, take a linen cloth, wrap it around the onion and hold it firmly in one hand. Squeeze very gently and the next thing you know, the onion will pop out and you will be left with an empty shell in your hand. Then you can stuff it."

Ferida was badly irritated by this dream. No one knew how to stuff an onion better than she did. Seyda had shown her the semi-boil trick years ago. She was getting old, repeating herself. Ferida had shooed her out of the kitchen with a clattering of pots that she knew gave her a headache. In the morning, when it finally dawned on her that Seyda was dead, Ferida let out a dreadful scream of remorse. She had sent her own mother away with an aching head.

Ferida's sobs swept through the house as she washed her mother's corpse. Khatoun and Mertha helped with the shroud, tying it under Seyda's naked feet in double knots so that the last storm that swirled all bodies together on judgement day would not disperse her limbs.

She was buried in the same grave as her husband, surrounded by friends. Khatoun stayed at home and left her room only to greet the funeral procession on its return. All day a steady stream of mourners made their way to the compound. The older women, who remembered Seyda as a girl, wept most. They had lost a friend, and with her gone, their own future was an open book.

Thooma found himself haggling with the toothless postmaster, trying to put into words what had passed, so that the news would reach Iskender as gently as possible without costing the earth.

The second telegram arrived and Iskender pinned it on the wall next to the first. Birth and death stared back at him, side by side. It was his doing. He was the one that had pulled his family apart looking for a better life. He'd uprooted them and scattered them to the wind. What was it his mother always said? 'Together we are a bundle. Apart, a bunch of sticks.' He wanted to see her smile again, but in the only photograph he possessed of her, Seyda looked faded and serious and from now on always would. Iskender searched for a cigarette, eventually lighting the longest stub he could find on the windowsill. He was done with Aleppo. For the last ten days he'd been trying to get a decent offer for the restaurant. Whenever he thought a deal was struck he woke up the next morning unable to remember who had promised what the night before. If only he wrote things down. And the loan... Enough with haggling. He stubbed his cigarette out, smoothed down his moustache and eyebrows in the mirror behind the door and, pulling on a clean jacket, went to see his friend Dickran Domasian. A bottle of *raki* later and the restaurant was gone. No more *Zankagadoun*. Baron Domasian had wiped the debt clean in return for the papers and keys.

Digin Iskuhi almost ruined the provisions she packed with her floods of tears.

"A mother is the eye of the needle through which the thread of life passes. You're on your own now, son," she said clutching Iskender to her chest and dragging her runny nose across his clean shirt.

He took few possessions with him, preferring to scatter them amongst his good friends in the city instead. A book here, a collection of letters to the Prelate, most of his clothes to the church. He left at dawn on a friendly mule, his remaining belongings packed behind him. The sun rose as he climbed the hill and the sweat trickled down his face and into the open neck of his shirt. The sour smell of his own armpits burned in his nostrils and brought on a black depression.

He took longer than usual to reach Ourfa, worrying everyone who was expecting him. He'd stopped at Baghshish on the way to spend time with Sophia and found himself unable to leave. Sophia, big sister, met him at the door in matriarch black. All of the children, even the Pests (who were no longer pest-like but quite sensible for their age) were in mourning for Seyda. Abdanour and Sammi both took time out from the fields to sit around the fire with Iskender and Old Glore Boghos opened his best bottle.

"I knew I wouldn't see her again," Sophia said. "The last time she was here, on the way back to Ourfa, she gave me these," she flicked the gold hoops in her ear.

"*Mayrig* always wore those."

"I know..."

Brother and sister spent a week reminiscing under the sycamores until they were done. Iskender left the Glore Boghos household with bundles of food and letters of comfort for Ferida (along with a recipe for apricot leather that had so far been denied her). Iskender promised to plant the parsley seeds Sophia gave him around their mother's grave, spurred on his mule, and in another day found himself in Garmuj, Khatoun's old home.

He was surprised at the strange sense of calm that greeted him. The dogs lay where they were, barely lifting their ears as he passed. He could hear boys in the distance arguing over a ball —a strangely familiar and comforting sound. It was Ferida who broke it by leaping from the doorway with a sharp slap to his face and a howl of tears.

"What took you so long?" she cried, "So much has happened without you." She ran inside and reappeared moments later carrying Afrem. She bundled the baby into Iskender's arms. "Look at his beauty spot," she said, "Just like yours – just like Baba's."

Iskender gazed down at his son. There was something in the shape of the infant's brow that he recognised, like an old photo presented to him again after a long time. He smiled. Looked up. Khatoun stood in the doorway, greeting him with a nod. Shy, like a newlywed after their months apart.

They took to her old room awkwardly, Iskender scraping the crown of his head in the low doorway as they entered. And there he stayed as Khatoun continued her confinement, infuriating Ferida who made salty soups and served pickles and garlic with everything in an attempt to prise him away from his wife's side.

"Why don't you leave her alone with the baby?" she hissed over lunch. "It's *indecent*. You'll *exhaust* her. People will *talk*." And still, the days passed and Iskender lay cocooned with his young family, watching the room move through the thin layer of muslin that tented them in.

One night, after pushing another tart stew around the plate, Iskender begged Ferida for something sweet to eat before he went back to the room.

"Only if you sit with me while I make it," she scowled.

Iskender laughed. He perched on a kitchen stool and raked

the edges of the fire with a *sis* while Ferida boiled milk and broke eggs over sugar. She whistled at him and when he looked up, threw an egg in his direction.

"A house without a door," she chuckled as he caught it.

"What?"

"The egg."

"The egg?"

"It's a house without a...never mind. *Agh*, Iskender Miskender, go back to sleep."

Iskender turned the egg over in his hand watching his sister. Ferida's movements were sure and graceful in the kitchen, her lips less pinched. She grabbed a jar of pistachios from a high shelf, shelled them, pounded them into fragments and sprinkled a handful over the dish she'd made. She tested the temperature with the back of her finger, scooped a portion onto a plate and put it on the table next to Iskender.

He held the egg up to her like a prize. "A café," he said grinning.

"A café?"

"Yes. With a garden."

"Now who's talking in riddles?" Ferida flapped the dishcloth in his face. She took the egg out of his hand and cracked it on the table with a laugh.

"Boiled. Think I trust your slippery fingers in my kitchen? So, you were saying – a café? I don't get it."

"It's not a riddle," Iskender smirked, "it's an answer. You love cooking. Nobody can make deserts like you. Why don't we open a little café and sell confectionery?"

"Don't be stupid," Ferida said shelling the egg and popping it into her mouth in one go, "you hated the restaurant. You were terrible at it. Why would you want to start again?"

"It's completely different. A smaller venture – fewer outgoings. I'm surrounded by women – you all cook. We do it family style. Open it on the outskirts of town so that market people can stop in on their way from the farms. We could make a fortune."

Ferida stared at him. "You've lost your mind," she said tapping her temple. "You'll never find such a place."

The small bungalow he found was one of a series that had been abandoned along the market road close to town. They painted it white, cleared the courtyard of weeds and arranged tables and chairs around the old well in the centre. The dirt floors were stamped flat, the furniture scrubbed clean, the walls slapped with lime. For days, until they were done, inquisitive neighbours turned up with scarlet geraniums in pots, eager to look the place over. The courtyard was soon a riot of colour.

Ferida took over the kitchen and Mertha served the customers. Thooma poured the drinks and Iskender was always there, smiling, greeting everyone with a broad grin. Their busiest days were Saturdays when whole families gathered together to gossip in the courtyard, displacing the usual knot of men who came with their *tavli* in hand and insisted Iskender build a shelf for their *narghile* so they could leave them overnight. Suddenly, in the middle of nowhere, the café had become a great place to socialise.

"See," Iskender told Ferida, "people pass this way all day. All we have to do is take their money."

Perhaps that's where he is, Khatoun thinks, tucking her watch back into her dress. He's 'doing the money.' Either that or playing chess. He should have been home hours ago. It's a pattern, she muses. At a certain time in our lives we draw a pattern and then repeat it all our lives – a little to the left, a little to the right, but always falling, eventually, into that pattern. She bends to kiss Afrem and tucks him in. The scent of cloves from the dress has permeated her fingers. She crosses over to the chest to rinse her hands. Above the bowl of water a small hand mirror hangs from a nail by a loop of fabric. The glass has a single crack running across it, splitting her face in two. She shifts from side to side trying to marry the contours of her reflection but somehow, however she stands, one eye obliterates the other. Slowly to the left, slowly to the right and over her shoulder she spies Iskender watching from the doorway. He walks across the room with exaggerated purpose, leans against the wall and slides down it, slow as melting wax.

"Ahhh," he settles his back against the plaster and pats the space in front of him, "come here, my little bird."

Khatoun sits between his legs, her back to his chest, and bends forwards to unlace his boots. He tugs gently at her headscarf, pulls it away, unpins her hair and lets it drip down her back. She peels off his socks, takes his feet in her hands and massages the

thick yellow skin around the big toe. Since they've been married
he's changed. Not the taste and smell of him. Not his pattern —
that's steady. It was something else.

She'd watched him at the café with the customers. His hands
always shaking when handling money. If someone mentioned
the bills, he laughed and took a drink. Found it easier to wave
customers to their seats, telling them to pay 'at the end of the
month'. Only the end of the month never came. He could write
down numbers but not take cash. Khatoun had tested him.
Handed him money to run over to the bank but he always 'forgot', stuffing the bag into a drawer instead. And in the evenings,
the small talk around the *tonir* stretched later and later into the
night with yet another and then another bottle. His breath was
sour in the mornings and he was no good to talk to until well
after lunchtime.

And while she'd been watching, Khatoun's hands had been
busy. In the beginning, the newborn Afrem had fed voraciously,
pinning Khatoun to her room. But before long, he'd become dis-
tracted by a menagerie of strange creatures that appeared fluttering above his milky head. Green worms, scarlet spiders, gossamer butterflies. Khatoun cut up all the scraps she could find
and made toys for Afrem and Baby Alice. When their room was
full, an arkful of stuffed pets found homes with the neighbourhood children and then, since she had needle in hand, Khatoun
was soon doing hems and alterations and just like that she was
back on the Singer running up dresses and coats. Little by little,
the small change grew. At the last count Khatoun realised she
had taken in twice as much money than the café had, in half the
amount of time. And all from her confinement in her bedroom.

"Men are fragile," her mother had cautioned, "they need to
think they hold the world in their hand. Bury the money and
pretend it's a gift from God when the time comes."

Iskender is holding Khatoun close, his cheek against the slope
of her neck, one hand twisting a strand of her hair as he mutters
the same line over and over in English, which she doesn't understand. The crickets sing. Gently, Khatoun pulls away and stands
up in front of him.

"I want to show you something," she says. She drags the dress out from under the sheet by the window and shakes it out in front of her.

Iskender nods his approval, "It's beautiful."

Khatoun brings the dress over to him, letting the full skirt billow to the ground – a deep sea of shifting blues. She crouches down, slides her hand under the mattress, careful not to disturb Alice, and pulls out a cloth bag. She unties three knots and empties a rain of coins onto the dark silk. Iskender looks at it, bemused. Khatoun reaches back under the mat and brings out another bag and then another. She unties them both and empties the contents into the pile. Iskender laughs, searching her face for clues.

"What is this?" he asks.

"It's…a gift from God," Khatoun mumbles. She clears her throat, "It's money I've made without thinking. Taking in sewing."

Iskender's hand reaches up to his lips. "Oh," he smiles, "I didn't know you were…doing anything."

"There's enough here to pay off our debts."

"Our debts?"

"Yes. There's enough here to pay off our debts and buy another machine."

"*Another* machine?" Iskender's fingers search his breast pocket.

"I could teach some young girl," Khatoun nods. "Or Ferida could help me."

"Ferida?"

"Yes. She can cut and baste. Do the ironing."

"But she's busy," Iskender says, opening up a pouch of tobacco and rolling himself a cigarette. "She works for me at the café. She's the chef…the pâtissière."

Khatoun is silent. Iskender stands up with a sigh and crosses over to the window. Only he is tall enough to look out of it. He taps the unlit cigarette on the wall. Outside in the courtyard a pair of slippers shuffles across the floor. Baby Alice stirs under her quilt, her eyes opening wide, searching the room for a moment before rolling back in her head as she turns to the wall.

Iskender fingers the polished glass on the window ledge. He blows imaginary dust off the collection then picks up a perfectly spherical aquamarine pebble and presses it into his forehead for a moment before returning it to its place. When he turns to face

Khatoun his tears are already lost in his thick moustache. She crosses over to him, picks up the hem of her dress and wipes his face, offering him a corner to blow his nose on.

"I'm your *husband*, not your son," he laughs, but blows anyway.

"It's a bad idea," Khatoun says, "forget it."

Iskender shakes his head, "No, it's a good idea." He pulls her in. She can hear his heart beat, his chest rumble.

"You're not angry?"

"No."

"Sure?"

"Sure as an egg is round. Or oval – elliptical, actually – but as sure as an egg is an egg. It's a good idea. I'm just...thinking about my father. What he would have said."

Khatoun pauses. "You won't have to handle money again. You can just add it up. Like you were taught to. That's what you're best at."

Iskender laughs, "True. And you'll rake it in, I know." He clutches her tight, pressing her face into the scratchy wool of his waistcoat and clears his throat.

"Somewhere in the world the sun is already rising. Hearts are being broken. Love is being found. The sea laps at the shore. We're lucky if, in our lifetime, we find one thing that is constant. I pray that whatever sands the wind may lift and carry with her, she will leave you at my side." Iskender lifts Khatoun's chin and strokes her face where a button has imprinted into her cheek. "Take Ferida," he says, "I'll figure out something about the café. Maybe even a pâtissière with a smile. It is your small stitches that will keep us together."

Aram Bohjalian

The Pink House, Assyrian Quarter, Ourfa, Easter 1910
Khatoun

The onion is surely King amongst vegetables. The luminous skin wrapped around the fleshy inner layers comes in many shapes and colours. There's the red onion, sharp and nutty and excellent in salads. The yellow – your general kitchen helper that makes you cry the most. The fist-size onion you can crunch into like an apple, or silverskins so small they look like God's pearls dancing in a pickling jar with coriander seed. Some onions come rainbow hued, the bulb bursting with purple, the tapered ends fading to a milky green, while others shine pure white, the delicate, papery leaves fluttering to the floor like unwritten letters. Ferida's favourite is, of course, the simple brown; a misnomer as its golden skin glows like the sun in a perfect dawn.

Sweat an onion in oil and it will thicken any sauce. Slice it thinly enough and it will turn into butter in the pan. Onions can be grated, sliced, stuffed, preserved or eaten raw to bring in mother's milk and purify the blood. Cut one in half and place it in a dish, the wound exposed, and it will suck up bad smells. Wrap a grilled onion to your chest while you sleep and it will loosen your phlegm. Bound to the soles of your feet for flu? Nothing better. An onion should be firm on the outside but yield to your wishes when cut. It's important to select wisely, to discern what may lie under the glossy exterior. Imperceptible soft patches on the surface will reveal black mold under the fragile skin, rendering the onion unfit for consumption. An onion, like most things, can lie.

Khatoun leans forward and plucks a feather from the onion hanging in the fireplace. The onion spins on its thread for a moment then swings like a pendulum. A single feather remains impaled in the flesh next to six pinpricks from which the feathers have already been plucked. One a week since Lent began. Next week, the last feather will go and it will be Easter with Mass, a string of visitors and egg fights in the church square (some dyed, naturally, with the skin of an onion). Khatoun sniffs the tip of the feather she's plucked, wipes it on her skirt and sticks it in her hair. She takes the *sis* and turns the coals over in the grate to release their heat. A warm eddy spins the suspended golden orb once more, the skin reflecting the glow of fire like a miniature planet.

Suddenly, the door behind Khatoun opens and a tower of laundry enters, collapses and hits the floor. Khatoun startles and the coals tumble and spit in the grate.

"*Agh!*" Serpuhi tuts, standing over the pile. "Oh, sorry...*Digin* Khatoun, I didn't see you." The young girl holds the door open with one foot and hops in after the clothes, the remaining laundry in her arms. "I thought everyone was asleep."

"Me too. You surprised me. Come. Bring a chair, sit and we'll fold together."

Serpuhi gathers up the scattered clothes and drags a stool next to the fire. Flap, fold. Fold, pick. She pulls the pile of clothes apart nervously, her fingers worrying at countless imaginary specs until Khatoun reaches out and stops her scraping a shirt collar raw with her fingernail.

"It's only a little dirt," she says, her voice dropping to a whisper, "I promise not to tell Ferida."

They fold and stack the clothes into neat piles on a sheet covering the floor. Dresses to the right, breeches in the middle, diapers all over.

Flap, fold. Fold, smooth. Serpuhi's slipper jiggling on her foot.

She wears the same blue and white checked smock that saw her through her last three years at the Protestant Orphanage. Still buttoned up to the neck, the white collar framing her delicate features, only now the dress is held in at the waist by a sash and no longer skimming her ankles. Her unruly hair is tamed into a simple braid and she wears small gold studs in her ears, a legacy of her mother's along with her startling blue eyes.

"She must have been beautiful, your mother" Khatoun says, watching the young girl work by the light of the fire.

"I have a photograph." Serpuhi draws a crease down the edge of a napkin with her thumb and adds it to the pile. "I'll show you tomorrow."

She's one of the new girls; been living with Khatoun's family for a month now, creeping around the house like a wraith and getting under Ferida's feet.

"Like an English tea-cup," Ferida had complained after the first week. "One day she'll shatter, mark my words. She needs bone-marrow soup to ground her!"

Khatoun hands Serpuhi more diapers. "Do you remember her?" she asks. "Your mother. Or your father? Do you have any memories of him?"

"No." Serpuhi's hands are busy with the flannel squares. Flap, fold, fold, smooth. The tangle of sleeves, bibs and hems is quietly tamed. The coals in the grate crumble and Iskender's clock laboriously begins to strike the hour across the other side of the house.

"Well," Khatoun says, patting the last vest on top of her pile, "it's getting late. You must be exhausted. Leave the laundry now and go to bed. Everyone else is already tucked in."

Flap, fold. "Except for you."

Khatoun laughs. She stands and reaches for the *sis*. "This is my time. The house is quiet and I can think without people tugging at my skirts. This is when I get to be myself."

She feeds the fire, burying fresh coals under the embers. The distant clock finishes the hour but Serpuhi makes no move to leave.

"Easter next week," Khatoun says, nodding at the twirling onion in front of her.

"Hm," Serpuhi shrugs. Flap, fold, fold, smooth. Eyes intent on her lap. "I hate Easter."

"You hate Easter?"

"Yes."

"That's an interesting thing to hate." Khatoun sits down again and waits.

Flap, fold. Fold, flap.

"They gave me an egg." Serpuhi's hands are still now. "A red egg. It was Easter. Easter, eighteen hundred and ninety-six." She looks up at Khatoun. "I was two years old and I don't remember much. But I do remember the egg. And the cold. The rest is mixed up. Things I remember, dreams, bits I've heard from people over the years."

"The nature of all stories."

"I definitely remember the cold," Serpuhi's fingers pick at bits of fluff stuck to her dress, "and his smell. Wood. He was a carpenter, my father. Strong. Quick. Like the fire, they said. And my mother; she was the wind that fanned his flames. Yes, she was beautiful. They say her eyes were bought from a merchant on the Silk Road. Lapis, was the colour. We lived in Zeitoun, friends with our Turkish neighbours and then suddenly not. How does that happen, *Digin* Khatoun? One day you love each other, the next, you're enemies. Infidel, they called us. *Giavour.*"

"Yes," Khatoun nods, "*giavour*. That's what we are to them."

"And my father went to the mountains with the others, the Hunchaks, so that if trouble came, they could defend the town," Serpuhi sighs. "And it did come. First the villages burnt to the ground. Then our town. It went on for months, and in the end the Six Powers intervened. The Europeans. And in the amnesty the Turks said that if the leaders of the 'uprising' went into exile, the ordinary people would be left in peace. But that didn't happen. Not for my family, anyway. They wanted 'the Hunchak, the troublemaking *giavour*.' So they came to our home looking for my father.

My mother threw the washing over me, still damp. There was a gap and I could see. They pushed past her, took my brother from the crib by his foot and swung him against the wall. He never made a sound. Nothing. Then, small bangs, click, click, click, click, like that. Her eyes. Her heart. Her head. Her belly. My mother fell down and was quiet. There was blood everywhere. All over our just cleaned clothes. I stayed where I was. Quiet. My father never returned. It was Armagan *Hanum*, the Turkish neighbour who found me and cleaned up the mess. My mother's friend. She already had seven of her own and she couldn't keep me so she sent me to Marash, to the Protestant Orphanage. It was Easter. Eighteen ninety-six. I was two years old and when I arrived they gave me a red egg and straight away, a boy with no hair smashed it. I lived there ten years and they taught me to sew. My handwork was good so they found me a place with *Digin* Aghavni and she sent me here. The rest you know." Serpuhi's fingers pick at the long thread of lint she has rolled out on her dress. She looks up at Khatoun. "I like it here," she says. "Next time, I don't want to see anything."

"*Next* time?"

"Yes. There's always a next time. Each time they tell us it's over, they lie. Look at last year. Half of Cilicia burned to the ground. Adana ruined. The schools, missions, churches. And all the people who took refuge, gone in the flames. Why would they do that? Why would they run to a place like a church for safety when they *know* the Turks will burn the place down?"

"Perhaps they think the church is safe. They have faith."

"That's not faith; it's stupidity. To the people that don't have faith, it's just a building. What do they care if they burn it? Anyway, it's *because* of our faith that we're persecuted."

Khatoun thinks for a while before answering. "Yes," she nods. "Faith, like everything, has its shadow. Darkness has light. Heat, cold. Summer is followed by winter. But it's the winter rains that give life to everything we grow the following year. It's not a straight line – it goes round in a circle and you have to reach the bottom before you can go up again – like a water wheel. Empty, full, empty, full – it has to go under before it can go up again, full. Like you. You are incredibly fortunate. Blessed, in fact."

"*Blessed?*" Serpuhi is stunned.

"Yes. Not many people can say their mother gave them the gift of life twice. Once, the day you were born and again the day she died."

Serpuhi stares at Khatoun, her face incredulous for a moment and then she erupts into laughter. "They told me about you. They said '*Digin* Agha Boghos says very little and what she says comes from another place.'"

"They said that about me? Another place?" Khatoun chuckles and draws a circle in the ashes with the *sis*. "Who said? I didn't know I was interesting enough to be the subject of gossip." The onion swings lopsidedly, its white feather pulling it to one side.

"No, *hanum*, not gossip, just talk."

"Of course." Khatoun pokes the ash. "There's a difference?"

Through their laughter, neither of them hears the door crack open and someone slide in behind them.

"Serpuhi!" Ferida snaps, the grey shape peeling away from her knees and padding over to Khatoun for a pat. "What are you doing here? Get to bed, *now!*" She heads over to the fireplace, her hair plastered to her skull, and Serpuhi flees the room leaving the laundry behind. Grundug yawns, turns a little circle at Khatoun's feet and settles down on the sheet next to the clean clothes.

"Stupid girl," Ferida says, nudging the piles of washing with her foot. "Look at how this has been folded! I'll have to do it all over again in the morning. And what are *you* doing? Hanging about like a kitchen-maid. Don't you need your sleep with three children and a husband to look after? *Oosht!* Off to bed!"

Khatoun stands up and stretches. "Ferida, Ferida, Ferida," she sighs, "I was having my first conversation with Serpuhi and now you've frightened the life out of her. The way you treat her, she *will* shatter like a tea-cup!"

"The way I...? *Barab glir!* She has the balls of an ox that girl. This house is too full of girls and if you give one of them special treatment they'll all take advantage. You're the one that should keep them in line – not chit-chat-chit-chat with them till the sun comes up."

"Feed them carrots, you breed donkeys."

"Let them eat our seed and lay their eggs in another barn. Then you'll see."

"Not these girls. They're family now."

"Yes, one big happy family. The girls? Pah! You didn't have enough of your own, you had to add half a dozen orphans? Lie down like a carpet and the whole world will walk over you." Ferida bends down, hissing like an old boiler. "Go on, go to bed. Take my lamp – I'm half blind anyway. Grundug can show me the way. Go." She starts transferring laundry to the tabletop, tut-tutting the whole time. She bends down for more, kicks a coal into the grate and notices the onion.

"There's only one feather!" she cries, casting around to see if the other one has fallen. "When I left it there were two. Some-one has taken the feather out. That's my job. I count the feath-ers till Easter! This is going to confuse all my calculations." She whips around irritably but apart from Grundug, the room is empty, the door clicking shut.

Khatoun takes two steps along the corridor and stops. *Asd-vadz!* She's forgotten the lamp. Never mind, she can make her way. There's enough light spilling in through the windows to light up the corridor. Angular chunks of moon splash across the tiled floor that runs alongside the enclosed courtyard. Khatoun stops at the French doors, looking across the damp flagstones. The patio is filled with ferns that thrive in the shade, elegantly grouped around the stone fountain that sends rainbows dancing

across the wall at a certain hour each day. Right now it is dark
except for a thin strip of light flickering under a door on the
opposite side. The girls must still be awake, sitting up in bed,
giggling and telling stories. Probably deciding which poor boy to
torture this week. She'll have to watch them in church tomorrow. Her girls. Poor Ferida.

"You're not a matchmaker!" she can hear her say. "They're
girls you've hired to help you. That's what they are supposed to
do – help you. It's enough that you provide for them without
encouraging their frivolity. Anyway, God chooses spinsters to do
his work. If everyone got married who would take care of the
chores?"

Khatoun stands watching the moonlight play across the courtyard. Ferida's right, of course. All people on earth have their
own path. Everything we do has been done before, but each time
it's different. Like having a child. It's the most ordinary thing in
the world, giving birth, and yet each time, each baby born, is a
miracle. How can a single act of love curl flesh into shell-like
ears that hear, open eyes that see and beat a heart that is inhab-
ited by a soul? How many lives are being created right now, as
she stands here? And how many are on the way out?

'Only two things we can be sure of in life. One, we're born.
Two, we die.' That's Seyda's voice in Khatoun's head now.

And still, even though our lives share the same bookends, every story in the world is different. Like a river splitting, joining,
sinking into sand. Even if people go through the same experi-
ence collectively, each person will have a different story to tell.
A hundred men herded together and shot – each one will have a
different death from his neighbour's, and yet, in the reporting,
it would just be another hundred men herded together and shot.

A hundred men herded together and shot. Khatoun presses her
forehead against the cool glass and closes her eyes. These days it
was not unusual for women to lose all the men in their family –
father, brother, husband, son – in the same sharp moment. They
seemed to have come full circle.

For as far back as she can remember, it's been the same. Harmony. Massacre. Uprising. Reprisal. Repeat. Just two years ago,
in the summer of nineteen hundred and eight, Armenians had
taken to the streets with their Turkish brothers to celebrate the
downfall of the Red Sultan, Abdul Hamid, *liberté, égalité, fra-*

ternité! The caliphate was dead, the constitution restored. The Young Turks were in power. The bloody days of massacre and uncertainty that had orphaned thousands like Serpuhi over the years were supposedly over. They were friends now, facing a new, democratic Turkey together, their past 'differences' forgotten, and then...

Khatoun opens her eyes. No more strip of light under the door. The girls will be whispering those boys' names into their pillows. Boys that will most likely 'disappear' one day.

"Next time," Serpuhi had said. How many nights had Khatoun lain awake herself, imagining her sons dragged away under the pretext of something or other, never to be heard of again? Call out a man's name in the dark of night. It could be pleasure, it could be pain. Hate turns its ugly head towards men, but it is women who get stung by the tail.

And how strange this house would be without men. Her sons; one still on the breast, the other already learning to read on Grandpapa's lap. Grandpapa Thooma, her father; interested only in politics these days and smoking hashish and talking nonsense. And Iskender, her husband who smiles, who nods, who uses his hands, but whose words to her have all but disappeared. He drinks more and has a smoker's cough and their lives, although spent together under one roof, are simply like phantoms that inhabit the same air. And yet...if his presence were gone, how empty this house would be.

She remembers the night Iskender held her in his arms and she watched him cry for the first time. Back then she'd thought it was wounded pride that had made him weep, only now she wonders if they could have been tears of relief.

It had taken months to close down their café with its pretty, walled garden. Each week they told their customers that the following Saturday would be their last. But somehow the warm weather dragged on, and it wasn't until the chill air of winter made sitting in the courtyard uncomfortable, that the customers had drifted away, leaving the hard-core whisky crew to their backgammon until a heavy snowstorm in March stranded even them at home. The shutters finally came down in April. The yard was swept clean, the potted geraniums replanted and the order for ice blocks cancelled.

Iskender paid off their loan and with the small amount of capital left, sent Khatoun to stock up on fabric and buy a second machine. He made Ferida go with her, telling her to stay 'practical' and not let his wife come home with armfuls of exotic stuff. Khatoun, of course, had other ideas.

"Why make day dresses for little profit?" she'd argued. "Everyone can sew those. I want to get the stuff people dream of and turn it into reality." And so, despite Ferida's vigilant stance under the shelves of striped cotton, they came back with armfuls of shimmering tissue and jewel-coloured silks.

She started with wedding gowns and was soon dressing whole families of guests, who trooped over to the house for fittings en-masse, filling the small courtyard with filthy jokes and cigarette butts. The news spread and before long, a never-ending stream of ornate wagons arrived to spirit her into town. Khatoun spent long days behind the fine grille-work of the women's quarters in Ourfa, entertaining the Pasha's wives with her designs. She'd return late at night, reeking of perfume, her head full of stories, her arms full of gifts.

It was *Digin* Aghavni, her old sewing teacher, who'd suggested she take on 'some of the poor misfortunes from the Protestant Orphanage' to help.

"Feed them and put a roof over their heads while you train them. When they start to sew for you, give them a small commission. And don't be too soft; you'll already be giving them family and that is priceless."

Lolig was the first to come. A chubby teenager with cheeks like ripe tomatoes. She worked hard, finished early and spent the afternoons playing with Baby Alice and Afrem. She had an uncanny way with babies and was the first to notice when Khatoun fell pregnant for the third time, presenting her with a little red hat she'd crocheted before the news was officially out. With Lolig in the house Ferida happily dropped sewing ("My poor stabbed fingers! *Kaknem!*") and returned to the kitchen, shooing Khatoun's customers away from her swept floors.

Iskender, with no café to distract him, retreated into the background behind a cloud of cigarette smoke. It suited him to stay at home surrounded by books, occasionally poring over the accounts. He was proud of his wife. There was something about the way she cut fabric, allowing it to breathe and settle around the body like a caress. If love was needed, it was stitched tight into the bodice. If happiness was missing, a giggle could be slipped into a soft gossamer *décolletage*.

Before long, Khatoun had exhausted the fabric stalls in the Gumrik *Khan* in Ourfa and had to take to the road, travelling to Aleppo or Damascus (and once as far as Haifa) to find materials for her voracious customers. Iskender stayed cloistered at home during these trips. He hadn't the stomach for travel any more and so he hired Khatoun a bodyguard with his own mule, instead.

No one knew exactly where Bulbul came from, he spoke so many languages. Khatoun once saw him converse with an old nomad woman who had no ears, using his hands the same way she did. Bulbul was as tall as Iskender but filled his height out with weight. He had the barrel chest of an athlete and lean muscular hips. Dark skin, black eyes. Quick in movement, slow to anger. Bulbul never spoke about family and since no one knew if he'd ever been married, a certain amount of evil gossip followed him everywhere, which he gracefully refused to acknowledge.

As time passed, Khatoun's clientele grew so numerous, the walls of her parent's compound were hard pressed to contain them. Ferida was sick of the constant traffic and claimed the disruptions were ruining her cooking. With fabrics taking over the storage space and buttons landing in the soup, the talk of moving dominated the fireplace each night but was somehow always forgotten in the whirlwind of activity the next day. Khatoun's roots were in this little place with its clear mornings and hazy afternoons and so life continued as normal, in a jumble of people and sewing and food, for several years until the spring of last year. Nineteen-oh-nine.

It was heading towards Easter. First the migrating birds began to sing wrong — their songs high and brittle. Then the storks got confused about their nests, many of which had been thrown from the rooftops in a recent effort by the municipality to clean up the skyline. As Easter approached so did an ominous air. People began to have bad dreams and the market place slowly turned hostile.

The Young Turks, their 'brothers' they had fought side by side with to restore the constitution barely a year earlier, had split into two factions. Both believed that all Ottoman subjects were equal under the new constitution. But only one faction, the Modernists, considered the minorities subjects; the Armenians, the Assyrians, the Kurds, the Greeks, the Jews — all the peoples that had populated this land for generations.

The other faction did not. Headed by the ultranationalist triumvirate of Enver, Talaat and Jemal, the party jockeyed for, and then took control.

"Turkey for the Turks," they called. The chant began, spread like fire and soon the whole country sang it.

"*Türk için Türkiye! Türk için Türkiye!*"

The killing began in Adana at the end of March. In one short month, twenty-five thousand Armenians were killed by blood-crazed mobs that swept through Cilicia in a wave. In nearby Mersin harbour, the warships of seven nations watched the massacres from sea but did nothing to help. The newly formed government turned a blind eye; took no steps to stop the killing and claimed no responsibility. And then, just as suddenly as it had started, it was over and life went back to the same as before.

Neighbours continued to do business with each other, people said hello, but friendships had stretched thin and it was impossible to tell what lay beneath the surface of a smile. It was no longer safe to travel and Bulbul took a leave of absence, promising Khatoun that Iskender knew where to find him if he were ever needed again. Her travels abroad curtailed, Khatoun decided it was finally time to pay a visit to her old friend, Aram Bohjalian.

Aram would have been a suitor if Iskender had not snapped Khatoun up first. He'd been their closest neighbour when they were children, his parents owning the fields next to theirs in Garmuj, their sheep mingling during the day. They'd hated each other at first, and had only become friends when Aram presented Khatoun with a runt lamb that had been rejected by its mother. They nursed it together, named it Samra and pretended it was their child. While a group of their friends had danced and banged pots as wedding drums, Aram had lifted the makeshift veil from her face and everyone hushed, waiting to see if he would dare kiss her. He'd winked at her instead and run off with the antique lace, pursued by the gaggle of shrieking girls.

Aram had played out many different endings in his imagination over the years and was devastated to return home from college one summer and find Khatoun married and gone. He refused all offers to meet young women after that and threw himself into business instead. He secured an office next to the bank, called himself a 'Financial Advisor' and got paid handsomely for telling others how to save – or spend – their money. He encouraged so many people to take out policies on their life that his friends joked about the kickback he must be getting from the fat suits at New York Life.

His mother (who never forgave herself for not acting faster and nabbing Khatoun as a bride) kept Aram up to date with Khatoun's news. Each child she saw born, "could have been yours; would have been mine!"

Even at work he heard about Khatoun through several clients who marvelled at the 'Little *Ermeni*' who had perfected couture *a la Franga* and could sew faster than anyone; whose dresses made neurotic women serene and their husbands passionate and fertile. And then, after almost a decade of not seeing her, before the Adana troubles had stopped her trips to Aleppo, he'd bumped into her there, in a fabric store.

She was busy haggling over silks with a shopkeeper, nodding quietly as the oily-faced Greek pulled stuff out from under the counter, insisting that she would never see anything of the kind this side of China. Standing next to her were the first and second wives of a wealthy gentleman Aram knew. The two women were quick to draw their veils as he approached and retreat into the background, but Khatoun turned to greet him, her face open and friendly.

"Where are your pigtails?" he asked, peering over her shoulder.

"Aram Bohjalian! Up in a bun," Khatoun laughed, patting the simple twist at the base of her neck as if she'd seen him only yesterday.

Aram was delighted to find her so unchanged and deliberately missed his departure, hanging listlessly in Aleppo an extra day so that he could accompany her party back to Ourfa via Harran. The two veiled ladies pretended to be scandalised as he followed them to the *khan* and helped Bulbul with their luggage, and they teased Khatoun mercilessly each time they stopped and he stuck his head into their carriage to check on their welfare.

"He *never* married?"

"No."

"How many years since you last saw him?"

"Eight. Maybe nine."

"And you're sure you never kissed him when you were a little girl?"

"No! Yes – I'm sure."

"Hmm."

"*That's* why he looks so hungry!"

"Better not let your husband see him!"

But Iskender had been delighted to meet him, and before long Aram had become a regular fixture at the dinner table, often sleeping the night with a blanket next to the *tonir* and setting off for his office at dawn. One evening he took a magnifying glass to Iskender's books and was happy to report the following morning that, by all accounts, Khatoun and family were getting rich.

"You know you should move, don't you?" he told them over breakfast, his eye on Khatoun's growing belly. "First of all it's not safe to live out in the open like this these days. Politics are too unsettled. I don't trust the Young Turks any more. Secondly, you need a bigger house for your…um…growing family, and thirdly you need the space to run a business from home. Then you won't have to travel as much. Store, live and work under the same roof and you'll save overheads. And, lastly, or fourthly, if there is such a thing, once you get a house with extra rooms you can always rent them out if all else fails. So," he dipped his *choereg* in his tea and took a soggy bite, "come and see me when you're ready."

The day she felt ready was warm and humid and Khatoun was out of breath when she arrived at Aram's office.

"Ouf!" she pushed the door open and stood with her hand on her hip, panting heavily. Aram shot out from behind his desk and swivelled his chair round for her to sit on.

"You climbed the *stairs?* In your condition?"

"That's what *I* said," Ferida yelled, reaching the top of the stairs herself and following Khatoun into the room. "She doesn't care. She doesn't listen to me. We walked here. *Asdvadz!* All the way from Garmuj!"

It was a swift deal. Aram knew of a house already – safe in the Assyrian Quarter. He'd be back in a minute. They were to relax while they waited for him. They sipped cool glasses of water and Ferida gulped down her coffee, upending it over a saucer and nodding favourably a few minutes later, just as Aram returned with a carriage to take them to see the place.

As soon as they stepped over the threshold into the airy, tiled hallway, Khatoun felt as if she'd come home. For years she'd had recurring dreams of a house with endless corridors that led to endless rooms. In the dreams there were secret chambers hidden behind fireplaces that twisted and turned into more rooms. Every time she turned a corner, the dream house got larger, and at each junction she had the sensation that she was just about to find out the answer. To what, she never knew. But walking through the pink plastered rooms of the house with Aram at her side, she'd had the exact same sensation.

Ferida had skipped ahead, her nose leading her straight to the kitchens like a hunting dog where she slapped her face and yelped at the discovery of cavernous rooms with huge boilers and plenty of pantry space.

"Look," Aram had pushed Khatoun along with an almost imperceptible touch, his fingers spread wide between her shoulder blades as he guided her through the rooms. "You'll have a parlour for fittings and Iskender can have himself a library. There's a huge salon in the back where you can spend evenings spread out like Pashas, and a handful of storerooms off the kitchen you can turn into workrooms. And then there's upstairs with five bedrooms, so, finally, your parents can be surrounded by their grandchildren *and* have somewhere to disappear to when the noise gets too much. And the *pièce de résistance* – Ferida will love this – your own petite *hamam* – no, *please* don't climb the stairs in your condition! You can see everything later. I promise, there is room for everyone."

He'd already worked everything out and knew all the unusual features to the place, like the hidden back staircase, the secret storage nooks and the star shaped skylights that lit up the floor of the entrance hall. He beamed down at Khatoun and she took his hand in hers, kissed the back and then, before he could snatch it away, turned it over and lightly pressed the palm to her lips.

"Thank you," she whispered, "I love it – I want it. The Pink House. Can I afford it?"

Aram waved his hand in the air and opened his mouth as if

to speak, only the words got stuck. He began to cough and retreated backwards down the corridor.

"Yes — you can afford it," he managed before whipping round
and skipping into the kitchen after Ferida. "I'll get the papers
prepared."

And so they had found it. Khatoun's dream house.

They'd moved in within the month, selling the farm in Garmuj a few weeks later to a Turk, home from Mosul with his Arab
wife and five daughters.

Solomon was born in the Pink House. Her third child. And
in the last year, six girls had followed Lolig from the Protestant Orphanage, overflowing as it was in the aftermath of the
Adana massacres. First, Gadarine and Margarit. Sisters from Sa-
soun; already employed as finishers for their fine embroidery
and delighted to move from their cramped quarters into a room
with natural light and air. Then the two gentle flowers, Hasmig
and Manoush, swift as rivers on the machines. Bzdig Shoushun
came next, and lastly Serpuhi. All of them orphans, although it
seemed strange to call them that. The youngest, Bzdig Shoushun,
helped with the children while she perfected her sewing but the
others were already young women and the talk almost always
centred on love.

The house was fat with life. Everyone had a bed that could
stay put, including the girls in their courtyard dormitory. No
more rolling the mats away and sweeping dirt floors. They had
a bathroom, hot water and an indoor toilet. Half a dozen machines were running daily. Business was booming.

And yet, open the doors to the street and ask someone. Are
we neighbours? Are we friends?

See what they say.

Khatoun can hear Ferida talking to herself in the kitchen ("I
don't talk to myself. I think out loud. It's different,") and gets
moving. If Ferida finds her dawdling in the corridor, "*Kaknem,*"
and "*Eshou botch,*" is all she will hear all the way to bed.

She reaches the cavernous entrance hall where long shafts of
light illuminate the floor in the outline of a star. In front of her,
the heavy wooden doors leading onto the narrow street are bolted shut. To her left is the parlour, as Aram called it, decorated

in European style. Khatoun and Mertha had studied several Parisian magazines before ordering the low, damask sofa and two
armchairs which they'd placed at angles to each other, separated
by ornate tables, as in the photographs. Potted plants stand on
the floor by the widow, framed by thick, floor-length curtains
held back by tasselled swags. The room is aired once a week,
before the ladies come to visit. In fact, they have renamed it 'The
Ladies' Room', as Thooma and Iskender never venture past the
door, preferring to sit and smoke in the room filled with books
across the hall that Iskender calls his office.

First, Khatoun climbs the stairs. Stone gives way to wood, silence to
the creak and whisper of escaping dreams. The upper floor curls
like a snail around the central courtyard and Khatoun takes the
long way round so she can pass each bedroom before she reaches
her own.

First, her parents' room. Her mother wearing dresses now,
the village *shalvar* put aside. Finally, in their old age, a large
wooden bed that stays put day and night. It sits on high legs,
away from prying insects, and is situated near the window for
air. Her father's satisfied snores reverberate through the door.

"May the light greet you tomorrow," Khatoun whispers, "and
God age you on one pillow."

Along the corridor to Ferida's room; her slippers, as always,
by the door, ready to go. Inside the room her belongings are still
in bundles even though they moved in over a year ago. And no
bed for Ferida, who prefers the cotton-stuffed mattress on the
floor she swears helps her back. At the end of the corridor is the
hamam with its large copper boiler. Once a week the girls light
the wood fire under the water tank and the whole household
files in, two by two, to sweat and scrub in the little room. The
rolls of black sweat and dirt sluiced down the drain with silver
bowls. The knots in Khatoun's back unravelled with olive oil.
Bath nights end with the smell of peeled oranges and the clatter
of wooden shoes down the stairs.

Next to the bathroom is a spare room, filled for now with
household linens and Ferida's unused bed frame. Bzdig Shoushun is currently 'borrowing' the bed while on night-call for the
children. Next to the small room is a large dormitory, the children's room. Khatoun opens the door. Empty. She checks under
the beds. Pokes at the quilts. Nobody hiding.

Around the corner she pushes through the double doors that lead into her bedroom. It is dark, fragranced by shoes. Iskender lies across the bed fully dressed. Earlier tonight he'd written a poem to his *Trio of Innocents* and there they lie, a tangled mess of limbs and damp hair, including the baby. Solomon is surrounded by pillows, safe in his own little cocoon, his lips occasionally moving as if latched on to her breast. Alice and Afrem are uncovered – their blanket wrapped around Iskender's head like a turban. Khatoun moves towards them wondering whether to take them to their own room or leave them be. She sits on the bed. She could just lean over and squeeze in at the very edge, right next to Solomon. Maybe head to toe. The floorboards groan. Iskender moves.

"Christ has risen," he says. "He's taking me with him. You can't judge a book by its cover. There are pages and pages and they all stink. May you live in the light, Amen." He clutches his stomach and groans.

"Did you eat onions?" Khatoun laughs. Iskender opens one eye and looks at her through layers of sleep.

"You can crack an egg but not an onion, thanks be to God," he smiles, then crumples into a frown. His hand reaches out and pats Baby Alice on the leg. "Ah, the little lamb. Let's slaughter the lamb for lunch. Put the blood of the lamb on the door. Keep the locusts away. Bring me the knife. Quick."

Khatoun heads out into the corridor once more. She will wake Bzdig Shoushun and get her to help move the children. On nights like these, the demons have found their way into their haven and she'll have a hard time undressing her husband and getting him to sleep again. Who knows what it is tonight. The house is safe and she has come home. But walls are only stone and plaster, and life and death can slip in through the cracks. Damp patches take a while to show. Within the walls may seem like paradise, and tomorrow's sun will shine bright and light up the world in a perfect dawn. A simple spinning orb. But the sun, in all its blistering simplicity, like most things, can lie.

Am I Still a Woman?

Ourfa, June 1912
Khatoun

A cool breeze drifts in the window. A flap of light hovers birdlike above the bed, spilling across one eye. Early morning. Downstairs, in the street below, the bustle and cry of life continue. A snatch of conversation, the clattering of hooves, the arched song of a vendor. They reach out to her but are far away, removed.

Khatoun knows Ferida is there; can hear the shuffle of feet on the *kilim*, smell the starched cotton tucked around her as calloused hands turn her first to one side and then the other, removing the bloody sheets from beneath. A damp cloth sweeps across her brow. The room is thick with orange blossom and antiseptic. Footsteps retreat across the wooden floor. The door cracks open and in the gap between her and the rest of the world she hears the cry of a newborn child. And the sky clouds over and the rain drops hard and her whole life becomes a dream. A patchwork of faces that blend into one.

Unlike his two brothers with their lusty cries and pummelling fists, he'd come late, Voghbed. Khatoun's fourth child. He would be her last. A small, dry baby that was slow to cry and quick to sleep. Before he was born, Afrem, now an inquisitive seven, had lain next to Khatoun, one hand resting on the tight globe of her belly, watching the small movements become agitated after a meal.

"Is the baby eating too?" he wanted to know. "Is it hot in there? Or cold?" And when his mother was asleep and couldn't answer any more questions, he'd pester big sister, Baby Alice.

"How did it *get* in there?"

"Daddy kissed Mummy."

"Do they still kiss?"

"Yes."

"When?"

"At night. You'll understand when you're older."

"Will I get a baby if Umme Ferida kisses me?"

"No – it's a special kiss."

"I want one."

"Shut up and go to sleep!"

Solomon, barely three at the time, was confused. Brothers and sister were *bigger* than him. How could another one fit inside his mother's stomach? As the youngest, he was used to getting spoiled, and instinctively knew that this would come to an end as soon as that baby got out of his mother's belly and into his bedroom. Solomon had been asleep between Iskender and Khatoun; sailing across the world on the huge wooden bed that had been built inside the room, jealously clutching his mother's hair when her labour had started.

Khatoun had been dreaming – searching for a quiet place to relieve herself. Every time she found a deserted spot and was just about to lift her skirts, someone appeared and struck up conversation. She eventually woke up sweaty and desperate. She untangled herself from her son and sat at the edge of the bed searching for her slippers with her foot when a familiar, sweet smell invaded the room and soaked her legs.

"At last," she said, rubbing her belly.

Iskender rolled over, his arm landing across Solomon's chest. "What is it? *Asdvadz!*" he yelped, his fingers flying to his face. The previous night he'd walked over to Ephraim Terzian's place after supper, begging him to use his tools to dig out the tooth that had been nagging him for months.

At first Ephraim had refused, "I'm a silversmith, not a dentist! A bangle or a candlestick and I'm your man, but a tooth, no. I'd rather poke your eye out with a *sis*." It wasn't until a couple of drinks and a game of dominoes later that he'd agreed to peer into the gloomy recess of Iskender's mouth.

"Bad news boss," he'd said, straightening up and mopping his face. "It's not just *one* but *four* that need to go." He'd disappeared into his workroom, returning minutes later with a leather roll of implements that he unfurled across the table. "Suck these, drink this," he'd said, handing Iskender a handful of cloves and a glass of *raki*. "You're going to feel as if a mule has kicked you in the face for a while, but by the end of the week you'll be fine."

Iskender had only just got to sleep when Khatoun's voice

broke into his dreams, and jumping up in a panic had made him feel worse. The vinegar soaked rags draped over his jaw were nauseating. He needed hashish for the pain. He hobbled out to the balcony to raise the alarm, crept back into the room and curled up on his side next to Khatoun, where he lay until Ferida finally kicked him out. He dropped into a chair on the landing, balancing his forehead on his knees, and found that if he moaned like a cat in heat, it helped. He was still there an hour later when the midwife hurried past, rolling her eyes at his sorry state. Ferida stuck her head back out the bedroom door.

"Go and find somewhere else to mope, you *dungulugh!* Your wife is having a baby. Go on. *Oosht!*" Iskender struggled to his feet. Despite his best endeavours he never seemed to be in the right place at the right time. There was always a huge chasm between him and everything that was happening around him. He slunk downstairs into the kitchen, and finding the last of the hashish gone, poked about in the drawers for something medicinal to drink, settling, finally, into a chair near the grate with some rubbing alcohol.

"Pomerania. Pomerania. Po. Me. Ra. Nia," he muttered between sips.

The girls were up and soon the clattering of half a dozen machines rattled through the air. Shortly after breakfast (which nobody touched), just as Lolig had the children sorting buttons in the workroom, another son burst into the world in a shock of red hair. The house erupted into cheers and the sewing was forgotten as Ferida yelled down into the courtyard. The girls gathered around the fountain, shading their eyes from the sun, clamouring for a look at the swaddled baby held in her arms but the look on Ferida's face was not right. And then Mertha ran down the stairs for more sheets, her skirts dragging a river of blood behind her. And Thooma skipped out the back door without his jacket, returning twenty minutes later with a doctor whose name no one could pronounce. The doctor disappeared into the bedroom and the midwife called over the balcony for more sheets.

When he finally emerged, Doctor Heimlichstrauser crept down the back stairs to the kitchen and lit up a cigarette. Iskender sat gripping a cloth to his face as he listened to the man's strange accented Armenian. Bile was dancing in his guts, sending a burning stream up to his throat. His face was heavy with pain, swollen to twice its size by the wads of gauze packed around his bloody gums.

The doctor flicked his match into the fireplace. "The placenta was attached to the wall of her uterus," he said impassively, his grey eyes pale as ash. "It's very rare, but it does happen occasionally. When the placenta emerges it pulls the top of the uterus with it – in effect, very much like pulling a stocking inside out. This is what happened to your wife. I managed to coax the afterbirth out but I'm afraid her womb has inverted. I can try to replace it by hand and hopefully she won't need further surgery but it will cause her great pain."

Iskender retched into the fireplace then wiped his lips with his handkerchief. The doctor crouched next to him and leaned into his face.

"I've given her some morphine and I'll do what I can, but she will need to go to the hospital. Your sister – Umme Ferida? – she doesn't want her to go but I'm afraid she may not realise how serious this is. The simple truth is, either we get your wife to hospital or…not." He took a drag of his cigarette and exhaled two long streams through his nostrils. "Do you understand?" He peered into Iskender's face then gave him a tiny tap on the cheek, just under the eye. "First, let's get your wife to hospital. *Then* I'll get you something nice for the pain."

Lolig (who'd left the children with their buttons so she could eavesdrop) promptly stepped into view. With a nod from Iskender she turned on her heels and ran, returning shortly with a carriage and their fretful friend, Aram Bohjalian, who paced the kitchen in tight circles until Khatoun was carried past and deposited in the waiting phaeton.

Two days later, Khatoun woke to the crow's flap of a nurse's uniform, her breasts heavy, her body on fire. The manoeuvre had been unsuccessful and they'd had to operate, slicing into her – ribs to pubis – later that day.

"When they'd finished…" Ferida spat, "she was no longer a woman."

A fever kept Khatoun in and out of delirium for a week, during which Ferida went to war with the hospital.

"You don't feed her enough! The sheets are filthy! Nobody sits with her! You just leave her lying there…"

Eventually the doctors allowed Khatoun home so the hospital staff could get on with their jobs without tripping over Ferida, who'd taken to sleeping stretched out on the floor by the bed, one eye open, ready for the slightest opportunity to harangue the young nurses.

The breeze lifts the curtain and another splash of sunlight warms Khatoun's face. The baby has gone quiet, his cries replaced by the melodic 'hampourner, bachigners,' of Mayreni, the wet nurse who'd been brought in to feed him. Khatoun has never seen her but these last few days at home have been filled with her singing. Voghbed – her last born she has not yet held, fed by a woman she has heard but not yet seen. There goes another one. Every thought, a pattern. Clear and sharp one minute, spiralling across the ceiling the next. And underneath it all, a constant fire in the belly, an unquenchable thirst and an itching-itching nose.

Downstairs, the girls are hard at work filling orders. Tac-atac-atac-atac, the machines go. Tac-atac-atac. There are children playing in the narrow cobbled street under her window, their voices carrying in on the breeze. Khatoun can make out the high, reedy pitch of Baby Alice's laughter amongst the others. *Alice.* Time to stop calling her Baby. Alice, with her long, gangly legs and the gap in her teeth, who still loves her dollies and is uncomfortable around any boy that is not one of her brothers. And like a metronome, above the harmonious sound of children, Mayreni's song still singing,

The girl went and slept in the garden,
And the wind opened up her chest.[4]

Footsteps run down the narrow street, stop, turn and run back again. The swallows pierce the heavens with their cries. Water splashes as the youngsters sprinkle each other with raindrops that have collected in a large barrel by the door. Ferida's voice is shrill as she leans out of a window and yells at them.

"You'll taste my slipper if you don't shut up! *Oosht*, off with you! Your mother is sick!"

And a shard of pain rips through Khatoun, opening her chest

---

4 Anonymous. Traditional song sung by girls in Habousi Village.

into a starless night that drags her up into its core. The city sparkles below. Her people and the fragile years of peace that have passed. Her children. Her family. The girls. She gathers them all into a blanket and casts them out into the firmament like a fisherman with his net, watching friends and husbands and children scatter. Where will they land? They are jewels she never managed to stitch down and the Pasha's wives will be disappointed that they are lost to the wind, dissipated for years, destined never to be sewn into that fabulous neckline. Never mind – they will shine where they land – less is more,

Her lover went to see her
And with a pretty 'kerchief, covered her heart.

Her lover. Where did he go? She can smell him in the cigarette smoke that enters the room before he does. He loves her. He adores her. He believes that love alone – the simple beat of his heart – is enough to sustain her, to keep her his. So he leaves her be, imagining that children and sewing and food and kitchens and rooms full of furniture and clocks are enough. How can you be lonely, surrounded by people? His love pins her to the wall – a mirror image, a photograph of her former self. He nurtured everything once. It was he who tended the thick courtyard of flowers outside their café but now he's buried his spine in his books and his answer for everything is another drink. "Just going for a walk," he'll say and Ferida will roll her eyes as he slips out the door tapping his watch with one finger or two to indicate how long he will be. And as the hours pass and Khatoun watches the walls, her love slips away with the shadows until only his smell remains,

The girl's lover has gone to Aleppo,
Asked for the price of the clothes,
Opened his purse of gold pieces,
Returned home with armfuls of gifts.

The sewing machines downstairs fall silent and the girls file into the courtyard chattering quietly as they unwrap their lunch. Khatoun opens her eyes and Ferida swims towards her, a bowl of soup in her hand.

"Are you awake?" She moves closer, strangely tender, and another shape materializes where she'd just been standing. Mertha.

"*Amma*," Khatoun's voice is thin, dry.

"Shush. Keep your energy, child. Everything is fine. The baby is beautiful. You just get well so you can hold him." Mertha sits next to her daughter and takes the bowl and spoon from Ferida. Warm, salty rice steeped with lemon slides into Khatoun's mouth. Her mother, smelling of vetyver, feeding her. Past her mother, her eyes search the room, recognise nothing.

"Where are my dolls?"

"Your dolls?"

"Be quiet. Set your mind straight," Ferida's voice booms from the corner.

"Life doesn't go straight."

"Of course not," Mertha smiles. "Here, *hokis*, have more soup." She slips another spoonful into her daughter's mouth.

"It's a circle," Khatoun says.

"Yes. It's a circle. Here."

"And at the end...we join the beginning again?"

"I don't know. Eat up. We need you to gain weight, get your strength up."

"And all the weight that people lose – where does it go?"

"Into the air. Just one more spoon..."

"The crazy people on the street with no homes," Ferida barks from over by the dresser. "You think they're talking to no one? No, they're talking to the lost weight in the world. It doesn't just vanish. It sits on park benches, waiting."

Mertha laughs, "There'll be a lot of me to talk to then – if I ever manage to stop eating so much!" She pats her sturdy body and stands.

Ferida stops rearranging stacks of medicines on the dressing table, crosses the room in a stride and cleans Khatoun's face with cologne. She takes the tray and swims out of sight again.

The sounds from outside move with the light, slanting across the floor the other way now. On the other side of town Khatoun can hear prayers begin. Her mother lies down next to her, stroking her arm.

Khatoun is four years old again, playing in the yard with a pile of lentils. A red one, a red one, a red one, a stone. A red one, a red one, a stone, a stone. Her brother, Gabriel, is playing nearby, drawing circles in the dust with a stick. He walks over to her and watches her game for a while.

"Give me some," he says.

She shakes her head. "No." They're hers and she isn't in the mood to share.

"Please," he whines.

"No!" she looks up at him defiantly. He stares back for a moment and then grabs a handful of the pulses and runs. She chases him out of the compound and into the fields. Running. Running. Her mouth dry. Her heart pounding. Gabriel is nowhere to be seen. The cotton is scratching her legs. It's in her mouth, in her hair, in her eyes. She can't see anything anymore. She is in a cloud, suffocating.

The soup is up and she can feel hands patting her back as she heaves into a bowl stained with rust. There is salt water dripping into her eyes. Sweat and seawater and rain. Her mind is on fire. And there, in the middle of the flames, Gabriel, her brother. Only now he is broken. His train has crashed and he will no longer be going to university and her mother is crying as they bring him home wrapped in a sheet. And when they wash him clean they discover a smile on his face; imprinted there because the train crashed just as he was dreaming of his girlfriend who was about to remove her bodice and let him fondle her breasts for the first time. He died with his lips parted and will always be happy as his beginning meets his end. And now there are strangers in the room and the rust from the bowl has stained her front red and her stitches are coming apart. They'll have to stretch her out on a rack and wind her entrails out and hang them up to dry. The baby in the next room cries for someone. But not her. Will he know she's his mother when she returns? Or will he forever inhabit that space between them, searching for love? Khatoun reaches out for her little one with the blood red hair but he is just out of reach, and there are hands pulling her up, removing her clothes with the stench of vomit and sweat encrusted in the front and her love is pulled out of her and handed to a man with a strange voice.

The German doctor is back with his dead fireplace eyes. She can hear his thin voice singing, the refrain sung by Ferida and her mother.

"It's another infection."

"Another infection?"

"And what?"

"Fever...too high."

"And where?"

"The hospital."

"The hospital?"

"Again? *Kaknem, eshou botch, vay, vay, vay!*"

"If not?"

"...a distinct possibility."

"Lord have mercy!"

"*Asdvadz bahe!* Take her."

And then strong arms lifting her and still, those snatches of song,

The girl's lover has gone to Aleppo,
Asked for the price of the clothes,
Opened his purse of gold pieces,
Returned home with armfuls of gifts.
The pretty girl, her heart has now opened!

And her heart is now open but nothing can fill it. It is an empty hole and she herself falls into it with no wings to save her. And down she goes and the air rushing by her is cool and soothing to the bright pain behind her eyes and soon, she knows, she will find her dead brother, her dollies, her flame-haired child and her love for her husband. When she reaches her end she will find, once again, where, oh where, oh where to begin.

Allegedly

Ourfa, Summer 1915
Khatoun

Ourfa, the Eye of Mesopotamia. Situated at the crossroads of ancient highways, it nestles in the warm, fertile valley between the Tigris and Euphrates Rivers; the cradle of civilization. According to legend it was the first city to re-emerge in the world after the Great Flood. The birthplace of Abraham. The spot where Nimrod, the Babylonian King, later flung Abraham onto a burning pyre for refusing to worship pagan gods. Where Jehovah intervened, turning those flames into pools of water and the coals into sacred fish — still alive and swimming in the pleasant Dergah gardens to this day. To the north and west lie the barren limestone foothills of the Anatolian massif with its distant, fortress-like villages clinging to its precipitous sides. To the southeast, a sea of cotton and wheat fields stretch all the way to the horizon — past the biblical city of Harran, last stronghold of the Sabians, worshippers of Sun, Moon and planets.

Born as Urhai to Nimrod of Babylon, Ourfa endured centuries of conquest and change. The Hurrians, the Amorites, the Hittites — everyone wanted to dominate the strategically placed city at the heart of all trade routes. The Assyrians elevated the place into a prosperous political and cultural centre. The Seleucids fortified and renamed it Edessa. Under the Parthians it became a Royal City; the capital of Osroene for almost four hundred years. And in the first century BC, Dicran the Great included it within the new boundaries of Armenia, and many Armenians migrated to the city. It was in Ourfa that early Christians worshiped freely and built their churches. The Crusades passed through twice, in between which Zengi of Niniveh turned the churches back into mosques and it wasn't until sixteen-thirty-seven that Ourfa, having swung for centuries between Islam and Christianity, finally settled down as part of the Ottoman Empire under Murad IV. A flourishing, articulate city filled with Turks,

Armenians, Assyrians, Greeks, Maronites and Jews. A city where the fez mixed easily with straw boaters, the veil with abundant, loose hair. A place where any combination of beliefs was acceptable, particularly if it were different and somehow complicated by weird embellishments from all paths of religion.

And if you were to stand amongst the crowds lining the streets today, you would be excused for thinking there was some grand procession approaching. A carnival perhaps, or a religious ceremony. All roads leading into the heart of Ourfa are packed with people jostling for the best view. They're hanging out of windows and standing on chairs in unshuttered shops. Over there, a family of five have crowded on the back of a mule that looks ready to collapse. The air is thick with expectation, suffocatingly hot and strangely quiet despite the number of people.

Khatoun stands in the sun shading her eyes. She's hooked Solomon by the collarbone, tucking him in close. Alice stands next to him with Voghbed on her hip and Afrem leans away from them, his long legs twisted into a scribble like his father's. Ferida is there too, jostling with the crowd behind them, her elbows sharp jabbing wings, her face set in a scowl. She's been arguing with Khatoun all morning.

"*Asdvadz!* In this heat? You're crazy! It's not safe. What do you think they'll learn? Voghbed is still a baby, for God's sake. Iskender, *babam*, stop her!"

But Khatoun had been adamant. "This is not the first and it will not be the last. I want the children to see. Let the eye tell the tale."

Iskender had waved his hands in the air, disappearing into his room under Ferida's hurled slipper and she'd had no choice but to follow Khatoun, dragging scarves and *shalvar* out of her room to disguise them all like Kurds before they set off. And now they stand waiting along the side of the road in the baking sun with half the city. Sweating, moving. Surging forward.

And here it comes.

First, the smell. Recoil. Then shuffling and murmuring and clouds of dust followed by people. A ribbon of people. Tufts of hair, hollow thighs, bloodied feet. The majority are women. There are no young men amongst them – just a handful of children and weightless grey beards seemingly carried along by air.

In the distance, a migrating Kelaynak bird calls out, and apart from a startled call in reply, the only sound is the shuff-shuff-shuff of feet passing by. Not a shoe in sight, all of them dressed in rags and many naked, causing some gasps from the crowd, *ooh* and *ah!* Tittering. The women walk on, oblivious. Some, the lucky ones, have belongings strapped to their backs. Soft limbs drape soundlessly from their bundles, a thin little arm, a blackened leg. The stench is overpowering and an enterprising youth and his sister are doing brisk business selling strips of orange peel to stuff up the nose. And there, a vendor with iced water and lemon. Another with nuts in cones.

And still they come, the line of people that stretches back as far as the northern suburbs. And yet, it is whispered, these are only the remnants. The survivors of groups ten times this size. Shuff-shuff-shuff under the scorching sky. A woman stops, folds in on herself like paper and crumples to the ground. The procession shifts around her but keeps moving, avoiding her with no attempt to move her aside.

Urhai. Edessa. Al Ruha. Ancient City of Prophets. A crossroads. A market. A collection point. A dump. Ourfa today is a holding pen for exiles – a teeming concentration camp rife with disease. The khans – hearth and home to travellers for centuries are now little more than prison cells. People arrive in the morning, die in the afternoon and are dumped in mass graves at dusk. All summer they've been coming. The ones that survive are regrouped and sent across the border, ending up who knows where under the desert sun. For now, the majority of the caravans are herded together into the Millet *Khan* near the Turkish armoury, and it is towards this cramped and filthy destination that the procession is headed.

"Why are some of them naked?" Alice asks, her face scarlet from heat and embarrassment. "Who's taken their clothes?" When nobody answers she pulls off her headscarf and holds it out towards the shuffling crowd. It hangs from her fingers, untouched. "Why won't they take it?" she asks, flapping it impatiently. Suddenly she is jerked backwards, Ferida's calloused palm covering her face. The headscarf is gone, snatched from her fingers in a cloud of dust and horse's hooves. Voghbed is now wailing in Ferida's arms. Alice strains forward, past Ferida's grip, and watches her scrap of clothing dance away on the tip of a bayonet waved by a smiling gendarme. A venomous hiss slips through Ferida's lips.

"You see!" she spits, "You put us all at risk with your stupid games!"

"I'm sorry..." Alice starts to cry, but Ferida is not listening. She has her face inches from Khatoun's, the veins in her neck like knotted rope.

"Happy? Happy now?" she shouts. "Why do you want your children to see this? What will they learn? They'll have time when it's our turn. Enough!" She elbows a gap in the crowd and herds the children in front of her. "You can come if you want or you can stay and watch, I don't care, but these kids are going home."

Alice hesitates for a second, torn between mother and aunt but a vicious cuff to her ear gets her moving. She reaches back, grabs Khatoun's hand and pulls her along with them. Ferida kicks and swats people aside until she has the whole family in front of a narrow gap between houses.

"Down here," she says, pushing them ahead. "Stick together and for God's sake Alice, shut up! Stop crying."

They wind their way through the alleyways, Ferida handing Voghbed over to Khatoun and moving forward to take the lead. Khatoun brings up the rear, her face ashen, her eyes swollen. The streets are empty of people, the houses firmly shuttered. Apart from the few dogs stretched out in the gutter, not a soul can be seen. They are either lining the roads where the marches are coming through, or sitting upstairs, their chess pieces moving silently across the board as they tiptoe from room to room in self-preservation. Chess, a good waiting game.

When the first caravans had come into town, people had stood side by side to watch them, the Armenians muttering prayers, their Turkish friends shifting their feet in embarrassment. But something had happened just days ago that had changed things. A boy (apparently not much older than Alice) had yelled something at an old man in one of the marches. A joke, perhaps. Who knows what he'd said or why, but further along someone else had pushed the same man and then a stone had struck him square between the eyes. The man fell without complaint and a gendarme rode up. People held back, melting into the shop fronts in fear until they saw the gendarme laugh. He directed his horse right over the old man's body and the crowd gasped and then cheered as his bones cracked. A momentary pause, like a wave receding and then they began to spit and howl, pushing and shoving to see who would fall. Since then, similar stories had surfaced and Armenians hardly dared come out to greet the caravans any more. It only took one incident, the snatch of an apron, a horse rearing for the crowd to turn ugly.

The sun whips the sky. The cool breeze that usually sweeps through the alleys has disappeared and a thin layer of dust covers everything. The markets and shops are closed and for once the family are not forced to wind around endless stalls, sidestepping the hawkers and their globules of spit. In a short while they reach home and Ferida takes a string of keys from her pocket, fiddles with a padlock and unbolts the large double doors. She stands with one arm up, holding the door ajar and ushers everyone in under her sour armpit, slamming it shut behind them. She slots the large wooden beam into its brackets across both sides, leans against the heavy wood and exhales. The lilting strum of a *saz* fills the hall from Iskender's office and Mertha emerges from the corridor leading to the kitchen, her arms outstretched to her grandchildren.

"You're just in time for lunch," she beams. "I've made beans and *pilaff* and boiled an egg for you," she smiles at Alice.

The children kick off their shoes and race across the hall in bare feet.

"*I* want an egg!" Afrem shouts.

"Me too!"

"And me!" The boys chase Alice towards the kitchen and disappear, the door slamming behind them.

Ferida sits down and pulls off her shoes, cursing under her breath.

"What's the matter with you?" Mertha asks. "You look ill."

"*Me?* Ill? Ask your daughter," she jabs a finger in Khatoun's direction.

"Khatoun?"

"I'm fine."

"So what's going on?"

Ferida grinds her foot on the floor, finding a seam between tiles to file away at the thick yellow skin on her heel. "It's your daughter who's sick. Sick in the head. She took us — all of us

— to see the marches. She says she wants her children to see everything. Says they'll learn about life that way. At the risk of getting their throats slashed. *Asdvadz*. If you ask me, there are some things nobody should ever see." She picks up her shoes and heads towards the kitchen, her feet sliding into her slippers as she goes.

Thin columns of light shaft down from the ceiling. Another song starts up on the *saz*. The sweet smell of hashish hangs in the air.

"Well. You shouldn't be outside in the sun," Mertha says, poking at the children's shoes with her foot, arranging them into a neat row by the wall. "You'll ruin your eyes once and for all. That's what the doctor said." She smiles at Khatoun, turns and heads towards the kitchen, her stout, comforting figure retreating into shadow. "I'm feeding the kids."

"There were children their age in the march," Khatoun whispers to the empty room. She follows the shafts of light up to the domed ceiling and the hallway bleaches white. She leans against the wall, turning her face to the side, pressing it into the soft plaster. Cold, smooth, damp. Black blooms where the lamps stand. Khatoun breathes slowly, the drum of her heart calming, the pressure behind her eyes subsiding. *Tac atac atac atac*. The clatter of machines vibrates through the walls.

Past the fragrant cloud seeping under the door of Iskender's office and on to the workrooms, Khatoun pauses at the door. As soon as she enters, the sewing stops and the girls stand.

"Sit down," Khatoun waves her hand at them, "or is it time for lunch already?" She crosses over to Margarit who is clutching a pair of *shalvar*.

"Beautiful work," she tells her inspecting the bright coloured embroidery that circles the ankles.

Margarit smiles, "Peacocks. Like home."

Khatoun traces the birds with her finger. When she looks up, the girls are still standing, watching her.

"What?" she asks. "What is it?"

One pair of eyes darts to the next, then the next, then the next. A chair creaks. Margarit takes the *shalvar* from Khatoun's hand. "We heard you went to see the marches today."

"I did."

The rustle of silk tissue.

"I went. And I took the children. I wanted them to see it with their own eyes, not hear wild stories about it, that's all."

"And?" Serpuhi is staring at her from her seat by the window.

"It was a mistake."

The clamour breaks and questions fly.

"What did they look like?"

"Do you know where they're going?"

"Which towns are they from?"

"How many...?"

"Stop." Khatoun holds her hand up to stem the barrage of questions. "One at a time. It's mostly women and children. Nobody knows where they're going. They've come from everywhere – Samsun, Erzerum, Trebizond. Here and there they stop and regroup so unless you ask them, it's impossible to tell."

The girls shift uneasily.

"Kharpert?" Bzdig Shoushun asks.

"I don't know. Maybe. Probably."

"Sivas?"

"Marash?"

"Is it just big towns, or are they evacuating all the villages as well?"

"What does it matter?" Serpuhi interrupts. She snips a beard of coloured thread from the back of a heavily beaded cuff. "Eventually they'll take all of us. Cities. Villages. Farms. Wherever we've come from, we're all going to end up in the same place."

Before Khatoun can calm the girls down, a sudden, urgent banging at the front gate sends them into a greater frenzy. Grundug howls in the courtyard and Bzdig Shoushun starts to cry. "I pricked my finger," she mumbles. "I almost ruined the *shalvar*." Nobody moves. The banging starts up again.

"I'll go," Lolig says, grabbing a *çarshaf* from a hook on the wall and throwing it over her dress. She sticks two fingers in her mouth and whistles. "Grundug! Come with me. Come!"

The girls sit, unpicking their tacking, scissors poised over ragged seams until Lolig's sunny face pokes around the door once more. "It's for you, *Digin* Khatoun. It's *Begum* Şenay. She says she has a fitting."

Khatoun slaps her head with her palm. "Of course. The time. It ran away today." She hurries out of the room, smoothing down her hair. "Serpuhi, the *a la Franga* evening gown in gold tissue and the rose peignoir. Bring them to the parlour please."

Three women sit on the overstuffed European armchairs in the Ladies' Room. Two of them veiled completely in simple green, the other wearing a lighter, ornate pink, embroidered with gold.

"May God's peace be upon you," Khatoun says, her fingers skimming a line from heart to forehead.

"And upon you. And blessings to you and your family," her visitor counters. They kiss. Eyes, hands, faces.

Lolig appears at the door, deposits a tray of thimble sized coffee cups and a pitcher of water on one of the low tables and disappears again. When they are alone, *Begum* Şenay peels off her outer layer and lets it drop to the sofa. Folds of creamy flesh pillow about her. Pale, waxy skin, big brown eyes and a full set of gold teeth. She stretches out her arms and a cloud of rose envelops her.

"I'm so excited!" she beams, clapping her hands, setting the bracelets jingling, the flesh aquiver below. "I can't wait to see what you've done. When my husband sees me in these dresses he'll forget that skinny bitch Orlan and remember why he married me!"

The two veils on either side giggle and stamp their feet in glee. A tap on the door and Lolig and Serpuhi sail two beautiful gowns in, their faces averted. The two veils stare at them as they leave, nudging each other behind Şenay's back. Across the hallway the mournful tune of Iskender's *saz* plays on.

One of the veils heaves *Begum* Şenay to her feet while the other pushes from behind. *Begum* Şenay scoops up her dresses and disappears into a small antechamber separated from the main room by a heavy velvet curtain. With much giggling and slapping of flesh she disrobes and squeezes into the first dress; a Parisian cut designed for scandal with its tight bodice and bare shoulders. She dances into the parlour, suddenly light on her feet, twirling like a little girl. The veils *ooh!* and *ah!* and prod at her monstrous décolletage.

"*Orospou!*" *Begum* Şenay laughs. "All men love a whore in the bedroom!" Her friends ululate as if they were at a wedding party.

"You'll be a mother in no time!"

"Or die practising!" They dance around her waving their hands, almost crying with laughter.

Khatoun stares at them quietly, fingering a small fold of cloth stuck with pins. "You look beautiful," she nods. "If you stand still now I can finish the hem."

Begum Şenay stops dancing and stares petulantly at Khatoun. "Ouf. What's the matter with you today?"

"Nothing," Khatoun shrugs. "Just my eyes. They're giving me trouble today." She takes a handful of pins and slips them between her lips.

Begum Şenay steps up on a little stool, the gold tissue lighting up her glorious breasts. "Rubbish!" she snorts. "Something else is bothering you."

The *saz* stops playing and the house falls silent. Across the hall, Iskender's chair scrapes back and he pulls himself up by the edge of the table. He coughs noisily and spits into a handkerchief.

"Aha! An argument with your husband," *Begum* Şenay smiles. "That's it, isn't it?" The veils lean in to each other and whisper. The sound of Iskender clearing his throat bounces down the hall as he shuffles towards the kitchen.

"No," Khatoun shakes her head. "No problems with him."

"Well, what then? I don't want you to ruin my dress with whatever is making you miserable. Get it out. *Hayde,* we're all friends here. Maybe we need to burn lead over your head and throw it in water to catch the evil eye."

"No. It's just me." Khatoun tugs the silk over Şenay's wide hips, smoothing the material down. "I've been arguing with everyone today."

"See, I *knew* it. Why?"

Khatoun strokes the skirt of the dress to the floor and surveys the hem. "I went to see the marches arrive and my family are upset. I took the children with me." She folds two fingers of fabric up from the bottom and secures it with a pin.

"To see the pilgrims? Why would you do that?" Şenay rotates a fraction on the dais and Khatoun continues to pin. "Of course your family are upset. In this heat with all those people! No wonder you look sour."

"You sound like Ferida."

"Your sister-in-law? Ouch! I don't look like her too, do I?" The two veils giggle and slap *Begum* Şenay's thighs.

"No."

"Allah is merciful. But you still haven't answered me. Why should the pilgrims concern you? They're just people being moved because of the war. Why would you want to see them?"

"I don't know." Khatoun leans back for a better look at the hem.

"So, what did you see?"

"Not much."

"Then why are you so sad? Really, Khatoun, I don't want you to ruin my dress with your mood," Şenay teases. "I need sex in here, not sadness!"

Khatoun laughs. A short hiccup of air.

"Well? What did you see that's upset you?"

"Women. Mostly," Khatoun says pulling a pin out from between her lips. "I saw mostly women. And children."

"So? What were they doing?" *Begum* Şenay inches around on her podium.

"Walking."

"Walking?"

"Some of them."

"Some of them?"

Khatoun stands and adjusts the shimmer around *Begum* Şenay's shoulders. "I saw some children walking. Others carried."

Begum Şenay looks at her friend. "How so? Carried? Why? Are they sick?" Her hands flutter up to her throat.

"Some. Some of them are sick, yes."

"And the others?"

Khatoun shrugs. She crosses over to the door and calls for Lolig who comes running in wiping her mouth with a cloth. "I'm sorry to disturb your lunch," Khatoun says to the girl. "Can you bring me some more of this gold from the work room?" She turns back to face Şenay. Alice and Afrem run past the door and thunder up the stairs, laughing. Dust dances like smoke in the chinks of light filtering into the room through the shutters. The two veils peel back a corner of fabric and sip their water. Shortly, the door pushes to and Lolig enters, carrying a bolt of cloth and some scissors. She waits for Khatoun to cut off a section then leaves.

"I'm going to give you another layer here," Khatoun says stroking Şenay's bodice. "It'll be softer – more alluring."

Begum Şenay steps down, allowing Khatoun to drape her with more fabric.

"How young?" she whispers.

Khatoun pats her breast.

"Babies?"

Khatoun nods. The dust swirls in the sunlight. "Some. Most of the babies are left behind."

"What do you mean? Left behind?"

"In different places. There's a tree by the walls to the north of town. The one covered with rags. I heard they drop them in the shade of that tree."

"The prayer tree?"

"That's the one."

"And…"

"They carry on walking."

"Don't be ridiculous!" *Begum* Şenay flaps at the gossamer tissue around her face. "Who would leave their baby under a tree and carry on walking? I mean, anybody could just come up and steal it. That's nonsense." She takes a step back and squeezes onto the sofa between the two veils who immediately lean in and start fanning her. She plucks at the neckline of the dress for a moment before getting irritated. "Stop! Take it off. I'm too tired for this today." Her hands flutter about her face and then fall in her lap. The two veils heave her up and deposit her behind the velvet curtain once more and she reappears a few minutes later, fully covered.

"I'll do some work on this before I see you again," Khatoun says, fingering the Parisian dress. "It should be ready the day after tomorrow."

"*Merci, hanum. Merci,*" Şenay says, retreating from the room, touching her heart and folding into the embrace of her companions and out of the door. Khatoun can hear them at the gate, screeching at their man, Bayram, for falling asleep in the phaeton. With a "*Hayde!*" they are gone and the house is finally silent.

Khatoun wanders into the kitchen and lifts the lid off a pot. Everyone else has already eaten, thundered upstairs and flung themselves into bed for siesta. She piles her plate with beans, takes some bread and an onion and heads for the courtyard. The fountain dribbles water and a small bird with a blue chest stands at the edge, eyeing her. It takes three hops and cocks its head to the side. Khatoun flicks a crumb across the tiles and watches the bird sweep it up into the eaves. She soaks up the juice on her plate with her bread and crunches into her onion. When she has finished she takes her plate to the kitchen, mixes yoghurt and water in a glass and heads upstairs to her room.

Iskender lies sprawled out on their bed like a star. She puts her glass down, tentatively moves his arm aside and slides in next to him. Iskender coughs, reaches out and buries his head in her neck. Khatoun closes her eyes, inhales her husband's garlicky sweat and floats out over the desert and into the blinding sun.

The light is dazzling, hurting her eyes. Below her, two hawks circle in wide lazy arcs, searching for prey. They call to each other mournfully, their wings tense. Somewhere a child cries – a miserable wail that not even a breast would comfort. And then the world opens up and Khatoun falls, jerking to a stop. She's on the ground, covered in dust, heart thudding. If she runs fast enough, she knows, she'll be able to fly again. The sun glints on her bangles as she prepares for flight. Like a well-honed athlete she stretches out her fingers, arches her back and begins to run. Faster and faster and she's in the air, coasting low over the scrubby terrain. The sensation is exhilarating, a memory of previous flight, but before she can soar her skirt snags. The more she tugs, the more she gets entangled. Blackened tree branches burst out of the earth and pull her down, piercing her organs. She watches her blood spread, a flower blooming over the earth but can't open her mouth. The birds circle above her and that teething baby wails for its mother and the earth beneath her opens up and again she falls with a lurch that leaves her skin stripped from the bone.

Iskender is leaning over her, shaking her gently. Someone is tapping at the door. "Wake up," he croons. "You were shaking in your sleep."

Khatoun sits up and massages her arm. The tapping at the door continues.

"Yes?" Iskender calls out.

An eye, half a pair of lips and a fragment of nose slide around the door.

"There's a man waiting downstairs. He told me to give you this," Lolig waves an envelope in the air and Iskender pads across the floor to get it. Inside is a note, scrawled in childish writing. He reaches for his glasses and scans the piece of paper.

"It's from *Begum* Şenay; she wants you to go to her house as soon as you can. Her man is waiting downstairs to take you. She says not to worry about her dresses, she has something for you but you must get there as soon as possible." He removes his spectacles and rubs his eyes. "Is everything all right?" he asks.

Khatoun nods. "Everything's good. Lolig, tell Bayram I'll be down in ten minutes."

"Yes, *Digin* Khatoun."

Minutes later Khatoun steps out into the balmy air in a fresh dress and headscarf. Bayram stands in the shade by the door in traditional stripes and cummerbund. He smiles when he sees her, extends his hand and helps her up into the covered wagon. He leaps into the front seat in one bound, displaying the lithe body he works so hard to maintain, and they set off through the streets at a pace. A handful of shops have already opened and a scattering of people are milling about, getting on with afternoon chores. Everyone seems to know Bayram, particularly the women and they call out to him as they pass. He delivers jokes like letters, leaning back in his seat with his fez pushed up at a rakish angle, guiding the horse and cart through the narrow streets of the Assyrian Quarter and on to the prosperous tree-lined avenues surrounding the Dergah Gardens.

As soon as they arrive, Khatoun deposits her shoes in the nook in the wall and is admitted into the women's quarters behind the fine grille work. The patterned walls are cool to the touch, the polished floors slippery as glass. Through a door, carved and inlaid, *Begum* Şenay is waiting, seated in a large room encircled by low divans, her unslippered feet powdered white. The air is thick with incense, the room illuminated in a fine cobweb of light. In front of *Begum* Şenay, a polished tray steams with tea and a young girl immediately pours a glass for Khatoun as she settles down onto the cushions.

"My most honoured guest, Khatoun *Hanum*," *Begum* Şenay bids in formal welcome. "Please join me." She waves the girl away with a flicked wrist. As soon as they are alone she leans across the table, a finger to her lips. "I've asked you here for a reason," she whispers to Khatoun. "Move closer."

Khatoun shifts her cushion until the soles of their feet touch.

Begum Şenay drums her fingers on her glass. She smiles. Takes a sip of tea. Exhales.

"My husband and I have weathered some storms."

"I'm sorry..."

"No need to be sorry. That *orospou* Orlan with udders is the one suffering right now. But between my husband and me... things are good again. Thanks to you."

Khatoun laughs, "But I've never even met him."

"And nor will you. He doesn't fraternise with women – not *decent* women, anyway. *Orospou, tangos, çaças,* definitely!" she spits on the floor. "Anyhow, I consider myself in your debt. I could never wear the dresses you make me in public...but in private..." she laughs and lowers her voice again, her eyes on the door. "He wants children, so anything I ask for these days he gives me." She sits back on her cushion and takes a sip of tea, pearls of sweat beading her upper lip. "You probably think I'm stupid but I knew nothing about the marches other than what I had been told. That they were pilgrims. Families, relocated out of harm's way. After you spoke to me I came home and questioned my women." Abruptly, without warning, Şenay slaps her face hard. "Nobody *ever* tells me anything!" she screeches. "I'm ignorant! Stupid! All I care about is clothes and perfume and sex. That's what everyone thinks. But that's all I *have*. That's all I am *given*." She is heaving with sudden tears; her pale face blotched with anger and a neat pink handprint. "I *will* be a mother, *Insha'Allah,* and all the gossiping will end!" She throws herself into Khatoun's lap, her flesh rolling in waves as she weeps.

Khatoun bends over her, a hesitant hand hovering over her shoulder. "I'm sorry to hear of your troubles," she begins.

"*No!*" *Begum* Şenay screams into Khatoun's skirt. "I don't want *anyone* sorry for me!" She heaves herself back into a seated position just as the door opens and the skinny girl who served tea ventures tentatively inside.

"*Siktir git!*" *Begum* Şenay screeches, hurling a glass at the unfortunate girl. "And don't come back until I tell you!" The glass shatters against the wall and the door slams shut again. *Begum* Şenay blows her nose into her hand and wipes it clean on the hem of her robe.

"Give me more tea," she says, stabbing her finger towards another glass. "Please." She swallows the drink in one go, dabs delicately at her lips and lets out a huge sigh. "*Vay, vay, vay*. Khatoun *Hanum*, in the hours since I last saw you I have learnt a lot. I have heard the truth and probably a lot of lies but it has brought me somewhere and that is *here*." With a flourish and an awkward lean, she pulls out an envelope from under her seat. "My husband wrote it for me. Don't worry, I paid him for it." She slaps the packet down on the tray, displaying all her gold teeth in a filthy laugh. "From my lips to his pen."

Khatoun stares at the envelope. "What is it?"

Begum Şenay tilts her head back and smiles. "A release form. He's working with some military tribunal. The Divani Harp. He gave me this to take to the Millet *Khan* where the pilgrims...the deportees are kept. I have permission to take half a dozen girls to help me in my home. And three for you. Only...if we find any babies...I take them too."

Khatoun looks at her friend in disbelief. The seal on the envelope is red, thick, stamped with a heavy hand.

"Let's do it," *Begum* Şenay whispers, heaving laboriously to her feet. "Let's go now and get those girls before he wakes up and changes his mind!" She puts a finger to her lips, tiptoes to the door and yanks it open, grabbing the young girl who has been eavesdropping by the hair and slapping her viciously across the face.

"How many times have I told you not to spy on me!" she screams. "Go and get my carriage and have Binnur and Alef wait for me in the courtyard." The weeping girl flees and *Begum* Şenay ushers Khatoun out of the room, leaving the warm red and gold Ottoman carpets patterned with the ghostly imprint of her powdered feet.

They slip through the corridors until they reach an enclosed garden where half a dozen women sit in the shade near the fountain. Two of them peel off and follow Şenay and Khatoun through an archway into another, smaller yard where a covered *araba* with two horses is waiting. They heft Şenay into the cabin, chattering as they climb in after her. Thick drapes enclose them, the heat of the long day stuffed inside. The clashing perfumes and stale air give Khatoun an immediate headache and she loosens the buttons at her neck as Bayram cabrioles into his seat and they lurch off.

"You'll have to wear this when we get there," *Begum* Şenay

says, throwing a *çarshaf* to Khatoun. "Cover up completely. It'll make our lives easier. And let me do all the talking, you just nod and do what I say."

By the time they reach the Millet *Khan*, Khatoun is feeling sick. She pulls the curtain open and lets a sliver of cool air in. Bayram dismounts and bangs on the *khan's* wooden doors. A trickle of sweat snakes down Khatoun's face and the sea roars in her ears. After several repeated knocks, a small door cut into the gate opens and a gendarme clambers out. *Begum* Şenay slips her hand through the drapes and hands the sealed letter over.

"Let's see how long this takes," she snorts. The gendarme disappears and within seconds the gates creak open and they are admitted into the *khan*.

With the heavy doors slammed shut behind them they pull the drapes open and are immediately hit by the smell. A high wall encloses a yard packed with mules, donkeys and horses — all of them shifting disdainfully away from a mangy pack of dogs foraging in their dung. Khatoun takes a shallow breath and looks up. Thin streaks of pink tear across the cobalt blue sky. A lone star is visible.

Above them, on the second floor, a balcony runs the length of the enclosure. At first it looks as if washing has been hung over the railings to dry, and then Khatoun makes out a face and then another. Hundreds of people are draped over the balustrade, watching them silently, their faces just discernible in the waning light. The gendarme who admitted them tells their party to stay put and disappears with the letter. The horses twitch uneasily, spooked by the scavenging dogs. Bayram curses and scrapes the sole of his slipper on the edge of the wheel.

"Sit inside and don't move," *Begum* Şenay orders Binnur and Alef. The girls nod, happily retreating behind the curtains. A few minutes later the gendarme reappears.

"This way." He leads *Begum* Şenay and Khatoun across the yard into a long dark room. A small iron bed lies next to the wall, a dirty sheet hanging over a length of wire that runs alongside it. The bed is unmade and the room smells stale. Cigarettes, feet and sleep. In front of the cot, near the only window, a large desk sits buried under a mountain of paper. A uniform sits hunched over the paperwork, head in hands, cigarette smouldering in the overflowing ashtray in front of him. As they approach the desk he rubs his face and looks up, a single black eyebrow framing his mournful eyes. The skin around his cheeks is pockmarked, his lips thin and flaky. He's left his shirt unbuttoned at the neck, allowing a promiscuous tuft of black hair to escape. He shifts his elbows back, lifts himself from his chair a few inches.

"Welcome, welcome," he says, clearing the phlegm from his throat. With a lazy wrist he gestures for them to sit, which they decline, then sags back into his chair. "So," he says fingering the letter, "you've come to get some girls."

"Yes," *Begum* Şenay nods, her bosom manoeuvring itself to eye level. "I need half a dozen women to help in the home and my friend here needs a handful as seamstresses. She's sewing for the war effort. Uniforms," she indicates Khatoun behind her.

The officer looks them over and nods. "Good. Take them. Less for me to deal with." He reaches into his pocket, pulls out tobacco and papers and rolls a cigarette, ignoring the one burning in front of him. "My duty is to safeguard the security of our borders. These people are spies, subversives and troublemakers – the ones that are left." He lights the cigarette and exhales. "Asker will show you upstairs. Take whomever you want – at this point they're all ugly. Useless to me or my men." He lifts himself out of his chair, slumps down again and dismisses them with a wave of his hand.

The gendarme leads them back through the quadrangle. Up a flight of stairs, two soldiers sit playing *pishti* on the landing. After a brief word, they scrape back their chairs and unlock the door behind them. The gendarme excuses himself "to urinate" and Khatoun and Şenay squeeze past the soldiers into the room.

The place is buzzing with flies, the smell of human excrement overwhelming. Several thousand women and children are huddled together, bound together by their own stench and there is hardly enough space to breathe. Despite this, *Begum* Şenay bats the smell away, picks up her flesh and moves forward, resplendent as a ship on the ocean. Sadly for her the floor is so thick with people and the room so dark she can't go far. She stops, strikes a dramatic pose and is about to speak when a commotion breaks out at the other end of the room.

A narrow door opens onto the street which is higher on this side, the *khan* having been built on a slope. Two men appear, their faces covered with cloth, one of them brandishing a torch. They poke about with their feet and yell muffled curses at the exhausted people. Anybody that doesn't move or yelp in pain gets dragged to the end of the room, sprinkled with lime and thrust out the door. At least two dozen corpses are flung onto the wagons lined up waiting along the street. The men are just about to leave when *Begum* Şenay speaks.

"Stop! Your torch. I need it."

The gravedigger scowls. One of the guards who followed them in whispers in his ear and sullenly he hands it over.

"Where are you taking them?" *Begum* Şenay asks. "The bodies?"

The torchless man shrugs. "Outskirts of town."

"Will you bury them?"

"Of course. With great ceremony," he snorts, the door screeching shut behind him.

Begum Şenay reaches for Khatoun and drags her close. "Let's choose our girls and get out of here," she whispers. She takes a deep breath and holds the torch up, illuminating herself beautifully. "We've come to take some of you away," she announces. The room remains silent, the travellers watching her dispassionately. "I said, we are here to *save* you," *Begum* Şenay smiles.

Silence.

"What my friend says is true," Khatoun says, switching to Armenian. "We have a paper allowing us to take some of you home with us. Tonight. Now."

Still no response.

A bent silhouette appears in the doorway to the gallery. "Listen. Listen to them. I know the truth when I hear it. Listen to what they say." The shadow approaches and extends a bandaged hand.

"Pastor Ghizirian. Follow me." Bare feet, one of them dragging. The remnants of pastoral robes. He leads them outside onto the balcony. A glorious magenta sky. Bodies wrapped around each other like pack dogs.

"You say you have permission?" he asks. Deep gullies from nose to chin. Eyes thick with crust. Beard, oozing in patches.

"Yes," Khatoun confirms. "This is *Begum* Şenay – her husband works with the Divani Harp."

Pastor Ghizirian nods. "And how many souls can you save?"

"Nine," Şenay beams. "Six will come with me; three will go with Khatoun to help with her sewing."

"I see." The pastor dabs at one of his sores with his bandaged hand. "And the girls that come with you – what will happen to them?"

"They'll live in a big house and have a good life."

Pastor Ghizirian smiles at her and nods. A rheumy tear slips down his nose and he strokes it into his tattered beard.

"I promise they'll be looked after," *Begum* Şenay continues. "My husband gave me his assurance."

"Your husband," the pastor says. He leans against the balustrade, taking the weight off his bad foot and the sky darkens to a deep bruise. "*Insha'Allah*. This way. Follow me."

He leads them to the far end of the balcony where a handful of women sit around a *mangal*, warming scraps of bread. They make space for him as he approaches and listen quietly as he bends down and whispers. They nod and mutter, occasionally looking over at *Begum* Şenay and Khatoun. Eventually one of them stands and approaches Khatoun.

"I am Armenouhi," she says kissing Khatoun's hand. "God bless you. I will go and live with the *Bayan*. This is my friend Arshalous, she will come and live with you."

Arshalous hobbles towards them on filthy wrapped feet. Shorter than Khatoun, she wears a tattered dress that ends at her knees. Dark eyes and thick eyebrows that almost meet in the middle. There is something child-like about her despite her skin – pinched like an old woman's and yellowing. Her lips part into a wide grin and several front teeth are missing. She touches her hand to her heart and bows her head before disappearing into the dark room.

"Arshalous will find some others," Armenouhi says. "And this," she indicates a tiny creature by the fire, "is Hripsime. She goes wherever I go."

A young girl sits huddled in a filthy blanket, her hair shorn to stubble. Her face is black with soot, her eyes closed as she dozes. Armenouhi nudges her awake and gestures with her hands. Slowly Hripsime stands, the blanket dropping from an extended belly, obviously in the last months of pregnancy. She stares blankly at Şenay and Khatoun.

"She doesn't talk," Armenouhi says. "We don't know whether she can hear or not, only that she never speaks."

Pastor Ghizirian puts his arms around Hripsime's shoulders

and kisses her sooty forehead. "Please take her with you," he says. "If this baby survives, a part of all of us will live. If I can save just this one, I will die happy."

Khatoun reaches out to Hripsime and is about to take her in her arms when *Begum* Şenay stops her with a grabbed wrist.

"Not yet," she smiles at the pastor. "We'll take her, but maybe we should leave the blanket for someone else." She slips it from Hripsime's shoulders and steps back as it drops to the floor. "It's *alive!*" she mouths at Khatoun, shuddering.

By now Arshalous has returned with six more women. The gendarme that accompanied them seems relieved. He's been hanging outside, sticking his head in at intervals and now he barks at them from the doorway, "Hurry up. I need to piss again."

"Uncouth lout," *Begum* Şenay snorts. "Ignore him." She pushes the women ahead of her, holding the torch high. As they trail back through the dark hall the voices follow.

"Remember Antranig, from Sivas."

"Haik from Erzinjan."

"Arevalous, Apraham, Apel. From Kharpert. Remember us."

"Go with the light."

"And the light remain with you."

The door bolts shut, the gendarme darts down the stairs and the guards playing *pishti* look up from their game in irritation.

The women are halfway across the yard when the officer calls out to them, two streams of cigarette smoke snarling out from under his nose.

"Happy?" he asks, tossing the crumpled letter they gave him into the courtyard. "By the way, *Bayan*, your two women left – said they'd rather walk home than stay here another minute."

"But I told them to stay put!"

"What can you do? Young girls. They never listen. We had a nice chat. I offered them an escort but they refused. You'll probably find them on the road home. Hope they're safe, unchaperoned like that."

"Thank you for all your help," *Begum* Şenay snaps back. "I'll be sure to tell my husband."

The *araba* is just where they left it, only now the gendarme with the leaky bladder sits next to Bayram, gesticulating wildly as he regales him with stories. Bayram seems rapt, holding a bottle in one hand and a cigarette in the other.

"Bayram!" *Begum* Şenay screeches. "Smoking? Drinking?"

The gendarme takes the bottle out of Bayram's fist and flicks the cigarette away. "He was only holding them for me while I took a piss."

"Again? What's wrong with you?" *Begum* Şenay snaps.

The gendarme laughs. He sticks the flask into his pocket and leaps down. "You haven't taken the pretty ones have you?" he asks. "The pretty ones are worth cash to us." He makes a fist with one hand and pokes his finger in and out as he saunters past.

The sky above is black, pinpricked with stars. The moon, a silver sickle. The veil enveloping *Begum* Şenay billows like an angry cloud.

"Hey, *pezevenk!*" she calls after his retreating shadow. "Maybe if you kept your little prick in your pants it wouldn't be burning with syphilis. Or was that a present from your mother?"

The air freezes and the gendarme stops. Above them, the exhausted travellers hang still and Pastor Ghizirian can be seen in the light of the *mangal* working his lips. Nine women melt into one behind Khatoun and hold their breath. And then, the sound of one person clapping. The officer, watching from his doorway.

"Asker – get over here!" He dismisses the gendarme with a curt nod and walks up to *Begum* Şenay, stopping inches away from her, his eyes bright. "*Vay, vay, vay,* what I'd do for a woman like you!" he sighs, a long exhale of rancid breath. "Go on, get out of here and take your precious cargo with you before you get me into trouble."

He extends his hand, helps *Begum* Şenay climb up next to Bayram and stands aside as Khatoun and the girls scramble over each other's laps into the back. Slowly, he walks their fillies to the gate, slaps one on the rump to set them off and laughs.

The heavy gates slam shut behind them with a thud. The Millet *Khan*, hearth and home to travellers for centuries. Ourfa, most civilised of cities, welcoming to all. The scent of roses is overwhelming. As the *araba* trundles away Khatoun pulls the curtain aside for air and looks back. Two figures guard the entrance, one standing forward, the other hanging back. A cloud obscures the moon, the officer's laughter soars over them with jagged wings and when the moon reappears, the figures have gone. Not even their shadows remain. The Millet *Khan* is silent.

Like a Plum

Ourfa, Summer 1915
Khatoun Agha Boghos (dictated to Iskender Agha Boghos)

Their two heads almost touch. Khatoun and Iskender Agha Boghos, husband and wife, bent over the desk in his room. Paper, ink, pens. The contents of Iskender's drawer scattered in front of them.

"There are sonnets, and they're fourteen lines. And haiku which are short – two thoughts balanced with a connecting one. And epic poems that are a book long. And then of course, there's how to organise sentences together to makes verses. And rhyming, which is when we make words sound the same. And alliteration…"

"Shush," Khatoun says, her hand on Iskender's lips. "Slow down."

"Yes," Iskender exhales. "Slower. Yes." He's over excited. His wife had come to him. In his office. Asked for his help. He didn't know what to say. Where to begin.

"Words," he sputters. "There are just words. Let's start there. With simple words."

"Such as?"

"Ah…" Iskender strokes his moustache. "Ummmm…"

"Ouagadougou?"

Iskender laughs. "That's the name of a place."

"A place…you want to go to? I've heard you say it many times."

"No. Maybe. I don't know. I simply like the name; the way it sounds in my mouth. Oua ga dou gou. Round, like a plum." He swivels in his chair and points to the wall, "There it is." Coloured pins, squiggly writing, a curling brown edge. His map of the world. Unframed. Stuck to the wall with mastic. He reaches up and taps some of the pins back in place. "Beirut. I always wanted to go there. To take you. Our honeymoon that never was. Kathmandu. There too. And other places. All over the map." He waves his hand in a graceful arc over the fading world.

"Why?"

"Ah. Different reasons. The mountains. The sea. The culture. A little peace for everyone. And you?" He reaches out, tentatively lifting Khatoun's chin, smudging it with ink. "Where would you go?"

Khatoun closes her eyes. "My old bedroom. You sleeping. Leafy patterns on the wall from the trees outside. Peppers drying in the sun. A sky, blue as a bird's egg. That's where I would go."

"See. You don't need my help. That's poetry. Let's write that."

"No." Khatoun shakes her head. "That's the past. This is now. Let's write this. You always said poetry comes from the heart? Then write this. I'll say the words, you write them down."

"As you like."

"I like."

Iskender picks up the pen, fills it with indigo ink, taps it, blots it, reaches for a page of vellum.

"Ready?"

"Ready."

Those Mothers.

they come from Kharpert, from Van and Marash,
walk broken, blood feet staining the ground.
the women hold children, place them around.

a hundred small voices migrating like birds,
in a day, they are gone.

did you take one, my sister, as a thing of your own?
give it your name? find its wood comb?

tell me, oh sister, as more of us pass
will our friendship turn dust? will it last?

will you choose me plump raisins and brush out my hair,
touch feet under the blanket? will we still share?

I drape you in silk, shroud myself in white muslin
walk to my church, watch my people turn ashen.

will you cry for me, old friend, as I walk my goodbye,
think not I am earth but a bird free in the sky?

tell me, oh sister, as most of us pass
will our friendship turn dust? can it last?

Walk

Ourfa, August 1915
Khatoun

A dove croons above, making them start. *Begum* Şenay looks up and frowns at the pale pink streaks threading the sky.

"That's deep enough," she murmurs, "you can stop now."

The gardener empties his shovel, leaps out of the hole and scrapes his boots clean at the side. *Begum* Şenay smiles graciously and leans into his neck.

"You know I'll be wearing your balls as a necklace if anyone hears of this."

The gardener nods, steps back a pace and relights the cigarette he'd tucked behind his ear. The dug earth smells fresh, edible. Khatoun stands amongst the shadows behind *Begum* Şenay, her arms around Hripsime, who droops around the bundle in her arms, protecting it from the night air. The shadows sigh, the dove flutters to the ground and a light breeze stirs up the scent of jasmine and honeysuckle. The bird hops forward, dips its beak into its chest, ruffles some feathers and trills. This time an answer echoes from the orange trees.

"Hrrrrooo hrrrooo!"

"Shht! *Siktir git* birdie!" *Begum* Şenay flicks her *çarshaf* at the dove. "*Siktir git* or shut up!" She looks up at the grilled windows and grimaces. "*Hayde*," she mouths to Khatoun, her hand agitating tight, nervous circles in front of her. "People will be waking up soon."

Khatoun nods. She steps out from under the jasmine, pushing Hripsime ahead of her.

"It's time, *jan*."

Hripsime stops in front of the hole, kneels, and uncovers the baby. Perfect. Pale blue in the dawn. The stubborn dove cocks its head to one side and then the other. "Hrrrrooo," it croons. *Begum* Şenay kicks a clod of mud in its direction and the bird pecks at it. "Hrrrrooo." Şenay is about to flap like a hawk, her *çarshaf* suddenly useful when another sound stops her. A shapeless tune hummed so low, so as not to disturb the infant, it is barely audible.

"She has a *voice* now?" *Begum* Şenay asks, staring at Hripsime. Khatoun shrugs. It's the first sound she's heard from the girl since they sprang her from the Millet *Khan*. They hang back, unnerved, not wanting to disturb.

It is not long, Hripsime's odd little melody. When she finishes, she hands her baby to the gardener who steps back into the hole, places it on the bottom and clambers out again, a trickle of earth showering the child as his boot slips. The dove has found some tasty morsel and is flicking it silently back and forth in its beak. Khatoun helps Hripsime to her feet and *Begum* Şenay gives the gardener the signal to start shovelling again. With expertise, he takes a rose bush and plants it over the child, digging a circle around the roots to catch water. When he is done, the women hurry to the back entrance of the walled garden and *Begum* Şenay bids them good-bye.

Khatoun walks fast, urging Hripsime on. She wants to be home before anyone sees them and she keeps to the alleyways, stepping around the dogs that sleep huddled together in the gutters in pairs. Both women are wearing baggy *shalvar* and flowered headscarves, same as the cotton farmers south of the city. Khatoun carries a basket under her arm. Shrivelled but highly valuable potatoes and a handful of spinach. If anyone were to stop them, the potatoes would be a handy bribe. Fortunately, the streets are empty and before the sun can expose them they are at the back door that leads straight from the narrow alley into their kitchen. A grey shadow leaps to its feet as they enter and nuzzles Khatoun's palm with wet kisses.

"Grundug!"

"You'll get yourself killed one day," Ferida's voice hisses from the corner next to the stove. She stands with an exaggerated wheeze, crosses over to the table and hands them each a glass of tea. "And what is *she* doing here? I thought she was supposed to deliver a baby any day now?"

"She did, *jan*. It passed with the light."

"And now what? Now there's no baby she's been discarded?"

"Sent here to recuperate, away from prying eyes."

"*Kaknem!* I suppose you're still bleeding, aren't you?" Ferida's eyes slice the air between the two of them. "She shouldn't be out of bed. Are you both stupid?" She stares at Hripsime with pursed lips and suddenly, with no warning, begins to cry. Short, angry little sobs escape her lips as she thumps her chest a few times then slumps into the chair and rolls her head from side to side on the table.

"*Vay, vay, vay,*" she moans. "*Vay, vay, vay.*"

Hripsime crosses over to her and puts a hand on her shoulder, "Umme Ferida, stop. You'll hurt yourself."

"*Vay, vay…*what?" Ferida sits upright and stares at Hripsime. "She has a voice now? I thought she couldn't hear or speak?" She talks to Khatoun, ignoring the fact that Hripsime is inches from her face.

Khatoun nods, "She has a voice. She can hear you, *jan.*"

"*Asdvadz!*"

Hripsime pulls a chair out and settles down next to Ferida. "Please don't cry, Umme Ferida," she says, cradling the warm tea in her hands. "God took my voice with my husband and he has given it back to me now that our Sirvart is in his embrace. My little rose is buried and at peace now."

"*Asdvadz hokin lousavore.* And your name?" Ferida asks, wiping her nose on her sleeve and crossing herself. "Have we at least got that right?"

"Yes. My name is Hripsime. Hripsime Aznavourian."

"And where are you from? How far did you walk before you got here?"

"All the way," Hripsime says with a wry laugh. "I don't know. Far."

"Potatoes," Khatoun declares, holding the wrinkled spuds up. "*Begum* Şenay gave us some. And a little spinach."

"Hm," Ferida stabs her chin in Hripsime's direction and snorts. "Her dowry? That'll go a long way."

Khatoun busies herself with her basket, unloading the precious vegetables and wrapping them in a cloth before storing them deep in a crock. She refills their cups and joins the others at the kitchen table. Grundug sighs, coiling himself back around Ferida's feet now that everyone has settled. Hripsime takes a sip of her tea and sets it down in front of her, her fingers tracing the flowered rim of the pretty cup. She looks up at Khatoun and Ferida and shrugs.

"I walked here from Erzerum. We had a farm near Tortum. It's very different to here. Rain, rivers, a waterfall. Our summers were filled with apricots and cherries. My husband was a fruit farmer. Like a butcher smells of meat? He smelt of fruit and blossom. A big man. Some would say fat, but to me, perfect. His smile was like the sun. Vartan. Always telling jokes, filthy jokes. Always at the wrong time, too."

"Apricots. Now that would be a fine thing today," Ferida sighs.

Hripsime digs into her pocket and brings out a clump of dust. She wipes it clean on her sleeve and hands it to Ferida. "Plant it. It's the kernel. I sucked on it for weeks but it might still grow."

"Thanks, *jan*," Ferida inspects the seed briefly before pocketing it with a smile.

"It was a Sunday. We were packing fruit, despite church. We had to get them out before they spoiled and *tap!-tap!-tap!* with his stick, Becki Baba, the night watchman, came round in the daytime to call our attention. The order was to pack our belongings and be ready to leave in three days. They were moving us because of the war they said. Out of harm's way. I was not yet showing. I thought, 'I'll be okay.' They said, 'Just the women, children and elderly'. They would take Vartan the next day to join the army; to build roads. All of the men would go. My father, my uncles, my three brothers, my sister's husband."

Hripsime rummages in her pocket again and brings out a rag. "The tea. It's making me sweat." She wipes the back of her neck and her forehead and carries on, talking in between dabs.

"Our last night together Vartan and I made love – of course we did – even though my mother-in-law told me not to because of the child. In the morning I packed a parcel of food for Vartan and we collected in the town square to say goodbye. All the women were there and it rained tears from heaven. A group of gendarmes took the men in a long line to the outskirts of our village. I knew as he left that I would never see Vartan again. He knew too. When the square was empty I found his parcel of food. Neatly left, like he would, on the bench. An hour later we heard shots. Then we saw smoke over the hill. My mother came to my mother-in-law's house and together we crept through the orchards towards the next valley. We knew the paths. Half of the women came slowly-slowly through the trees and bushes. Our men had been tied together with rope and attacked with axes.

The few that had survived had been shot. That was the shooting
we'd heard. And then the soldiers had started a fire to get rid of
the bodies but the rain put it out. That's why we have good apricots in Tortum – the spring rains."

Hripsime coughs and spits stickily into her rag. She takes another sip of tea. "My mother was looking for my brothers when
I found Vartan in pieces. I gathered him together and began to
dig a hole with my hands to bury him, like the other women
were doing. But before I could finish, the gendarmes came and
ordered us back to the village. They told us the men had been
trying to escape, that they had been shot as deserters. Ashes,
soot, mud, blood and rain. I left Vartan there unburied and gave
my voice up to God. Until today," Hripsime smiles. "Now I have
buried the last of him."

Ferida shakes her head. "I'm sorry about the baby." Her hand
is resting in the soft patch between Grundug's ears where she's
been absent-mindedly picking at his hair. As she stands he follows her over to a large earthenware pitcher, hoping for another
pat. Ferida pours water over her hands. "Not now, *shouniges,*"
she says, scrubbing her fingers with a small brush. "I need to
make bread." She takes a lump of dough that has been resting and
pummels it flat. "The bastards," she mutters banging the bread
onto the floured surface. "We hear the same story again and
again – ever since they declared *Seferberlik.* 'We need the boys!
We need the men! Our army needs you.' Army? *Kaknem!* They
know our women are helpless without the men. And where is
this grand army of men they have taken? Dead! Every single one
of them. Used like pack horses to get the roads built and then
what? Chopped down like trees." She lifts the circle of dough
and slaps it onto the smooth sides of the oven. A soft sizzle accompanies the heart-warming smell as the bread immediately
begins to bake.

"At the beginning of the month they took all the young men
from Ourfa too – Armenians and Assyrians. Thousands of them
sent to build roads outside town, at Kudemma and Kara Keopru.
They took their guns and gave them shovels and picks. Work,
work, work." She slides a perfect circle of warm, flat bread onto
the table and Khatoun tears off a piece, dipping it into her tea
and popping it in her mouth. "Only about thirty Assyrians survived," Ferida mutters. "They took the men and..." she claps her

hands together, the flour dust puffing into a ghostly little cloud, "*Kara Keopru* became *Kurmuzu Keopru*. The Black Bridge is now Red." She slaps another piece of dough onto the oven. "Bastards."

Outside, a distant *azan* echoes from the rooftops and the local rooster, bereft of his mates, though miraculously still alive, replies.

"The call to prayer is so beautiful," Hripsime says, her head to one side. "Even though it's not for us."

"Don't believe everything that is heard," Khatoun says. "Trust the eye, not the ear."

"What?" Ferida asks.

"It's the opposite to the *azan*...Iskender told me...never mind." Khatoun goes back to the bread, pulling off another piece and eating it.

"Is it one God, Khatoun *Hanum*?" Hripsime asks her. "Is it the same God that watches us all and sees us fight amongst ourselves like children? I've often wondered that." She coughs again, another phlegmy issue into her rag. Khatoun hands her a clean handkerchief and Hripsime mops up her face and neck. "Because it doesn't make sense. How can everyone be sure that their belief is the right one and everyone else is wrong?" She traces the veins along the smooth work surface of the wooden table with her finger.

"What are you talking about?" Ferida spits. "One God? For all of us? Have you lost your mind? We're all different." She slides another circle of bread onto the table. "Eat. *That* is God. God is my hands and your womb. In her crusty eyes that can still sew. That rooster outside? He's God as much as the idiot on the other side of town singing his song. Existence. That's God. I'll tell you something, though. People that think they're doing God's work? They're the worst, not the best. There's another opposite for you. 'God told me to do this!' Pah, of course he did, with a nice personal message in your ear. One God? At times like these I wonder if there even *is* a God."

"You sound like my mother," Hripsime says. "Ouf." She pushes her chair back and stands. Her mouth opens as if she is about to say something, but instead, she clutches her head, sways against the table and crumples to the floor, taking the cups with her. A pool of blood blooms from under her *shalvar*.

"You see! I told you she shouldn't be out of bed!" Ferida yells.

She scoops Hripsime's skinny frame into her arms, kicks the doors open and pushes through the girl's dormitory into a small room at the back. Khatoun pulls the quilt off the simple metal cot and Ferida lays Hripsime down. The other girls, woken suddenly and dragged in their wake, clamour round the door in a tight knot, their faces still creased by sleep.

"Serpuhi, a basin of water," Ferida snaps. "Arshalous, help me undress her. One of you, get me a clean nightdress. Hasmig, Manoush, sheets – rip them up. I need bandages."

They strip Hripsime naked. She is red hot to the touch with a loose pouch of belly and sores oozing along the length of her spine and crusting the inner edges of her knees. She is bleeding heavily between the legs. The smell of iron and rotting flesh.

"*Oosht*, all of you. Out!" Ferida barks, using a hastily folded pillowcase to stanch the blood. "This isn't a market place. *Vay vay!* Let's have some air. Lolig, you finish the bread. Bzdig Shoushun, the children. Washed, dressed and fed. I made yoghurt. Look on the shelf, under the cloth. *Hayde!* Let's get moving!"

One by one the girls unfurl from the doorway leaving Arshalous in the room with a basin of water. She soaks a sponge, dribbles water across Hripsime's chest and wipes her limbs down. Khatoun settles at the top of the bed, cradling the girl's stubbly head in her lap. Ferida scoops up the bloody clothes from the floor. A small square of sunlight blinks at the window and the fountain bubbles merrily outside in the courtyard. Hripsime opens her eyes, squinting against the light. When she sees her friend Arshalous she breaks into a smile.

"Arshalous *jan*," she whispers, "I had a funeral. I have seen my Sirvart find her way to heaven!"

"I know."

"You should see her now – soft and round and happy. There in the corner," she points to the light dancing by the window. "Now I know there is a God – my mother was wrong."

Arshalous continues to wipe down Hripsime's feverish body. "You found your voice," she says. "You sound funny." Both girls giggle which leads to a coughing fit that wracks Hripsime's body. Eventually she stops and lies still, breathing heavily through her mouth.

"Enough chit-chat! Can't you see it's killing her?" Ferida barks, straightening up, the pile of soiled clothing clutched to her chest. "Ever since finding her precious voice she's been *gederderuhgederderuh* about God non-stop. As if a girl her age knows anything about God. She should never have been allowed out of bed in the first place. Now I've got a lot more work to do. Her first baby, no doctor, dehydrated, thick with disease...My back's already killing me and now I've got to boil wash this and make sure Lolig doesn't poison us with her ridiculous cooking. Don't any of you do anything stupid. In fact, don't do anything at all. I'll be back." She slams out the door.

Hripsime closes her eyes. Arshalous covers her feet with a damp rag and sets to cleaning the wounds crusting her knees with a sponge and sliver of soap.

"Thanks, *jan*, I hope someday you have someone to wash your feet." Hripsime coughs. "*We are all headed for death but we go courageously.*' It was written on a rock. Somewhere between here and home. There were hundreds of messages scratched in the earth by the people who'd gone before us: '*God walks by your side,*' and '*Do not deny God for soon we will be in His bosom.*' They seemed to get more desperate the further we walked. It made my mother spit. 'There is no God!' she'd say and one day she took a stick and wrote '*The mother denied the child,*' which is what we said in our village, when everything went upside down. My auntie used to argue with her – 'There *is* a God and he will save us.' She was younger than my mother and pregnant like me. 'We're having twins!' she used to joke. Twins. They split her open like a fruit on the road. They had a bet – was the baby a boy or a girl. They held her down and sliced her open. It was a boy. They stuck him on a bayonet and held him up to the sky. First he was wriggling and then he died like a little bird. My auntie watched the whole thing, a pomegranate split open and then she closed her eyes. My mother refused to eat after that. What food she found she gave to us. She passed away soon after. But always, to the end, 'There is no God! There is no God!'"

With this she falls silent and the room is peaceful, the rustle of sheets and trickle of water the only sounds. The sunny block of light from the window moves around the room, elongating into strange shapes across the wall and Hripsime begins to snore.

"Let her sleep," Khatoun whispers slipping out from under her. She takes the bowl and sponge away from Arshalous. "We can dress her when she wakes." She inspects the wounds and covers Hripsime with a light quilt before settling on the floor next to the bed with Arshalous.

A small spider swings on a thread underneath the simple bed frame. Above them the floorboards creak, sending down a shower of plaster as the children jump out of bed and hit the floor running. A series of chesty coughs follow Iskender down the stairs and into the kitchen. Eventually a door slams and the mournful tune of lost love on the *saz* winds its way through the house. The tac-atac-atac of sewing machines begins, the street sounds awake, a distant dog howls for its mate. Hripsime seems at peace, her chest rising and falling under her bony hands. Her face shines with perspiration; a gentle smile spread across her face.

"She's my sister," Arshalous says watching the spider spin its web under the bed. "Not my *real* sister but you know...sisters of the road. We met in a camp in Malatia and were in the marches together ever since. I *did* have a sister. Arsinee. She had the long-est hair. My mother used to say 'Your hair is a spider's web for husbands. You catch them in it and they can't escape!' Hey little spider – is that true?"

She puts her finger out, snags the insect under the bed then flicks her hand and watches the spider drop from a thread, dan-gle there for a moment then hurry back up. Arshalous drags it back to its web. "She finds food, Umme Ferida, doesn't she? They say she grows potatoes in her pockets and herbs in her shoes. Is that true?"

"No. Yes. She does find food but no, she doesn't grow anything in her pockets but yes, she has grown mint in an old pair of shoes on the roof."

"So did my grandma. She planted in anything that held earth. Shoes and jars and pots. And she grew herbs and perfumed things and she made medicines and teas and her cooking was the best in the village. We lived in a white house and there was a hallway between their part and ours, and the animals lived downstairs – it was lovely and warm in the winter. Not every one in the vil-lage had a kitchen so people were always cooking at our house, but never mind, my grandmother loved our neighbours. We had a flat roof and there was a bridge to the next house and another to the next one and the next and on and on. And people used to come and go that way to get their medicines, over the roofs, and we used to play up there. It drove my mother mad. She said we were like mice – upstairs downstairs all day long. Moug, she called me.

"One day we were on the roof and they shouted 'Stay up there – don't come down, lie down and be quiet!' and soldiers came and my father and uncles left with them with all their stuff tied in bundles. My grandma cried even though Grandpa was still with us, and when he tried to talk to her she hit him in the chest. My mother closed the door so I couldn't see, but I heard them anyway. Then all the women came to our house, cooking like we were going to have a feast. Loaves and loaves and loaves of bread. It was crazy. And like a bazaar, everything was out - the blankets, the sleeping mats, the carpets – and the Turkish ladies came to buy things. Some stuff was sold. I know that because my mother cried when she counted the money, saying it was a crime. She got my handiwork and Arsinee's out of the dowry chest and put it together with the things she had made as a girl. The things we had all sewn – birds and flowers and our names, she rolled them all into one bundle with her jewellery in the middle and she sewed it into a pouch and wore it around her belly.

"A few days later all the villagers met outside the church. Some people were staying behind with new names and they stood at the side of the road and watched as we left. My friend Hagop stayed behind and he wouldn't look at me. He had a new name. Hassan. Instead, he threw stones at a cat. He'd never been mean before and it made me wonder if changing your name makes you suddenly hate cats."

"I don't think so," Khatoun says with a smile.

"Well. Boys can be stupid sometimes. I wanted to bring my bird along but mother said no. That was sad because the bird sang and would have been great company. I let him go from the rooftop the day we left. He was called *Janavar*. He didn't fly far, so he's probably still there, in the village. We had a donkey too, that we did bring, and we sat in baskets on either side with little bags around our necks filled with nuts and raisins and bread to eat.

"In the beginning there were lots of people with carts and mules but not for long. Every night animals and people disappeared. The first night we camped under the stars outside a village and it was fun – although I missed my father and uncles –

especially Uncle Shnork who liked to tickle and tell jokes. There were some boys there and we made a campfire and told stories. In the morning the boys were told to gather together and then they walked into the hills with the gendarmes. They smiled and waved when they left and then they were gone. I thought of Hagop Hassan and how he was maybe better off in the village, even though he'd turned mean. Only little boys were left with us now, like my brothers. One was five, the other seven – a bit like yours.

"The women were all crying and wanted to stay but as soon as the sun was high they made us walk again. We walked and walked and walked – I thought it would never end. As far as I could see behind us there were people and in front of us too. One night the soldiers told us bandits were coming and they could make them go away if they had some things to give them. All the women gave stuff; money, jewels, bracelets. It was all thrown down onto a big blanket that the gendarmes tied up and carried away. That night the bandits came anyway – chettes they called them. It was very dark. There were clouds over the moon. I was asleep when they came, screaming like devils, and my heart went bang in my chest. I saw girls like me pulled from their mothers and carried away. My mother threw dirt on my face and quick-quick cut off my hair without me even noticing until it was too late. People were running in all directions. I saw my grandfather opened with a knife. It went in so clean – like he was a doll and he stood there bright red then fell down. Next morning I found my mother alive but her eyes were too big for her head. My two little brothers were gone and my sister Arsinee had blood between her legs and a broken face. She looked at me then took her long hair and cut it with a knife like my mother had done to mine. My grandmother wouldn't walk with us that day. She sat in the dirt, kissed me and said she would see me another time. Our donkey had disappeared with all our stuff. It was me, my mother, my sister, my aunt. We had our needlework and some bread but that was all.

"The walking continued. Some days we walked until our feet bled and at night we lay under the stars. I used to try and count them but I always fell asleep before I could finish. I love the stars for that – whoever comes, whoever goes – they're always there. Every morning I saw dead people. My mother told me never to step over a dead body. She said since we couldn't bury them in the normal way we could give them respect by not walking over them. The ones on the road you wouldn't want to go near anyway. Black and full of worms and stinky. One day my aunt disappeared. My mother said the river had taken her. Then my sister was snatched again, by Kurds this time, and never returned. Then it rained. I hated the rocks and the wind and the insects, but I liked the rain. You can drink the rain. Some people ate the grains they found in horse's mess. Not me. Sometimes food would come from somewhere — women with blue lines on their faces with yoghurt and milk. We stopped at Malatia and that's where I met Hripsime and *Djibour*. *Djibour*, because she never stops talking. Why are you smiling?"

"Nothing," Khatoun pats Arshalous on the knee. "Carry on. You were telling me about *Djibour* who never stops talking..."

"Yes. She and I would sneak around together when nobody was watching, looking for things to eat. She was at the *khan* when you came to get us but she didn't want to go and live with the *Bayan*. She wants to go to the end of the march and wait there. She was promised to Altoun in America and she wants to be somewhere he can find her when he comes looking. Do you know where the marches end, *Digin* Khatoun?"

"I...No. I don't."

"Do you think Altoun will know where to find *Djibour*?"

"Yes. I'm sure he will."

"Good. She'll be married then. It was in Malatia my mother got a disease. She told me not to come near her — to forget her. So I did. One day I missed her so I went back to where she had been but she was gone. This is all I have left." Arshalous bends forward, unpicks some tacking along her hem and pulls out a piece of fabric. Inside the simple muslin fold is another piece, stiff and sour smelling. She hands it over to Khatoun.

"This is for Umme Ferida. To make yoghurt. My grandma gave it to me to carry all the way from home. You have to warm milk to make it. If you can find some."

"Ferida will know what to do, *jan*. Thank you."

"And this. I have this from my Grandma too." Arshalous slips her hands into her underwear, rummages around and pulls out a small pouch. "I'm sorry. I had nowhere else to hide it. It's medicine milk. Milk of the poppy." She leans back against the wall and smiles, a pink sliver of tongue in the gap where her front teeth should be. "I'm lucky nobody tried to mess with me because they would have found it and that's worth twenty souls at least, Grandma said."

"Yes, God smiled on you," Khatoun says quietly. "Is that it? Do you have anything else hidden?"

"No. Just me."

"Just you."

"Yes." Arshalous tips her head in her friend's direction and smiles. "And Hripsime."

"And how old are you?"

"I don't know." Arshalous fans her fingers out in front of her. "Something more than this. We celebrated my birthdays in the summer in Erzinjan but I don't know how many. My mother was waiting until I was a woman to promise me and I don't think I am yet. Do you know?"

Before Khatoun can answer a sudden squeal comes from the kitchen followed by frantic footsteps down the corridor and Ferida bursts into the room.

"It's Loucia!" she cries. "Loucia is here!" She wipes her hands on her apron, spits on her fingertips and reshapes her eyebrows. "Get cleaned up and go and see her. She says she's here for you and she can't stay long. *Hayde!*"

It was a rare woman that could intimidate Ferida, but if that mantle were to be worn by anyone it would have to be Loucia, her elder sister who had emigrated to Damascus with her family years ago. In the last year she had moved back to Aleppo and letters had been tracing back and forth as often as was possible. Since *teskeres* had been revoked it was virtually impossible for anyone to travel and inconceivable that an unaccompanied woman should reach Ourfa from Aleppo. But here she was. Alone. No sign of her husband or three lanky children.

Khatoun gets up from the floor and dusts off her *shalvar*. "Wait here, Moug," she tells Arshalous. "If you need anything, come and find me."

"*Hayde!*" Ferida yells, flapping her apron at Khatoun. "She hasn't got all day!"

Loucia has already been shown to the Ladies' Room and there she sits, on the sofa, feet crossed neatly at the ankle. Khatoun has only met her a handful of times — the usual weddings and births

— and over the years Loucia has become solid — stout makes her sound fat. Rather, she is like European furniture, the fabric of her dress stuffed and straining at the buttons. Her bun is so tight it pulls the corners of her eyes up and her feet could easily be in a pair of shoes three sizes larger. She sits beaming at her attendant audience, one hand clutching a row of amber prayer beads, the other a small crocheted bag.

Mertha and Thooma sit opposite, swallowed by the large horsehair armchairs and there is suppressed mayhem from all four of Khatoun's children who have run in to see their little-known aunt. Khatoun pushes them away good-naturedly and perches on the edge of the sofa just as Iskender sticks his head around the door. He stares at his sister in disbelief and she laughs at him.

"You are too thin brother and I know it's not from lack of food!" She grins as Ferida elbows through the door past Iskender with a tray of pastries in her hand. "Even in times of war Ferida will keep us fat!"

Ferida swats her sister's comments away. "This is the last of the batch and it's stale. There's no more flour, butter or sugar, so enjoy."

Iskender hovers in the doorway clearing his throat until Ferida hands him a single *kurabia* on a plate. "I'll be in the little room," he mouths backing away, the plate balanced on upturned fingers.

The family swarm Loucia, watching her eat the lightly dusted pastries as they bombard her with questions. She swallows and nods, answering them in-between mouthfuls.

"I'm here for an hour."

"The family are fine."

"Yes, all of them musicians. Aleppo? Well, Aleppo is changing." She ends the meeting with a wave of her hand. "I promise I'll speak to you all again but I need a quiet word with Khatoun first."

Mertha and Thooma gather the children and shuffle out of the room, dawdling at the door, reluctant to lose sight of this magnificent woman. Only the promise of a repeat visit in the near future prises them out of the room. Ferida reorganises the biscuits on the plate, slips two into her pocket and disappears.

Finally they are alone. Loucia stuffs her beads in her bag and produces a clean, white handkerchief.

"Right. I'll get straight to the point. I hear you sprang some girls from the Millet *Khan*." She dabs at her face.

Khatoun nods, "Nine in all. Three are here, four now if you count Hripsime. The others are with a friend. It was her idea. The friend. Without her, it would have been impossible."

"Yes. *Begum* Şenay." Loucia gathers a pile of crumbs and deposits them into the jardinière next to her. "A stupid woman with a heart of gold. If it weren't for her husband she'd be a prostitute you know. Like her mother. Like her sister. Even her aunt was... well that is another story but yes, *orospou* stock, the whole family." She takes a bottle of cologne from her bag, sprinkles it onto the handkerchief and wipes the back of her neck. "Anyway, that's irrelevant. What's important is that she got those girls out of there. For that, we are in her debt. However..." she pauses. "She has to give them up."

"Give them up?"

"Think about it. What does her husband want those girls for? *Tavli*? *Pishti*? Chess?" Loucia inhales the cologne, waves the handkerchief in the air between them then exhales heavily. She leans forward, her dress creaking like a galleon. "This is how you do it. Talk to your friend, slowly, slowly; a few hints about her husband, his desires, his wandering eye. I know *Begum* Şenay. Soon she'll want those girls out of there and that's where I come in. When your friend has finished playing with her Armenian dolls she can send them to me." She sits back and dabs at her neck again.

Khatoun can feel her cheeks going pink. This is unjust, this way of depicting her friend to whom they owe a lot. She'd liked Loucia until a minute ago. Now she is not so sure. She nods at her sister-in-law, her lips tight.

"I've made you angry," Loucia says, eyes sparkling. "Good — that's what I meant to do. Obviously from your reaction you trust your friend. That's reassuring, because I trust your judgement. But still — *I* wouldn't trust her if I were you." She laughs. A trill like a bird. "Confused? Excellent! Now you know me. They call me the Devil's Advocate."

"The Devil's Advocate?"

"In a certain circle of friends — it's the way I argue. Anyway, listen to me. If your friend doesn't get sick of those girls, someone else in that house will. It's a snake pit, in case you hadn't already gathered. So much venom there I wouldn't accept a cup of tea. Eventually they will want to discard them. I'll tell you what to do then. Keep your mouth shut and your ear to the ground and we can help them — and a lot more too. It'll all become clearer in time. When you need to get word to me, go and visit your old friend, Aram Bohjalian. Yes, him. Your bookish accountant. Don't look so surprised. Books have deceptive covers. Other than that, I want you to promise me that you will stay indoors. It's not safe to wander the streets any more — despite your wonderful peasant disguise this morning." She helps herself to another pastry, wraps it in her fragrant handkerchief and tucks it into her bag, "For the road." At the door, she pauses for a moment, weighing something up. Her eyes search Khatoun's face before she leans forward, her dress wheezing at the seams. "One more thing. I'm going to send some friends to see you from time to time. Ever heard of Mgrdich Yotneghparian?"

"Mgrdich? Of course. He's a legend."

"A legend?" Loucia hoots and the unmistakable sound of a button popping off and rolling across the floor accompanies another creak as she rocks back on her heels. "I like that. A living legend. Anyway, some friends of mine will come and see you and I'd appreciate you helping them out in a small way now and then. You know, food, shelter, arms." She hoots again. "Only joking!" She envelops Khatoun in a hug, leans into her ear and whispers. "You can die in a storm or you can step outside and pin down the tent before the storm takes it." She kisses her sister-in-law on the forehead and puts her finger to her lips. "And when people ask you — you haven't seen me. Ever."

The children have been waiting in the hallway, hanging about on the staircase, and the clamour starts all over again with them shadowing Loucia through the kitchen into the back alley where she hurls handfuls of sweets up into the air. When they straighten up again, fists full, Loucia is gone.

Despite the brevity of the visit, Ferida is happy. Colour has flooded her cheeks and her feet slip across the scrubbed floor with ease, her bad knee suddenly oiled and working like a ballerina's.

"Didn't she look well?" she beams. "Like an English lady, my sister Loucia. Like their old Queen Victoria!"

"Yes," Khatoun agrees. She's exhausted, her eyes aching. Too much has already gone on today and it is only mid-morning. "I think I'll lie down for a minute. I'll be upstairs." She heads towards the front staircase, sticks her head in on Iskender and finds him asleep in his chair. She tiptoes over, watching the breath flutter the edges of his moustache. He opens one eye, startled.

"Reykjavik," he shouts, one hand flinging out and stabbing the map on the wall. "Oh. Sorry…I thought you were Loucia for a moment. But of course, that's impossible. What would my sister be doing here?" His chin drops, he lets out a sigh and his eyes roll back in his head. Khatoun leans forward and slips the empty glass out from between his fingers.

"I'll be upstairs with the children," she whispers. "Call me if you need anything." He snores.

Bzdig Shoushun has gathered the children into their bedroom. Her workload has doubled since there's no more school for the boys. *Seferberlik* again. Afrem is sitting on the floor in the corner, protecting his pile of paper and pencils from Solomon who is pummelling him with fat, sweaty fists.

"No! You can't do a drawing!" Afrem yells. "It's *my* paper and I *need* it!" Solomon wails even louder when he sees his mother at the door.

"I want to draw" he cries, "and Afrem won't let me!"

Two dolls swing listlessly in a hammock by the window. A pile of wooden blocks towers above the menagerie of stuffed insects covering the floor. Bzdig Shoushun sits in the middle, her eyes filled with tears.

"I'm trying to keep them happy," she says, "but I can't." She turns to Solomon. "Listen, Afrem needs his paper to do his classes. It's not a game. Leave him alone and come and play with me." She stretches her arms out and tries to coax Solomon over, but he runs towards Khatoun grizzling instead. Alice stands aloof, a crochet hook in one hand, a red woollen hat in the other.

"They've been arguing since Auntie Loucia left," she says. "They're disturbing me."

At this moment a pile of clothing erupts and Voghbed sits up, crying. He wanders over to Khatoun tangled in a sheet, a pair of pale blue trousers dangling from his hand.

"He's wet himself," Alice says wrinkling her nose up at her brother. "You smell of *tshishig*."

"Go downstairs," Khatoun tells Bzdig Shoushun, "and dry your eyes. I'll look after them. Go on. Go."

Bzdig Shoushun picks up the scattered toys and piles them into a basket. She casts her eye around the room and with a quick bob, flees.

"What is the matter with everyone?" Khatoun asks the children. "Have we been mean to poor Bzdig Shoushun? Don't forget, she's only a girl like you. Maybe we ate too many *kurabia* and the sugar has got to you. Or maybe..." she turns to Solomon, "Maybe you swallowed a cockroach? You look like a cockroach, waving your arms around like that. In fact," she leans over her son, "I can see your wings growing." Solomon looks over his shoulder and laughs.

"That's not wings! That's legs like a cricket! I'm turning into a cricket!" He takes off across the room, bouncing in a frenzy. Voghbed sits clapping in glee at his mother's feet before jumping up and doing his best to imitate his brother. Then Alice throws her crochet down and begins to twirl on the spot.

"And I'm a butterfly!" she cries, swirling her skirts out as she spins around. "I'm a yellow butterfly!" Only Afrem hangs back, still serious until the noise in the room grows too loud and he too throws his wad of papers up into the air and they all dance like lunatics in a rain of schoolwork. Solomon runs to the window, attempting to open it so he can throw paper down into the street and Khatoun has one arm around his waist, just about to lift him down from his rickety chair when an unearthly howl rips through the house. They run en masse to the balcony, thinking it to be Grundug, and look down into the courtyard where the old dog likes to sun himself in the mornings. It is not Grundug but Ferida wailing at the top of her lungs, lashing out at the plants around the fountain. She throws her head back and claws at her dress, ripping the bodice apart in a burst of buttons that is quite unlike her, as she looks past them, up towards heaven and cries.

At that moment there is a gentle cough behind Khatoun. Arshalous stands on the landing clutching a wet rag, her feet bare.

"I'm sorry, *Digin* Khatoun," she says. "I came to tell you. It's Hripsime. I was stroking her gently and she opened her eyes and smiled at me and now she is gone."

A Flock of Birds

Ouzounian Street, Nicosia, Cyprus, October 23rd 1969
Ferida

So that's me. I'm dead. Me. Ferida. Iskender's sister. Everyone's Umme. That's me huddled at the foot of the bed looking like I'm about to climb off. Yes – you thought everyone died peacefully in their sleep looking as if they were about to float down a river with their hair undone. Well not me.

I had a fight with death at the very end. Saw it coming, didn't mind, relaxed into its arms and then remembered where I had put the *dolma* scoop. You see, you need a long smooth instrument to scoop a courgette out cleanly. Tomorrow it's *dolmas* for lunch and as I felt myself slip from life – before I had entered the tunnel of bright light – I remembered the scoop. It was up on the roof where I'd caught the kids using it as a telescope – trying to burn out their eyes by looking up at the sun, stupid *dungulughs*. If I didn't get out of bed and bring the *dolma* scoop down to the kitchen, no one would be able to dig the pulp out of the vegetables. So, I sat up, almost touched my feet to the floor, but death had me by the ankles and that was that. A brief struggle and I gave up and lay in a heap.

In a few hours (hopefully before I go stiff) someone will find me and stretch me out into some kind of elegant pose. Imagine that. For the first time in years my body will be unbent – soft, pliable – and no one will complain at my hunched shoulders ever again. No, they'll cry because I'm dead and even though we all know it's coming, we still weep and wail at the time.

So, I'm dead. Now listen and I'll set you straight on a few things. I have something to tell you but if I open my mouth and a flock of birds flies out you have to catch them, all of them, hold them close to your heart and never let them go. What I'm going to say has to be held tight in the palm – not twisted and turned into a story for later. Oh no. This is just between you and me.

You see, people always spoke to the others and slid around me silently. Because I scared them. They thought I knew nothing about life but what did *they* know? I knew love. You want to know how long I cried for my dog Grundug when he died? Months. Yes, grief fades with time but it takes a long time passing for memories to turn happy. I remember Khatoun telling me, in her way, what had happened to Grundug and the slam it gave to my heart. We try to bury memories with the dead but every now and then they spring up like ghosts to haunt us. Grundug had died in the winter and I remember seeing a shadow in the courtyard and thinking it was him and the pain hit me that he was gone. And I looked up at the sky and counted off the months and it had been a whole winter and some of spring and *still* I was crying for my dog. So laugh at me, but let me tell you – loving animals is not stupid. No. Your animal loves you through everything. Whether you are married or not. Or ugly. Or a bad seamstress. Or the elder sister, the maid, the cook, the floor-sweeper with the rickety legs, bad back and slipper in hand. Yes, our pets love us. And Grundug – let me tell you – he saw it all. He knew what I knew and sat patiently by my side while I lost my child.

Ah, now you're listening but I'm well ahead of my story here, so be quiet and wait.

I knew from an early age my path was different. My sisters all got married – plucked like ripe fruits from my side while I began to wither. I wasn't really interested then. Men seemed stupid to me, and women even more so. People joined up together for no reason other than their parents thinking they would make a good match – no talk about feelings. No whisper of love. In my mind, love is what makes marriage and family.

I have watched mothers with their children and they cannot help but love their child. But ask them how they feel about their man and they will tell you words like "respect" and "gratitude" and "sadness" because they are widowed, but they rarely say, "I will lay down my life for him." No, for men and women, sometimes you have to wait, like I did, to find true love. Patience is an egg that lays great things.

So the years slipped by and people spoke of me as if I was never going to hear their stories but I heard them all. I saw the looks and the heads shaking as my years passed. And then more passed and I earned respect from other women and then, by then, where were we? My brother was an alcoholic; don't let's waste words. He would drink until everything came spilling out of his eyes instead of his mouth. He could tell you many things once, but even though it still went in, because of the drink, he filled up with sadness and that's all that came out. I could have slapped him many times, my older brother. He saw and loved what he had in front of him but could he tell anyone? No. Just that pathetic note at the end of his life. Well, it was too late. A human being needs to hear those words. "I love you". Trust me – I am one that knows.

And more years passed and it was war. You want to know how painful it is to survive? To watch shadows of yourself pass by in an endless stream with their hair unbound? To catch the eye of some young woman, still pretty despite disease, and say good-byegoodbyegoodbye as her feet throw up dust? The shame of living as corpses gathered at my door and I had nothing to give them – just water and a pat on the head before I limed my hands rid of them. I couldn't feed them all. Why delay death for them? Prolong it? I got to know the smell of death long before it caught up with the flesh and I got sick of it. Sick of the stench of pain and injustice and begging and refusal and shutting off my heart. That must be why it happened.

He came to our house and like everyone else I said how lovely he was – sweet, charming, polite – even to me. He noticed me in a small way – asked after my health – and I noticed him barely at all. And then, if I'm honest, I remember thinking one day that if I would or could or were not who I was, I might have liked him in that way – but my life was different. And so he came and we loved him, all of us, like an Auntie loves a boy and one day he came to the house and it was my birthday – and he took me in his arms to tell me "*Bon anniversaire!*" and it was different. It hit me like a slab and from nowhere I fell, fell into love.

And where does that come from? One minute you are simply a friend and then 'click' a key turns and all you can think of is burying your head in their neck and smelling the warm, sweet air that nestles there. What is that? What does it?

Is it that you catch them looking at you in a surprise moment, unawares? Or that they then hold your gaze once caught? Is it that when they draw away from a friendly hug you imagine your neck elongating so that your face can dive headlong into the pool of warmth at their collarbone? Or that you kiss 'hello' in line with everyone else and the corner of your lip accidentally catches the corner of their lip and your stomach sinks into your deep wet sea and your knees want to buckle and you realise? Is it that they lean across you and you catch their smell and you want your hair to smell of them — that if your hair smells of them the way you want it to, it means you have loved them good— the way you suddenly want to?

Once he was in my mind, I couldn't get him out — he was there constantly, everywhere I turned. And I knew lust and desire and joy at the casual mention of his name. That soft brown skin, my lips hungry to suck. His arms around me. Oh, I dreamt of his arms long before I felt them. He would stand near me, just feet away, and my body would arch towards his. If I had taken a knife, I could have cut the air between us, fed it to the birds and watched them fall to the earth like stones with the weight of it. I dreamt of him touching me everywhere. Under the moon, watched by the sun, by the light of the fire, in my hair, my breasts, my thighs. Thinking about him even now turns me to flame, and I'm dead. Just think about that.

It was at the Pink House. He came often — at times when everyone else would be asleep. That was most of the day in those times. We slept to avoid hunger and heat. And I slept in the kitchen because it was cool and because I knew that sometimes he would come. And when I let him in we never spoke of what was between us. But the way he held his head high and slid his eyes over to me — my knees would drop and my stomach would turn and I would flood and have to leave the room. And the thud of my heart broke down walls.

And you would come to the door and I would let you in and do anything that you bid of me. My own life meant nothing and the risks that you brought gave shape to my life. I would carry anything for you — take it wherever you asked. And one day your hand touched mine as you passed me a package and you held it there. And my heart flew through my veins, trembled in the palm of your hand and I shut my eyes and you moved behind me and I felt the heat of your chest as you put your lips to my neck. And we moved towards the darkness where not even the shadows slept and we lit it up with fire.

And you never knew that I carried you a child. A tiny little thing — just a few months in my womb — and Grundug sat with me the night that I lost her. There was nothing to see — just blood and blood and blood — and I sat in the bathroom and poured water over me in bucketfuls and our child was washed away. Never mind, never mind. I was past bearing children — that much I knew. I was not one of those women ripe into old age — I was barren from misuse and only the thought of you could fill my breasts with heaviness. I had no place being a mother. With a child everyone would question my morality and forget that I had conceived in love. And *that* is what matters. I mothered love and not one person knows.

And one day he left. You want to know how? Vanished. Came to the house, broken and torn and told us bad news. I nearly dropped to the earth when I saw him. Held his face in my hands, carefully, as if it were the most precious thing in the world, and Khatoun sewed him together. I cradled his face, drank it in. I only took the cigarettes so I could pass them to him, to touch him again. And later, on the roof, Khatoun stood with one arm around Iskender, the other on *his* shoulder as he lay casually against her leg. And was I jealous? Yes, but I loved Khatoun more because she could be close to him and I couldn't. So I shut my eyes and flew though her body into her hands to feel his warmth.

And eventually we were alone and I said very little as I undressed him and bathed his sweet body. Let it seep away, I told him. And I meant it to myself because I knew he would go and I wanted it to be over already — I didn't want to visit that pain at all. And my face…my face was burning when I left the white bathroom. And that was the last time.

He left me something and I tell you, I was too scared to open the rag he had pressed to my heart. Too scared even to touch it, so I gave it to Khatoun. When she unwrapped it and I saw his gold teeth, I knew that was all I would ever own of him. That, and the memory of his smile.

So lift up my pillow as you strip the bed and find those nuggets of gold I have kept safe all these years. And say what you want – that I was mean, I hid my gold in my mattress, I knew nothing of life and I died alone, without love. And I'll laugh, because only I know.

Mgrdich Yotneghparian

The Pink House, Assyrian Quarter, Ourfa, October 23rd 1915
Khatoun

The skies were in labour
The earth was in labour,
And so was the crimson sea.
And in the sea a small red reed
Was also in labour.

And out of the reed came smoke
And out of the smoke came flames,
And from the flames dashed forth
A blond youth

With fiery hair,
And a flaming beard,
And his eyes were two blazing suns![5]

"Don't open it!" Ferida screams. "Don't you *dare* open it or we'll all be killed!" She's clutching her favourite *pilaff* pot over her head, ready to hurl it as frantic banging threatens to separate the back door from its hinges.

"Don't you even go *near* that door," she hisses, raising the pot even higher. Who she intends to hit is uncertain, but the tone of her voice is enough to stop Khatoun halfway between kitchen table and thudding door. The banging stops abruptly and Khatoun looks at Ferida with the sprinkling of *pilaff* littering her shoulders and cautiously moves past, pressing her face against the peeling blue paint of the door.

"Maybe it's someone we know," she mouths.

---

5 *The Birth of Vahakn*, Pre Christian, Anonymous. Translated by Gerald Papasian. Copyright 1987 by Gerald Papasian. Thanks to Gerald Papasian and Nora Armani; *Sojourn at Ararat*.

Another huge knock slams against her cheek and the ancient hinges screech at the force.

"What if someone needs help?" she says, rubbing her face and reaching for the bolt, not yet daring to spring it.

"So help me God – if you open that door I will brain you!" Ferida snarls.

Too late. With a flick of her wrist, Khatoun undoes the heavy metal rod and slides it back, turning the key with her other hand. The door flies open and the stench of sweaty meat and cordite lands, large and bloody at their feet. Up in a flash, their intruder slides the bolt back into place, drags the dresser across the door, scattering dishes everywhere, and spins around to face them. Ferida screams, her *pilaff* pot finally released from her grip and clattering to the floor.

Standing in front of them, eyes wild, face black with soot, is their old friend, Aram Bohjalian. He is almost unrecognisable from the genteel, bookish person they know. Gone are the spectacles, the French-cut boots and fine suits they recognise. Instead, he sports a head-dress tied across the forehead, a rifle in one hand and Ferida's meat cleaver (just acquired) in the other. The hair escaping his filthy headgear is long and tangled and, despite the current length of his beard, he wears a smile. A jagged, unruly flap that curves from ear to mouth, exposing the whole left side of his jaw.

Ferida screams, staggers back against the table and retches all over the floor. Khatoun rips off her apron and plunges it into a pitcher of water and holds it up to Aram's broken face. His eyes dart around the room, casing the shadows that loom and scatter in the flickering light. He smells rank, sweaty, like rotten lamb. He leans back against the dresser, pries the dripping cloth from Khatoun's fingers and pushes his face together with a sharp intake of breath.

"It's over," he says, the words sliding over his tongue in a bloody mess. "Mgrdich is dead."

And just like that the noise outside stops. The bells fall silent, the high-pitched scream that has been constant this last hour vanishes and the desperate footsteps echoing through the alleyway disappear into a hole.

Ferida stops swabbing the floor with her rag-draped foot and Khatoun stands motionless, her fingers still dripping. The silence scares Grundug, who's been sliding around their skirts, getting under their feet. Convinced he's done something wrong he slopes off under the table, tail between his legs. And then the cacophony outside starts up again.

Khatoun pushes Aram into a chair and peels the wet apron from his face. "I can sew this together," she says inspecting the gash. "Hold it in place for now." She presses the apron back into his cheek and wipes her bloody fingers on her dress.

Behind them a door creaks open and Iskender's skinny frame looms in the half-light.

"I heard banging," he says groggily.

"Yes."

"Everything all right?"

"Yes, *jan*..."

"We're fine!" Ferida's apron flaps impatiently. "*Oosht!*"

"You're sure..."

"No," Aram shakes his head and winces in pain. "It's over. Mgrdich is dead. The Turks have captured the Armenian Quarter and everything is in flames. This is it, Iskender, *efendi*. The end."

Iskender stares into the kitchen, shifting from foot to foot. "Oh," he manages eventually, through fingers and moustache.

"I'm going to stitch Aram's face back together," Khatoun says. "I need a sharp needle. Boil a pot, Ferida." She crosses over to Iskender and pauses, burying her face in his chest. His arms reach around her and they stand there together, creaking like floor boards until Iskender lets out a sigh, leans down to kiss his wife on the head and steers her out of the door.

"Good. Yes. You get a needle, I'll get some drinks." He follows his wife down the corridor and returns moments later, a flask under his arm, a nest of shot glasses clutched together in yellowing fingers. He pours several drinks and hands a glass to Aram, who stares at it.

"Oh! I'm an idiot!" Iskender says, slapping his forehead. "Let me help." He lifts the cup to Aram's lips and, with a sideways tilt, messily slips some of the dark liquid into the good side of his mouth. "This'll work wonders...ouf...sorry. It's just a dribble. From Scotland. My special reserve. It'll be a long time before we see any more of this, so enjoy." He throws down a shot himself and pours an immediate refill.

When Khatoun returns she finds Ferida out of her stupor, sorting clean rags out from a large sack of cuttings. A pot of water is bubbling over the stove and Khatoun plunges two needles into the flame, watching them glow red momentarily before settling down next to Aram. She takes a reel of cotton from her pocket, unwinds and licks the end and threads both needles. From her bodice she extracts a small vial and measures out two drops of liquid into a glass of water.

"Milk of the poppy. Drink it," she urges, holding Aram's face together as he lifts the glass to his lips. "And sorry, but I have to do this. Put the glass down, yes. Now hold onto the table leg and don't let go." She takes a length of rope and ties Aram's hands together around the table leg. "I'm sorry, *jan*, not for long, just squeeze tight." She soaks a rag with alcohol and carefully cleans the area around the wound. With a razor and held breath, she removes as much hair as possible from around the jagged flesh. A deep moan rumbles up from Aram's belly and Ferida slides in behind his chair. She takes his head in trembling hands, holding it in front of her like an unborn child, her tears slipping down the inside of her nose and onto his headdress. Slowly, with precision, Khatoun inserts the needle into his flesh and stitches him back together, finishing off with the second needle.

"Talk now," she says, snipping the thread at the end. "You won't be able to later." She undoes his hands and dips the needles into her glass of whisky before taking a swig.

Iskender has been stoically watching the water boil. He turns back to face them, his face grey. "Finished? Good." He slides a packet of cigarettes across the table to Aram, which Ferida nimbly intercepts, taking one for herself. She lights it and hands the packet to Aram, offering him the flame from her match, her fingers tenderly cupping his.

"Tell us everything," she says softly, sitting back. "We haven't seen you for months."

Aram slumps forward over the table, the adrenaline already abandoning his body. His hand shakes and he smokes so slowly, an inch of ash quivers at the end of his cigarette. He drops the whole thing into the ashtray in front of him and watches it smoulder. His face is curious to them now. A patchwork of what it once was. When he opens his mouth to speak, Khatoun notices for the first time that he is missing two teeth. He touches the stitches gingerly then pulls off his head covering and buries his filthy fingers in his hair.

"I don't know where to start," he sighs. "The one person who could have saved Ourfa is dead and our hopes have died with him." He snorts, inhales too deeply and begins to cough. "We are lost," he says when he catches his breath. He looks around the table at his friends, takes his glass and holds it to his lips but cannot drink. Sudden, great sobs wrack his body. Ferida throws her cigarette down, stubs it out on the scrubbed floor and pats his back like a dog.

"He put the bullet here," Aram weeps, pointing to his forehead. "Here, where it's written. He took his own life right in front of me. And that's it. It's over." He wipes the tears into his beard and whimpers. "Mgrdich was the only person alive who could have saved Ourfa."

"Trouble maker," Ferida retorts. "That's what he was."

"Sht! Let the man speak!" Iskender says, hushing his sister with a raised finger. He turns back to Aram. "You were in the Armenian Quarter?"

"Yes."

"With Mgrdich Yotneghparian?"

"Yes. With Mgrdich and his men."

"What were *you* doing there?" Ferida asks. "I didn't know resistance fighters needed accountants."

"We were friends. I was fighting, not accounting."

"Fighting? *Asdvadz!*" Ferida crosses herself.

"I was there when the police came looking for Mgrdich. They broke in through the roof and it went badly, depending on whose viewpoint you take. It was the trigger for the resistance, which is what Mgrdich wanted..."

"And now the whole Armenian Quarter is in flames?"

"Yes."

"With everyone trapped inside..."

"Yes."

"Surrounded?"

"Yes."

"And the hero that started it all just *killed* himself?" Ferida shouts. "What kind of hero is that? All he did was prove that if you resist you end up dead, just like everyone else!"

"Ferida!" Iskender yells. "Sit down! Let the poor man catch his breath. Can't you see what he's been through?"

Ferida flings herself into her chair and downs her shot with a grunt. Khatoun has been listening quietly, jabbing at the spool of thread with a needle. She stops, looks up at Iskender and then across at Ferida. "You know I knew him," she says, sticking the needle under the collar of her dress and slipping the cotton reel into her pocket. "Mgrdich. God rest his soul. I smashed his egg with mine one Easter and he was mad – said I wasn't a lady."

"You were *friends*?" Iskender asks, his cigarette stuck to his lip. "You and Mgrdich Yotneghparian?"

Khatoun shrugs. "Neighbours. Friends. A long time ago. The brothers used to trade, they had a *khan* and we knew them that way. Mgrdich and I were the same age. We used to meet at church. Easter. Christmas. Mgrdich wasn't really friends with anyone, although all the boys loved him."

"The girls too," Ferida snorts.

"He was troubled. Even back then. They said it was being an orphan made him wild. 'He prefers horses to school and rifles to books,' that's what they said. His brothers had to send him away in the end. The older two, the sensible ones, Nerses and Kevork. Mgrdich ended up in the desert with tribesmen, Arabs, Kurds, I don't know. They say he was a nomad, really, in his heart. Anyway, that's where he learnt to ride and hunt. Out in the desert."

"Bet that's not all he learnt!" Ferida scoffs reaching for another cigarette and lighting it. Aram has slumped forward in exhaustion, his head resting on his arms, his face turned to the side. Outside, life is in turmoil but there is a sense of calm in this smoky kitchen. The pots are boiling on the stove, hissing and spitting as if beans and lentils are all that matter in the world. Grundug has buried his nose in his armpit and is busy snuffling out fleas. Every now and then he looks up, sneezes and wipes his nose with his paws.

Ferida exhales two perfect streams of smoke from her nostrils. She taps her cigarette into the ashtray, pokes the mound of ash with the tip.

"He came here, you know. Your friend." She takes another drag and casts her eye around the table. "About a month ago. Dressed like some Arab. Didn't tell me his name, but I knew. Said he was a friend of our sister Loucia's."

"Don't talk rubbish," Iskender says, ash dropping from his lips. "Now *everybody* knows this Mgrdich?" He pats at the ash with his finger, working it into the grain of the wood. Ferida ignores him and continues with her story.

"He was looking for Khatoun. When I said she wasn't available he gave me a basket to give to her. Said it was bread and could she carry it to Mariam *Hanum* in the Armenian Quarter."

"Mgrdich's sister," Aram mumbles.

"Exactly," Ferida rolls her eyes.

"And?" Iskender asks. "What did you do?"

"What do you think I did? I took it. He said they needed bread so I took it. Heaviest bread I ever carried. Two men followed me all the way there and back. Armenians dressed as Turks, but I knew. Kept their distance and watched me like a bird watches its nest."

The pause that follows is so long Ferida wonders if she actually spoke the last words or just thought them. Eventually, Iskender shakes his head.

"Why would you do such a thing?" he asks. He reaches for another cigarette, lights one from the other and slides the pack over to Aram. "Help yourself. After this I'm back to roll ups, so smoke."

"I did it because if I didn't, *she* would have," Ferida juts her chin in Khatoun's direction. "Your wife would have gone and got killed on the street and then what? Children need their mother."

The pot on the stove spits. Khatoun scrapes her chair back, gathers cups and spoons and starts to make tea.

"He could be very persuasive, Mgrdich," Aram murmurs, the good side of his face resting against the table, the puckered side up. "Even when we were small he had us organised into gangs against the Turkish boys." He sits up, eyes red with exhaustion and reaches for his glass. He takes a swig, swills it around in his mouth – the sting good against the sharp pull of stitches. "I can't believe it," he says. "I can imagine anyone dead except Mgrdich. He was too alive to die."

"Too alive?" Ferida laughs. "What does that mean? Shine too bright and God will put out your light. And if not God, your jealous neighbours."

"Amen."

"Yes," Aram sighs, "not everyone liked Mgrdich."

"He was a hot head, that's why," Ferida says. "People died because of him. Look at the people of Garmuj. Just weeks ago. That's her people, remember," she indicates Khatoun.

"Nobody could have predicted that," Aram says. "He was holed up in the Garmuj caves because there was a price on his head. A lot of people were ready to betray him – fools who believed that if they fingered Mgrdich the persecutions would stop. It was impossible to trust anyone. And someone did betray him. When Mgrdich got to the caves the army already knew about it. They surrounded him but his men had arms and managed to hold their ground. They slipped out when the soldiers went for reinforcements. Followed them out in disguise. Walked right past the sentries and nobody realised until they were long gone. Reinforcements arrived. Caves were empty. It enraged the Turks."

"Who took it out on the people of Garmuj. Tortured and killed them, including the poor mayor," Ferida says. "We know all this. But how is that protecting your people? Letting them die for you?"

"It's the government who torture our people, remember that," Aram says. "And they'll use anything as an excuse."

Iskender clears his throat, "Exactly. If they had caught Mgrdich in the caves they would have killed the villagers as conspirators, and if he hadn't turned up at all they would have killed them for sheltering a criminal. They make up whatever excuse is needed at the time."

"You're right, my friend," Aram sighs. "The pressure to surrender was strong. A few of Mgrdich's men did give themselves up just to keep the peace. They were killed instantly and still the people of Garmuj were tortured."

"Well, he's dead now and that's that," Ferida says. "*Asdvadz hokin lousavore.*" She clears a space on the table for Khatoun's tray of teacups. "And now what?" She accepts a cup, watches the steam rise for a moment then pushes her chair back impatiently. "*Kaknem.* I can't sit here drinking tea. I'm going up to the roof to see what I can see." Iskender stands as she passes, hovering over his chair clumsily. "What?" she asks him. "What do *you* want now?"

"Nothing," Iskender shrugs. "Just…keep low and…um… keep out of sight."

Ferida smiles. "I'll keep low," she says. "More importantly, don't let your wife open that door again." She darts daggers at Khatoun. "I'll light the fire in the bathroom and have a bed made up for Aram. And you," she looks across at the shattered man, "you're not going anywhere. I want to wake up and see your lovely face for a few more years." She gives him a disjointed grin and creaks out of the room, Grundug loping after her up to the doorway where he stands whimpering.

"Go on. Go with her, Grundug," Iskender tells the dog. Grundug turns to look at him. Normally, he isn't allowed upstairs and that's distinctly where he heard Ferida's slippers heading.

"Go on, go!" Iskender slaps his hand on the table and Grundug drops his head and tucks his tail between his legs. "*Hayde! Oosht!* Go with her!" Iskender yells and the frightened mutt finally pushes the door to and scampers up the back stairs to find his mistress, totally confused.

Iskender stands, holds his drink up high and places his other hand over his heart. "My beautiful mother, Seyda *Hanum,* God rest her soul, told me that if I said a prayer for someone, an angel would sit on their shoulder. To the people of Ourfa, my people, may the angels please come and sit on your shoulders because I can't think of any other prayer to send you right now. Amen." He swills his drink around in his glass and knocks it back in one.

"Amen," Khatoun whispers.

"Amen."

"And now..." Iskender declares to the ceiling as he pulls at his waistcoat and pats the gold watch nestling in his breast pocket, "I'm going up to the roof too." His shoulders are at awkward angles and his shoes seem to have ants in them, and yet he doesn't move. He belches into his cheek and blows the air out in a stream. "Aram," he says, still looking up at the ceiling, "you are welcome in our home. Khatoun will look after you. I am going to check on the children first and then I'm going to see what is happening." He breaks into a cough, excuses himself and is gone.

Khatoun and Aram remain at the table, their tea untouched. The lamp is almost out and they sit in the gloom trying to make sense out of the noises that find their way in through the cracks in the walls. In the distance the demons are howling but there is a void between the warmth of this kitchen and what is taking place across town. Doors are locked and people with any sense are inside. Life has slipped underground and dares only rattle the windowpanes. It's a long while before either of them speaks and in the silence the furniture swells and creaks, exposing the flaking blue paint of the wooden chairs, the ancient cracks that snake across plaster. Khatoun stretches, reaching her hands out in front of her and cracking her fingers. She wipes at the crust that has collected in the corner of her eyes.

"What happened to Mgrdich's little brother, *Azdoo Peepuh*? Is he still alive?"

Aram laughs. "God's Eyeball — what a shot! Yes, he was alive when I left him but wounded. Their sister is dead, *Asdvadz hokin*...she was defending the church. His wife, Elizabeth, I saw just before I came here. Alive but wild with grief." Aram pauses, takes a rag from the pile on the table, rolls it into a little ball and stuffs it into his pocket.

"Khatoun, it doesn't matter who is alive now. We'll all be dead soon — it's just a matter of time."

"I know," Khatoun nods, "but some of us will survive. Some-one will live to tell the story. May God grant it be one of us."

"*Insha'Allah*," Aram sighs.

"Come on. The roof?" Khatoun pushes her chair back and offers Aram a hand.

"So we can watch our city burn? Yes, we should witness it. You'll have to push me up the stairs, though." Aram takes her hand and staggers to his feet.

They wind their way up the stairs slowly. Aram is exhausted. He feels as sick as the day he smoked his first ever cigarette. Heavy in the stomach and legs, weightless in the head. When they reach the roof, the sky is a murky purple, a pall of black smoke hanging over the Armenian Quarter to the west. The moon is lost somewhere and only a few stars can be seen behind the fine dust of ash that floats in on the evening breeze.

Ferida is crouched by the balustrade, watching the sky change colour. Iskender stands further back; a tall, black squiggle sil-houetted against the putrid sky. Mertha and Thooma sit huddled together under a large blanket near the wall, Mertha distraught; her hands tugging at her hair, pulling it out in strands and wind-ing it frantically around her fingers.

"My brothers, my sons, my brothers, my sons" she weeps, unable to tear her eyes away from the billowing cloud in the distance. "Waaaaaaa! Mybrothersmysonsmybrothersmysonsmy-brothersmysons. *Vay vay vay!*"

"Bastards," Ferida says.

"Montreal," Iskender mutters to no one in particular.

"*Vay vay vay!*" Mertha's lament continues. "*Hanum! Bayan! Ben seni çok seviyorum.*" She wraps her hair into knots, her upturned face catching the dust that falls like rain. "They say they love us, but they love our blood more! I had to sit on top of her...to stop her running to the windows and looking out...'Baby Alice, not the window,' I said...but she saw everything...women and children, blood, blood, blood like a river, like a dream, like a game...'It's just a game,' I lied, 'only a game, they're going to chop down trees, not people...' but look! I lied! First they chop us with axes and now they burn us...look, look, the sky is thick with our smoke, we cannot see the stars...and my brothers, my sons, my brothers...there, out there! Waaaaa!"

"Shush," Thooma whispers. "Take a breath." He wraps his arm around her and she stops wailing only to sink her teeth into his sleeve.

Aram limps forward, settling at Iskender's feet, his knees hugged close to his chest. Khatoun stands behind him, letting Aram lean against her legs, one hand on his shoulder, the other snaking around her husband's waist as they watch the sky. The cloud belches upwards, bleeding across the heavens and obliterating the moon. The distance glows orange. The Armenian Quarter crackles gently – an eerily soothing sound from this distance. It is otherwise quiet. No human sounds. Above them, night closes in and a lone swallow sings somewhere – surprised by its solitude.

"How many people still trapped in there?" Iskender wonders out loud. "They know they're going to die but they still have some time. What do you do with that time? Fight? Hide? Run? Sit and wait for the flames?"

"I would run," Khatoun says. "Not away, but towards death. I would run with an open heart, my children in my arms, rather than have it come up behind me in some ugly way."

"Don't even say it!" Mertha shrieks. "Not even a word!"

"We could have avoided this," Aram says shifting his weight and pulling his shirt close against the chill. "If we'd listened to Mgrdich, we could have avoided all this bloodshed."

"Pah!" Ferida scoffs. "Avoided? How? It's *because* of him the city is burning!" She twists round to face Aram, her face lit red by the distant flames.

"This is not the time to argue," Iskender hisses.

"No, no, this is no argument. I'd love to hear how we could have stopped this," Ferida insists. "Perhaps we could learn something — pass on the advice."

"We could have fought," Aram answers gently, accepting another lit cigarette from Iskender. "Instead of waiting and defending ourselves we could have attacked. Fought. There were plenty of opportunities."

Iskender nods, his gaze still fixed in the distance. "And plenty of warnings. We should have seen the writing on the wall ever since Zeitoun. We should have followed their lead."

"What are you talking about?" Ferida laughs. "They got fucked in Zeitoun!"

"Ferida!" Mertha implores, covering her ears.

"They did!" Ferida crawls back towards the huddled group and sits opposite Aram. "The Zeitounis made their own lives hell with all their endless uprisings and, if you ask me, life more difficult for Armenians everywhere. And where did it get them in the end? Digging their own graves on the Rakka road!"

"Exactly my point," Aram says. "They were duped. 'Stop resisting, leave peacefully and we'll be lenient with troublemakers.' Like always. The Zeitounis were the first to defend themselves. This time they listened to the Turks and fell into their trap. Trust is what killed them."

"Wait. You said we could have avoided this, but so far all you've done is show us how futile resistance is," Ferida snorts.

Aram is calm. "If we had resisted *earlier* we could have avoided this."

"Earlier?" Ferida laughs. "When? All the young men are taken, the weapons are called in — what are we supposed to do? Gather the old women and children together and fight with cooking spoons?"

"Your meat cleaver would have come in handy," Aram says. "And it may still come to that, so let's not laugh too hard at our own jokes."

"Yes," Iskender agrees. "I'm telling you, Aram is right. Early resistance is crucial." He takes a clean handkerchief out of his pocket and spits grey dust into it.

Ferida sneers at her brother, "What are *you* talking about? You never leave your room unless a hashish cloud forces you out. Talk about resisting. Pah!"

She takes a swig from the bottle hidden in her skirts and hands it to Aram. He drips the alcohol into his mouth and cocks his head to the side, letting it bathe the inside of his torn cheek before spitting it onto the floor.

"Beginning to hurt," he says taking another slug and swallowing it this time. "The answer to your question is this, *jan*..." he hands the bottle back to Ferida. "We should have put up a fight *before* the boys got drafted, *before* our weapons were confiscated. At that stage, as you point out, it's already too late."

"Put up a fight? Unprovoked? Like Van..."

"...they won..."

"...at what cost?...And Zeitoun, and everyone else who's tried the same and ended up as bird food on the Rakka road."

"Unprovoked?" Aram holds up his fingers and starts to count them off. "Martial law. Labour battalions. Misappropriation of property. The hundreds of thousands of people dragging through here on marches. You saw them yourself! You have girls here who've told you first-hand what's happening to Armenians all over the Empire. What other provocation do you want? But no. 'Wait, wait,' the Prelate said. 'Don't fight back, don't resist, maybe it won't happen to Ourfa.' And then what? Our weapons were taken and as soon as the populace was unarmed, they attacked. A thousand Ourfalise dead in one day."

"I tried to sit on her," Mertha cries. "'Baby Alice! Don't look!' But she ran to the window and saw everything! *Vay vay vay!*"

"We here survived by luck alone," Aram continues indicating their group with a circled hand. "Maybe we woke up late and weren't in the street that day. Who knows what stroke of fate saved us. And since then? All of us prisoners in our own homes."

"Except for you. Out, playing with the bad boys." Ferida spits on the floor.

"I had no choice. They were making arrests. My name was on a list. I chose to disappear instead."

Thooma lets out a long sigh, breaking his silence from over by the wall. "We live with our heads in the sand."

"We do indeed, Baron Khouri," Aram agrees, his voice becoming more animated, unlike the Aram they thought, up until now, they knew. "We could have – no, *should* have – acted earlier. It was the church elders that held us back. They said that unless a specific announcement came that Ourfa Armenians were to be exiled, Mgrdich was to sit tight."

"A raft, floating in the sea," Iskender mutters to the sky.

"Despite all the arrests, the deportations, the witness reports, no one was ready to listen to Mgrdich until after the notice went up to hand in our weapons," Aram continues.

"Well, that's the final step isn't it?" Thooma says. "Make people defenceless, then go in for the kill."

"I don't understand why everyone agreed to hand in their weapons," Khatoun says. "It doesn't make sense to me."

"Because failure to hand over metes out punishment," Iskender replies. "Another dozen killed. There were plenty of villagers who bought guns just to donate, to avoid trouble."

"Anyway, it was after that that people finally began to listen to Mgrdich," Aram says. His voice flows with excitement. His hands flutter and dip into the folds of his shirt, twisting the ends around his fingers and letting them go again. "In order to gain time, Mgrdich told us to donate our guns, but only those that were defective or broken."

"That'd make a good pile!" Thooma laughs. "I had a pistol, belonged to my father once. Useless. The only thing it ever killed was a rat — I hit it over the head with the handle. It must be somewhere."

"Find it!" Aram jokes before continuing. "So, as the government began to confiscate weapons, Mgrdich began stockpiling them, preparing for battle. A lot of people still held on to the hope that we wouldn't get the same treatment as in other towns."

"That's what I don't understand," Thooma exclaims. "The Armenians always think other people are reasonable and level-headed even though there is evidence of their brutality right in front of them. We're stupid; as a race we must be amongst the most stupid people in the world."

"Thooma," Mertha cries, "please!"

"We're not stupid," Aram shakes his head. "Just stubbornly optimistic."

"What? Giving up all means of defending yourself and hoping that no one will harm you is *optimistic*? It's downright stupidity," Thooma shouts. "As soon as we were unarmed Talaat let all the miscreants out of jail so they could carry out his dirty work.

And there you have it, a thousand of us dead in one day." His arm sweeps out in a large arc as if he were clearing a table of its contents.

"I knew it was coming...that day the moon covered the sun... it was warning us. I tried to sit on her..." Mertha wails, "but she ran to the window to see...'Baby Alice, not the window,' I said...but she saw...men with axes and bayonets...knives from the kitchen...blood, blood, blood like a river..."

"Khalil Bey and Ahmed Bey," Ferida spits into the ground. "*Kaknem peruned.* I shit on your faces."

"The Armenians are not stupid," Iskender says calmly, ignoring the passionate outburst surrounding him. "There was confusion over the fate of Ourfa. The orders from the government were for total annihilation, *kiamilan imha*, of Armenians in the provinces of the Empire but *kusman imha*, partial annihilation in other places. Particularly places populated by a lot of Europeans. Look at the big cities. Look at Constantinople where there are foreign witnesses. The Armenians there are treated differently. We were outside the boundaries here – that's why we believed our fate could be different. Then the borders were changed which included us in the province of Diarbakir and at the same time the order was issued that all Armenians were enemies of the Muslim State – to be eliminated. It opened the gates."

"Yes, yes, *hanum, bayan, efendi, efendi* to our faces but they chop us just the same!" Mertha howls, dragging the blanket with her and slumping at Khatoun's feet. "Why? Why? Why?"

Thooma stands alone at the balustrade smoking furiously. "Why? Because they hate us. Because we have better jobs and work harder and send our children to school and educate our girls and learn foreign languages." He rants over his shoulder, his profile sharp and angular against the glowing sky. "Because we sleep in beds, because we love our families, because we have two arms and two legs, because, because, because. Who in hell knows why!" He flicks his cigarette over the edge into the street below.

"They don't hate us," Iskender says, "they hate what we stand for. In every thriving city they see us and people want to emulate us – to wear Western dress, to become more global. To travel. And that challenges the nationalists, the ultraconservatives, the fundamentalists; our values are threatening their control over people, so they blacken our name and hate us for the very same things they want."

Thooma turns to face them, "They claim to be enlightened on one side but on the other it's all about how many *giavour* they can kill and how much closer they'll get to paradise with its gushing fountains and dark-eyed *houris*."

"When you meet the unbelievers in the jihad, strike off their heads." Aram reaches up to his puckered face, his fingertips tracing the stitches that pull angrily at his swollen cheek, "I imagine the poor fellow that did this to me is severely disappointed." His laugh is hollow and Mertha lets out a little sob.

"Whoever kills, unless for a soul, or for corruption done in the land — it is as if he had slain mankind entirely. And whoever saves one, it is as if he had saved mankind entirely. Isn't that also in their book?" Khatoun asks.

"Yes, it is," Iskender looks surprised. "As with everything, there are two sides or more to every story. War itself is terrible — look at what's happening throughout Europe right now. But it is religion that turns war evil. We can carve out territories over a dinner table and argue politics with educated fervour, but when 'God tells us' we are right, we become despicable and bloody. We take carte blanche to commit the worst crimes in the world. People are just selective in the way they interpret things."

"They're murdering us because we let them. Because we're stupid," Thooma persists, walking over. "What about that farce with the ransom? Not bad enough that everyone gave in their guns, we were stupid enough to go along with the ransom too. Six thousand *gurush* for the return of all prisoners and our continued safety? Extortion, that's what that was. Once they had their pile of gold, they killed all the prisoners and turned on anyone stupid enough to be in the street." He pats Mertha on the hand, remembering too late that she was one of the women who ran to hand in their gold bangles in the hope that it might save lives.

The sky is shedding large flakes of ash and the Armenian Quarter glows a fierce red. The group pass round the bottle, even Mertha taking a healthy gulp before handing it back to Ferida who washes out her mouth and spits soot onto the floor.

"That day is burnt in here," Ferida says, tapping her head. "It was noon, the hottest part of the day. The children were outside, playing with the neighbour's girls. Everything seemed normal. Then it went quiet. A single moment of silence and I remember looking up from my *dolmas* and then, that sound I had never heard before. Like a woman in childbirth, but worse. The hair rises on my skin to remember it. And suddenly people everywhere. Running, screaming. Madness. Dragging the children indoors. Pushing the neighbour's children out the back to their grandmother..."

"A day like that and then everything goes quiet and you think the worst of it is over. Everyone is friends again, *efendi, efendi*. And again we end up here,"Thooma sighs. "It's senseless."

"Yes, senseless," Ferida says, "for us to end up here. But Aram, you still haven't told us everything that happened. After all this time of not seeing you, how did you end up here?"

"How did I end up here?" Arum drums his fingers on his knee. "It began about a month ago, after the deportation order came in. After the slaughter. Everything had calmed down. Relatively. It was September twenty-ninth. I was in the Armenian Quarter. We were in the middle of a meeting, figuring out the next move, when the police came looking for Mgrdich. They surrounded the house saying they were looking for deserters. They knocked a hole in the roof and began to break in from above. The first policeman to jump down was shot in the head. The soldiers outside went berserk. They began to shoot at us from all directions. It was exactly what Mgrdich had been waiting for. He opened his hand, the bird flew and the church bells rang – the signal to begin the resistance."

"We heard them," Ferida says.

"Church bells ringing as a sign to pick up arms," Mertha weeps. "It's sacrilege!"

"Church bells that had been *silent* for twenty years, don't forget," Iskender says. He looks at Khatoun, recalling the day he'd been at her house trying to muster up the courage to ask for her hand when the Apostolic bells had rung out the last time. Khatoun never averts her gaze, staring ahead at the smoke billowing across town from the rooftop, just as she had done then.

"That's *why* Mgrdich used the bells," Aram explains. "Twenty years ago the Turks rang them to announce the massacres. Mgrdich was just a kid with a slingshot, running around the hills fetching ammo for the resistance. But it made an impression on him; *our* church bells, *our* massacre. This time he had his little brother ring the bells as a sign to resist. People responded immediately. Those that could. Finally, we were going to fight." His face lights up for a moment beneath the red sky. "We seized the police, got their guns and began defending ourselves. They surrounded us, then sent in an envoy asking for calm, saying the police had made a mistake and if we gave up there would be no reprisals."

"Honey-tongued envoys, dripping with lies," Iskender says.

"Exactly. But Mgrdich had waited too long for this opportunity. He sent back a message, laying it bare. No deal. The first night passed quietly. We dug in and set up barricades. In the morning the army arrived expecting to carry out a massacre like they had in ninety-five. They advanced from numerous positions and we let them. The lone voice of one Moslem priest was heard pleading for peace and then even he shut up."

"Yes. We heard that too. I was right here, on the roof," Ferida says. "Watching from that corner. Couldn't see anything, just heard the ruckus and his voice above it all. On and on he went. Pleading to God, to Allah, the wives, the mothers, the fucking mules…"

"Well, his pleas went unanswered. The Turks kept coming. When they'd advanced deep enough into the Quarter we attacked. It was amazing. They were stunned, suffered heavy losses and had to retreat. They thought they had another Musa Dagh on their hands. They were embarrassed; that's why they sent in so many troops after that. Maybe six thousand regulars and another ten thousand fanatics."

"Oh yes," Iskender sighs. "The boots marching past the doors. Khatoun hid the girls under mountains of fabric. Just to be on the safe side. Even the walls shook."

"We were completely surrounded," Aram says. "But we played them like idiots. Kept drawing them in. The alleyways, the side streets – they were so easily trapped. We had the upper hand for a long time. But about a week ago it was clear we were losing, simply by numbers. We only had about three hundred fighters, mostly civilians, including the women. And out of those, perhaps fifty of us properly trained to use weapons, Mgrdich's sister and wife amongst them." Aram accepts the bottle from Ferida, takes a sip and continues. "We were under constant shellfire and running out of ammo. Most of us down to hand weapons. I knew it was over days ago. We'd lasted a month."

"And?" Ferida asks.

"And?"

"You knew it was over and then suddenly you turn up in our kitchen with your face undone."

Aram stares at Ferida and exhales, slowly, deliberately. "And I kept some bullets. Mgrdich always said it would be better to die by your own hand than murdered. I saw families torch themselves because they had no bullets left. Mothers and children doused in kerosene, sitting calm, waiting. My first thoughts were to get out and come here. To tell you I love you." He looks around the group. "All of you. And I have bullets."

"And I still have that gun," Thooma declares. "Somewhere."

"It won't be necessary," Aram says, his voice steady. "I brought my Webley." He digs into his waistband and extracts a revolver. "Six bullets," he pronounces, flicking it open and showing them the full chamber before snapping it shut again and placing it on the ground between them.

"The children..." Mertha whimpers as everyone stares at the revolver, "...they're..."

"...downstairs. It's okay, *Mayrig*..." Khatoun takes her mother's hand in hers. "Shhh."

Iskender flicks his cigarette over the balcony and takes the final two out of the packet. He crushes the pack, lights both cigarettes and hands one to Aram. The two men consider each other for a long time without speaking, the silence between them eloquence itself.

"So," Iskender says eventually, pushing the gun towards Aram with his foot. "What's next?"

Aram groans, picks up the revolver and slides it back into his belt. "I don't know," he shrugs. "You love each other. You stay indoors. You dig a hole and bury yourselves or run headlong, unafraid and naked to your destiny. Take your pick. After today, we vanish."

"*Agh*, Mgrdich," Ferida murmurs, standing. She stretches up in time to catch a sliver of moon behind the ashy clouds and starts to laugh. "*Mgrdich tekrar oynamış!* Still up to your old games. Are they true – all the crazy stories we heard about his life?"

"Probably," Aram smiles.

"I heard he stole a whole stack of carpets once, in some kind of disguise…"

"Stole them *back*, you mean," Aram snorts. "Yes. From under their noses. *And* sold them for arms. They belonged to Armenians once. Requisitioned and stuck in a warehouse. The guard on duty was so confused. Told his boss, 'Of course it's empty, *efendi*. You came here twice already and took everything!' The boss was furious. Those carpets had been under lock and key for years. Mgrdich liberated them, and then, for a laugh, rode to the town square in yet another disguise, screaming, 'Who is this damned Mgrdich? Wherever he is, I'm going to find him and kill him!' before he rode off."

The huddle of people on the roof laugh. "*Oyna*, Mgrdich! *Oyna*! Keep playing!"

Aram leans forward, takes Ferida's hand and pulls himself up. "And now, Ferida *jan*, if I don't get to bed I'm going to evaporate. Your whisky has worked wonders."

"The bathroom first," Ferida says. "You stink."

"Thank you, Aram," Thooma calls out as Ferida leads Aram down the stairs. "We're glad you're safe."

"Goodnight."

"God bless you."

"The light be with you."

"And with you."

Slowly the family unravels, wandering the perimeter, picking up shoes and cigarette butts and taking one last look at the belching city before following them down into the house, leaving the roof empty. A small patch of darkness where they sat on the floor is all that remains and soon that too is buried by the ash that continues to fall and settle like sifted flour.

In the bathroom Ferida has cut and pulled the clothes from Aram's broken body.

"Let it seep out of you," she says, pouring warm water over his naked back. "I'll be back with clean clothes. Let me go and burn these before I catch your lice." She holds his tattered clothing to her chest and is about to leave.

"Ferida *jan*."

"Yes?"

"What I said upstairs…I meant it."

"You said a lot of things."

"You know what I mean."

"I know what you mean, *jan*. Me too." She puts her hand on the door but he stops her again.

"I have a question."

"What?"

"Why do you always fold down the backs of your shoes?"

Ferida turns and stares at him. "Because I can't reach down to cut my toenails. When I wear the heel up it pushes my foot forward and my nails dig in…"

"Sht," Aram puts his finger to his lips. "Come…give me your foot and your scissors. I'll cut them…"

At their bedroom door, Thooma takes Mertha's ashy cheeks in his hands and kisses her on the nose. "You better wash this pretty face before you go to sleep. And no more crying. We'll find out in a few days what has happened to everybody. Until then we stay calm." He gestures at Khatoun to get her mother into bed. "I'm going to sit up for a while. Iskender and I have a few things to discuss." He takes a few steps backwards, turns and winds down the stairs to the little office where he knows a lump of hashish is waiting with the last of the scotch.

Mertha leans her face against the wall, waiting until she hears the office door click shut downstairs before allowing Khatoun to lead her to her bed. The covers are still in a jumble on the floor where they were hurriedly thrown earlier. Khatoun eases her distraught mother out of her clothes and sponges her down with a cloth soaked in rose water.

"My heart cannot take this," Mertha weeps. "My sons, my brothers, your uncles and aunties, their children, our friends! They're all out there somewhere! Look at us in this house. We feel safe, but the walls lie. That should be us out there – falling to the ground as ash!" She buries her head in Khatoun's lap and sobs miserably.

"Have faith, *Mayrig*," Khatoun croons. "The only way to cheat death is not to fear it." She undoes her mother's headscarf and combs through the feathery locks. "Come on, sleep now. We're all together and we'll be safe – I know it." She moves her like a child, lifts the patterned quilt from the floor and covers her.

She pauses at the door, waiting to hear the change in Mertha's breathing that signifies she is asleep. As she is about to go, her mother's sleepy voice calls out.

"Khatoun?"

"Yes?"

"You were right to let Aram in."

"Yes."

"But please don't open the door again. Promise me."

"I promise. Goodnight now. Sleep."

"Go with the light."

"Stay with the light. Goodnight."

The shadows engulf the room as she slips out into the corridor and closes the door behind her. Slowly she makes her way down the hall towards her room. As she turns the corner, past the bathroom, steam seeping under the door, Grundug standing guard, she hears voices. Bzdig Shoushun murmuring softly and the low whine of Alice crying coming from the children's quarters. She stops and listens for a moment, trying to make out what they are saying before entering the room. The boys are asleep in their beds. Only Alice is awake, wrapped in Bzdig Shoushun's arms in the middle of the room, a lamp flickering on the floor in front of them. As soon as she sees Khatoun, Alice stands and runs to her mother, flinging her arms around her neck.

"Hello," Khatoun smiles. "What are you doing awake?"

"I'm sorry, *Digin* Khatoun," Bzdig Shoushun says. "The poor girl can't sleep. She's scared."

"Afrem told me the whole city is on fire!" Alice wails, "And they're going to burn us down!"

"No," Khatoun says firmly. "Nobody is going to burn us down – only you, if you jump up and knock over the lamp like you almost did. Come on, let's put you to bed." She leads Alice to her bunk, waving Bzdig Shoushun out of the room with her hand.

She curls her body around her daughter's, letting the girl rest her head on her arm, the lamp throwing patterns onto the wall next to them. She strokes Alice's hair, watching the patterns dance. "Are you still awake?" she asks after a while.

"Yes," comes the whisper. "Are you?"

"Yes, *janavar*. Otherwise how could I be talking to you?"

"Ha!" Alice shifts closer to her mother, their heads touching. "You sounded like you were sleeping."

"No, not sleeping, just dreaming."

"What are you dreaming about?"

"What am I dreaming about? Let me see...I am in my bedroom in the afternoon – the late afternoon in summer. It's dusk and I am lying on my high iron bed and the light coming in the window is beautiful. The curtains are two layers of fabric; cream over turquoise, the light soft blue. Outside I can hear the birds and the sounds of other people. I can hear music and rattling, like a piece of machinery. Then I hear some conversations in the distance – I don't know what they're talking about and every now and then there's a bell – and then a sneeze and a dog, yes, a dog – the white one with brown paws like he's wearing *goshigs*. And I feel happy here, it's my secret. It's peaceful because I am alone and at the same time I want to share it. To open the curtain and float out the window and over the rooftops. The sun is a soft blanket and I'm happy because I'm at home. It's a very fragile place, just like an eggshell, and I have to hold it gently otherwise I will shatter it." She pauses to kiss Alice on the head. "That's where I go to be happy. Now you do the same. Tell me your favourite place to be in the world."

Alice looks at her solemnly in the dim light, her eyes the same dark hollow of her father's. She twists her braid around her finger.

"My favourite place in the world is in Grandma Mertha's farm and I'm still little," she says. "I remember the kitchen in the garden. The colourful cloths on the floor covered in tomatoes and peppers you made me promise not to put in my mouth. My favourite place in the world is our bedroom in that house and the big bed on the floor we all slept in together. Looking at the shadows on the wall."

"Let's go," Khatoun smiles. "Shut your eyes and let's go there now." She pulls the covers up and tucks them in around her daughter. Gently she begins to stroke Alice's body, patting her gently along the spine as she curls into a ball. "There you go," she croons, "we're back at Grandma's in the big bed on the floor. In front of you is the wall and the sunshine is coming in the window through the trees behind us. What do you see?"

"I see lacy fingers playing games. Little hands and birds like angels."

"And what are the fingers playing with?"

"A butterfly."

"A butterfly? How lovely. Is the butterfly flying?"

"No, she's eating...now she's flying."

"Let's go with her. Let's be butterflies. Open your wings and dance up into the sky. Up. Higher and higher with the wind. Up through the clouds. How soft the blue is. Like an egg in a bird's nest. And there's a bird and she's singing to you."

She begins to sing and before long a soft shudder slips through Alice as she finally releases into sleep.

It is only as Khatoun slides her arm out from under Alice's head and sits on the edge of the little *divan*, rubbing it back to life, that she notices Ferida hovering in the doorway. She has taken her slippers off and now slides noiselessly across the floor, her face tense, stretched tight like a drum.

"Aram's gone," she whispers. "I went to get rid of his clothes and when I got back he was gone. I've searched everywhere, but there's no sign of him. Both doors, back and front are locked from the inside. I even searched under the bed we made up for him; nothing."

"Where could he have gone?" Khatoun asks. "You left him in the bathroom?"

"Yes."

"Maybe he got hot and went to sit down somewhere."

"I'm telling you, Serpuhi and I have been through the whole house; the girls' rooms, the kids', everywhere," Ferida hisses. "Not even Grundug can sniff him out. Everyone is in bed except for those two sinking a bottle in the office. I haven't said anything to them."

"But if the doors are locked how did he get out?"

Ferida shrugs, "It's as if he were never here except that his gun was on the kitchen table with the bullets still in it. And this. I found this in my pocket. He must have slipped it in somehow." She hands Khatoun a rag, mottled brown with dried blood. At first it seems as if that is all there is but as Khatoun handles the fabric she feel something hard inside. She looks at Ferida, puzzled.

"Go on. Open it, see what's in it," Ferida says.

Khatoun unravels the cloth — a scrap from the kitchen which

is wound around a piece of paper. Inside the crumpled paper, two gold teeth.

"What does it mean?" Ferida asks, looking at the beautiful script that flows in a single line across the page.

"I don't know," Khatoun shrugs. "Either we never find out or we ask Iskender to read it to us."

"Not now," Ferida snatches the paper back and shoves it in her pocket. "Maybe later."

Khatoun holds the teeth up for inspection, and then they hear it. Somewhere, somewhere over the roofs and under the sickle moon they hear the unmistakable sound of laughter escaping; but when they run to the balcony and look up, the world is silent and all they can see is the sky shifting, pale as a dove's feather with falling ash.

Our Neighbours

Ourfa, Summer 1916
Khatoun

Hunger. A reversal of nature.

Ask anyone who has been truly hungry and they'll tell you the same thing. It eats you from the inside. Hunger hollows you out and then fills you with nausea. After a while your muscles atrophy, your vision blurs and it becomes difficult to hear, despite the constant sound that dogs you. That low, never-ending drone that shifts like the waves, sometimes lapping, sometimes crashing on a rocky shore. And then there are the voices that accompany your every move – not that you move much. Some of them recognisable from long ago, others new, calling you forward before your time, occasionally soothing, more often terrifying in their fervour. And all of this goes on under a confusing swirl of distant conversation in a world that surrounds you but no longer contains you.

"Feed me."

On the other side of the city, beyond the furthest roof the eye can see, the inmates of the prison are starving. Hunger floats from their lips and carries across town, drowning out the song of birds, shadowing the call to prayer.

"Feed me." Their voices lift in the wind and land nowhere. The whole city is in famine and every morning the sun rises, pokes her bony fingers into shadowy doorways and illuminates the pathetic remains of some wretch that didn't last the night.

The Armenian corpses are buried in ditches on the outskirts of town, clutching each other in an embrace of tangled limbs and half-lost hair. Their fingernails grow into each other, hooking infant to parent, lover to friend, rooting them to their unmarked graves that will sprout scarlet poppies one day. Moslem corpses are wrapped in a shroud and made note of. Five yards of cloth, a cake of soap and five *gurush* for the lucky undertaker. No wonder corpses are presented half a dozen times. Bodies have become barter. A hidden ring in a loose flap of skin. A pair of embroidered slippers. Rich, virgin hair in an easily sliced braid. The dead don't care. For the most part they grin and are to be envied – they no longer feel hunger.

Ferida had found her that morning – had almost walked past her, she was bundled so small in the corner. At first Ferida thought she was alive – that she had been fed – she was smiling so peacefully. But the girl didn't respond to the startled shriek that accompanied her discovery. Her eyes remained open, calm, holding her last thoughts in that glassy stare. She'd been dreaming of home. Above her, the wide sky echoing with laughter as her brothers ran back and forth to the well, dropping stones in to see how deep it was. Her mother yelling at them as always, her floured hands streaking white against her red apron. The dogs were yelping, the chickens running for cover, the brook busily churning the mill at the side of the house. It was early morning and a constant stream of women passed her as they came for their bread.

"*Pari louys*, Nairi," their skirts swayed past. "Good morning. Are you feeding your dolly?"They smiled, red apple cheeks and chestnut hair and the morning was pleasant and the smell of bread sweet. Soon she would go inside and help prepare lunch while her brothers went to school. Soon she would eat and the pain in her belly would subside. Soon, very soon, she would lie down with her grandmother for their afternoon nap, and they would sleep curled up on the floor with the breeze cooling their feet. Soon.

A tentative shove with a foot and she'd toppled sideways, still happy. Ferida sprinkled lime from her special reserve over both doorway and child and waited for One-Eyed Osman, the only Muslim with a cart who'd touch the infidel corpses, to arrive. He'd accepted her coin with a shrug and tossed the girl's body on top of his pile.

Since then, Ferida has scrubbed her hands three times and the girls are still on their knees scouring the flagstones with brushes, indoors and out.

"I said hello to her," Moug says, scrubbing tight circles into the floor. "Just yesterday. She wore a red hat. Did One-Eyed Osman take that with her?"

Lolig tucks a strand of hair behind her ear. "Must have done, there was nothing left but lime. I spoke to her too, several times. Skinny little thing with nasty feet. She came from the mountains, from some village, north of Erzerum. Always muttering about the river and how each year some young boy would almost drown. She walked all the way from home to the desert then made her way back here. As if this place is any better."

"Yes. Why come back here?" Moug asks.

Khatoun takes a sip of her tea. "Maybe she was looking for someone."

"Who?" Lolig asks. "Who could she know here in Ourfa? I don't get it. Surely things must be better in Aleppo, why come back?"

"Maybe she was on her way to her village," Moug shrugs, "and only got this far."

"Probably," Khatoun says. "Returning to something familiar. Like the Kelaynak bird. Everyone wants to go back home, especially if they've been forced to leave. Even if home was no good we turn it into paradise up here," she taps her head. "We prefer the safety of what we know to what we don't. A lot of people don't like anything new or different."

"That doesn't make sense," Moug says, her face pink with the exertion of scrubbing. "Every day is different. We never live the same day twice but we're not afraid to get up in the morning. At least I'm not. I like the morning."

"Good," Lolig laughs. "You can get up early and make the tea from now on."

"Giggling and laughing?" Ferida snaps, stepping back into the kitchen holding her broom by the neck. "A poor girl died from hunger on our doorstep this morning and you find it funny? I want these floors shining by lunchtime. The whole city is filled with disease and we won't be laughing with typhus stupor in our brains. Now get scrubbing. And you..." she glares at Khatoun, "haven't you got sewing to do? Your girls are getting lazy in the workroom."

Khatoun picks up her cup and heads towards the workroom, winking at Lolig and Moug as she goes.

The sewing girls are taking a break, leaning over their machines and gossiping as they share weak tea. They sit up as

Khatoun enters and start tugging at seams and rearranging materials under their Singers.

"*Pari louys*, *Digin* Khatoun," they chime in unison. Khatoun waves them down, drifting from machine to machine, checking what is left to be done. The orders for dresses have continued despite the wretched state of the city. There is nothing like war to widen the gap between those that have and those that don't, and sequins and frills are still in high demand. It seems the hungrier people are, the more they need to distract themselves with frivolity.

"Did they take the girl away?" Bzdig Shoushun asks.

"Yes. One-Eyed Osman came."

"Poor little thing. All alone in a doorway." Bzdig Shoushun blows her nose. "I feel so guilty. If only we could have fed her."

"And all the others like her?" Serpuhi asks. "We can't feed everyone. We don't have the resources. Look at us — if it weren't for this place we'd be in exactly the same situation. And why guilty? You didn't cause this famine."

"I know — but I can't sleep at night, thinking about it. It eats away at me." Bzdig Shoushun takes a fine pair of scissors and starts to snip away at some embroidery that has gone wrong.

"Sleep?" Gadarine moans. "I get two hours if I'm lucky. During the day I manage to keep myself occupied. Sewing these beautiful dresses, I forget that we're in war, that people are dying on our doorstep and we are virtually prisoners in this house. Every night I wake up in a panic and nothing I do can comfort me back to sleep. I'm so tired I can hardly see in front of me."

"It's because you push your fears into the dark," Serpuhi says. "And when you sleep the darkness wakes up. Everything you've shoved back there comes alive and eats at you. That's why I maintain a temper — if something bothers me I get it out right there and then."

"Oh. That's why you're always smashing dishes," Bzdig Shoushun smiles, "to keep calm."

"Maybe," Serpuhi holds up the bodice of a dress covered in gold tendrils for Khatoun to see. "At least I get a good night's sleep and my sewing is better than yours because I can see straight."

"But then you have broken dishes and Ferida to deal with!" Gadarine quips, a quick darting look at Khatoun.

"*One!* One dish in all the years I've been here. Well, one dish and a teacup. And they were both accidents."

Khatoun waves her hand in the air. "I think that's enough gossip for now. We need to keep working so we can feed ourselves. Thank God we still have orders."

"*Park Asdoudzo.*"

"Thank God? Hah! I'm sure we should be grateful, *Digin* Khatoun – but personally I hate making these stupid clothes for rich fat women who have no idea what's going on outside their doors." Serpuhi tugs at the knots on the underside of the bodice. "We do all this work for them and they act like they love us but in reality we're nothing to them. *Giavour.* None of them would think twice if we had to leave or if we died of hunger. They wouldn't even notice so long as their dresses were made on time."

"That's not true," Khatoun says, crossing over to the young girl and picking up the dress. "We have many friends who work hard to give us business. They could easily go to another seamstress and then we'd be starving as well. This is beautiful Serpuhi, *Begum* Şenay will be delighted."

She hands back the dress and heads to the rear of the room, settling down at her own machine set up on the floor. She unfolds a gossamer shawl, part of a wedding trousseau, and begins to unpick the scalloped hem where it has puckered. After a while the chatter stops, the sound of fabric rustles through the room and the starving girl is forgotten; a pebble dropped to the bottom of a well.

"At least we're still together," Khatoun whispers, unravelling a string of stitches. "Some of us, at least." As the silver thread pulls away hundreds of little hexagonal sequins rain into her lap, an iridescent galaxy of familiar faces. There, with her ever-arched brow is sister-in-law Sophia nudging her, a young, frightened bride, into opening her wings. And there's Anni – surrounded by an ocean of children who are now fatherless. And Sammi, their father. Poor, bright Sammi who could ride faster than them all but still got caught and hacked to pieces by a mob he must have known. And her father, Thooma, high on hashish these days. And Mertha, her mother, frail as an onion skin ever since she woke up, her hair in disarray, to find no news of her beloved brothers;

the two of them vanished into thin air like the whole Armenian Quarter. No bodies to grieve for, no watch to pocket or ring to touch, just ash that she had watched from the rooftop and dusted casually from her locks. And the stitches unravel and there is Seyda of the red hair and Aram and his broken face and Iskender and her four children, thanks be to God, and Ferida and the girls. And the machines continue to hum as they have over the years, binding them all together.

Bang! The door flies open in the usual way and there, standing in the sunny triangle that spills in from the hallway, is Ferida.

"Good," she barks. "Glad to see you all working at last. Bzdig Shoushun, when you finish, go and help with the boys. Serpuhi, since you hate making these stupid clothes so much you can come with me. We have carrion to buy so I can make lunch. Chop-chop," she claps her hands and disappears down the bright corridor that connects the workroom to the rest of the house.

Serpuhi folds away her sewing and adjusts her headscarf. "Why me?" she complains. "I hate going out."

"We need food," Khatoun shrugs. "Just stick close to Ferida and do what she says."

"Yes. Nobody messes with Ferida," Gadarine grins, "especially if she has Grundug with her."

The girls roar with laughter. "That mutt is half blind!"

"And lame…"

"And stinky…"

"Not to mention the messes he makes in the courtyard," Bzdig Shoushun slips in under her breath. "It's disgusting."

"Grundug is like Ferida's son," Khatoun says. "And despite his age he's still a good deterrent…"

"Yes, nobody dares come near for fear of catching mange!"

"Then you'll be fine, Serpuhi – you've already got it!" Gadarine yanks at Serpuhi's braid and Serpuhi turns from the bowl where she's been washing her hands and flicks water at her.

"Serpuhiiiiiiiiii!" Ferida yells from kitchen, "Lunch time *today*; not next week!"

The sun is already high when they set off, poor Grundug dragging behind on a leash. He droops his head and looks at Serpuhi, willing her to let go of the rope so he can sniff his way back to the cool flagstones under the kitchen table. A playful breeze scatters litter along the cobblestones and the stench of refuse fills the air. The trio slip through the uncluttered lanes to the market place. Once, it bustled with women elbowing each other over apples and apricots. Today the *meydan* is empty. The smell of spice lingers but the stalls are bare. The pyramids of fruit and vegetables have been replaced with strips of cloth laid on the ground and scattered with a handful of home grown produce. Bands of children squat with outstretched palms, defecating where they sit. A few shops are open for business and in the far corner Etci Tosun The Meat Man stands in his doorway, his shoes covered in sawdust. His ears sprout hair thick as a sheep's tail and his fleshy nose dissects a single grey eyebrow that curls up into wings at the sides. He lounges in the sunshine, using a knife to clean his filthy nails. He looks up as they approach and cracks a yellow-brown grin.

"Ah, Ferida *Hanum*," he beams as she pushes past him into the shop. "Always a delight to see your beautiful smile."

"*Siktir git*, Meat Man," Ferida barks. "Serpuhi, tie Grundug to the post outside and get in here." She turns to face the bachelor (who, had he not loved whore-mongering so much, might have had a decent wife to clean him up a bit) and holds out a handful of coins.

"Don't even think of cheating me. I want something edible – not gristle and bones and none of that spongy *kak* you call goat. I can tell horse meat when I eat it."

The eyebrow quivers and Etci Tosun the Meat Man exhales a little laugh. He shivers theatrically, his belly quivering as he adjusts the drawstring of his *shalvar*.

"You make me so hot when you're angry. I have just the thing for you, mistress – no gristle, no sponge, just a few bones. That is, if you like pigeon." He smiles, his eye slithering appreciatively over Serpuhi as she bends down to tether Grundug.

"And where did you find pigeon?" Ferida asks, slipping between Serpuhi and the Meat Man. "There isn't a bird left alive in this town."

"Ah, the secrets of the trade," Etci Tosun says tapping his nose with a grimy finger. "You interested or not?"

"I'm interested – but you'll be splitting them open so I can check for maggots before I leave."

"Maggots, pah! You insult me, Ferida *Hanum*; if you weren't such a handsome woman I would be offended."

Ferida waves her hand in his face. "Enough, *pezevenk!* Now show me the birds."

"Birds?" Etci Tosun feigns surprise, elaborately counting out the coins in his hand. "But you've only given me enough for one pigeon!"

"Listen to me, *dungulugh*. I need to feed twenty people – I need more than one measly pigeon."

"Well..." the Meat Man scratches his head, tipping his chin back and looking over her shoulder at Serpuhi. "I have orders. People in high places."

Ferida turns her back on him. "Serpuhi." She puts her hand out for the little purse hidden in Serpuhi's skirts, extracts two more coins and spins back to face the butcher.

"Give me five birds."

"Three."

"Four, or I'll let it be known you're pilfering doves from *harem-lik* gardens with your *orospou* friends."

Etci Tosun's face breaks into a fetid smile. "You are stupendous, Ferida *Hanum*! Four birds for the lovely ladies coming right up."

He disappears into a back room and returns with a bloody parcel. Ferida sniffs as he opens it for her inspection. She peers into the birds' bony cavities and shoves the package to the bottom of her bag with a nod.

"They'll do."

"See you tomorrow, my partridge!" The butcher grins, leaning against the doorjamb and pretending to inspect his nails once more, forcing them to squeeze past his bloodied paunch as they leave.

"You stink bad and you're a rotten thief," Ferida retorts, hustling Serpuhi out into the sun. "If one of my girls gets sick I'll be roasting *your* tail."

They have only gone five paces when they remember poor Grundug. His leathery rope is still tied to the post outside the butcher's shop but Grundug is no longer attached. The tether has been severed and a tiny damp spot on the threshold indicates where the mutt's nose lay just moments before.

"Lost something?" Etci Tosun asks.

"My virginity," Ferida snaps, scanning the *meydan*. "Grundug!" she yells, shading her eyes against the sun. "Stupid dog. He's taken off for home again. I'll give him the slipper for this."

"Maybe he was hot, Ferida *jan*. Poor Grundug…he's old," Serpuhi starts.

"*I know how old he is!*" Ferida snaps back. "He's *still* supposed to be our guard dog. Come on, let's stop dawdling. We need okra – there's a girl at the other end who sometimes has them. Damn okra – it's the only thing I can't seem to grow."

As they step around the defecating children there is a sudden cry at the far end of the street. A group of Turkish soldiers start battering down a door whilst a woman shrieks from behind the latticework of her window above. As the soldiers swarm in, the guttersnipes rouse themselves from the filth and run towards the commotion.

"Deserters!" they yelp, looking towards the sky – for who knew what delights could fall from the pockets of a fleeing army boy! In minutes mayhem has erupted across the rooftops as the soldiers leap from window to roof in hot pursuit of three barely dressed youths. The woman continues to screech as her house is ransacked and the shutters slam shut in adjacent homes. Ferida stops where she is.

"More bastards who couldn't afford to bribe their way out of the army. We don't want to see this. Come on." She turns on her heel and slips down an alley, hurrying Serpuhi ahead of her. "That's our shopping over for the day. Deserters? My *boutz*! Hungry men out for blood more like it, chasing kids for cash." She bustles past a door, narrowly escaping a bucket of soiled water being emptied into the street.

"*Kaknem!*" she yells.

"Serpuhi! Serpuhi!" someone hisses and the two women whirl round.

"Serpuhi! Here! This way!" A pretty young girl in a flowery apron stands in the doorway clutching the empty bucket. "Serpuhi *jan*, it's me, Shakeh!" Her blonde hair bounces in ridiculous ringlets as the girl beckons them over.

"Shakeh?" Serpuhi gasps, rushing to her friend and throwing her arms around her neck. Above them one of the deserting youths briefly considers suicide before spying a balcony on the other side of the street. He disappears for a second then is suddenly airborne, hurtling through the air as shots are fired after him. Ferida watches him crash through a window before turning to Shakeh.

"Do you mind if we come in for a moment?" she asks. "There's going to be soldiers in the street in about five seconds and you never know when they get a bit frisky."

"Yes, yes, of course! Come in, quick." Shakeh stands back and they duck into the courtyard and slam the door shut. "I can't believe it's you!" Shakeh yelps, hugging Serpuhi over and over. "This way – keep your voices down." She leads them across the tiled patio towards the kitchen, glancing above her to the balcony that runs along the inside of the courtyard one storey up. When they are safely seated around the kitchen table, she turns to them smiling.

"Where have you been hiding?" she asks Serpuhi. "I haven't seen you since you left *Digin* Aghavni's. That must be six years ago."

"*Me* hiding? I've been at the Agha Boghos house the whole time. It's *you* who disappeared. You never came back to church – nobody knew where you were. We thought you were dead."

Shakeh crosses to the interior door and leans against it, listening. The sound of singing carries through the walls from a distant room and she relaxes a little.

"Well I'm alive as you can see, I just don't go to certain places anymore," she whispers. "I'm not allowed. The man who hired me...I started off sewing dresses for his sisters and wives. That was a few months after you left. I was too busy to do anything other than sew at first and then...well...after a while he took me as his third wife."

Ferida shakes her head. "Three wives? What does a man do with them all? No, no, no, spare me the details. I can imagine." She scrapes her chair back, and heads for the stove. "I see water boiling. You two catch up – I'll make some tea." She busies herself at the range, searching out cups and spoons with precision.

Shakeh smiles at Serpuhi. "They're good to me," she says quietly, "the other wives. I mean one of them hates me – the Ugly One, but the other wife treats me well. That's her singing. The Ugly One doesn't like *her* either. They used to gang up on me but that stopped when they realised I was happier in the kitchen than...anywhere else." She accepts a cup of tea from Ferida then crosses over to a stoneware jar and removes the cloth from the top. "*Choereg?*" she asks.

"*Choereg?* Just one," Ferida says stuffing the whole thing into her mouth. She nods her approval. "Not bad – you make them?"

Shakeh nods. "It's what I do. Bake, pickle, sew, clean. The usual. It's getting harder – food is scarce but he seems to have connections. But that's enough about me. Tell me what you've been doing these last six years." She passes a pastry to Serpuhi. "Married?"

Serpuhi gobbles and laughs. "Don't be silly!" She looks over at Ferida then takes a breath. "There *was* a boy..." she pauses as Ferida's back stiffens, then continues. "There was a boy...at church...but he disappeared..." her voice trails off. She picks at the seeds decorating the *choereg* and slips them into her mouth with her finger.

"Did he have a name, church boy?" Shakeh asks.

"Nerses," Serpuhi nods, "Nerses Terzian." A tear drops out her nose and Ferida starts.

"Terzian? The silversmith's boy? I know his father...knew him...Ephraim. He could dig out a rotten tooth..." She shakes her head. "Bastards. Not them...you know..."

Down the corridor the singing gets louder, the mournful ballad trying to escape the thick, stone walls. Shakeh dips her *choereg* into her tea.

"She's singing to her bird," she says. "He's traditional, our husband. Keeps his women inside and covered. Except for me. I can go to the market. And my hair? I have to wear it like this for him, curly curly, no veil." She crumbles pastry into her mouth and turns back to Serpuhi. "So, if you're not married what do you do?"

Serpuhi rolls her eyes. "Sew dresses."

"She's good," Ferida says. "Got a fine hand. Beautiful embroidery." She pats Serpuhi on the arm, gets up and wanders over to the range with her tea, poking into the cupboards, surreptitiously checking to see what's been stored away.

"*Digin* Khatoun has a good business," Serpuhi says. "There are ten of us sewing girls and we keep busy. You'd think people had more serious things on their mind than dresses, but no, they seem to want them even more."

"Ten of you!"

"Yes…but…" Serpuhi falters when she sees Ferida's expression.

"Nobody knows who's in the house and we'd like to keep it that way," Ferida says. "Understood?"

Shakeh nods. "House? Girls? I know nothing."

"We had a hard time right after the Armenian Quarter burnt down but then the orders came flooding in," Serpuhi continues. "In fact, we're busier than ever, but now they bring their own fabrics because we can't get them."

"All the cloth merchants are dead," Ferida says, "that's why."

"So now they dig up some fancy fabric – curtains, tablecloths, their grandmother's trousseau – and come running to us, hoping *Digin* Khatoun will solve their problems with a dress. And she always does."

At that moment the *haremlik* door flies open and the room erupts into chaos as a half-naked little boy runs through the door and disappears under Shakeh's skirt. He is closely followed by a heavy-set woman in vile green.

"Barış! Come here!" The green dress shrieks. "I'm going to skin you alive!" The little boy skitters across the floor and retreats under the table clutching a string of beads behind his back. The woman in the dress stops to catch her breath and takes in Shakeh's guests. She glares at them, her hands on her hips, her bosom heaving. "And who said you could entertain, Shakeh?" she asks disdainfully. "And handing out food? Don't you know there's a famine in the city?" She grabs the *choereg* jar and peers inside to see what's left.

"This is a friend of mine from *Digin* Aghavni's sewing school and her sponsor, *Digin* Ferida," Shakeh says. "And this," she gestures towards the woman, "this is my sister."

"Sister? Don't put us in the same category," the woman sneers. She smoothes the fabric of her vivid housedress over her square hips. "I am Fatima, first and favourite wife of Hakim Kadir."

Ferida takes Fatima's hand and brings it to her lips. "Fatima *Bayan*, what a pleasure to meet you. We were passing and came in to pay our respects. And may I say, that is a beautiful dress you have on, the colour suits your complexion most amicably."

"Thank you," Fatima smirks. "I was wearing a set of beads that highlighted the outfit perfectly but the brat took them." She peers under the table. "Go on, swallow them you little half-breed. I hope you choke!" She stamps her foot and Barış shimmies further back beyond her reach.

"I'll get them for you, sister," Shakeh says. "You go back to your rest."

"You're damn right you'll get them for me," Fatima snaps. "And when you do, send the mongrel in to see me so I can beat him senseless."

"Yes, sister."

"And stop calling me *sister* you ugly beanpole!" Fatima shouts. "And tie back your hair! It's...obscene." She turns back to Ferida. "These young girls — they have no idea of manners these days." She swivels on her heel and sweeps out the kitchen.

"The Ugly One?" Ferida whispers as Fatima's footsteps retreat down the corridor. "Please don't tell me the other one is even uglier."

"The Ugly One," Shakeh nods. "I like what you said about the dress."

"*Süslü püslü*," Ferida grins. "We have to go — it's getting late." Slowly she bends low enough to stick her head under the table. "Come here little boy — give your auntie those cheap nasty beads before you swallow them. If you do we'll have to pull them out of your bottom like worms." She straightens up, grinning broadly. "Handsome little chap," she says, one eyebrow raised, "Blonde curls."

Shakeh nods. "Fatima couldn't have children so...I...he...belongs to the family."

"He's beautiful," Serpuhi smiles as the little boy crawls out from under the table and hands Ferida the necklace.

"Worms?" he asks.

"Yes, worms," Shakeh says taking the beads from Ferida. "Let's go and give them back." She hoists Barış onto her hip and they walk through the cool leafy courtyard to the back gate. "I'll come and visit," she smiles. "The Agha Boghos house in the Assyrian Quarter. We're neighbours. I'll come soon."

"They call it the Pink House."

"The Pink House."

"Yes."

The women kiss and hug and pinch little Barış's cheeks before stepping back into the flat glare of noon outside the gate.

"We're late," Ferida grumbles. "Mertha's going to be at the window pulling out the last of her hair."

"Why don't we go back the way we came?" ventures Serpuhi, eyeing the narrow street that winds through the overhanging houses in front of them.

"I don't know," Ferida muses, "I think we'd better keep going – it's longer this way but better to get there in one piece than run into those thugs again. *Hayde*, let's go." She sweeps ahead clutching her birds to her chest.

Their detour takes them north towards the old Armenian Quarter. A year has passed since fire demolished the whole quarter but an acrid smell pervades. The walls that once stood tall now tilt in blackened ruins.

"Two thousand years up in smoke in two days," Ferida mutters as they grow closer. "Locusts. Swarmed through and picked the place to bits. It's a crime. It's all a crime."

Around the corner and they run into a pair of women sitting in the rubble at the side of the road. The older of the two has her face turned up to the sky, weeping. Her companion, the opposite. Knees to chest, face hidden in a threadbare dress. A comma to her friend's exclamation mark.

"What now?" Ferida mutters. She stops, sizes the pair up then walks over to them. "What are you doing here?" she asks. "In the rubble?" The younger woman refuses to look up, the elder shakes her head miserably.

"It took us months!" she cries. "Months to find our way home. We've bribed and hidden and done unmentionable things to get here and this is what greets us!" She waves her hand around her. "From the camps in Rakka to Aleppo to here, searching, searching for Mr. Leslie and look what we find. Ruins! Nothing but dust where our house used to stand!" Her hands flap at her sides like lost birds.

"Mr. Leslie?" Ferida asks. "The Reverend Francis Leslie, the American missionary?"

The old lady nods and wipes her chin of tears. "When trouble was brewing we gave all our valuables to Mr. Leslie for safe keeping. Jewellery, the deeds to the house, my husband's life insurance with the New York Company. Everything. Now he's disappeared and let us down."

Ferida squats down next to the two women. "Who told you to come looking for Mr. Leslie?"

The woman shrugs. "What else is there to do? Who else is there to look for?"

"I have some news for you," Ferida says. "Mr. Leslie didn't let you down. On the contrary, he would have done anything to help us, poor man." She pauses for a moment and shrugs. "Mr. Leslie is dead."

The younger woman looks up and Serpuhi jumps at the sight of her face. One eye is half-closed, the other missing altogether – a cavernous hollow burrowing into her skull where it should be instead.

"I told you he was dead," she says, her mouth pulling to the side, displaying a handful of broken teeth. "Only a few of us have a second chance." She laughs as she stands up, almost cheerful. "So now we know, *Tantig*; we have nothing. We are nothing." She starts to sway, moving her feet in some strange dance.

"Where are you staying?" Ferida asks as Serpuhi backs away from the dancing girl.

"Staying?" The young woman throws her head back. "Don't *stay* anywhere! Blow like the dust. The wandering souls lost between Heaven and Earth, that's us." She dances closer to Serpuhi, glaring at her through her one distorted eye.

"Shut up, Zagiri," the older woman says turning to Ferida. She taps her temple with a grubby finger. "She's not well," she mouths.

"So where do you go from here?" Ferida asks.

The older woman shrugs. "We thought we might find something here. We've been to the desert and back. We wanted to stay in Aleppo but you need a special permit so we made our way back. I hoped to find more than this."

"Hah!" Ferida scoffs. "There is more but you would never have got your home back – even if it were still standing. Anything left habitable is housing the Turks fleeing the Russian front at Van and Tiblis."

"Haven't they taken enough?" the auntie cries. "They took our men, our valuables, the clothes from our backs. Now they take our homes? *Eshek siksin!* Take them! Rot in them!" She spits between her feet.

"They are," Serpuhi says. "Rotting in them. They say 'ghosts' are choking them in their sleep."

"Peasants," Ferida clears her throat and spits too. "I have nothing against peasants but this lot are full of straw. Half of them poisoned themselves already using bronze pots to cook in, the rest are so stupid they burn the roof beams for firewood and wonder why the roof falls in on them while they're asleep. Ghosts? My *boutz*."

Zagiri hops from foot to foot, chuckling. "Dig a hole big enough for someone and you'll fall in it," she sings, lifting her skirts to her knees.

"Zagiri, keep your clothes on," her friend warns.

Ferida watches the strange dance. Zagiri circling Serpuhi menacingly, her skirts brushing her thighs. "Listen, you two can't be in the streets. It's not safe." She clutches the package from the butcher to her heart and groans. "Got anything to eat?"

"A handful of okra I saved since Aleppo – we were going to cook it for our first meal. But where to cook?"

"Okra? There is a God. Come with us," Ferida sighs. "*Hayde*, follow me. We have to move though – we're late and people will be worried. You can share our food and have a bed for the night. Tomorrow we'll figure something out." She sticks her hand out and helps the older woman up. "Ferida Agha Boghos, pleased to meet you."

"Vartanoush Maghakian. God bless you, Ferida. *Agh*, my bones!"

By now the streets are deserted, shuttered against the afternoon sun. Ferida strides ahead, talking as fast as she can in an effort to get everyone moving at the same speed as her babbling.

"So, you gave your lives to Mr. Leslie."

"Everything," the woman nods. "It was either that or the Ottoman Bank or Mr. Eckart, whom my husband didn't trust. Many people hid things in their homes; dug holes and buried them in the yard to come back for later. I would have done except that we had no yard. We trusted Mr. Leslie; he was a personal friend."

"Scratch your own head with your own nails!" Zagiri shouts.

"Ferida!" Serpuhi calls from behind. "She's taking her clothes off!"

"Just keep her moving," Ferida yells over her shoulder. Zagiri skips along between them, her dress unbuttoned, her hair loose. Vartanoush is panting with the effort of keeping up with Ferida and valiantly ignoring the girl unravelling behind them.

"How did he die, Mr. Leslie?" she asks.

"Depends who you ask. Poison is the short answer. His wife was having a baby and when she went to hospital in Aintab he stayed behind to look after the Mission. He was going to join her but the battle began in the Armenian Quarter and he got stuck here. Once it was over he was told to report to government headquarters. They were interested in his relationship with 'suspicious' Armenians. He was threatened and bullied. At the end of October he was found dead with a suicide note on his body."

"He killed himself? *Asdvadz!*" Vartanoush cries, making the sign of the cross.

"*Eshou botch* he killed himself! He was a scholar. The note they found on him was a fake, written by an illiterate – my brother told me."

"What do you mean?"

"Everyone knows it was forged."

"Why? What did it say?"

"Nobody was to blame and he was taking his own life with poison. What was fake was it referred to the battle of Ourfa as a 'revolution.' When Mr. Leslie was alive he was always in hot water with the authorities for calling it 'self-defence'. You see, the idiots couldn't even remember that and get the language right."

"Poor Mr. Leslie. And all the stuff he kept for everyone? Our deeds and papers?"

"Stuffing the coffers of government officials by now. My brother Iskender can tell you more when we get home. He follows the news. Doesn't talk much, so people jabber away in front of him like he's deaf. Give him a whisky and you'll be surprised at how much he knows. He doesn't trust those Eckart brothers either, although by all accounts one of them is a good egg. The other one, Franz, well, he preaches all high and mighty about God but in reality he loathes us Armenians. A missionary straight from hell."

"That's what my husband said."

"He was right. All the stuff given to Eckart for safekeeping just made him richer. He betrayed everyone who trusted him.

Sold some of them out after giving them refuge. Lots of people have come looking for him to get their stuff back – just like you with Mr. Leslie."

"And?"

"He laughs in their faces."

"How can anyone be so heartless?" Vartanoush asks. "Surely someone in the government could force him to pay up. You would think that anyone who survived the marches and made their way back home would deserve a little pity."

"Fuck pity!" Ferida spits. She stops, takes a deep breath and turns to Vartanoush, "Sorry. It's just that I've had a hard day so far and profanity gives me release. Have to watch my tongue at home. Can't say anything without offending someone."

"No offence," Vartanoush smiles. "I feel like that myself sometimes."

"Anyway," Ferida growls, setting off at a slightly gentler pace so that Serpuhi and Zagiri can catch up, "there is no pity in this town. And the government is the worst thief. As soon as the resistance was over they swarmed the shopping district, sealed up all the Armenian shops and confiscated everything. A supposed 'committee' came from Constantinople. Thieves! First they set up headquarters, which they furnished with stuff they'd confiscated – all the best rugs and everything – then they auctioned off the rest. Didn't have a clue about prices. Some stuff was sold for nothing, the rest was overpriced. God knows what, if anything, reached the crooks in government. The store rooms were ransacked before the auctions even began. The inventory was jigged every night so the auctioneers could line their pockets too. What was left? Iskender knows more than me, he'll tell you everything when we get home."

"Ferida!" Serpuhi cries from the rear. "Her *underwear!*" A hundred yards behind, Serpuhi is struggling with Zagiri's naked breasts.

Vartanoush looks back and shrugs, "It's pointless. Nobody can stop her."

"Never mind. We're here now. Quick." Ferida ducks into the cool back alley that leads to the kitchen entrance. "Mind the lime on the doorstep. We had an accident this morning." She takes the keys from her pocket, jostles with the door and hustles the others inside.

Lolig is the one to greet them, her hair undone and eyes red. She jumps up from her seat by the range as the door opens.

"Ferida *jan*..." she starts.

"Not now, Lolig! Go and get water so our guests can clean up. And where's Grundug? The stupid mutt ran off again."

"Ferida *jan*..."

"Not now! Can't you see I have women here who need help?"

Lolig bolts with Serpuhi and the two women. It is Khatoun who slips back into the kitchen with the end of Grundug's leash in her hand. She hands the slippery rope to Ferida.

"He's in the courtyard, sister. He made it back. I think he was looking for you. His throat was cut. There were children after him. I think, maybe...I think, maybe they thought they could eat him. I covered him with your apron. In his favourite place by the fountain. Go."

Keep Quiet and Sew

Ourfa, October 1919
Alice

I never spoke much but I could raise my eyebrow in a way that said it all and this was the look I gave Sarkis when he insisted he keep my photo, saying he'd wear it over his heart forever.

Sarkis was the most beautiful boy I'd ever seen. Some may have thought he was too pretty, that he looked like a girl, but to me he was perfect, like Jesus. Curly black hair, pale skin, dark eyes, eyelashes, long-long. His lips met mine often when the stars were out and the moon wasn't looking and on those mornings I woke up damp with Umme Ferida looking at me funny. But there's no sin in dreaming is there? He was tall and slim and as elegant as his auntie — without her sour air. Sarkis was my first love and we were engaged and torn apart without ever having spoken a word. Talking was saved for the wedding night right before you lie down on that clean, white marriage sheet. And we never got there.

I was sixteen when he asked to marry me and he was two years older — already a man. We lived in the pink house in Ourfa, in the Assyrian Quarter. The war was over and Umme Ferida kept telling us how poor we were but really we were rich because we had each other. That's what my mother said. The churches were open again and that's where I saw him for the first time, with his Auntie Tatou and sister Sylvie, all of them dressed up like something out of a book. My brothers poked fun at them behind their backs but Ferida said they were family now and we had to be nice. Auntie Tatou's daughter, Isabelle, had married my uncle Adom and because of that, Sarkis and Sylvie were allowed to visit our house after the sermon on Sundays.

At first I didn't like him but then I caught him looking at me in a certain way and before I knew it, the dreams began and I became sick with his love.

It was his sister who followed me to the baths. I saw her looking at my naked body as I scrubbed in the steam, whispering to her friends and nodding as they checked I was all in one piece with wide enough hips. She smiled at me in my dress later, offered me a slice of orange and I knew she would tell him that I had pleased her.

They had no parents left, Sarkis and Sylvie, only their sour Auntie Tatou and so it was Sylvie who came to the house with his proposal, bearing gifts. Two gold bracelets twisted together like snakes with rubies for eyes that had belonged to their mother. Everyone talked. Talk talk talk and then my father took me aside.

"No more sitting on my knee," he teased, "you're getting married, little girl."

The priest conducted the engagement ceremony under a fat moon on our roof and we exchanged rings. Plain gold for him, an emerald for me. We didn't speak but I knew that he loved me. I knew he was the one that had sent Sylvie to spy on me, and the thought that she had seen me undressed made me burn, as if it had been him. When I shut my eyes I could see our future together – all the places we would go. I could smell it in his hair as he brushed my cheek with his lips that night, the night we were promised to each other and the dancing began. My life was before me and it smelt of the sea.

The days that followed were like a dream. I had never been in love before and here I was – first time and already loved back. My father was happy, my mother too. My brothers – they teased me about indelicate things, made me blush and Umme Ferida curse. She slapped my head for listening and dragged me into the kitchen to cook. And with my mother I began the embroidery for my chest. Flowers and stars and the letters of our names twisted together in silk thread. S.A.S.A.

And I was going that way, like a blind girl, all foolish, chest open to his love, dreaming of our future together and suddenly-suddenly they told me it was over. Poof. I was no longer engaged.

I sat at the machine and cried into my sewing until my mother took all the silks away from me and gave me calico instead. She said she was afraid I'd ruin her orders and we needed them badly.

I felt sure Sarkis had loved me but he'd dropped me just like a stone in a well. Hadn't even come himself – only sent Sylvie one evening to return the engagement gifts we'd given him. I knew it was her fault, us breaking up, and after that day I never spoke to her again. Strange spirits follow bad energy. We knew always to be careful of what we said in troubled times, lest we inadvertently curse someone, what with all the strange spirits agitating around us. Even at the baths we kept our backs turned and Sylvie came late to church and stood apart from us, near the door.

It was my little brother, Solomon, who told me about the letter. He said it was from Sarkis and he'd read it but that nobody knew. He'd found it in our father's office, partly burned. I waited for someone to mention it to me but my parents never said a word. They acted as if Sarkis were dead. Nobody talked to me about my heart, only Solomon, who asked if I had heard it crack when it broke. He offered to teach me chess to heal it. Pawn, king, queen, but my mind wouldn't stay.

Eventually my mother told me about the letter because she couldn't take my tears any more. She said Sarkis had pleaded in his letter to come and talk to me but my father had refused. "He's nobody to us," he'd said and thrown the letter into the fire.

It was Umme and Mamma who agreed to let Sarkis come in secret after I begged and begged and begged them. They arranged it for one evening at ten o'clock when my father and brothers would be asleep.

The three of us, Mamma, Umme Ferida and I were sewing when Sarkis knocked on the back door. Umme Ferida let him in and brought him to the workshop. He'd brought a friend — a boy I had never seen before. They'd just finished work and had run to the baths before coming. They entered our house in a cloud of cologne and cigarette smoke. I could see Sarkis had been crying like me. Mamma stood back. Umme Ferida stood between us and acted the go between.

She told the boys it had not been necessary for them to come. She was behaving as if this were a small problem that hadn't even bothered us. She said that since the engagement was over Sarkis could no longer visit but he'd been allowed this once as a favour since he was a relative. Then she asked him what he wanted.

Instead of replying to her, he came over to the sewing machine and asked me to stop what I was doing. I did, but kept my eyes turned away from his. I could hardly hear his words because of the roar of the sea in my ears.

"Speak to me," he said. "I just want to hear the beauty of your voice. Please. Say something."

I leaned over to Umme Ferida, who had followed him over, slipping her body like wire between us, and whispered in her ear.

"Alice wants her photograph back," Umme Ferida said, straightening up, her hand already out.

That's when he burst into tears right there in our very room.

"No! Her picture will stay with me until the day I die," he shouted. "Since I can't have you, the photograph will be my love and it will stay here." He banged his fist to his heart.

This is when I turned to face him and gave him my eyebrow. I don't like exaggeration, even when my heart is broken.

"You may not believe me," he said, "but I mean it. I love you. It wasn't me...it was...it was...it was the worm came out of the tree and ate the tree."

And then there was silence. We waited for an explanation and he opened and shut his mouth and twisted the buttons on his coat and tried to force out a sound but although his heart was full, his mouth was empty. After a while, my mother stood up. Usually she didn't say much, just watched everything and I wished she hadn't spoken then because I really did want to wait and hear what he had to say. But my mother always chose her moments carefully.

"Never mind, Sarkis," she said. "Go with God's blessings." Then she turned and left the room.

This left Umme Ferida and me alone with the boys. Sarkis was so close I could have reached past Ferida's shoulder and touched his beautiful face. I could smell his sweet breath, could see the blue vein beating in his neck. His hands were trembling and I thought he would do something stupid at any minute and I prayed that he would.

Umme shuffled her feet and put her hand in her pocket. "To conclude this visit," she said, "I think you should have this back." She held my emerald ring out to him but he shook his head.

"I want her to keep it," he said, "as I intend to keep hers." He pulled a chain out from under his shirt and the ring I had given him was hanging there. I saw his flesh, his sweet collarbones and the soft black hair at the top of his chest. I turned away from him again and pushed at the wheel of my sewing machine. Tac-atac-atac-atac, it sang.

"As you wish," Umme Ferida said, dragging him by the elbow to the door where his friend stood waiting.

I could feel his eyes on me the whole time. Sick black birds burning a hole in the back of my dress. I wanted to do something but I couldn't. The air was thick like molasses and I was pinned to my seat with no air in my throat. Tic-tock tick-tock I heard the clock and tac-atac-atac-atac, the machine, and then a cold breeze and slam! the door shut and only then did I turn around and he was gone and my mother was there in his place.

She walked over to me, her arms stretched out wide and she took me in and held me close, and then came Umme and she was crying and that made me cry too. We sat at the machine, all of us, and howled like dogs and if Grundug had still been alive he would have trembled at our feet. The ceiling above us creaked and shed plaster and my father shouted over the balcony, wondering what the hell was happening now! and Mamma went out to the fountain and looked up and said we were telling sad stories and remembering friends no longer with us and to go back to bed. And she looked at me and put her finger to her lips. Be quiet, she was saying. Not just for now, but for ever.

So I will keep quiet and sew. What good are words anyway? Words are nothing but hot air and vibration that disappear into thin air. Not like people who can appear forever in dreams. Hot and wet and smelling of the sea. Words are nothing but dead birds dropping. Words get you nowhere.

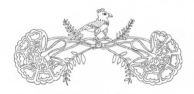

Words

Ourfa, November 1919
Khatoun

If she could take a needle and thread to her lips she would. She'd
stitch the top to the bottom with precise, even stitches. Black
thread, a sharp needle, done. Khatoun studies her face in the
mirror. Startled hair, puffy eyes. She's had eyes following her all
day long. Ferida, watching her silently, her mouth thin and puckered. Alice, trailing her like a shadow, weeping pools of grief.
A hundred guests shifting their eyes to the floor whenever she
passed and Adom, her own brother, covering his face with his
hands, the look in his eyes haunting her nonetheless. For was it
not his wife and unborn child under the earth today? And were
they not Khatoun's words that put them there?

She drops the cloth back over the mirror. All the mirrors will
stop today along with the clocks, and, uncounted and unseen,
the day will disappear into the air like ether and only foolish gossips will keep it alive – passing it down generation to generation
with their embroidered truths. Khatoun snuffs out the lamp and
steps outside into the alley behind the kitchen. She'll need to
walk far to outrun the shadows tonight. She turns south towards
the Dergah Gardens, holding close to the wall, eyes sharp, voice
buried, mind busy-busy.

It had been spring, a full moon, when Ferida had come muttering to Khatoun that Alice was sick.

"She's sleeping late, pushing her food around the plate and
getting up in the middle of the night to sit on the floor of the
roof half-naked. She's going slow like an idiot," Ferida tapped
her forehead, "and spending far too long in the bathroom. If
she washes her hair any more she'll get pneumonia and if we
don't get to the bottom of this she'll waste away to nothing." She
threw the laundry onto the table and began tugging at the sheets.
"Something is not right," she muttered into the folds. "Trust me,

I know." And so Khatoun did what any mother would do. She kept quiet and watched.

Ferida was right. There were midnight talks with the moon dressed practically in air, and the mornings were half over before Alice sat down at her machine — although her sewing miraculously improved. Her appetite seemed to have vanished but the angular slant to her cheek seemed to have more to do with an emerging beauty than sickness. Alice was quiet, that much was true. But sullen? No. That was a spinster's notion. Someone who had never known love.

When she thought no one was watching, Alice's face glowed; her eyes lit up with dreams that left her cheeks pink and a furtive smile playing her lips. Her hair smelled of spring rain caught in the barrel outside the door and she paid great attention to darning every small hole that appeared in her sleeve or stockings. And there was more. A name muttered secretly into the corners of rooms that slid along the walls in a long soft sigh and disturbed the moths around the lamplight. At first all Khatoun could make out was a hiss.

"Saaaassssssisss," Alice would breathe. Sometimes she would give in to that smile and at others it looked as if her heart were about to crack. Which is, of course, what it was about to do.

Love. Those early days. Smelling your love on every breeze. Touching where they have touched, grazing your hand over their fingerprints, your body alive with desire. If you could just lean your shoulder close enough or find some way to take their lemonade glass and feel their flesh under yours. A hand or a brushed finger. The sweet agony of not knowing if they want you the way you want them even though their eyes are on you whenever you turn. The heat of not knowing, burning the air between you. Other people everywhere, eyes too many, the sound of the sea in a shell in your ears, darkness and blinding light, warm breath just paces behind you and then a lock of hair lifted from the nape of your neck. It's enough to drop your knees and make you fall endlessly through deep sky and sea and into their arms. So.

Khatoun was not so old that she couldn't remember the first days of love. She'd been the same age as Alice — younger even — and could still recall the heat and terror of fire in the sky and the brush of Iskender's breath at her neck. She knew without a doubt that her daughter was in love. But with whom? It was obviously someone they knew – this was not a love affair with thin air. But who could it be? Alice rarely left the house and if she did venture beyond the walls, it was always with family. Where could she have met this boy that was so valiantly disturbing her sleep?

"Saaaasssssssisss?" Khatoun tried whispering into the room, but of course there was no reply.

Spring turned to summer. A dry, dusty summer thick with the kind of heat that leaves you blind in your room by midday. After lunch (meagre as it was) the whole house would sink into a stupor, Alice taking to her bed, her coverlet of pale blue satin kicked to the floor, the jug of water covered with lace to protect it from flies and a delicate flag of palms fashioned into a fan in her hand. There she'd lie, stirring the warm air, the sweat pooling between her breasts until sleep finally took over. At dusk she'd pull on some clothes and head downstairs to join the family, the smile on her lips infuriating Ferida who knew that *that* was what was turning her vegetables ripe before their time. Khatoun said nothing. She didn't want to draw attention. The more people watching, the less there'd be to see.

It came to the hottest day of the year. The roof ablaze with white heat, scalding to the feet, even in slippers. Ferida and Khatoun leapt between the washing lines, exchanging one load of laundry with another. Stiff shirts into baskets, damp bedding over the lines.

"Alloooo!" a thin voice called up from the street below, faint at first, growing more insistent with each call. "Alloooo?"

Ferida crept over to the balustrade and peered down. It was so bright up there she couldn't see anything below. She shut her eyes, screwed up her face for a moment then opened them and sighed. "People," she frowned.

"What do you mean *people*?" Khatoun asked.

"There's people at our door," she scowled. "What do they want? Whatever it is, we've got nothing to give them."

Khatoun laughed at her sister-in-law. "You like visitors," she teased. "It gives you something to do. Tell me who it is." She sniffed at the armpits of her dress and began fixing her headscarf.

"Relatives. Yours," Ferida spat after another look. "Now we'll have to feed them."

"Relatives?"

"Your brother's wife's mother, what do they call her, and her nephew and niece. She's holding an umbrella. Lace!"

Khatoun laughed. "A parasol. That's Tatou. We'd better get out the cutlery."

"That's what I mean. Who needs visitors? Locusts. Thieves. *Kaknem!*" Ferida hung her head over the parapet and called down. "Hey! Up here! Hello! Welcome!" She waved frantically and the thin voice downstairs 'allooed' back again. "Wait there – I'll be straight down!" Ferida yelled. She dragged the basket of sheets over to the staircase pushing Khatoun ahead of her. "You go down and let them in; I'll finish this and follow you. Go on, go down, you shouldn't be in this glare anyway with your eyes."

When she got downstairs Khatoun found Alice hanging by the stove, the kitchen door open already. Tatou stood in the alley-way, her lace umbrella shading herself but not the two young-sters sweating by her side. She smiled elegantly and tilted her head at an angle forcing Khatoun to reach up to kiss her.

"How delightful to see you," Tatou said, planting a kiss in the air.

Khatoun ducked back into the kitchen and beckoned them in. "Come in, out of the heat."

Tatou shook her head and shimmied backwards a step. "Im-possible, my dear. I'm far too busy." She tapped the pretty wrist-watch, worn on the same hand that held the parasol aloft. "The children wanted to see you, though, so I said I'd ask. If it's not convenient they can accompany me, but…"

"No, no! Of course. Sarkis, Sylvie, come in!" Khatoun ushered the sweaty teenagers past her into the kitchen. "We love young company. Welcome!"

Tatou smiled and arched her neck dangerously. She looked pleased with herself and, despite the heat, made no move in ei-ther direction, in or out. Instead she glanced around theatrically before dropping her voice to a whisper. "Spoken to your brother recently?" she asked, giving her parasol a quick twirl.

Khatoun shook her head. "Adom? Not for weeks. Why?" She wished Tatou would either come in or leave instead of keeping her hovering on the doorstep like this. "There's nothing wrong, is there?"

"*Au contraire!*" Tatou paused then let out a great sigh. "*Agh*, I really should wait for your brother to tell you himself but, since

I've started, I feel obliged to continue. I hope I won't regret it. Well, I'll spit it out...my darling Isabelle is expecting. Your brother Adom is going to be father at last!"

Khatoun let out a gasp, "Oh! How wonderful!" She took Tatou's face in her hands and gave her a clammy kiss on both cheeks. Her brother and his young wife had been trying desperately for a baby for years. They'd tried everything and, having exhausted every available herb and ointment left in the city, had all but given up. It truly was great news. A new baby in these times.

"Yes, it is wonderful," Tatou beamed. "Of course, I shall have to tell them I told you. I hope they're not angry with me. How oddly impulsive I can be sometimes. And please don't tell your parents — I think they should hear it from your brother himself, don't you? Personally I detest gossip. Anyway, I must go, I don't want to keep them waiting. I have a man lingering at the end of the street, ready to take me there. Shall I send your love?" She dipped her head into the kitchen and with an, "*à bientôt, enfants,* try to be good," turned on her heel and stepped delicately away over the cobbles.

"Good," Ferida said, joining Khatoun at the door as Tatou sailed away down the alley, her umbrella held at a fetching angle. "One less for lunch. And *what's* so wonderful? Why're you all grinning like idiots?"

"My brother's having a baby," Khatoun smiled.

Ferida swatted the air with her dishcloth. "And that makes you *happy*? Pah!" she huffed. "Half the kids in this country are starving, the other half orphans. What do they want more children for? Who's going to feed them?"

Khatoun laughed, opened her mouth as if to reply but simply shut the door instead. She slid the heavy bolt in place, turned, and saw it.

Saw Alice rooted to her spot by the stove and Sarkis standing opposite, the air between them trembling so much it sucked the life out of the flame Ferida kept trying to light on the stove. So, here it was. How obvious. Her brother's wife's mother's brother's son. Close family. Sweet, dark-eyed Sarkis with the poetic hair, ridiculous eyelashes and girlish lips. He stood as far away from Alice as the kitchen would allow, one foot twitching in the corridor, ready to flee.

"Alice?" Khatoun called out. No answer. "Sarkis?" She dragged the name out like a whisper and the flame flickered, burst to life on the range and immediately went out again.

"*Kaknem,*" Ferida muttered, licking her fingertips.

"Tea, Sarkis?" Khatoun asked.

"Hm?"

"Tea?"

"Yes, *Digin* Agha Boghos," the boy replied, his eyes never leaving his boots.

"It's fine, Sarkis, you and Sylvie can call me Auntie," Khatoun said.

"Yes, *Digin* Auntie."

Khatoun suppressed a smile. "Would you like some tea?" she asked.

"Yes."

"Yes *please*, Auntie," Sylvie rolled her eyes at her brother, walked over to the stove and bent over Ferida's sputtering flame. "Let me help." She blew onto the grate as Ferida struck another match and the flame took.

And that's how they discovered that love had blossomed in their own kitchen.

Sarkis had had free access to their home ever since he and his sister moved in with Tatou, their closest living relative. They were orphans – the only two left out of a family of twenty from Trebizond on the Black Sea. They missed the comfort and mayhem of family life and had become regular visitors to the Agha Boghos household, the youngsters huddling together upstairs for hours telling stories and making up games until Tatou sent a man to accompany them home.

As time passed, Sarkis had slung his gaze towards Alice. And, despite never having spoken a word to him (preferring to disappear behind the boisterous banter of her brothers) Alice had noticed. What girl wouldn't? He truly was a beautiful boy. Tall, with broad shoulders and slim hips, he had long, unruly hair, a chiselled face and delicate fingers – perfect for goldsmithing, the craft he was learning. Sylvie was older than him by two years and had assumed the role of mother. She wore her hair scraped into a bun instead of braids and preferred plain colours to checks or stripes. It was Sylvie who spoke for her brother that day, when he and Alice had peeled out of the room separately and the plates were being cleared.

"He wants to marry her."

Ferida choked on her pickle. "Alice? Don't talk *kak*. She's still a baby." A door slammed down the hall and frantic foot-steps dashed towards the roof followed by the muffled sounds of Iskender yelling from his office.

"Ferida!" Khatoun raised her eyebrows. "The walls. They hear everything."

Ferida spat the pickle into her hand. "Why? What have I said? All I know is that that daughter of yours has turned into a moody dog of late. Who could possibly want to marry her? Why? What's going on? What have I missed?"

Khatoun stood looking at her with doleful eyes, shaking her head.

"I think I can speak for my brother and possibly Alice as well," Sylvie explained. "I believe they are in love. They seem to have discovered each other while none of us was looking."

"*Asdvadz!* How long has this been going on?" Ferida sputtered. She turned on Khatoun. "Did *you* know? Is this what all this strange behaviour is about?"

"I don't know how long and no, I didn't know and yes, this strange behaviour is called love," Khatoun smiled.

"Love? Pah!"

"Sarkis is besotted," Sylvie said, quietly. "He can't sleep. He doesn't eat. He says he's happy to wait until Alice is older but he doesn't want to lose her."

"So why hasn't your Auntie Tatou requested her hand?" Khatoun asked. "She is your guardian."

"Yes, what does Auntie Tatou have to say about all of this? I'll wager she's as much in the dark as we are!" Ferida snapped. "This is not the proper way to conduct this. I mean, what are you? His go-between? You're his *sister*. What right do *you* have to come here and ask for an apple? Just because everything is upside down because of the war, doesn't mean you can take your lives into your own hands. There's the proper way to do things. If we drop our ways we lose everything. And there I was thinking you were *sensible*."

Sylvie stood her ground and scraped the dishes into a bowl. "Our ways are changing, out of necessity. Auntie Tatou may be our guardian, but she has different views on life. My brother is eighteen. A man already. I simply did as he asked. The question is, do you accept the proposal? If not, we'll never mention this again. If you do, I brought this." She wiped her hands clean on the borrowed apron, reached inside her skirt and handed Khatoun a small bag. "Our mother's. There's a ring as well but Alice will get that later...when the priest blesses their engagement." She stepped back and stared at the two older women.

Khatoun undid the drawstring, opened the pouch and pulled out two gold bangles. She gave one to Ferida who bit into it, nodded her approval and handed it back. The bracelets sat together beautifully, two snakes twisting around each other, their ruby eyes bright.

"This is very generous, Sylvie," Khatoun said. "I'm sure they mean a lot to you." She took off her glasses and rubbed her eyes. "Give me two days. I'll ask Alice how she feels. From what I've seen, I'm sure she'll accept, but I have to talk to her father. It's only right. Two days. I'll send someone to your Aunt's house with our answer. Probably Afrem." She put the bangles back into the bag and slipped them into her bodice, patting to show they were safe.

The moon hung pale and fat. It was one of those evenings the sun could be seen slipping away on one side of town as the moon rose directly opposite. Alice wore a simple cream dress with a high neck and lace-edged sleeves that set off the gold around her wrist. Sarkis had grown two inches since the proposal. And a moustache. Almost. The lovers stood side by side on the rooftop and practically ignited when the priest blessed their engagement, allowing them to touch for the first time. Iskender had commissioned a ring, a simple gold band which Alice slipped onto Sarkis's finger. In return he slid a brilliant cabochon emerald on hers, his hand sticking to hers as the dancing began.

Ferida sat in the corner with Sylvie, turning peppers and onions over a small charcoal fire. "In the old days we'd have had a whole lamb for an occasion like this," she muttered.

"Yes, stuffed with apricots and pine nuts from Lebanon," Sylvie sighed. "And meat balls with yoghurt soup and barley."

"I suppose you think you can cook," Ferida teased. "We'll see, soon enough." She had a soft spot for the girl. Sylvie had no plans for marriage but had chosen life at her brother's side instead. Once he and Alice were married they would all come and live in the Pink House with the Agha Boghos family rather than take Alice off to Tatou's place, which was much too small. The thought of fresh input excited Ferida. It was a rare woman who could enjoy her place in life as secondary to others, especially these days. She might even enjoy the company in the kitchen. If the girl behaved.

"Turn them over. Don't let them burn," she said with a smile, "I'm going downstairs for a minute."

The whole family had gathered on the roof for the party. Even though the war was over people rarely got together outside church and when they did, food was scarce and something to raise in a toast almost unheard of. Luckily, Iskender had friends. Ferida was sick of the sharp burn of *raki* in her throat and wanted some of the smooth gold of imported whisky hidden in his office – the 'emergency supply' that never seemed to completely disappear. She creaked down the stairs, cursing her knees. Everyone was smiling. The lovers were engaged, the music was playing, they'd even found small birds to roast on the *mangal* and as the moon rose higher, not one person remarked on the absence of Aunt Tatou.

The winds came early that year, shaking the leaves from the trees in the Dergah Gardens. The shutters were bolted but a fine dust entered through the cracks anyway, stinging the eyes. The weather was changing and the winds brought sickness and insanity with them from the desert. They brought rumours too, and several ugly stories began to circulate and slip in under the door with the dust.

"Something's not right," Ferida hissed while they sat at the back of the church. "Look around. No one is speaking to us. I don't know what it is but I can smell it and I don't like it." Khatoun had noticed too but everyone else in the family seemed oblivious; the men as per usual and Alice, well, her head was up in the clouds with love.

Khatoun leaned into Ferida. "The absence of something is always more difficult to see than the presence of something," she whispered.

"Stop the riddles," Ferida hissed back. "Talk to me in a language I can understand."

"It's the difference between a boil and the cancer. You see a boil on your face; you know how to treat it. With cancer you could be half dead before you know it has eaten your lungs. Something is going on. I can sense it through what people *aren't* saying and I don't like it either." She fiddled with the buckle on her belt and smiled at her waxy neighbour who steadfastly kept her eyes on her prayer book.

Later that day, there was a knock at the kitchen door. Sylvie stood on the doorstep alone, the *pilaff* pot she'd borrowed the week before clutched to her chest, her blotched face strained with anxiety.

"Looks like the boil is about to burst," Ferida muttered as she let her in.

Sylvie walked over to the table, put the pot down and erupted into sobs.

"I'm sorry," was all she could muster.

"Told you I could smell it," Ferida said, grabbing the saucepan so viciously, the lid went flying. It clattered noisily to a stop by the stove and Khatoun bent to pick it up.

"Calm down, Ferida. Let Sylvie tell us what happened." She turned to the young girl. "Take your time. Tell us everything."

Sylvie shook her head, her fingers tracing the same whorl in the wooden table she had played with a few weeks ago.

"Talk to us," Khatoun urged.

"Yes, spit it out girl!" Ferida shouted.

Sylvie wiped her nose on her sleeve and looked up. "The engagement is off."

"*Off*?" Ferida yelled. "How can it be *off*? It's only been *on* a few days!"

"Ferida! Sht!" Khatoun got up to check the corridor and pulled the door to again. "Stop shouting. Let the girl speak freely."

Sylvie sat at the table looking ill. She lifted her shoulders and dropped them again. "Sarkis has changed his mind. You know… our parents are dead and he thinks he'll be abandoning me if he gets married and," she wiped her nose again and continued, "he thinks he's too young to marry."

"Pah! If you're going to make up stories, you'd better make your mind up first," Ferida snapped. "Which is it? Is he afraid of *abandoning* you or is he *too young*? I thought we'd all agreed that you would be coming to live with us. How is that abandonment? This sounds like rubbish to me."

Sylvie shrugged and opened her mouth but did not speak. Eventually she reached down and picked up the hem of her skirt and blew her nose. "I only came to bring the news," she mumbled into her hair.

Khatoun had been watching quietly. She got up and disappeared down the hall to Iskender's office, returning a minute later, the pouch holding the two bracelets that Sylvie had given them in her hand.

"Don't worry," she said to Sylvie. "I'll tell Alice. It doesn't matter what the reason is. The engagement is off, that's all. And once an engagement is off it can't be fixed. You'd better take this back to Tatou." She handed over the bracelets and patted Sylvie's hand as she ushered her outside. She closed the door, leaned against it and exhaled.

"You weren't very helpful, Ferida," she said, shaking her head.

"Me?"

"Yes. You. All your shouting. It shuts people down. I would have liked to know more. It doesn't add up. That boy was besotted. I saw the fever on him. I don't believe Sarkis changed his mind. I believe it was changed for him."

"Yes. By that sour-faced, pretentious auntie of theirs, I'll bet. Anyway, like you say — what does it matter? It's off and we'll never know why. You think anyone will tell us the *truth*? Never." Ferida slumped over the table and held her face in her hands. "Now what are we going to say to Alice? The idiot girl — it was her first love! How do you ever get over that? You don't! You take it to the grave with you." And then she began to cry.

Rage blew the shutters open that night and the moon hid behind the clouds. Lightening lit up the sky in the distance but there was no rain — just a howling wind that settled before dawn. The next morning, the sky was an endless blue, the breeze clean. A sombre household swept the dust out the doors and mopped down the floor. The sewing girls kept their chatter bright and business-like. Buttons, hooks, hems. After lunch the windows onto the courtyard were thrown open and the machines began to hum. Alice's brothers crept up to her room and tapped on the door but she stayed inside, refusing all offers of food.

It would have been over, dead before winter except for the note under the door. Neither Khatoun nor Ferida could read and when Solomon confirmed that the words passionately scrawled across the front of the envelope were '*To Alice, my Beloved,*' they were forced to pass the letter over to Iskender whose hands shook as he scanned the script written across the thick cream paper.

"That boy wants to come and see my daughter, let me see – '*to explain,*' he writes here. Explain what? Abandonment? Embarrassment? Dishonour?" He crumpled the note and threw it into the fireplace. "Over my dead body."

Nobody knew how Alice found out about the letter and Solomon kept his part of the bargain and said nothing about eavesdropping, or sneaking the semi-charred piece of paper up to his room where he pored over it with Afrem's dictionary before panic made him burn it completely. He even kept his gaze steady as he kicked Alice under the table when she wondered out loud one morning if such a letter might have existed and, if it had, what it might possibly have said and how cruel it would have been to keep such an important missive from the person for whom it was intended. Ferida almost boxed Alice's ears for starting up with her nonsense but Khatoun pushed her plate to the side, slid her glasses up her nose and studied her daughter.

"There *was* a letter and it was burnt," she pronounced. "Sarkis said he wanted to see you. To explain."

"And?"

Ferida dropped her greens into the sink. "And what? Your father wouldn't let that boy back in this house now. What are we? Fools everyone in the neighbourhood can walk all over?"

"Mamma?"

"Ferida's right. Your father won't have him in the house."

"And you?" Alice began weeping again.

"What about me?"

"Will *you* let him come and see me? So he can explain?"

Khatoun looked at Alice then Ferida. Then she remembered Solomon who was watching the whole exchange with his mouth open, a scrap of bread inches from his lips.

"Son, go upstairs and see what your brothers are doing," she said. She slipped her hand into her pocket, took out an onion and bit into it as Solomon slunk out of the room affecting nonchalance. When she heard the bottom stair creak she turned to Alice.

"It will have to be at night, when everyone is sleeping. Your father must never know. Sarkis works late – he can come here to the kitchen, by the back door, after work. He can bring one person with him – his sister, whoever he wants, but that's all. We three will be here and Iskender and the rest of the house will be in bed. Ferida will arrange it."

"Pah!" Ferida said and spat into the sink.

The clouds hung low, not a star in sight when Sarkis arrived with a friend, late, as arranged. The women were waiting. Alice sat in the corner over her mother's machine, pretending to sew. They had expected the exchange back of rings but Sarkis had refused. He said he wanted Alice to keep the emerald he'd given her and he would carry her photo next to his heart for ever. Alice kept her lips tight, her hands busy. Sarkis stood as close to her as Ferida would allow and was eventually dragged outside, crying like a baby, by his friend.

"It still doesn't add up," Khatoun said to Ferida when Alice was tucked up in bed later that night. "Except for the fact that he obviously still loves her, he didn't explain anything."

"Yes, he did. He said plenty." Ferida wiggled her finger. "He told us 'the worm came out of the tree.' That's someone in his own family. And we don't have to think hard to know who."

"Perhaps," Khatoun mused, "it's time I visited Auntie Tatou."

Tatou's rooms were small and stuffy, filled with stuff she'd hoarded over the years. It was a mystery how she still had all her porcelain, her carpets and knick-knacks. Khatoun walked around the room fingering things carefully while Tatou spoke.

"My late brother's, God rest his soul,"Tatou watched Khatoun trace the delicate curls around the feet of a wooden clock. "And this is my mother's – and that belonged to my husband, *Asdvadz bahe*. Everything reminds me of someone. It's such a comfort. Especially since I am alone now."

"Alone? What about Sylvie and Sarkis?"

"Yes. Of course," Tatou smiled. "Sylvie and Sarkis. My little orphans, pillows between myself and loneliness. Such lovely children. Still a little provincial in manners, but on the whole, charming children."

"Children?" Khatoun put down the china egg she had been fingering. It sat in a little gilt throne on the table.

"Obviously! Why else would they have acted without my knowledge and created such unhappiness for everybody? An engagement? *Vay, vay, vay!* They brought shame upon themselves and your poor daughter with their rash behaviour. Who knows what people think of poor Alice now? And what must she think of us?"

Khatoun perched on the *divan* next to Tatou. "Alice is fine," she said. "Sad, naturally, but I don't think she blames Sarkis."

"Of course not. Who could blame the boy for coming to his senses? He realised his whole life is ahead of him. What would he do married to a girl like Alice at this age? Last time I saw her she was still playing with dolls. Can you imagine her a mother?" Tatou giggled and patted Khatoun's knee. "Come now, drink your tea. They're children, thank goodness. They'll get over it."

"From your lips..." Khatoun picked up her tea and studied the cup nestling in its paper-thin saucer.

"Beautiful, isn't it? I still have the whole set, from Paris,"Tatou smiled. "One day I'll go back. They say the French army is coming to Ourfa. The Allies. Perhaps I'll go back with them."

"Do you remember it?"

"Paris? Only that I was happy there as a child. We always meant to return, but life changes. I got married, my husband got a good position with the government, we stayed here. Now I'm a widow with not even a brother or sister alive. And despite all those years of service we got nothing. My husband left me naught but trinkets and books, except, of course, the light of my eye, my darling Isabelle."

"And a grandchild on the way, *Insha'Allah!*" Khatoun held her tea up in a toast.

"Oh yes! *Masha'Allah, Le Petit Prince.* I just know it's going to be a boy. I felt him kick as I stitched up her dress. He's growing so big her belly split the seam right here! I took the needle and thread to it right away."

"While she was wearing it?"

"Of course."

"Oh...no...that's..."

"What?"

"Never mind. A superstition."

"I simply can't wait. My grandchild will be the most important thing to me, not that I expect you to understand." Tatou

smiled, leaning in as close as her stays would allow, "I mean, what
is loneliness to *you* surrounded by all that family? How many
children do you have – four? And still one brother miraculously alive and two sisters somewhere in the world and even your
parents and that gaggle of girls living under your roof. Sewing,
stitching, busy, busy, growing vegetables in your pots and pans
and so many of us dead in the marches. Burnt, raped, starved in
the desert. You seem to sail through life so easily, Khatoun. One
day you'll have to tell me your secret."

Khatoun took a sip of her tea. "We are fortunate, it's true. But
we also lost people we love."

"Yes, yes, some uncles, some *friends* in the resistance. Perhaps
if it wasn't for those friends, that futile opposition, the people
of Ourfa may have had a different fate. Still..." Tatou sat back
again. Observed the clock tick. "Some people crave solitude,
a little time to themselves. Others fear it – they want family
around them at all times. Let me ask you something. What does
life mean if you are alone? If you're not feeding somebody, do
you still get hungry? I don't know if I do. I eat simply because the
maid puts the plate in front of me. If there was no one to prepare
food for, would you even bother to eat? Some people get very
confused – whose life do they live once family has left them?"

"You live your own life."

"But what *is* your own life? Every mother knows you give up
your life for your children. Think, Khatoun. What would you be
if I took that family of yours away from you? Why do you suppose Ferida stays with you? You think she likes being little more
than a servant for her brother and his family? Of course not. She
stays because without you she is nothing."

Khatoun put her cup down on the lace covered table, her smile
never faltering. "I'm not sure I agree, Tatou. To me, it's a simple
case of desire. Desire is what gives your life meaning. If you
know what you want, your life is validated. You have a purpose
– a goal – no matter how small it is. If you're hungry, you know
what you want to eat. It's when people are depressed that they
complain that they don't know what they want. Happy people
have desires and they know what they need to fulfil them. They
say things like, 'oh, I fancy some *choereg* and hot tea,' or, 'I would
kill for some stuffed vegetables right now.' Wanting something is
what makes you live life. Although I do believe that sometimes

you have to find that desire. To create your purpose – to stitch it into your life."

For a moment Tatou was silent; then she threw her head back and laughed.

"Happy people want *choereg?*" she chuckled. "I don't understand a word of what you just said…stuffed vegetables? Please! My sides. You obviously don't have enough to do if you can spend your day thinking up ridiculous theories like this. I never knew it before, but you're *so* like your husband. I always thought he was the dreamer and you were the practical one, but *non!* By the way, talking about him, how is he? Iskender? Still…how do you say…melancholic?"

"Not melancholic, no. Iskender is one of those people who really does love solitude. He's angry about Alice, right now, of course. One minute she was his little girl, suddenly she was a woman in love. Now she's broken hearted."

Tatou slapped her cheek and sputtered with laughter again. "Please Khatoun! You're going to kill me with you absurdity! Alice is a *child* – what can she possibly know about love at her age?" She wiped her eyes with a scrap of lace and lowered her voice into a whisper. "And to go back to your theory about desire – you'll find that the people who *want* something in this world are always the ones who are *never* satisfied." She rang a little bell at her side and a maid in starched black and white appeared. "And now, Khatoun *Hanum*, do you need anything else? If not, I am going to get Angelig to clean up the room so I can take a nap. I'm afraid you have exhausted me with your impossible views on life. I'll have a headache right now if I don't lie down immediately with a cloth over my eyes."

Khatoun stood up. "I'm sorry about the headache, Tatou. Thank you, no, I have everything I need."

"Good." Tatou grabbed Angelig's arm and pulled herself out of the chair. She took Khatoun by the elbow and led her down the rickety staircase to the front door where she paused, her face split by a wedge of light that fell in as she pushed the door open onto the street.

"Before you go, Khatoun, a word of advice. Don't encourage Alice's nonsense with talk about love. Let her be a child a bit longer."

"I was younger than Alice when I married."

"Yes. Just like me. Arranged, of course. But all this talk of love is fantasy. You can't expect me to believe that you loved your husband when you first married him. He was old enough to be your father, for God's sake!"

Before Khatoun could reply, Tatou reached out and covered her mouth with her papery hand, "Don't say it. Even if you thought you were in love with him. Love is like the seasons – you start with spring, youth, passion and soon you end up with winter, cold, snow. And then they die anyway. Believe me, Alice will get over it – if you allow her to. Don't, for pity's sake, fill her head with any more of your ridiculous fantasies. I couldn't bear any more youngsters weeping around the place. Really, Khatoun, you act as if somebody caused this break up. They're just adolescents who have come to their senses and in a few weeks they'll all forget about it and we can return to normality."

"*Insha'Allah,*" Khatoun said and then, as she paused on the step before leaving Tatou's house, the words slipped from her mouth like birds taking flight. "Did you ever love, *Digin* Tatou? Do you know what it's like to have had love in your heart and to lose it?"

Tatou opened her mouth but before she could speak Khatoun reached forward and, in the same way Tatou had moments earlier, covered it with her palm. "They say someone must die so that those left living can appreciate life. My wish for you is that you discover..." Before Khatoun could finish her sentence, Tatou had stepped back and shut the door in her face, the unsaid words hanging for a moment with nowhere to land before scattering to the skies with the slam of the door.

It was the beginning of winter and the mountains were covered in snow. The air was crisp, the sky bluer than ever in summer. In the eighth month of pregnancy Isabelle, Tatou's only daughter, sat up in bed just before dawn, declared she was hungry, belched and felt her heart stop. When the doctor arrived the tip of her nose was cold and the child in her belly was motionless. She was buried a day later in a tall box, child still in belly, a light drift of snow falling over the earth.

Khatoun has reached the Dergah Gardens, the leafless trees dancing in the sky. The ground is crisp, the air sharp. They were just words that had slipped from her mouth. And what are words? Nothing but hot air and vibration. Only the bitter cold can make you see them. But sadly, words never get lost. Words last longer than matter – longer than anything you may have or have lost. Words are what, if anything, remain.

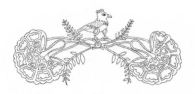

The French

Ourfa, April 1920
Khatoun

The back alley leading to the Pink House is only six feet wide; the flagstones worn smooth with age, a slippery drain running down the middle. In the past, the doors leading into the kitchens would have been thrown open to drink in the cool air. Today they are bolted shut, as they have been for years, the locks on some so corroded that if you were to try and open them you'd be met with a rusty screech of protest.

Running along both sides of the narrow lane, thick walls of impenetrable stone soar up three storeys to roof terraces where a few wild sheets flap in the breeze. The windows that look out onto this side of the street are mere slits – too small for shutters and dark enough not to require grille work to keep the women inside safe from the wolverine stares of men.

Ferida is standing at one of these windows on the second floor. She's sliding from side to side in the darkness, trying to make out who it is banging at the door below without them seeing her. Squinting up at her from the alley, one hand on her hip, the other shading her eyes from the sun, is her sister Loucia.

"I can see you," Loucia laughs, catching sight of Ferida in the gloom. "Any chance you could stop hiding and let an old auntie in off the street?"

"Sht!" Ferida hisses, gesticulating wildly before she disappears from view. Moments later the kitchen door screeches open and a bony hand reaches out, plucks Loucia by the elbow and drags her in.

"Wait! I'm not alone," Loucia says, pushing someone inside ahead of her. A boy, leather violin case in one hand, a bulging sack in the other. Ferida ignores him, slams the door shut behind them and slides the bolts back into place.

"What are you doing here?" she asks, spinning round, wiping her hands on her apron. "And where in hell have you come from?"

"Yes, and hello to you too, sister. We've come for a visit. From Aleppo via Baghshish and yes, it was hell. I wouldn't recommend it. Now where's my kiss?" Loucia hugs Ferida and steps back to get a good look. "Oh my. Going a little grey aren't we?" She nods at the salty locks that part severely down the middle of Ferida's face.

"Happens to all of us," Ferida snaps back. "Just some of us paint it over."

Loucia roars with laughter and heads towards the table. "Youseff, son, say hello to your Auntie Ferida."

"Hello, Umme Ferida." Youseff towers over everything, limbs long and stick-like in dark clothing. He wears a fez which adds another six inches to his height, but his pimply chin, shadowed by the slightest of beards, shows him still to be a boy.

"Youseff?" Ferida stares at him blankly.

"That's what I baptised him," Loucia says, easing herself into a seat and unbuttoning her boots with an "Ouf!"

"Youseff? Your son? But he was a baby!"

"I'm eighteen now, auntie," Youseff shuffles backwards but Ferida is quick. She gets his cheek, tweaks it between finger and thumb and slaps him.

"Unbelievable; you look just like Iskender, doesn't he, Loucia?"

"Yes. Both dreamers. Though this one writes music, not poems." Loucia rubs her temples. "Can't we have some tea? I've got such a headache." She looks around the kitchen. "And where *is* everybody? What's happened in here? It looks like a morgue."

"Everyone's sleeping."

"*Sleeping*? It's lunch time – I thought I'd timed it just right!"

"Lunch time? Pah! It's one meal a day, these days," Ferida says. "We get up, work, sleep and then eat. After that, work some more, talk, bed. Somewhere in the middle, I suppose we pray."

"I see," Loucia muses. "One meal a day. No lunch. That's a bit upside down. You can't work on an empty stomach. Youseff – the bag." She snaps her fingers.

Youseff slips the sack off his shoulder and unleashes a cornucopia of vegetables onto the table. Onions, red peppers, tomatoes, beans, potatoes – a feast of fresh produce.

"From Sophia and Anni in Baghshish. I've got letters too. Why don't you wake everyone up so we can have a proper lunch – get the sewing girls to join us as well? We'll make it a celebration."

Loucia stretches her feet out in front of her and looks up at her sister. "I'll have that tea now, Ferida *jan*, and I'd love to soak these old dogs in cold water."

"You're the old dog," Ferida laughs, her hands already muddy with potatoes. "How do you do it — appear at my kitchen as if I saw you just yesterday? With all of this too! And I can't believe you're stupid enough to risk bringing him out," she jerks her head in Youseff's direction. "Mincemeat they'll make of him if they get him."

"He's my bodyguard," Loucia grins. "A rich little 'Turkish' boy with a violin. Nobody questions him."

"And you?"

"I'm just an old auntie with dyed hair. Who's interested in me?" Loucia flexes her feet. "Water? Maybe a handful of mint. There's some in the bottom of the bag." She pulls her skirt up, exposing her mottled calves and pudgy knees just as the door leading to the workroom opens.

Yawning and shuffling, hair in a mess, one of the sewing girls walks into the room, an empty glass in hand. She startles at the sight of the visitors, tilting her head back and glaring at them as if they are trespassing.

"Ah. And you must be Zagiri. How are you?" Loucia asks.

Zagiri stares at Loucia with her one good eye and then, puzzled, turns to Ferida.

"Where are your manners, girl?" Ferida snaps. "This is my sister, Loucia. Say something. And, since you're awake, make yourself useful — boil up the mint for tea and add some to cold water for Loucia's feet. Can't you see she's suffering?"

"I don't know her," Zagiri says, suspicion curling her lip.

Loucia laughs. "You do now! Come and say hello. Come on." She stretches her arms out and pats her bosom, releasing a cloud of white powder. Zagiri inches forward and Loucia takes the girl in, all angles and sharp bones, for a stiff hug.

"I'm going to get everyone up," Ferida says heading for the door. "I'll send Moug in to cook. And Zagiri, for God's sake, wake up, light the stove and stop gawping."

Zagiri boils the water and fills the teapot, her eye on Loucia the whole time. She pulls apart a bundle of mint, throws a handful into the footbath, tucks a sprig behind her ear and places a posy on top of Youseff's violin case before sitting down next to it. The house stirs to life as people shuffle out of bed. Thud, creak, the floorboards above them clatter. Alice and Afrem reach them first, skidding into the kitchen in stockinged feet. They stop inches in front of Youseff, the cousin they've never met before with his city clothes and smart boots. His hooded eyes and pale skin give him the melancholy air of a night person who finds sunlight harsh and he greets his cousins with a vague nod, stepping away from them and into the shadows.

"Is it true you have a violin?" Alice asks. "Where is it?"

Youseff juts his chin towards the table where his instrument lies in its box. Zagiri has one hand draped over the case, her fingers flicking the clasp open and shut, open and shut.

"I'm going to dance," she announces. "He's going to play and I'm going to dance."

The door swings open again and Khatoun enters beaming, her face swamped by a heavy pair of glasses that sit awkwardly on her tiny face. "Loucia! Youseff! I was just dreaming about you…there was a camel…and roses…and here you are. How are you?"

"Khatoun! Hello, hello. I am fantastic but the camel would have been handy. My feet are killing me. Excuse me if I don't get up. I'll be better in a minute."

"Sit. Relax."

"I will. Thank you."

"I'm going to dance," Zagiri says again. "After lunch. Youseff is going to play and I'm going to dance."

"And I'm going to make beans," Moug says, bursting into the kitchen. She jumps at the sight of Youseff by the wall then stands twisting her skirt and giggling until Ferida reappears, flapping an apron in her face.

"Put this on. Onions – chopped. Potatoes – peeled. Now." She pushes Moug over to the table and begins sorting vegetables into piles, handing some over to be washed. She takes a handful of little tomatoes, still clinging to the vine and smells them. She plucks one, strokes it against her cheek and chucks it to Khatoun, "Smell that. Ripe, rich earth."

Khatoun wipes the tomato on her blouse and bites into it. "Mmmm!" she nods her approval. "Heavenly."

"Yes, they kept well. Underground. So are we going to sit here all day being poetic about vegetables or are we going to cook the damn things?" Loucia chuckles, splashing her feet in the tin bowl. Moug is twirling her knife in her hand, trying not to stare at Youseff.

"Chop," Ferida yells, pointing to the mound of onions in their papery skins, "or *I'll* make you cry!" She takes a sharp knife and begins to slice the tomatoes, pushing the beans towards Khatoun to de-string. "And you," she turns on Zagiri, "stop click-clicking that violin case, and go and get everyone else up...and stop staring with your one bug eye; you're making me nervous!"

Zagiri lets the clasp go, pats the black leather case and walks out the room throwing the sprig of mint at Youseff as she passes.

"Oh aren't we busy!" Loucia grins, stepping her feet out of the bowl and onto a ragged towel with a groan of delight. "This is much more like it. So, apart from sleeping, how's work?"

"Quiet...busy. I'm sewing officers' uniforms now." Khatoun shrugs.

"So I hear," Loucia says.

"And blankets," Alice says.

"Even I'm helping," Afrem adds. "I find the stuffing for quilts."

"Blankets?" Loucia asks.

"For the orphans."

"Fifteen hundred – and more arriving at the American Mission each day," Ferida explains.

"We've made two hundred blankets and quilts so far," Alice beams.

"Excellent." Loucia steps her puffy feet onto a towel, rolls them around one way then the other. "Frankly, the orphans are a nightmare, if you ask me. I'm trying to do some rehabilitation. Get them back to family who've survived. Problem is, some of them are so young they don't remember anything – only the Turkish families they've been with since the war. Treated appallingly in some places but it's all they know. I have one who keeps running back to the folks that took him in. Not at all interested in joining his sister at the orphanage. 'My name is Osman, now,' he says, 'and I like their food better than yours.' Can't say I blame him. Orphanage food. Pah!" She winks at Alice, takes a pair of slippers out of her bag, throws them onto the floor and slides her feet into them. "How's lunch doing?"

"Cooking."

"You read don't you, Afrem?" Loucia pulls a sheaf of papers

from a fold in her dress and scatters them across the table. "Letters from Anni and Sophia."

Khatoun gathers the pale yellow pages up and tucks them behind a pot on the dresser. "Iskender can read them to us after lunch," she says.

Loucia nods. "Iskender should see them, I suppose. That is if he ever graces us with his presence. Where is he, anyway?" She flaps the heel of her slipper on her foot impatiently. "Where are all the men?"

"Sleeping."

"Getting their strength up, I suppose. For…what exactly?"

"I'll go…"

"No, Khatoun. Stay. It's you I came to talk to anyway."

"Here we go," Ferida says, clearing the table and attacking a pile of greens with a knife. "Never comes just for a visit – there's always more."

"Well, someone has to keep you up to date, tucked away in this house like wraiths."

"Tell us," Khatoun says. "What's the news?"

"In a nutshell; it's time to go."

"Go?" Ferida stops chopping.

"Yes. It's time to leave Ourfa. Maybe not tomorrow, but soon enough. Up until now you've had it good. You've been safe. Enough people in enough places love you and want to protect you. That's good – but it's coming to an end. For a start, the girls here are at risk and they make your lives more complicated."

Khatoun stares back, the thick lenses of her glasses fracturing her face.

"The girls never leave the house. Hardly anyone knows they're here."

"I know. But everything is changing and they pose a risk. Believe me."

Alice looks at her mother, confused. "I thought it was safe now and everyone would be coming home," she whines. "Why do the girls have to leave? Who'll do the sewing?"

Khatoun hands her a colander of beans to give to Moug.

"Does this have anything to do with the French Allies?" she asks Loucia.

"So you heard."

"Some."

"Heard what?" Ferida asks. "Is anybody going to fill me in? I thought the French were leaving Ourfa. Just like the British."

"They were," Loucia says. "Now they're dead."

"Dead?"

"Almost every one. They were massacred in the Shebekeh Ravine two days ago."

"Two days ago? How come you know all this and we don't?" Ferida asks.

"Because you never go out. And you're prudent. Female abductions are high right now. Everyone wants a home for their seed, doesn't matter your age."

"Moug! Alice! Cover your ears!"

"I got the news first hand at Baghshish when I was collecting supplies. Some of Sophia's family had jobs at the French Army camp. Basil, George, Mariam. Since Sammi and Abdanour were killed they've been doing whatever they can to keep the farm going. Exercised officers' horses mostly. Did the shoes. A lot of Armenians worked at the camp. Cooks, cleaners, whatever. Personally, I never liked the idea. Ever since the French took over from the British there's been nothing but trouble."

"It's been murder," Ferida snorts. "The worst winter since Year of the Snow, no food anywhere and the Turks and the French trying to kill each other with us stuck in the middle. So, what happened?" She reaches into her pocket for a half smoked cigarette and lights it.

"Just like you said. The French were leaving. They had twenty-four hours so they took down the flag and started packing. Everyone working for them panicked; couldn't decide whether to go home – impossible for some – or take their chances and move on with the army. Our lot went back to Baghshish. Luckily."

"*Park Asdoudzo*."

"The camp was on a hilltop and they still have snow and nobody wanted to be out in the cold so they managed to make it home in one piece. They'd given a map to a few friends – telling them to follow. The next morning the French began their departure – along with the poor souls who'd decided to go with them. They'd been warned, of course, but instead of taking the safe route across the plains to Harran, they followed the Turkish army into Shebekeh Ravine and were ambushed. Like all Europeans, they believed in the '*parole d'honneur*' of the Turk.

It was a blood bath. One of Basil's friends escaped — another smithy — and found his way to the farm at Baghshish. I came across him in the yard, covered in blood, *kak* and *tshish*. Pardon my language. He told me everything and we put him straight to bed. I'm surprised you didn't hear more. Once the massacre was over, the Turks came back here to celebrate. If you had gone out you'd have seen some grisly sights. You know..." she points to her head, "...on sticks. When I heard, I thought I'd better come and see you."

"Straight into the mouth of the dragon," Ferida snorts.

"Pah! The dragon has no teeth. Yet. But yes, your time is up. Until now you've had it good. But it can't last. The dragon will bite."

"What about all the talk of repatriation?" Khatoun asks. "The city is filled with refugees. Missionaries, orphans, people coming back from all over, hoping to rebuild. What's going to happen to them?"

"Yes, we've all seen the women running back since the Armistice," Loucia sighs. "They survive the walk to the desert, people dying like flies all around them and run back 'home' expecting to move into their old house again. And what do they find? Nothing but rubble. The ruins of their past lives, rattling around with a bunch of ghosts and no wood to hold the lock for the key in their hand. Frankly, I don't know what they expect. You'd think they'd know what to anticipate after all they've been through, but no. Always optimistic. Or is it stupid? Anyway, I'm rambling. What was I talking about?"

"The women," Moug says from the stove.

"Yes, the women. And where are those optimistic women now? All over the place, living off thin air. You have one of them here. Zagiri Hovanessian."

Moug whirls round from the stove, her spoon slashing sauce over her apron. "You know Zagiri?"

"I do know Zagiri — she just doesn't know me yet," Loucia says, crushing a mint leaf and pressing it into her temple.

"Do you know her auntie too? They came together but she went to St. Sarkis and since then we haven't heard anything."

"Never heard of the auntie."

"Aunties of the road," Ferida explains. "Vartanoush went on, Zagiri stayed because we thought she had a bastard in the belly."

"It turned out to be an infection. After that we couldn't turn her away." Khatoun adds. "She's here now and that's it."

"Like a piece of furniture," Ferida says, rolling her eyes.

"She's not taking up space. No one else will sleep in the back room," Moug mumbles.

"Why not?" Loucia asks.

"It swallows people," Moug says with a shrug. "Like Zagiri's baby that wasn't and Hripsime and Aram Bohjalian..."

"Who asked you to speak?" Ferida shouts, grabbing the spoon from Moug and stabbing deep into the stew. "You're talking rubbish. Rooms don't swallow people." She takes a sip of the sauce.

"Zagiri likes the back room," Khatoun says. "It's so small she fills it completely. There's no room for shadows, no space for dreams."

"She's good at finding food, and that's worth something these days, I suppose. A pinch of salt," Ferida says, handing the spoon back to Moug. "One pinch – not more."

"And she's good with children," Khatoun adds. "Voghbed loves her."

"He even likes her face," Ferida says, shuddering.

"I like her face, too," Moug giggles. "It's funny."

"Who gave you birdseed this morning, girl!" Ferida snaps, swiping at the back of Moug's head with her hand. "Just shut up and cook!"

"This is precisely one of the things I came to talk about," Loucia continues. "The girls. They have to leave as soon as possible. They're at the greatest risk." She winks at Moug who is rubbing the back of her head. "Don't worry. I'll help."

"Where would we go?" Moug asks throwing a handful of salt into the bubbling pot. "I don't *want* to go anywhere."

"That's *it* Moug! You've said enough," Ferida explodes. "And that wasn't a pinch. Get out! Go and tell the girls to get ready for lunch. Half an hour. And don't fill their heads with nonsense."

"Yes, Umme Ferida." Moug unties her apron and hangs it up on a nail by the door.

Ferida watches her go and covers the stew with a lid, leaving a small gap for steam to escape. "That girl," she tuts. "Simple in the head."

"So, how many girls still with you?" Loucia asks Khatoun.

"Eleven," Khatoun answers.

"Well, there you go. Must be a strain on you, feeding all those extra mouths."

"Feeding which mouths?" Iskender asks from the door, his eyes puffy with sleep.

"Iskender!" Loucia says, clapping her hands. "Ready for some lunch, brother?"

"Lunch? Yes, yes, lunch is good. Lunch is excellent. Are you really here?" Iskender kisses his sister and sits at the table next to Alice, ruffling her hair. "When did we last have lunch? Must have been nineteen-sixteen. Yes, rotten pigeon. Made us all throw up."

Zagiri trails in next with Voghbed and Solomon – the two youngsters perplexed by the sudden change in their daily routine. They've been scrubbed and changed although Voghbed's hair still sticks up like a bird's nest in the back. Khatoun spits on her hand and tries to plaster it down as he slides in next to her. Thooma comes through the door next, Mertha fluttering beside him. She looks confused at the number of people in the room.

"Who are they?" she asks, hand at her throat. "Do we know them?"

"Yes, Mum," Khatoun shouts. "It's Loucia and her son Youseff from Aleppo."

"How lovely to meet you," Mertha says, waving at Loucia. "I thought you were dead."

Loucia laughs. "Not yet, *Digin* Mertha, although my feet will kill me soon enough!"

"I'm so sorry," Mertha settles down at the far end of the table. "That's such awful news to carry around."

Finally, the sewing girls troop in to say hello. Lolig with her rosy cheeks, Serpuhi and Margarit, Gadarine and Bzdig Shoushun; all smiling and touching their foreheads and eyeing up Youseff. Hasmig and Manoush enter next, holding hands, then Amina and Elise, the two sprung from the Millet *Khan* who shared Iskender's love of books, pocketing thin volumes as they come. The door opens one last time and it is Moug with fresh ribbons in her hair and a sprig of mint tucked into the bow. She slides into the kitchen behind Ferida's hot gaze and stops opposite Youseff. The girls bob and smile their hellos then set about laying the table; plates, knives, forks, *pilaff*, yoghurt and bread. One by one they take a bowl into the courtyard where they sit, ears pressed back like cats to catch the stray gossip.

Ferida sets the simmering pot in the middle of the table. It's been a long time since there was a feast like this in the kitchen and there is a satisfied silence as everyone digs into their food. The furniture creaks, the cutlery tinkles and everyone's bellies stretch, ooh, ah, slurp. After a while Iskender puts down his spoon, takes a healthy sip of *raki* and smiles.

"So what brings you here, sister?" he asks.

"Bad news I'm afraid, brother. I've already told the others." Loucia mops up the juice from her plate with a hunk of bread. "The time has come to leave Ourfa." She pops the bread into her mouth.

Iskender nods. "So, our time is up." He laughs, a short belch of air. "I've been expecting it." He pours another *raki* and waits for the water to cloud milky before continuing. "We think one awful chapter is over, but in fact the next is just beginning. I suppose this has something to do with the French leaving."

"What do you know?" Loucia asks, dipping more bread into the sauce.

Iskender takes a sip. "I heard they were leaving, and it was tense. That's all."

"Tense?" Loucia says. "Now they're all dead."

"I knew *someone* was dead!" Mertha beams across the table.

"Say that again?" Thooma leans forward.

"I knew *someone* was dead."

"What happened to the French?"

"*L'épouse du boulanger baise le boucher,*" Mertha remarks brightly.

Afrem's eyes dart nervously towards his grandmother. "*Allez-vous bien, Mamig?*" he asks.

"*Mais oui. J'écris avec une plume d'oie,*" Mertha giggles, scratching across the table with her finger.

Afrem smiles anxiously and his two younger brothers titter into their hands until Zagiri emerges from the shadows. "Come on, *Tantig*," she says, prising Mertha out of her chair, "let's go upstairs and play chess with the boys." She takes Mertha by the hand and holds the door open for Voghbed and Solomon, giving them a quick flick across the head as they pass. Alice nudges Afrem but he ignores her. Their parents seem to have forgotten them so she takes her brother's cue and shrinks back against the wall, out of the light.

Loucia dabs at her mouth with a handkerchief and waits for

the door to click shut. "What happened to the French? What can I tell you that you don't already know? They were herded into Shebekeh Ravine and slaughtered. Officially, of course, they've just 'vanished.' Later on someone will blame the *chettes*, the outlaws, whatever. But no one will ever get punished and soon it will be forgotten."

"I knew this would happen," Iskender sighs. "Ever since the Allies first came — starting with the British last year with their grand protestations about protecting us."

"Full of hot air," Ferida says. "Hot air out a donkey's ass. *Eshek siksin.*"

"At least the British were honest," Thooma says. "They knew their limitations. None of us were in any doubt that our situation would get worse once they left — and we all knew they wouldn't be here long."

"And the French? Did they promise anything more? Anything less?" Ferida asks.

"The Turks have always hated the French," Iskender says. "Never mind Paris fashion and finishing schools for the rich, deep down the Turk is not a Francophile. We've been on curfew since the day they arrived. Holed up here like phantoms, for months now."

"I know, brother," Loucia says. "And it will only get worse. Mustafa Kemal Pasha is gaining power and he's got Namuk Pasha, chief of Ourfa gendarmes, in his pocket. And that man hates everything foreign. French and Armenian."

"It's no surprise they came to a sticky end," Thooma says, offering Iskender a smoke. "The French. They poked fun at the Moslem way of life — were rude to the women, danced in the grounds of the mosque. They showed no respect at all."

"That could have been exaggerated," Khatoun says.

Thooma shrugs, "It's what I heard." He flicks ash into a plate and takes a drink.

"This is our problem," Iskender sighs. "Our lives are never our own — we always end up as pawns in someone else's chess game."

"I'm teaching my brothers to play," Afrem tells Loucia. "Solomon is really good — even Zagiri's learning."

"I don't know the rules," Loucia says. "But I do know that whatever game you play, the pieces are returned to the same box when you've finished; winner and loser. And now there are no more Allies left playing in Ourfa, which means one of two things. Either the Turks will be nervous about what they've done and treat us decently in case anyone's watching, or, they'll think they got away with it again and take it as *carte blanche* to start massacring us once more."

"Massacre," Iskender nods. "Historically speaking."

"On top of this, Mustafa Kemal Pasha is not happy with the way the Allies have been carving up his homeland. He's minutes away from taking over and he's a nationalist, so unless you plan on becoming a Turk I'd get packing."

"Mustafa Kemal Pasha," Iskender holds his glass up in a toast. "I salute you."

"Yes, Mustafa Kemal — a brilliant man, but not the best news for Armenians. He wants a Republic. A Democracy. For the Turk. Not for us. Minorities have no protection here now. Look at how fast the British Allies left once he dangled the Mosul oil-fields in front of them. And now look at the French."

"Politics," Iskender muses. "They call themselves *allies* but the British and the French had their own fights between them. The spoils of war — who got what, where, when. No wonder we dropped through the cracks. Every single promise made to the Armenians by the Allied powers during the war has been forgotten. Once again we've been sacrificed for political and economic gain."

"Naturally," Thooma says. "The stupid Armenians again."

"Aulis," Iskender announces.

"Aulis?"

"Yes. Euripides. *Iphigenia at Aulis*," Iskender starts. "Or was it Tauris? No, Aulis. That's where they sacrificed…"

"Oh, shut up, Iskender!" Ferida snaps. "Places, places. All you ever do is dream of places you'd rather be, not what is right here in front of you!"

"Just listen to you," Loucia laughs. "You're making my point for me! As you see, the minorities are completely unprotected here, at the mercy of anyone's whim. Mustafa Kemal wants the country for himself. He's already separated himself from the Ittihadists — thrown the blame on them for the massacres and the marches. Says they're the ones that dragged the country into the war in the first place *and* committed all the atrocities. He's busy in his fight against the Greeks right now but very soon his attention will turn back to us. And at present, despite their failure here, the French are doing a good job at keeping the peace in Aleppo. That's where you should be – not trying to eke a living out here. It's the end for *all* minorities and the sooner you get your heads around that the better."

"That's it?" Ferida asks. "Somebody doesn't like us so we just pack up and go? This is our *home*."

"It's just a house," Iskender sighs. "Walls and plaster."

"And if we refuse? What? My head on the end of a stick like some French boy's?"

"Ssst!" Iskender hisses, jerking his head in Alice's direction.

"Yes. Enough talk," Khatoun says, standing. "Let's clear the Ladies' Room, make coffee and have a song with Youseff on the violin. We can talk about this later."

Loucia smiles and stretches like a cat, the fabric straining at the seams across her large breasts. "Yes, Ferida *jan*, what about coffee?"

"I'll make it," Thooma says jumping up, "Ferida always skimps on the sugar."

"Some of us are sweet enough," Ferida says, gathering up dishes. "And sugar is precious. Can't grow that in my pockets."

"Maybe a drop of whisky since it's a celebration?" Iskender asks. "If I can find a bottle." He gets up from the table and takes Alice with him, an arm around her shoulder.

As the kitchen is cleared the sewing girls come back in from the courtyard with their plates. They jostle each other, competing for sink space.

"Is it true Zagiri's going to dance?" Margarit asks.

"She can't, I mean..."

"Her clothes."

"She always..."

"Enough!" Ferida snaps, slamming the *pilaff* pot down on the counter. "Enough chitter-chatter! Go and air that musty old room out so we don't choke to death on the dust in there. Move it – my slipper is itching on my foot!"

The girls scatter, the echo of "slipper, slipper!" trailing them down the corridor.

"Good to see that you're loved," Loucia chuckles.

Thooma turns to the stove, a cigarette stuck to his bottom lip. He watches the dark coffee bubble and rise in the *ibrik* over the flame. He raises the little pot, waits for the coffee to settle back down and balances it over the flame again. "So, Loucia, you come here with all this news – what have you got up your sleeve?" Cigarette ash cascades over the front of his shirt.

"Starting tonight, I take two girls with me when I leave. Over the next few months I take them all."

Khatoun pushes her glasses up her nose. "Two of them. To-day?"

"Yes. They walk out of here with me, someone meets us, and we're gone." Loucia pads round the table and puts an arm around Khatoun's shoulder. "I'm taking Zagiri. The other one is up to you. But whoever comes must be ready by dusk."

"Zagiri?"

"Yes. She's got a sister waiting for her."

"Zagiri has a sister?"

"A twin. A Bedouin took them, as a novelty. You know. Two of everything?" Loucia raises her eyebrow. Thooma coughs over the stove. "Apparently he was kind enough, only there were other wives, lots of children – you know the story. Jealousy, poison, endless fights. The wives used to strip them and make them dance together. Do lewd things to each other. Sisters – can you imagine? Anyway, Zagiri had had enough one day and fought back. She ended up like she is, left for dead in the desert. Za-belle, the twin, went to look for her. She found a bloody pile of clothes with an eyeball on top. Says it was a sign. Proof that Za-giri was alive. Eventually Zabelle came under my wing out of the desert at Ras-Al-Ain. She kept on at me to find her sister. 'She's alive, she's alive, she's alive.' You can imagine my surprise when I discovered Zagiri *was* alive and right here under your roof."

She reaches into her pocketbook and brings out a tatty-edged photograph. Two beautiful girls smile out at the world, their long hair rippling over their shoulders in waves. Identical, apart from the beauty mark above one lip.

"That one is Zagiri," Loucia says, pointing to the girl on the left. "Before her face was rearranged. Zabelle says she won't trust anyone. She needs a gentle touch. And proof. Maybe you should be the one to show her this, Khatoun." She hands her a drawstring pouch with something small and pea like inside. "Yes. The eyeball."

Khatoun takes the pouch and stares at the photograph under

the light, "You think you've lost everything and then you discover you have everything. I'll go to her now." She pockets the
photo and gets up to leave.

"By the way," Loucia asks. "How's your friend, *Begum* Şenay?"

"Still our best customer," Khatoun answers from the doorway.
"Even though the latest fashions don't suit her figure at all."

"Who do they suit?" Ferida sneers. "No waist, no bodice – just
straight up and down – women look like boys these days!"

"Still dressing like a whore for her husband?" Loucia asks. "Or
has she tamed it down?"

"Still *orospou!*" Ferida snorts. "*Süslü püslü.* Tame for her means
you can't hang your coat on her nipples."

Thooma bursts into laughter over the *ibrik.* "Ah, *Begum* Şenay,"
he chuckles, "where would we be without you?"

"And what about the girls she rescued from the *khan?*"

"Well…" Khatoun begins, "they ran away. One by one. They
disappeared."

"Ran away?" Loucia interrupts Khatoun. "I'll tell you where
they are. The prettiest, Armenouhi, is dead. She drank something that didn't 'agree' with her. Don't tell Moug. They were
good friends. Two of them are in America, married to farmers
in Boston. The rest are in Aleppo. I told you they wouldn't last
long in that snake pit. I went to see *Begum* Şenay shortly after
Armenouhi died. It didn't take much to convince her to help me
move all of them."

"She never said anything to me."

"What's to say?" Loucia shrugs. "Pay the monkey, and he'll
dance to your tune. Talking of which – come on Youseff, time
to give these folk some music. *Hayde.* Coffee in the Ladies'
Room."

The girls have already bundled into the room and pushed the
armchairs back to create a stage in the middle. Iskender and
Thooma hover in the doorway, both of them shy of this room of
European excess. The plants that once decorated the stands are
gone and several framed photographs have taken their place, the
family staring out of the silver frames in various stages, Khatoun's
belly swelling with each new child as the years progress.

Alice, Afrem and Solomon sit cross-legged on the floor,
Voghbed fidgeting in front of them. The tray of coffee cups is set

on a low table and the curtains tied back, letting the afternoon sun stream into the room through a halo of dust. Youseff takes up position in the middle of the circle, his pale face solemn as a mask. He removes the violin from its case and places it under his chin as the room hushes. He brings back the bow and, with a flourish and an almost imperceptible wink in Moug's direction, lets the music fly. He breaks into a smile and his mother starts to clap.

"*Yallah!! Masha'Allah!*" Loucia calls out. "Come on, everyone!"

Iskender and Thooma grin like schoolboys as they slip a little silver flask between them and the girls join in – their clapping banishing the parlour of all shadows. The youngsters on the floor giggle as their hawk-nosed cousin's face brightens with the music. Mertha is confused by the hubbub – it doesn't sound like church – but everyone seems happy so she grins and claps along, throwing in a fervent "Amen," every now and then. Loucia beckons for the silver flask, taking a quick nip 'for medicinal reasons', then another 'for her bones' and yet another 'for good luck'. Before long, her eyes have closed and she sinks into the sofa, snoring in perfect time to the music.

Khatoun looks around her. The music has lifted everyone's spirits. The room is alive with laughter and the odd line of song as the girls recall ditties from their past. For some reason she keeps thinking about the kitten Alice had when she was a child. A tiny scrap of grey and white they'd called Smokey. Alice had loved that kitten – feeding it milk sweetened with molasses and rubbing its stomach with a damp rag to help it urinate. It can only have been a few weeks old when Grundug brought it home gently clasped in his jaws. Alice had given up her dolls and carried the kitten everywhere, including to bed where she'd suffocated it one night, weeping inconsolably over its limp body the next morning.

"I know you loved it, Alice," Khatoun had told her, "but next time you get a kitten you shouldn't take it to bed. It needs its own space to grow. It died because you kept it too close." She'd hoped to find a replacement but no other cat would comfort her daughter and after a few years they'd given up on pets. She wonders if Alice remembers the kitten, now that she's tasted love on her lips and heard her heart crack for a man.

There is a pause in the music and before Youseff can oblige

with the next request, Iskender begins to recite a poem — one
that Khatoun has heard before, a long time ago,

> On the banks of the river, in the row of cranes,
> That one drooped its head,
> Put its beak under its wing, and with its aged
> Dim pupils, awaited
> Its last bleak moment.
> When its comrades wished to depart,
> It could not join them in their flight.

The room is hushed, the walls bathed with sunlight which
hurts Khatoun's eyes and sends her mind elsewhere, flat and
white,

> It is vain to dream any more
> Of a distant spring, of cool currents of air
> Under strong and soaring wings,
> Or of passing through cold brooks
> With naked feet, of dipping its long neck
> Amongst the green reeds;
> It is vain to dream any more!

Khatoun removes her glasses and rubs her eyes. The colours
around her bleed into one another. There is white light in her
head, the taste of flour in her mouth, the roar of the sea in her
ears. Iskender's voice reaches her from far away, his face floating
towards her like a head on a stick,

> And on the misty river-bank
> Its weary wings, spread for the last time,
> Point straight toward
> The Armenian hills, the half-ruined villages.
> With the voice of its dying day
> It curses immigration,
> And falls, in silence, upon the coarse sand of the river bank.
> It chooses its grave,
> And, thrusting its purple beak
> Under a rock, the dwelling-place of a lizard,
> Stretching out its curving neck

Among the songs of the waves,
With a noble tremor it expires![6]

He is applauded by a loud belch from the sofa.

"It begins with family," Loucia says, opening one eye. "Just like an onion. The skin on the outside looks shiny and golden but it is the layers inside that make you cry. Start at the heart – make a baby, give him brothers and sisters. Close them tight with your love as parents. Wrapped around you, your own siblings and parents – tight and oily. Friends wrap around that and then acquaintances – the skin. Might look good, but flakes off like paper. That is why you need to close down and look to your family. It took you a long time to start – it's worth an eternity to protect."

There is a pause as everyone looks at Loucia, her plump feet dangling a few inches above the carpeted floor. She belches again and Ferida crosses over to her, her hand stretched out.

"Give me the flask from inside your jacket," she demands. "If the whisky is that good, I want some!" She lifts the silver bottle to her lips, winks at Loucia and drinks as the music starts up again.

This time the door opens and Zagiri spins in, whirling towards Youseff, her hair loose, flicking about her like snakes. She has changed into a bright red dress with a sash tied low over the hips. She stamps her feet and lifts up her skirts, exposing her muscular calves, and a whisper trickles through the huddled girls. Ferida stares ahead, her body coiled, ready to leap forward if a single button should dare loosen on Zagiri's dress. Zagiri whirls faster, her bare feet sending up clouds of dust from the carpet. She plunges her hand into her bodice and the girls nudge each other. Ferida takes a minute step forward. Serpuhi covers her face and Bzdig Shoushun gasps. Zagiri digs deeper into her dress, her hand scrabbling frantically at the inside of her bodice. And then she spins, her feet lifting inches above the ground as

---

6 *The Aged Crane, Armenian Poems* Taniel Varoujan (1884-1915 Victim of Genocide) Translated by Alice Stone Blackwell, *Published by Caravan Books Delmar, New
York Reprint of the 1917 Edition. Thanks to Gerald Papasian and Nora Armani; Sojourn
at Ararat.*

her restless hand plucks the tattered photograph triumphantly from her bosom and holds it high above her head.

"Lelelelelele!"

The room erupts. All of the women throw back their heads and join as Zagiri ululates with joy and dances for her sister — sunlight and bare feet and dust — her upturned face a beautiful light at the centre of her dance.

A Mouse Nest

Aleppo, Syria, Fall 1922
Khatoun

Something in the rafters cannot sleep. For the last two hours it's been running the full length of the roof, pausing at each end. Either it has a nest at the far end and has discovered something delicious to eat in the roof right above Khatoun's head, or the nest of ravenous babies is tucked in above her and some rotting pigeon carcass is wedged in a hole above another sleeping family. The cheap roofing has made it impossible to gauge how large the intruder is, its scuttling is so magnified.

Perhaps it is friendly, perhaps it is not. Khatoun keeps her eye on the ceiling, watching the cracks in the plaster, wondering if anything will show itself. If it's a rat she'll have to lay poison. Then again it may be a lizard — in which case that's good. Lizards eat insects and who knows what kind of creepy-crawlies they have here. Poisonous. Burrowing. Parasitic. The scrabbling stops in their room and after a brief hiatus, takes off again, past the sleeping family, down the length of the roof to the far end of the building. Silence. Eight people sleep huddled together across the floor. The room thick with escaping dreams. This is their first night in their new home and nothing resembles the life they've left behind other than the colourful comforters they are wrapped in.

She'd signed the papers with an X.

"I can't write," Khatoun had shrugged when pressed for her signature. The Armenian clerk had opened her file, leafing back through the deeds of her home with trembling hands. One eyebrow shot up. There was her name, 'Khatoun Agha Boghos,' in the simple scrawl she'd been taught years ago. The clerk's hands shook so much, Khatoun let out a laugh. He stared at her, his bloodshot eyes begging her to sign her name and make his life easy.

The other man, the one with the greasy moustache who'd come into the room half way through the transaction didn't seem at all concerned. He reached over the clerk's shoulder, barely glanced at the simple X Khatoun had penned, muttered "Good enough," and slipped the papers into his pocket, yelling for more coffee as he left. That's when she knew for sure they'd been lying. Her signature was irrelevant. The Armenian clerk stared at her mournfully, the tips of his ink-stained fingers dancing across the filthy blotter. *Bang!* He stamped a chit with an ornate seal and slid it to her across the desk.

"Thank you." Khatoun smiled as she stood up. She reached over the pile of papers and shook his hand. "So, everything is in order. We are leaving of our own accord. You have the right to sell my property and will send me the proceeds. This is my receipt." She held up the chit stamped in red.

"Correct." The clerk nodded and bent back to his paperwork, his bald patch shining.

"And you?"

"Me?"

"Yes. When are you leaving?" Khatoun asked.

"I'm sorry," the clerk mumbled, his attention diverted to his suddenly leaky pen. "I can't talk. I have a lot of people to see."

"Yes. You do." Khatoun slipped the receipt into her dress and reached for the door to the waiting room. As soon as she opened it, Ferida stuck her face in the gap and hissed at the clerk.

"Gagosian it says on the door. Traitorous mother-fucker is what I say!"

The clerk's eyes never left his pen and Khatoun slipped out past Ferida and shut the door behind her. The small, stuffy waiting room was lit through a high window that was painted shut. The heat was unbearable, the floor an unemptied ashtray. Simple wooden benches lined three of the walls, and every time someone gave up their seat the packed room shifted along a space, allowing another couple to slip in from the corridor outside. Khatoun and Ferida walked past the line of expressionless faces, out into the breezy atrium with its potted plants that dissected the municipal offices and down the curved staircase leading into the sunlit street. With a simple X that meant nothing, their home had been sold and their life in Ourfa was at its end.

They headed back to the house. The house empty now of half its occupants. Loucia, true to her word had spirited the girls away in pairs in the last two years. Zagiri and Moug happy. Lolig and Serpuhi in tears. Gadarine and Margarit straight to America on a boat-load of brides which Hasmig and Manoush had refused; pledging themselves to each other and settling in Aleppo instead. Bzdig Shoushun was in love with a doctor, Elise and Amina busy gathering books for their refugee school in Aleppo and Moug was engaged to Youseff (what a surprise!) and living with him under Loucia's roof.

The neighbours had vanished in waves, their homes emptying in the night as families despaired of there ever being peace in Ourfa. There were no goodbyes. Everyone had their own private deals, their slipping out under a blanket of darkness, and each morning found another home emptied, the doors locked for a brief spell before they were prised open again and the contents ransacked.

Who stands looking across the city from her rooftop now, Khatoun wonders? Whose washing already slapped in her wind?

Empty of people, the rooms of the large house had echoed. The house with pink walls that coiled round its own heart – the courtyard – where she'd nursed and eaten and sat in the cool spray of the fountain. Where old Grundug lay buried under a flagstone and Ferida had grown medicinal herbs and potions. The bedrooms, shabby without beds, the spiders spinning madly in the eaves. The shadows slipping up and down the curved staircase, searching for footsteps to follow. The resplendent Ladies' Room with its carpet faded in blocks – darker where people had once sat on furniture that had been sold and transported in one go, like a theatre set. The curtains that had disintegrated when touched, a mesh of sunlight and cobwebs. The library, the office, all those books, that writing. The girls' rooms. The workroom. The machines. The fabrics. The buttons. The needles. The pins. The stitches. Who had it now?

It was Celine the Arab with the cobalt eyes who'd finally convinced Khatoun to leave. She'd spoken to her quietly as they sat on the roof, splitting seeds between their teeth, collecting the shells in their skirts. It was a late summer evening and the sun was operatic, streaking the sky ridiculous shades of magenta and orange as it disappeared.

"They won't be happy until Turkey is free of all Christians," Celine the Arab said, sweeping her arm in an arc across the rooftops. "That means everyone. Greeks, Armenians, Assyrians, Americans. You're one of the last — I don't know why you even stayed this long."

"I had to get the girls out first. And this is my home."

"Your home! Just like my mouse. I catch her all the time, take her miles away in my pocket and let her loose in the fields. A few days later she's back in my kitchen, laughing at me. 'This is my home,' she squeaks. It drives me crazy. If my husband finds her he'll crush her with his boot."

"What about the missions?" Khatoun asked, handing over more seeds. "The orphanages?"

"The Near East Relief is already packed up and heading to Lebanon."

"Are you sure? We hear so many rumours..."

Celine the Arab shrugged. "Who knows what's rumour any more? Who cares? Stories all come to the same end. But my husband told me to come here and convince you. He says to get out now and he'll help you. With his new job supplying the government...we hear things. Rumour, fact, the only thing we do know for sure is that everything is about to change with Mustafa Kemal."

"Iskender says he's a great man."

"Undoubtedly." Celine the Arab split another seed. "He has a vision — no more Empire, no more Sultan. And no more foreigners. In a matter of months Turkey will be born again. There will be chaos and bloodshed and this time you won't survive. Sell what you can immediately but set aside your most precious items. My husband will organise safe passage out of here for you and your family. With your valuables."

Khatoun laughed. "Valuables? What's the point? We'll be robbed on the road like everyone else. I'd rather travel light, take what is immediately useful. I don't want this life to follow us anyway."

"Khatoun *Hanum*, you don't build a new fire with old ashes, that's true, but take some things. Your sewing machine, at least.

Take what you want. It will be safe, my husband promised. He'll send a wagon here to fill with your valuables. Quietly. But do it soon. We'll keep your stuff at our farm until you're ready to move. When you're prepared, we'll send another wagon with two gendarmes – friends of my husband's. They'll accompany you to the border. When you cross into Syria you'll meet up with the rest of your belongings and stores of food."

"We don't have stores of food," Khatoun laughed again. "A pocket full of *bulgur*, some lentils…"

Celine the Arab shook her head. "*Hanum*," she smiled, "for a clever woman, some simple stones fall from your mouth. We have a farm. You will have stores of food." She licked the salt off her fingers and wiped them on her skirt. "Think about it. It needs planning. Send word with your youngest son. If anyone asks – he's delivering my dresses. But you should decide soon. Once rumour becomes fact it'll no longer be possible to sell anything."

"I'll talk to Iskender."

"Good," Celine the Arab nodded. She bunched her skirts together in her hand and stood. "I know what you're thinking, *hanum*. Why me? Why should some man I have never met go so out of his way to help me?"

"It is generous…"

"I'll tell you why," Celine the Arab smiled. "There are three reasons my husband holds you dear to his heart." She held up three fingers. "Duman, Galip and Hasad. Every time you made me a new dress I fell pregnant – including on my wedding night. Now I have three sons and a secure future and my husband blames it all on you!" She chuckles and extends her hand, helping Khatoun up off the floor. "Also, and this makes him angry – this new patriotism – getting rid of all foreigners? If I wasn't married, it would include me."

"But you're Muslim."

"I am now. But my family are Maronites. They never forgave me for changing my faith. My mother told me I was a fool to marry for love and my father simply turned his back on me. They live in Beirut, but when I visit my own city I am forbidden to see them. My parents have never met their grandchildren and they are so old now…*Insha'Allah*. So, *hanum,* my husband knows what it is like to be able to leave of your own free will, rather than be forced out of your home at dawn. He is married to it. Think about it and be in touch."

She crossed over to a bucket near the stairs and shook the seed chaff from her skirt. The sky shimmered mauve and the smell of cooking wafted up from below. Khatoun joined her, sweeping up around the bucket with a little broom and pan.

"A little supper before you leave?" she asked, dusting off her hands.

"No, no. I must be on my way. I'm staying with family tonight. Tomorrow I set off early, back to the farm."

"Tell your husband I'll think about his kind offer," Khatoun said. "I need to talk to mine first."

"Of course, *hanum*. But soon, yes? Soon."

Khatoun took a few days before going to Iskender. He barely looked up from his book as she slid into his cramped office and stood by his chair. He'd been ready to leave for a while – ever since Loucia had come to them two summers ago with the same story. Since then he'd slowly turned into a wraith, hardly leaving his room and eating only sporadically. The nights were filled with his ramblings but during the day it was not unusual for him to sit silent until the sun sank again. He surrounded himself with the shadows that had scared him for years. Now they were his friends. He nodded distantly at what Khatoun had to tell him, his eyes fixed on a crack in the plaster that snaked down from the ceiling behind his map of the world.

"Saskatchewan," he murmured, his finger still hooked in his novel. "Minn e so ta."

Khatoun took this as his tacit acceptance.

She began by visiting the handful of friends she held dear in the city, urging them to pack up and leave. Even at this point some refused to consider it. Their homeland was on the brink of a new era, everyone sensed that, and many believed modernisation would end their troubles and they'd be able to live peaceably with their Turkish neighbours at last. For others, the mere whisper of the word 'exile' was enough to send them deep into their homes from where they disappeared without trace during the night.

Khatoun spent the rest of the summer stripping the house bare and selling what she could. She started with the Ladies'

Room; the European furniture transported by mule and set up almost identically in *Begum* Şenay's quarters.

"Take this," *Begum* Şenay had muttered, handing a bag of gold coins to Khatoun. "That's for the furniture. And this – this is *very* important." She pressed a tight bundle into Khatoun's hand. "You *must* pack this with your belongings when you travel. Don't look in it now – just trust me. And if you take anything valuable don't hide it up *there*. That's the first place they'll look, *eshou botch* bastards. If you have to, the other end is safer. They like that less, unless you're a pretty boy." She wept as she watched Khatoun leave for the last time, the marble corridors echoing her footsteps, the grille work around her seemingly alive.

The sewing machines were checked over by Old Bastard Ilhan who gave Khatoun a surly fraction of their price, claiming they were all old and useless. The beds were taken apart, the carved wooden frames sold to a local carpenter and the family slept on the floor once again. Boxes and trunks were filled and emptied and filled again as everyone tried to choose what to take. The pots and pans for Ferida. The little Singer for Khatoun. The best rugs, the colourful bedding. It was all so familiar. Iskender wanted his worn leather chair and his world map, but his books he piled into the kitchen and fed to the fire. Solomon wanted nothing. Alice, her first pieces of handwork, minus those with Sarkis's name embroidered on them. Those flew into the fire with the books. Afrem packed up his chess set and Voghbed tried desperately to cage the mangy pigeon that sat on his windowsill each morning waiting for corn. Thooma took his cigarettes. And Mertha? Mertha took nothing at all, not even herself.

Grief had drained all the fat from her body, the sense from her brain, and no one blamed her for fading quietly into the walls as they were stripped bare. For taking to her bed one day, easing herself down onto the floor under the flowered quilt, a photo of herself as a young girl surrounded by brothers in her hand, and sleeping on through lunch. They buried her without tears near their old farm in Garmuj, the wild jabbering of geese accompanying her descent.

Just two months after Celine the Arab's visit, Khatoun was summoned to the municipality with all the other Armenians who still owned property in the city.

"We'll arrange safe transport and sustenance. There will be

no Deir ez-Zor," the greasy moustache had said. "These are troubled times for Turkey – it's best that you leave. You sign the deeds over to us, we give you a chit and reimburse you when we have sold it for you." He spent the few moments Khatoun was in the room trimming the hairs in his nose without looking at her. "Make an appointment with my clerk, Gagosian, and come back next week with the deeds." He sneezed into the mirror, wiped it clean with his sleeve and inspected his nostrils. And so, rumour had become fact.

A week later, Gagosian's chit tucked safely in Khatoun's dress, the family walked to the edge of town with their scattering of bags and met the wagon Celine the Arab's husband had promised. Two handsome gendarmes smiled as they helped them up under the canopy. One of them sat up front and guided the mule, the other led a spare horse.

It was strange to be travelling this road, knowing it was for the last time. A route they knew well, winding across the rich fertile plains towards Harran and on to Baghshish. They'd be bypassing both on this journey. No point going there now. The whole region was empty of people and horses; the Glore Boghos farm at Baghshish burnt to the ground. Instead they would turn off the main road and strike out across unknown territory towards the ever-shifting border and its endless checkpoints.

Ferida took the bunch of keys from her waist and hung them on the metal bar that kept the canopy up, listening to their jangle as tears slipped down her nose and into her lap. The sun rose, the churning wheels rocked them into a stupor and the trapped heat made them all sick and drowsy.

As she slipped into sleep, familiar voices slid in and out of Khatoun's dreams. Chattering tongues that swept along the path and sank into the red earth with a sigh. She heard the wind from high mountains singing of winter snow and the babbling brooks of spring. The murmur of old stories accompanied by years of laughter. The spit of bread baking on a flat oven. The crackle of fire snuffing life in the eaves. The screech of a hawk. The stifled cries of women who left their children by the well, the echo of love lost under their skirts. The wagon wheels rumbled over buried lockets and dropped dreams, past scraps of prayer etched into stone. And then, the fresh wash of thunderous water, which made Alice cry out as they crossed the Euphrates and left their homeland behind.

They spent the night by the river sleeping under a blanket of stars. It was shortly after they set off the next day, the clean air of the riverbank behind them, that they were stopped.

"We have the right to check for valuables. They may be stealing from the Empire." The irregular's uniform had seen better days and so had his teeth — simple black stumps that stank when he smiled. Above him, on the hilltop, a straggle of miscreants stood leaning on their rifles, grinning as their commander spoke.

Alice shrank back, behind Afrem, and Ferida reached over to squeeze her foot, a finger to her lips. The younger of the two gendarmes, the one with slate coloured eyes, dismounted. He sauntered over to the *chette* and spoke in a lowered voice. Moments later he lifted a corner of the awning, flooding the interior of the wagon with light. He searched out Khatoun and threw his hands up apologetically as she crawled over everyone's legs towards him.

"I can't stop the search, even with a bribe," he said. "Get your family round you and do exactly as I say. And excuse my language, *Bayan*. It's in your best interest."

Khatoun nodded and motioned for everyone to get down from the wagon.

"Women this side, men over there," the gendarme barked. "And no smoking." He snatched Iskender's cigarettes, lit two, gave one to the other gendarme and tossed the rest to the toothless irregular who stuffed the packet in his belt. Within minutes the small band of *chettes* had scrambled down the hill and were rummaging through the bundles in the cart.

The gendarmes stood smoking as the wagon was ransacked, their faces blank, their conversation trite. Iskender crumpled to his haunches at the side of the road, clutching his stomach, cursing the dozen gold coins he'd swallowed, begging them to stay put despite the roaring pain in his gut. Thooma turned his back — unable to watch the pale photographs of his beloved Mertha fluttering to the ground like dead moths. Ferida stood behind Alice, her feet digging into the earth, her toes gripping the coins in the soles of her shoes. She relinquished her bag with a sneer and watched the thieves toss it aside without noticing the carefully waxed seams of the hollowed out handles.

The brigands were becoming increasingly irritated as they tore through the family's luggage. There really was nothing of any value to be found. They had just begun to cast an evil eye

over the women when one of them discovered *Begum* Şenay's
bundle inside Mertha's embroidered quilt. As the bag ripped
open, a tumble of jewels fell to the ground and the men fell on
them, bickering. Ferida turned to Khatoun, her eyes wide with
shock.

"You see," the toothless commander said, waving an admon-
ishing finger at the two gendarmes. "They *say* they have nothing
– that they are destitute – but when you scratch beneath the
surface you find what these *giavour* are worth!" He pocketed a
length of glittering beads and told his men to gather up the rest
to share out later. "You can go now," he grinned at the gendarme.
"Pity you didn't think to look through their stuff yourself. But
then again, they must have paid you handsomely. Why else would
you be doing this?" He herded his gleeful band of *chettes* together,
threw his rifle over his shoulder and waved goodbye to Khatoun
as if she were an old friend.

The family got back into the wagon and sat in silence as the
gendarmes gathered up their belongings and passed them in to
them. When they finally began to pull away everyone sighed
with relief. And then Khatoun began to laugh. At first it was just
a slight shake of the shoulders but soon she was weeping uncon-
trollably into her palms.

"What's so funny?" Ferida snapped.

Khatoun wiped her eyes and kissed Alice on the cheek. "*Begum*
Şenay," she chuckled. "It's her joke. The jewels. They're fake. It's
costume jewellery she wore in her days as a dancer. She's had it
for years. Once she asked me to decorate a dress with it around
the bodice. A few days later she told me her husband hated it. He
said she looked cheap, but she continued to wear the dress until
he came home one evening with a beautiful emerald necklace
from India. Then she brought the dress back and asked me to remove the fake stuff. I replaced it with feathers. Much better. She
kept the fake jewels – said they might come in handy again one
day." Khatoun dabbed at her cheeks. "Every piece those thieves
took is paste – cheap glass and gilt chains."

"*Orospou!*" Ferida spat. "The cheap slut! *Orospou* Şenay *Hanum*
– I love you!" She slapped her thigh and roared with laughter as
the cart swayed across the desert scree.

The gendarmes were careful to avoid roads after that. For the
most part they followed the railway line towards Aleppo but

shortly before dusk they turned off the track into the low hills and followed a dry riverbed. An hour later they came to a halt and the gendarme with grey eyes pulled up to the wagon.

"*Digin* Agha Boghos," he called. "This is it. The border. This is as far as we go."

Khatoun lifted the tarpaulin up. The driver's seat was empty. The two boys sat on their horses, silhouetted against the evening sky. She beckoned them closer.

"What are your names?" she asked.

"Abdallah."

"Aref, *Digin* Khatoun."

"Here." Khatoun took Ferida's bag and snapped off one of the handles. The wax fell from the seam and she dug her finger in, pulled at a thread and offered the purse that slid out to Abdallah.

He shook his head and his horse took two steps back. "We were told strictly no tips, *Hanum*."

Ferida stuck her head out of the wagon, her headscarf wound round her neck, her hair a bird's nest. "Eat shit from a donkey's arse," she said, grabbing the purse from Khatoun and throwing it towards the boys. "Keep it, you did a good job."

Abdallah caught it in an easy swipe.

"No! Keep it. Share it," Khatoun insisted as he drew his arm back, about to toss it back to her. "It's not a tip — it's a gift for your children."

"Children?" Aref began to laugh. "Abdallah's not married. If he has children his mother will take a broom to his head!"

Abdallah grinned. He threw the purse back up in the air, caught it and opened his hands wide to show they were empty.

"Magic fingers!" Ferida joked, "That'll keep the girls happy. You'll definitely be married with children soon!"

Abdallah pointed to a gap in the hills. "The road is just over there, *Hanum*," he said, ignoring Aref who had thrown his head back and was howling like a wolf. "Nuray knows the way. Someone just has to sit up front with her and hold the reins. You'll see the lights of Aleppo in less than an hour."

Khatoun made way for Thooma to disembark.

"What a beautiful evening," he said as he clambered down and stretched out his legs. "Greetings, Syria."

"Once you join the road, let Nuray guide you," Abdallah told him. "There's a crossroads a few miles down and a café where

you should stop. The other wagon with your belongings is going to meet you there. If it isn't there already, wait for it. Don't
worry. We have to go. *Hayde* Nuray, guide these people well."
He bent to kiss the mule on the nose, brushing past Khatoun as
he turned his filly in the opposite direction. "Have a good life,
Bayan, and may *Allah* be with you."

"*Insha'Allah*. And with you."

As he spoke the moon slipped behind a cloud and the sky went
dark. When it reappeared, the two boys were already on their
way back to the hills, chattering and laughing.

"*Asdvadz bahe*," Ferida shouted after their retreating forms.
"God keep you!"

Despite the sudden drop in temperature, Ferida and Khatoun
couldn't resist peeling back the cover of the wagon so the sleepy
family could get some air. Above them, the stars pricked the cover of nightfall and the moon played games, slipping in and out
of the bruised clouds like a child. Nuray the mule meandered
through the pass to the road and before long the orange glow of
Aleppo's glorious skyline lit up the distance. The road widened
and as they turned a bend, there, in the middle of the desert, a
crossroads appeared.

A handful of wagons clustered around a low building next to a
makeshift tent. A scattering of travellers sorted through bundles
or sat at the rickety tables around an open oven where a family
of Kurds turned skewered meat over charcoal. A few stalls had
been set up and Afrem went to buy cigarettes for his father and
cool *tahn* for everyone else. As he stood waiting at the counter
for the green-eyed girl to fill up the glasses he felt a tap on his
shoulder. He turned around and for the life of him, could not
figure out who the man standing in front of him was until he
looked down at his feet. Next to the fine city shoes, covered in a
fine layer of dust, sat Youseff's violin case.

"Oh my Lord!" Afrem laughed, looking up again. "You finally
grew a beard!"

"Happens to the best of us," Youseff grinned, stroking his chin
proudly. He hugged his cousin and helped him carry the drinks
to the others. There was a huge cacophony of hellos and everyone lit up cigarettes – including Afrem who had never smoked
before but was not to be outdone by his cousin who stood expertly blowing smoke rings over their heads.

"That's yours too," Youseff said pointing to another wagon covered in canvas. "I've got a friend looking after it in case of thieves – although I already went through everything and there's nothing worth stealing." He laughed and Alice blushed, thinking of her delicate underclothes wrapped in paper for her future trousseau. "Just teasing," he mouthed.

Ferida grabbed his cheek and gave him a playful slap. "You must be in love. Last time I saw you, your humour was in your boots and you looked like a ghost."

"How is Moug?" Khatoun asked kindly.

"She's well, she's well. She's at my mother's house. She's good. Very good." Youseff took a last deep drag on his cigarette and flicked it away over their heads.

"I've got my sewing machine with me," Khatoun said.

"She was hoping you would have," Youseff replied.

"And I have cuttings of all my herbs," Ferida winked. "In case she's in need."

Voghbed started to dance, clapping and pulling at Youseff's coat as he sang,

> 'Your breasts are a snow white cathedral, your nipples eternal lamps.
> Oh let me become your verger and tend to your vernal lamps!'
> 'Be off, you foolish young suitor, my lamps to guard you're not fit;
> You're fickle and quickly distracted: you'd leave my cathedral unlit.'[7]

Ferida cuffed Voghbed round the ear as he gyrated past her. "Who taught you that filth? Don't tell me – I can guess. Anyway, that's enough. We should get in the wagon and carry on. I think my brother needs to get where we're going. Iskender *jan*, there are bushes over there. Go. We'll wait for you."

"I'm fine," Iskender insisted, waving irritably as he clutched his belly and smoked.

And so they were out.

It was late evening when they arrived in Aleppo, the sky lit gold by the lights of the city. Youseff drove one of the wagons ahead and they followed him through narrow winding streets

---

7 From *A Hundred and One Hayrens*, Nahapet Kuchak (Sixteenth Century), *translated by Ewald Osers. Published by Sovetakan Grogh, Yerevan, Armenian SSR. Copyright 1979. Thanks to Gerald Papasian and Nora Armani; Sojourn at Ararat.*

still jostling with people. It seemed as if all the races in the world
had converged on this place and everyone seemed to be shouting. Women hurried past, some of them with covered faces, others brazen in rouge and glitter that sparkled "follow me!" as they
swung by. The wagon narrowly missed a pack of dogs chased by a
man in a bloody apron, cleaver in hand. Somewhere above them,
a musician sang to his lover and she giggled with delight. The air
was thick with the competing aromas of food and incense, rotting garbage and heavenly perfume.

Gradually, the streets began to narrow until the walls almost touched above them and the throngs of people thinned
out. Voghbed reached his hands out and ran his fingers along the
soft, peeling plaster until Ferida slapped them into his lap with a
glare. Eventually, after much twisting and turning, they pulled in
through a set of large wooden gates and came to a stop.

"The Neighbourhood," Youseff called out over his shoulder.
"Your new home!"

Alice began to cry. The Neighbourhood was nothing but a simple *khan* centred around a courtyard. A well and two palm trees
sat in the middle. Thin strings of washing radiated out from the
trees to the compound walls. There were a dozen rooms downstairs and the same again on an upper level. Here and there, the
light from a *mangal* shone as people prepared their supper on the
landing outside their rooms.

"At last!" a voice called out from under the palm trees by the
well. Loucia lit a lamp and held it up, an overexcited Moug barely able to contain herself at her side. "I can't believe you're finally here! I was falling asleep." Loucia handed the lamp to Moug,
hugged Khatoun and Ferida and was about to squeeze the life out
of Iskender until he whispered in her ear. "Ah. Over there, at the
end of the courtyard. Youseff will show you. Youseff!" She called
her son over and gave him a spare lamp, lighting it quickly and
sending him scurrying after Iskender who was already half way
across the yard. The horses were led to a trough and watered and
a handful of belongings unloaded. Youseff's friend waved them
away, saying he would guard their valuables for the night and
they followed Loucia up a rickety staircase to the room they
were to sleep in.

"It'll only be for a while," Loucia said bustling around, arranging their bedding on the floor and ignoring their silence.

"There are a lot of families arriving these days. We need to see an end to the flow before we can relocate everyone. You'll see; it's total madness. We've got girls coming in from the desert – half of them covered in tattoos, most of them with no idea of who they are any more. Anyway, it may not look much but I'm sure you'll be happy here. All the other families are Armenian and everyone has plenty of stories. The well is good for washing but there's only one toilet. Most people use a bucket in their room and empty it down there. It's basic but clean – that much I can tell you. Your stuff will be safe downstairs. Youseff and his friend will be sleeping with it for tonight and in the morning we'll all be back to help you get settled. And there's good news for the girls – it's *hamam* for you tomorrow – the boys will have to wait another day."

"And there's hot stew!" Moug cried, carrying in a large pot wrapped in cloth and setting it down on a tablecloth in the middle of the room. "It's your recipe, Ferida *jan*. Not too much salt. I made it myself."

After Iskender had rejoined them and they had eaten, the family curled up to sleep on the floor, wrapped in their comforters. Tomorrow would see the beginning of their new lives. Khatoun was the last to retire and was still awake long after her family began to belch and snore, filling the room with their dreams.

She is convinced now that the scuttling overhead is a rat. The animal stops right above her and goes quiet. The moon slips her fingers in through the solitary window and a beam of light illuminates a crack in the plaster next to the rafters. Suddenly, two bright eyes appear and then a nose and then a face – small and white and innocent – a mouse.

"Hey, little Moug," Khatoun laughs, "what news?"

The mouse freezes as Khatoun speaks and then it is gone again, thundering across the roof to its family. Khatoun is wide awake now. She knows it's useless for her to try and sleep. On nights like these, the most peaceful thing is to get up and enjoy the time awake rather than fret in bed. She slips her feet into her shoes and shrugs on her jacket. Outside, she follows the narrow balcony to a small winding staircase that leads up to the roof. Someone has tied an old *kilim* across one corner of the terrace with bits of wire, creating a makeshift shelter. Underneath it there are several more kilims and half a dozen cushions. A forgotten tea glass lies dejected, a dead fly belly-up in the stale liquid. Khatoun settles herself under the little tent and pulls her jacket around her.

The moon is ripe, ready to burst. The city shimmers ahead as far as she can see. Aleppo, their new home. It smells of smoke and spices and dung and filth. Too many people and too many stories crowding in on each other, suffocating one another. Which old friends will she discover here and who in the new pack will prove to be real? The moon smiles down, a breeze plays with her hair. She slips her hand into the pocket of her jacket to retrieve her headscarf and finds, instead, a small bag. Perplexed, she holds it up to the light and laughs. It's the same purse she tried to give to the gendarmes Abdallah and Aref earlier. She opens it. The gold coins are still there.

"No tips," Abdallah of the magic fingers had said.

Khatoun smiles at the moon and holds the coins in her hand as she makes a wish, "But a handful of children for you, Abdallah, *Insha'Allah*. And may they live long."

She stands up, crosses over to the balustrade, takes one of the coins and throws it up into the air. It spins, caught in the light of the moon and falls, clattering into the street below. Khatoun watches it roll into a corner by the gutter.

Who will find it? A mother? A child? A desperate man? A pockmarked and lazy whore? What does it matter? Even a pebble dropped into the driest of wells can ripple and swell and cause floods somewhere across the ocean. Everything has its purpose; every person we meet, every star that collides, every cloud that takes shape. Even that stranger we bump into at the market place and brush shoulder to shoulder without acknowledgement. Our actions – like the ocean waves, the breeze in our hair, a simple X inked onto a page or the toss of a coin into a dirty street – all may seem random, unpredictable and chaotic. But they are simply the effects of energy, the harbingers of change.

"*Asdvadz bahe.* God bless you," Kahatoun sings out to her new home. "Halab. Alep. Aleppo. City of song. I am ready."

Index of foreign words

Word/phrase	Meaning
Agh!	Oh!
Amma	Mother
Araba	Horse drawn covered carriage
Arak	An alcoholic liquor mixed with water to drink
Asdvadz	God
Asdvadz Bahe	God bless you
Asdvadz hokin lousavore	May God enlighten his/her soul
Azan	Islamic call to prayer
Azdoo Peepuh	God's eyeball
Babam	Turkish familiar term for father
Bayan	Lady. Form of address to high-ranking woman (Turkish)
Barab glir	Empty cock (Armenian/Turkish)
Bastourma	Seasoned, air dried Armenian cured beef
Begum	Islamic form of address to women of substance. Appropriated by Begum Şenay from Begum Samru, one of the richest women in history
Ben seni çok seviyorum	I love you very much (Turkish)
Boubrig	Term of endearment meaning little doll (Armenian)
Boutz	Armenian slang for vagina
Bulgur	A cereal made most often from durum wheat. It is partially boiled, then dried
Çaça	Colloquial term for a woman of low status and loose morals. A dancing girl

Çarshaf	Simple loose overgarment
Chette	Thief, brigand
Choereg	Traditional Armenian sweet bread
Digin	The Armenian title equivalent to Mrs
Divan	A long, low sofa without arms, typically placed against a wall
Djibour	Cricket
Dolma	Vegetables stuffed with rice, meat and spices
Douvagh	Armenian wedding veil
Dungulugh	Idiot (Armenian)
Efendi	Formal address to a man in Turkish. Sir
Ermeni	Armenian (Turkish)
Eshek	Donkey (Turkish/Armenian)
Eshek siksin	Fuck a donkey (Turkish)
Eshou botch	Donkey's tail (Turkish/Armenian)
Gederderuhgederderuh	Blah blah blah
Giavour	Infidel (Turkish)
Goshigs	Little shoes (Armenian)
Gurush	Turkish money
Halvah	Sesame/tahini desert, often with embedded nuts
Hamam	The Turkish variant of a sauna
Hanum	Beloved; a form of address towards women in Turkey
Haremlik	Sequestered womens' quarters, usually with separate doorway
Hokis	Armenian term of endearment meaning darling, my soul
Houri	Virgin
Hrshdugig	Little angel (Armenian)
Insha'Allah	God willing (Arabic)

Ibrik	Small pot for making coffee
Jan	Term of endearment meaning 'love' or 'friend' (Armenian)
Janavar	Term of endearment meaning 'cheeky' (Armenian)
Kaknem	I'll defecate (Armenian)
Khan	Inn, collection of buildings where horses and people could rest
Kilim	A flat, woven Turkish rug
Kurabia	Armenian cookies dusted with sugar powder
Lokhoum	A confection of flavored gelatin coated with sugar; Turkish Delight
Mangal	Portable brazier
Masha'Allah!	An Arabic phrase indicating joy or praise. It is often said upon hearing good news
Mayrig	Diminutive form of 'Mother' (colloquial Armenian)
Menug parov	Goodbye (Armenian)
Meydan	Central marketplace
Mgrdich tekrar oynamış!	A colloquial rhyme in Turkish meaning 'Mgrdich still up to your old games!'
Muezzin	A man who calls Muslims to prayer from the minaret of a mosque.
Narghile	Water pipe
Oosht!	Shoo!
Orospou	Whore (Armenian)
Oyna	Play in Turkish
Pari louys	Good Morning (Armenian)
Park Asdoudzo!	Praise the Lord! (Armenian)
Petit Echo de la Mode	French fashion magazine
Pezevenk	Pimp (Turkish)

Pilaff	Rice cooked with vermicelli noodles
Pishti	A popular Turkish card game
Raki	A strong alcoholic drink made in the Middle East and Eastern Europe
Rojig	Solidified grape jelly preserve
Saz	A long-necked stringed instrument of the lute family, originating in the Ottoman Empire
Seferberlik	Law regarding mobilization, conscription and forced exile
Shalvar	A pair of loose-fitting pants
Shouniges	My little dog (Armenian)
Siktir git	Fuck off
Sis	Long metal fire poker
Soujouk	Armenian/Turkish dried cured sausage with garlic and spices
Souq	A commercial corner or market in an Arab city
Süslü püslü	Turkish for overdressed and gaudy
Tahn	Armenian yoghurt drink
Tango	Woman of loose morals. A dancing girl
Tantig	Term of endearment meaning 'auntie' (French/Armenian)
Tavli	Greek backgammon
Teskere	Travel permit
Tonir	Clay bread oven
Vay!	Wow/oh/ow!
Vordevan	Armenian slang for homosexual
Yerkchouhi	Singer/songstress
Yallah	Come on/Let's go (Arabic)
Zankagadoun	Armenian for belfry
Zurna	A woodwind instrument

About the Author

Victoria Harwood Butler-Sloss is Armenian-English and grew up on the island of Cyprus. She began her career as a dancer at the world famous Raymond Revuebar, trained at the Royal Academy of Dramatic Art and spent twenty years as an actress in TV, film and theatre in London. After getting married she moved to Los Angeles, started a family, continued to work in voiceovers and wrote her first opus, a trilogy beginning in the Ottoman Empire in 1895, following four generations of women until the present day. *The Seamstress of Ourfa*, is the first. She has also produced two short films, *Cyprus Summer 1974* and *A Flock of Birds*, based on a chapter from the book. She currently lives in Los Angeles.